SHADOW RIDER

By the Author

Unexpected Ties

Unexpected Sparks

Cross Purposes

Shadow Rider

SHADOW RIDER

by

Gina Dartt

2024

SHADOW RIDER

ISBN 13: 978-1-63679-691-8

This Trade Paperback Original Is Published By
Bold Strokes Books, Inc.
P.O. Box 249
Valley Falls, NY 12185

First Edition: September 2024

CREDITS
EDITOR: SHELLEY THATCHER
PRODUCTION DESIGN: STACIA SEAMAN
COVER DESIGN BY INKSPIRAL DESIGN

Dedicated to Aloy. May your adventures never end.

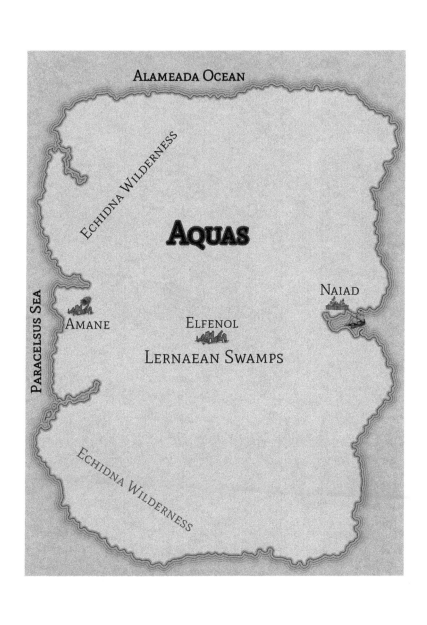

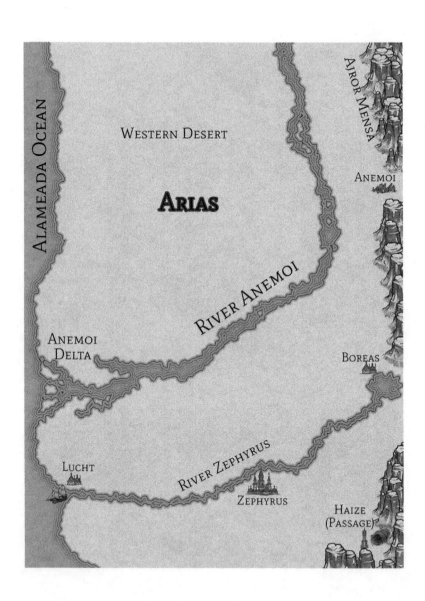

ALAMEADA OCEAN

WESTERN DESERT

AJROR MENSA

ARIAS

ANEMOI

RIVER ANEMOI

ANEMOI
DELTA

BOREAS

LUCHT

RIVER ZEPHYRUS

ZEPHYRUS

HAIZE
(PASSAGE)

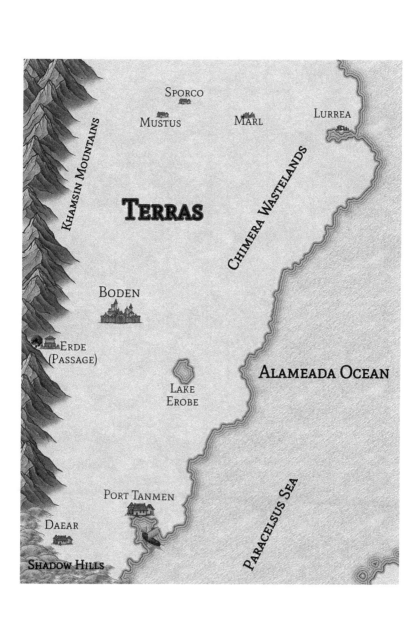

I

Shay noticed a tiny gleam from the black metal buckle near her stirrup and carefully smudged it with a bit of soot, knowing how dangerous even the slightest bit of reflective material could be. Nickering inquiringly, Onyx turned his finely boned head as she fussed over his tack, and absently, she smoothed over his forelock, stroking a line down to his ebony muzzle. Around her, the Rider station was already bustling with the foundlings mucking out the nearby stalls, grooms feeding and watering the horses, and the station master in the office grumbling about the early start to his day.

Beyond the large open door, mist drifted, making the predawn morning seem even darker as the white tinge to the vapor lights seemed to glow with a sharp, sparkly radiance. The warm smell of horses and manure and hay filled her nostrils as she gave a final tug to Onyx's cinch and slapped him on his neck, running a hand along his dark hide. Shay was about to mount when approaching footsteps and heavy exhalations made her pause and turn.

He was clearly a merchant, bearing several envelopes in his meaty hand. "Rider, I wish a word."

Frowning, she drew back her hood, letting it fall about her shoulders as she stared sternly at him. He didn't seem disconcerted by her gaze, as so many were, and she wondered if he dealt with Riders often. With an effort, she forced herself to be polite. "How may I help you, sie?" With no way of knowing if he bore title or not, she could only use the general if rather formal form of address.

He thrust the letters toward her, though she made no move to accept them. "I need these taken to Vokanus immediately." His voice was harsh, his manner abrupt, disdainful, as if he didn't really want to deal with her but was doing so only out of necessity.

Fury roiled in the pit of her stomach, but she merely stepped to the side, moving away from Onyx so the royal seal on the black saddlebags was clearly visible. "I'm not riding to Urodela," she said, trying to make this situation as least awkward as possible. "I ride to Zephyrus."

After all, the Merchant Cartel held no little power here in Naiad. It wouldn't do to unduly upset the members. But he didn't cooperate, apparently oblivious to the insignia that indicated she ran messages for the Queen and Council only. She was aghast when he dug out a small bag that clinked as he handled it, indicating it held coins, and thrust it toward her.

"I'm Shop Master Murross, and these contracts are important, girl," he said, impatiently, apparently misreading her reticence. "There's sufficient gold in it for you." As if that were her only motivation in life.

She knew those in Aquas tended to the myopic about those from elsewhere, but this was ridiculous. He was so intent on being superior, he didn't see what was right in front of him. She straightened, injecting a note of authority into her tone.

"I ride only for the crown," Shay said, no longer trying to spare his pride or avoid the uncomfortable situation. "I do not carry for a—" She barely avoided injecting the word *mere* before adding "shopkeeper."

He stopped and looked at her for undoubtedly the first time, seeing beyond the dark hair, dusky skin, and strange eyes that marked her as from the Shadow Lands, and at the leathers and cloak that bore the badge of royalty. He paled somewhat and lowered his hand.

"My apologies, Rider," he stammered. "I thought—"

"That I was merely a courier? Even the most inexperienced of us deserve more respect than you have shown, merchant."

She no longer held rein on her temper. She knew the rest of the world held her people in little regard, even though they birthed the only individuals gifted with the ability to navigate the Shadow Realm. It didn't seem to matter that without Riders traversing in minutes and hours what would normally take caravans days, weeks, or even months, much of the Five Nations' economy would be significantly different. She raked him up and down with a furious look, taking in the fine clothes, the fat belly straining his belt, the hearty jowls indicating he ate often and well.

"I must ride," she said shortly, instead of releasing the flood of invective that filled her throat. Turning her back, she gathered the reins and mounted Onyx in one, sinuous motion. As she touched his sides lightly with her heels, he sprang forward in an immediate gallop, leaving the merchant behind in a rain of dust, straw, and a strategically placed clot of manure that just happened to be by Onyx's near hind hoof.

She slowed Onyx to a steady trot when they reached Naiad's main thoroughfare, falling in with the early morning traffic as the vast capital began its day. As she rode, her temper cooled, and she regretted that she had allowed it to get away from her in the first place, hoping there would be no lasting repercussions. It would be too bad if that merchant turned out to be as important as he thought he was. The wealthy had influence even over the court. She tried to focus on her mission as, around her, people bustled about their business on the sidewalks, and carts, carriages, and wagons filled the streets, along with individual mounts winding their way while the early rays of the sun broke through the mist.

Up on the cliff overlooking the harbor, the white marble walls of the palace and the nearby step-pyramid of the Academy gleamed brightly, both powerful symbols of the city's importance. Not just Aquas's crown city, Naiad was capital to the entirety of the Five Nations, its wealth and power understood by all. Down by the water, the sounds and smells of the docks filled Shay's senses, making her itch to be free of all these people. Ignoring the shouts of shopkeepers hawking their wares and workers unloading goods from the high-masted ships snugged up against the wharves, she touched Onyx with her knee, guiding him up one of the side avenues leading to the city's main entrance.

Once she was free of the gate bureaucracy and riding along the dirt road winding west through the surrounding farmland, the tension in her shoulders began to ease. By the time she reached the towering obelisk that marked the beginning of the Path linking Naiad and Zephyrus, she felt like herself. The sky was cloudless, providing a sharp contrast between the thin shadow cast by the stone spire and the sunlight blanketing the verdant meadow, providing her the easiest of access. With a minor exertion of thought and energy, she rode Onyx into the shade at the base of the obelisk, and suddenly, she was in the Shadow Realm.

It was the place between places, where time and distance didn't quite exist, where stepping into a specific spot in one part of the world could take a Rider to another spot hundreds, even thousands of leagues away, bypassing jungles, crossing water, and traversing through mountains with ease. Many Paths ran between the various major towns and cities in the Five Nations, connecting them financially and politically, but only the Shadow Riders could follow them, carrying time-sensitive communications and precious goods. Shay had proved herself reliable and honest over the years, rising through the courier ranks until she'd finally been assigned elite status, riding for the crown itself.

The darkness surrounding her was impenetrable to non-Riders, but she possessed the unique ability to see through the greenish murk, though there was little to see beyond jagged, rocky, crystalline outcrops and the occasional spindly growths that weren't plants. The air was so arid and bitter that it was uncomfortable to breathe, and she pulled her scarf up over her mouth so that the moisture leaving with her exhalations was trapped and remained with her. Onyx, trained for these unnatural surroundings, responded obediently to the touch of her knees and heels as she guided him along the path that lay marked before her. Sound was muted, with the creak of saddle leather and even the thud of Onyx's hooves on the ground barely audible. Beyond that, the Shadows was oppressively still, though in that unknown expanse, things roamed freely. She didn't want to say lived, because she wasn't sure the entities that inhabited this place were alive. Despite that qualm, despite the constant sense of otherness, she didn't urge Onyx to move faster. She enjoyed the ride more than she perhaps should.

Barely minutes into her journey, the faintest trace of foreign sound brushed her ears. Shocked, she drew Onyx to a halt, her head swiveling as she sought to pinpoint the noise. As she listened, it grew more defined, finally becoming recognizable as the sound of battle. At first, she wasn't sure what to do, knowing full well the dangers of leaving the Path, of becoming hopelessly lost and never finding a safe exit from the Shadows. But she was also keenly aware that, as a Rider, she was duty-bound to aid anyone who might be in trouble, especially if it was a guide with a civilian. Sailing or traveling by caravan might take longer, but it was infinitely safer and far less unpleasant than to travel the Paths. Only civilians with the most urgent need ever made the attempt, so whoever it was could be rather important. Not that she valued them over a fellow clansman.

Taking a deep breath and squaring her shoulders whilst ignoring the uncomfortable sinking sensation in the pit of her stomach, she nudged Onyx off the Path and into the darkness, straining her eyes to pierce the murk. She rode carefully over the uneven terrain, guided by the grunts and clashes of metal on metal. When she was finally able to detect motion ahead, she swiftly reined in Onyx and jumped from her saddle, landing lightly on the ground as she drew both daggers from her belt. With a touch, she bade Onyx to remain where he was, knowing that he would obey, and cautiously approached until she was near enough to see what was going on.

Her heart sank as she saw the darting shadows. Wraiths. Formless creatures with red eyes that glowed as they attacked and razor-sharp claws that formed out of nothingness. One on its own was dangerous, but beatable. Two or three working together could take down a Rider and her mount within seconds. Except they didn't usually work together, nor were they found so close to civilization. Certainly not so close to a warded Path.

Yet Shay could see five of them, collectively fighting a woman who was not wearing the garb of a Shadow Rider. In fact, she didn't look like a Rider at all.

Solidly built, yet incredibly graceful, she was armed with a sword and shield that gleamed in the dimness, much to Shay's dismay. Any hint of light was lethal in the Shadow Realm. It attracted…well, it attracted wraiths at the least and, at worst, much larger and deadlier things. Even the woman's armor was reflective, shimmering in the dark, a silvery mail tunic over a black shirt with insignia that Shay belatedly realized was part of a uniform.

The woman was a marshal, a keeper of the law.

But it was more than that, to Shay's considerable consternation. The woman, though no older than Shay, had pure white hair, held back in a plait that fell halfway down her back. And though the irises were only a thin ring around pupils blown wide in the blackness, her eyes were a distinctive brilliant blue.

The woman was Undine.

Only one in a thousand were born Elemental. Sylphs commanded the air; Chthonic shaped the earth; Salamas forged fire; and the Undine wielded water on a world that was primarily ocean, making them the most powerful of all. Elementals used their abilities to make themselves extremely wealthy and politically powerful. All the nation's rulers outside of the Shadow Lands were Elemental. The Queen was. Practically all in the Ruling Council were. Shay had never heard of one who would work for as little gold as a marshal made.

What in the Lady's name was she doing in the Shadows?

But the question had to wait as Shay moved forward and slashed the nearest wraith, her blade digging deep. It wasn't like cutting flesh or bone. This substance was spongy and sinewy, like digging through sand, but the creature screamed in agony and turned on Shay, who dispatched it with a swift slice across the throat, although as far as she could tell, wraiths didn't breathe. But they did eat. If she and the stranger couldn't defeat these creatures, they'd be consumed. In the next step, she was ducking beneath the swing of the sword and snugging up behind the woman.

"Who's there?" But even with the terse demand, the woman fell naturally into the defensive position of them back-to-back as they faced the remaining four wraiths.

"Courier Rider Shay Kendrith," she stated, slicing through the air and catching a wraith, causing it to shriek, a sound that made her ears hurt and fearful of what it would attract.

"Marshal Keagan Riley." She slammed her shield into an approaching wraith, forcing it back. "I can't see."

Shay wasn't surprised. She was, however, considerably astonished and impressed by Keagan's ability to have survived this long with her senses hindered, all the while defending herself against this many wraiths.

"We can't stay here," Shay said, parrying a strike from swiping claws, the clash causing a streak of sparks. "This battle will draw more of them."

"I'm open to suggestions. Not even sure how I got here."

Shay filed that remark away to consider later. Then a flicker caught the corner of her eye, and she glanced over to see one of the wraiths draw something from within its form. It looked like a crystal, clear, cut into a diamond shape with ruby veins laced through it, about the size of a goose egg, but apparently heavy enough that the wraith needed both appendages to hold it.

Dear Lady, they were using tools now? She'd never heard of such a thing and braced herself for it to wield it like a hammer to crush their skulls, or to throw it at them. Instead, the wraith raised it into the air above its head, almost as if it were offering it up to some unknown deity. Shay barely had time to goggle at that oddity when the rock emitted a sudden flash of reddish light that blinded her. She cried out, looking away, spots dancing in her eyes. Behind her, she felt Keagan stagger, then slump back against her, downed from some unknown injury.

"Onyx, to me, now!" Shay screamed, panicked. "Come to me!"

Hoofbeats thundered toward her, the horse's dark form appearing in the murk, knocking aside two wraiths. Slashing wildly with one hand to keep the wraiths at bay, Shay dropped her other dagger and slipped her arm around Keagan's waist. In one motion, Shay heaved her up into the saddle before swinging up behind her and digging her heels deeply into Onyx's side. He sprang forward, ever trusting her lead, lunging into full gallop without hesitation.

Without direction, wanting only to escape, Shay didn't slow, shuddering as she heard the shrieks of the wraiths in pursuit. Worse, she began to hear other cries from around and in front of them as tiny sparks of red began to appear. At this point, she couldn't feel the location of any Path, nor did she think they'd be safe on one even if she could. The whole situation was so far removed from what she knew and understood about the Shadows that she was terrified. That left her few options. It went against all her training, her years of experience, and every instinct of self-preservation, but she could see no other choice.

With a surge that left her head aching, she tore open an entry immediately in front of her, a profoundly desperate and dangerous action. They could come out of the unmarked Shadows anywhere. Inside a rock face, over a yawning chasm, or even in the center of a city building. But since she was probably still near the island nation of Aquas, the chances were that they'd exit—

She barely had time to register the heaving swells below before they were plummeting twenty feet down into the turquoise depths of the Paracelsus Sea, the section of ocean separating Aquas from the rest of the nations. Losing her grip on both Onyx and Keagan, Shay forced herself not to panic, grabbing a deep breath before she hit the surface with a mighty splash. For a few seconds she remained still until she could right herself, natural buoyancy causing her to rise. Salt stung her eyes as she breached with a shout, drawing in sweet gulps of air to the very pit of her lungs. Whirling, she found Onyx gamely swimming near her, but no sign of the marshal. Sucking in another breath, she ducked below the surface, searching the sea water that seemed remarkably bright and clear after the Shadow Realm.

She spotted Keagan, a strangely graceful mass drifting down, unresponsive. Swimming strongly, Shay dove down and snagged the trailing cloak, yanking Keagan upward with her. Once they surfaced, she thumped Keagan on the back, gratified when water spewed from her mouth and she began to breathe raggedly, though Shay was unsure if an Undine could actually drown. She remained unconscious, however, and had a disturbing tendency to sink because of her armor. Treading water as she held her up, Shay tried to see how she was injured or, worse, if she was bleeding. That would attract as much undesirable attention as light did in the Shadows, but she couldn't see any obvious trauma or any trace of blood in the water.

Holding Keagan under her arm so she was easier to pull, Shay looked around, tremendously relieved when she saw land a reasonable distance away. Onyx was already swimming toward it, but he stopped when Shay whistled, waiting until she could swim to him and take hold of a strap on his saddle.

"Go!" She urged him on.

It was a miserable swim, with the horse taking most of the burden, but finally, she felt the bottom beneath her feet as they emerged from the gentle waves breaking around them. With an effort, she released the strap, took a stronger hold on Keagan, and began to drag her up onto the sandy beach. Staggering around rocks and driftwood until she felt safe enough to fall down, she dropped Keagan and splayed on her back as she stared up into the sky, wondering where she was.

Not far away, Onyx shimmied violently, shaking off the water as his penetrating whinny disturbed nearby gulls, sending them shrieking into the air. With a groan, Shay rolled to her feet and stumbled over to him. "Good boy," she said, thumping him lovingly on the neck before hugging him tightly. "You saved us all."

Digging into the salt-soaked saddlebags, she drew out a couple of carrots, feeding them to him as she praised his strength and courage. Then she stripped off his tack and dropped it onto the sand, freeing him to trot toward the nearest bits of grass growing sparsely at the edge of the jungle. From within the depths, sounds from more birds, mammals, and reptiles echoed, indicating an immediate lack of large predators, and, feeling herself relax just a little, Shay turned to the motionless form lying in the sand.

She supposed she should have attended to Keagan immediately, but she was a Rider and looked to her mount first and foremost. Besides, the woman would either survive or she wouldn't. Shay's medical skills were rudimentary at best, and if Keagan was seriously injured, she couldn't do much about it. But as she looked Keagan over, she couldn't find anything major—no slashes on her body or bruising on the head, no obvious wounds—yet she remained oblivious, unresponsive to Shay's exhortations.

She was pretty, though, Shay thought idly, even looking half drowned. Keagan's snowy hair framed strong, well-defined features, her long eyelashes throwing whisper lines across the high-boned cheeks. Her lips were thin, but it was a sweet mouth, a slight curve up at each corner even while she was unconscious.

Shay shook her head, realized she'd been staring, and forced herself back to the situation at hand. Unstrapping her bedroll from the saddle, she carried over the blanket that had remained dry within the sleeping pad and draped it over Keagan. She didn't know if it would do any good, but it made her feel like she had accomplished something useful. They were both drenched, but the day was warm, and neither was in danger of hypothermia. Their clothes would dry. In the meantime, Shay concluded that they weren't going anywhere unless Keagan showed some sign of regaining her senses.

Until then, she built a fire, not for the heat, but for the protection from predators, dragging over as much driftwood as she could find. Then she sat and began sorting through her saddlebags, taking inventory. Besides the carrots and apples she carried for Onyx, she had some dried meat, a few cornmeal wraps, and a small bag of travel mix comprised of nuts, seeds, and dried fruit. Not a lot, but enough to feed them for a couple of days if they rationed it. In addition, she had a few changes of undergarments, her throwing stars, some travel soap and shampoo, and brushes for both her and Onyx. She also had the standard survival pack that she had never used but was expected to always carry, which contained hand-drawn maps of the Five Nations, a compass, fishing line, hooks, bandages, medical ointment, and a small cooking pot. Strapped to her saddle was a sealed canteen full of drinking water and a coiled rope.

Last, but not least, was the courier packet that she'd been assigned to deliver that day to the court in Arias. That wouldn't happen now, she thought with a wince. Knowing the protocol, she inhaled sharply and tossed the packet into the fire without opening it, watching the flames turn violet as they consumed the pouch and its undoubtedly very important, very crucial diplomatic paperwork. Not only would she lose the commission, she thought morosely, but she would also have to pay a hefty fine for non-delivery.

Slumping back against the silvery bulk of a log, she sighed and stared grimly at the fire. How in the Lady's name had she managed to get herself into this mess?

II

Consciousness swam back like the slow approach of evening tide, inexorably creeping across Keagan's awareness. With it came a painful throbbing of her temples and an odd, penetrating emptiness. She wasn't sure what was going on, but she didn't like it. Her eyes felt crusted shut, and she had to force them open, breath escaping in a hiss as the light stabbed into her vision.

"There you are," came a low voice to her left. "I was beginning to think you weren't coming back."

Keagan made a pitiful sound and, with an effort, glanced over to see a young woman next to her. Probably the person who had come to her aid in the darkness, Keagan thought, as memories flooded back. Shay something. She was lean and possibly tall, though it was difficult to tell while she was seated in the sand as she was, cross-legged and leaning forward slightly as she regarded her. Long, thick dark hair flowed around dusky olive skin, wonderfully formed features, and dark, reflective eyes that held hints of silver, like a cat's eyes at dusk.

"You're the Rider," Keagan managed to say, disturbed at how weak and rusty her voice sounded. "What happened?"

"Something very strange." Shay's voice was quiet, contained, as was her body language. "I found you in the Shadows being attacked by wraiths."

"Is that what those were?" Keagan considered that information, and as she did, she became aware of other things: the strong rush of waves, the warmth and crackle of nearby flames, the soft brush of a breeze on her skin, and the brilliant glare from the sun. But mostly she finally realized what she wasn't feeling.

"Blessed Aigua!" She shot upright into a sitting position and nearly went down again as quickly, dizziness sweeping over her.

"Hey, take it easy," Shay muttered, grasping Keagan's shoulders, keeping her upright. "Are you okay?"

"No," Keagan said, struggling to sense what should be all around her. "I'm not." She reached out, arm shaking as if she had been struck by palsy, aching for the shimmering water laid out before her, an actual ocean of power that she could no longer touch.

She suddenly felt very small and very vulnerable. "I'm…what's happening to me?"

Shay regarded her, uncertainty narrowing her eyes. "I don't know. You tell me."

"Nothing," Keagan said, voice cracking. "I feel nothing. I should be bathing in all this moisture, but I can't feel any of it."

Shay blinked, clearly taken aback. "You are Undine, then. I was starting to wonder. All this water around should have had you on your feet hours ago."

Keagan rubbed her temples, wincing at the pain. "Hours?" she repeated blankly. "I don't understand."

"There's a lot of that going around." Shay hesitated, then rubbed Keagan lightly on the back, between her shoulder blades. It was unexpectedly soothing. "Can you tell me how you came to be in the Shadows?"

Keagan realized she no longer had her protective mail, nor even her shirt, though her sleeveless undergarment remained. A rough blanket covered her. Glancing over, she saw her uniform trousers tossed over a log, drying in the sun, along with her boots.

"My weapons?"

A small quirk touched the corner of Shay's full lips. "Long gone," she explained. "You dropped them in the Shadows when you fell. I wasn't about to go back for them, even if I could."

Keagan brought her fingers up to her temples, rubbing fretfully. "Those creatures…wraiths, did you call them? I think I've heard of them."

"They inhabit the Shadow Realm," Shay said, her tone grave, "along with many other things, but they're the most common. They're not usually found so close to established Paths, and certainly not more than one or two at any given time. Though you were lit up like a festival tree. Probably attracted every one of them within leagues, and their cries would have attracted others." She stopped suddenly, a furrow appearing between her thin brows. "Except they weren't shrieking, not until I started stabbing them. That's unusual."

"They were in the temple," Keagan said, struggling to put things into their proper order. "Five of them around the sarcophagus. When I confronted them, they dragged me through some kind of dark rip in the air into blackness. That was the Shadow Realm? I've heard of it, of course. Never traveled that way."

"Wait, are you saying you were in the world when they attacked?" Shay straightened, her face set as if in stone. "That's impossible. They don't exist outside the Shadows. They can't." She inhaled visibly, almost as if she were centering herself. "Wait. Start from the beginning. What temple? What do you mean?"

"The Temple of Aigua in the main square," Keagan said, feeling comfort in the recounting of facts, even as she strained to sense the moisture around her, probing that sixth sense like a bad tooth, devastated when it continued to be unresponsive, as if she had been suddenly struck blind or deaf. The water sense had developed at the same time as her breasts and her monthlies. She couldn't remember who or what she had been without it.

Shay nodded, apparently recognizing the location. That wasn't surprising since it was the third most recognizable landmark in Naiad after the Palace and the Academy. The huge structure of gleaming white pillars and statues, dedicated to the island nation's religious deity, the God of Waters, was located in the very center of the city. The other nations had their own gods, but Aigua was the most important. Of course, Keagan suspected were she from somewhere else, she'd think differently. Or even if she were someone else. She was Undine, after all.

Wasn't she?

That thought was so distressing, she shied away from it, refocusing on her explanation. "I'm a marshal. There's been a series of break-ins over the past year, thefts from museums and private collections. That's not normally my area, but the most recent theft involved an Undine attacked in his home when he discovered someone raiding his art collection, so I took over the case. I suppose it was only a matter of time before the temple was hit. When suspicious activity was reported in the early morning, long before it opened for the day, I was dispatched, along with a squad of patrol officers, to investigate."

Shay nodded encouragingly, and Keagan continued. "We discovered those creatures below in the catacombs, in the tomb of Heratherus."

"Heratherus? The warrior queen?"

"Yeah. They seemed to be looking for something. They had pulled off the cover of the sarcophagus and disturbed the body." Keagan paused, the horror of the sight lingering even now. The venerable bones were strewn about the tomb floor, along with the esteemed warrior's armor and treasure, tossed aside as if it were all garbage.

"One of the wraiths had a stone of some kind," she added, trying to put context to what she had seen. "I don't know what it was. It was carved into a diamond shape and had a ruby crystal running through it."

"I saw that stone in the Shadows." Shay shook her head, appearing both disbelieving and concerned. "Honestly, this behavior you're describing is hard to believe or understand. I've never heard of wraiths acting in such a manner, or of ever being able to exist in the world. It sounds impossible but…" She exhaled slowly. "I do believe you."

"Good, because it's what happened." Keagan faltered. "When they saw us, they attacked immediately. My men…" She bowed her head. "We weren't ready for that. We expected thieves. We got monsters. There's so little moisture in the catacombs, and we were completely surrounded by bedrock. I was able to draw on the nearest sewer lines, but it wasn't enough. They overwhelmed us. Three of us went down immediately. One of my men and I held them off a few minutes longer, but one got past his guard. They were so fast. Then two of them grabbed me. The one with the stone had another device. It gestured with it, and suddenly, this thing appeared. A hole in the air that led to darkness."

"An entry," Shay said softly. "It's how we access the Shadow Realm. I didn't think wraiths could do that. None of this makes sense."

Keagan couldn't disagree. "The next thing I knew, I was blind. It was so dark. I continued to fight, but I couldn't…" She thought furiously. "I couldn't draw on any moisture. My reserves drained away to nothing. I had only my weapons."

"There's no water in the Shadows. Or fire or earth," Shay said. "There's barely air. Just enough to breathe. Like being on top of a mountain. I wonder why they took you rather than kill you. Was it because you're Elemental?"

"Maybe," Keagan said, thinking furiously. "Does the Shadow Realm…no. Other Elementals have traveled through without losing their abilities."

"Perhaps that reddish light from the stone," Shay suggested. "It was very odd. It didn't do much besides temporarily blind me, but that was because of the contrast. I don't think it was that bright otherwise, but it knocked you cold for hours. You weren't injured in any way I could see."

Keagan looked down at her hands. "What happened then?"

"I called for Onyx, my horse. He came to me, I threw you over the saddle, jumped on, and got the hell out of there," Shay said, her words arriving slowly, as if she were thinking about what they meant even as she said them. "I believe you're right. They were trying to take you, not kill you, because otherwise, you'd already be dead. And they were so focused on you, they barely noticed me, even after I killed one."

"Where are we now?"

"I don't know." Shay suddenly looked uncertain. "I had to leave the Realm. More wraiths were coming, and probably other things, too. We came out over the ocean, fortunately not far from land."

"Where do you think we could be?" Keagan asked tentatively after a moment, when Shay seemed unwilling to speak further.

"It's late afternoon now, and the sun's setting over the ocean, so I'm guessing we're on the west coast of Aquas," Shay said. "I'm hoping that's the case. If we're on an island…" She looked out at the ocean. "I haven't seen a ship all day. And from what I remember, there aren't a lot of settlements on this side."

"There aren't any." Keagan put her face in her hands, rubbing her forehead. The pain was easing, and it seemed as if she could think more clearly. "The War destroyed this part of the nation. The land was devastated for centuries. It was left for the jungle to take. It was easier to rebuild in the east, and I don't remember hearing about anyone who ever chose to resettle here. We call it the Echidna Wilderness." She lifted her head and looked into those dark, flashing, strangely attractive eyes. "What do we do now?"

"We'll stay here tonight and begin our journey tomorrow," Shay said, returning the gaze steadily. "I don't dare try to enter the Shadow Realm. I'm a courier, not a scout. If I'm close enough, I can sense a Path, but who knows how long it would take to find one, and there's a lot more than just wraiths to worry about in there. Once the stars come out, I can narrow down where we are with my maps. It could be a long journey. We can hunt, of course." She paused. "If your abilities return, we won't want for water."

"And if they don't?" Keagan didn't even want to consider the possibility.

"Then we'll find fresh water along the way." Shay had a quiet confidence that soothed Keagan and kept her from feeling so lost. "We won't give up."

"No, of course not." Keagan looked over at the ocean. "And if we're on one of the islands?"

Shay didn't answer immediately, her expression darkening. "I don't know."

Then it was Keagan's turn to inject a note of optimism. "I know how to sail. In fact, I'm good at it. We can build a raft."

"Large enough for Onyx?" Shay said dryly.

Keagan glanced over at the big black horse grazing near the jungle's edge. "Ah, maybe," she said, uncertain.

"Are you hungry?"

Keagan blinked, considered the possibility, and realized she was famished. "I am. I haven't had anything to eat since supper last night."

Shay leaned over to the fire and brought out some leaf-wrapped packets that had been warming on rocks. "I did some fishing earlier," she said. "And I have some berries and roots I dug out."

"A positive feast." Keagan was delighted, unwrapping the white filet from the large leaf, the flesh tender and falling apart. It was seasoned somehow and tasted delicious, as did the roasted roots that resembled potatoes. "How did you know what was safe to eat? Do you do this often?"

"I haven't had to do it since I was ten and developed the Sight," Shay said as she devoured her own meal. "When it was discovered that I could walk the Shadows, I was taken to Aether for training, but until that time, my clan taught me how to take care of myself. How to herd, how to hunt, how to fish, how to identify and gather edible plants. The usual."

Keagan nodded as she tried to remember her geography lessons from the Academy. Aether had been the only nation that had survived relatively intact after the last Element War, but that was because they'd never had much to begin with. Not worth fighting over, in other words. Nor did their people give birth to Elementals as the other nations did. Primarily nomads, living for their herds of horses, their scattered villages and their single crown city were sparsely populated. It was their ability to create and navigate Paths that rebuilt the other nations into the powers they eventually became, bringing those people together and providing the capability of communication and trade. Ironically, Aether, as a nation, had been left with little more than what it had started with.

"Was it hard to leave your clan?"

Shay shrugged, but her gaze turned downward. Keagan suspected it had been hard. Especially when she immediately changed the subject back to her.

"What was it like for you? I've never met an Elemental." A bit of a twist marred Shay's mouth. "At least, not one that I could ever have a conversation with."

Keagan believed that. Elementals tended to hold themselves aloof from those around them, retaining a certain arrogance that their contribution to society was so much greater than those without abilities, conveniently forgetting that they were the ones who had waged the war that had nearly destroyed the world. She shrugged. "I never really had a clan. I don't remember my parents. I grew up on the streets in Naiad," she explained. "That changed when some marshals caught me lifting some coins from a merchant in the square. I pushed them away with a blast of water. I was eleven."

"Huh. I bet that was a surprise."

"They took me to the Academy," Keagan said. "I was terrified, but the people there treated me well. Suddenly, I had three meals a day and a roof over my head every night. They taught me how to control my abilities, along with all the rest."

"The rest?"

"Reading, writing, sciences, comportment, the whole thing. It took a while to catch up to the other students, but it was better than the streets."

Shay looked at her from beneath lowered lashes, her head bent over her meal. "Is that why..."

"I'm not rich and powerful?" Keagan asked dryly.

"I meant no offense, sie," Shay said quickly.

Keagan felt a pang. She was so used to that reticence around her, even with those she'd worked with a long time, that she had stopped noticing it after a while. But for some reason, she didn't want to feel it from Shay.

"I could have gone a different way," Keagan admitted. "Someone like me can make a lot of money. But I guess I…" She didn't know how to say it without sounding pompous. "I guess I thought it was more important to help people."

"Elementals are always helping people," Shay said in a mild tone, clearly not wanting to cause any offense. "They're the ones that construct the cities, nurture the fields, run the manufacturing, provide heat in the colder climates and coolness in the hot climates. There's even a couple that stop by yearly to recharge the crystals in my apartment so that my lights and kitchen appliances keep working."

"I know the advertising, but Elementals are always doing it for the sake of the company that employs them, which pays very well," Keagan said. "Look. I'm not saying that good isn't done. Many towns in Arias wouldn't last long without the wells the local Undine fills from the aquifers, and some places in Urodela wouldn't even exist if the resident Chthonic weren't easing the seismic pressure along their local fault lines. But sometimes it's better not to rely on Elementals to get things done. Look at Aether."

"Yeah. We have it so good," Shay said flatly.

"That's not what I meant," Keagan replied hastily.

Shay lifted her hand. "I know. Sorry. It's just that my work takes me everywhere, and it seems that others have so much, while my nation has so little. It's hard to understand, sometimes."

"I know. That's sort of why I do what I do. Not for those who have. For those who don't."

Shay nodded. "Okay. Maybe I get that."

They finished their dinner and then settled back against the log, looking out at the ocean as it caught the last rays of the sun setting behind the hills at their back. Keagan reached out again, straining, and thought she felt the faintest hint of acknowledgment within her. Not the rush of sheer power that should come from so much water, of course, but perhaps a promise that this absence wasn't permanent. She could hope, at any rate. She was more aware of Shay's lean form beside her as they sat in companionable silence, dusk settling around them.

"Do you see better in the dark, even out here in the real world?" she asked idly after a while.

"Yes," Shay said. "I can see everything. I don't remember what it was like not to see perfectly at night." She turned to face Keagan. "I'm sorry you've lost your abilities. It must be terrible."

"I'm trying not to think about it," Keagan told her honestly. For a moment, she grew lost in those eyes, wondering at the possibilities she saw there, and it seemed that perhaps Shay felt it as well, leaning forward ever so slightly.

But then a log snapped in the fire, sending up a wave of sparks, and the moment vanished. Vaguely disappointed, Keagan settled back against the log, and silently, the two of them watched as the last light died from the horizon and stars began to appear in the sky.

III

"I feel naked without my sword," Keagan said as they pushed through the jungle.

Shay glanced behind her, fighting back a smile as she saw the strands of snowy hair sticking to Keagan's sweaty forehead. Her face was very red from both the heat and the exertion. It had been five days, and the longer they were together, the less the marshal intimidated her and the more she liked her. Keagan was intelligent and kind and had a wry sense of humor, even while grumpy, as she was now. The way Keagan had yielded to her authority in their jungle, following her lead without question, also impressed her. It couldn't have been easy for an Elemental and revealed a humility she hadn't expected.

"If it's any consolation," Shay said, "I lost one of my favorite daggers in the fight, too."

"It's not."

Shay felt her jaw firm. "I dropped it because I had to throw your unconscious ass onto Onyx while fending off wraiths with my other hand."

"Oh." Keagan was quiet for a minute. "Sorry. I don't think I ever thanked you for that, by the way. Saving my life, I mean. Not for losing your dagger." She paused. "I don't suppose you have a spare."

Feeling sheepish at her display of pique, Shay pulled one of her longer blades from a concealed sheath on her leg. She supposed it was good that Keagan was finally beginning to think about defending herself rather than relying on her and Onyx. She handed the weapon back to Keagan, who accepted it with a sunny smile.

"Thank you."

"You're wel—"

Shay held up her fist, and Keagan immediately froze in place. Around them, all noise had ceased—the birdsong, the frogs, and the insects. Even the soft breeze wafting through the foliage seemed to die. Following them, Onyx also paused at her signal, lifting his head and flicking his ears, as if hearing something they weren't.

"What is it?" Keagan asked after a couple of minutes, keeping her voice low.

"I'm not sure," Shay whispered. "Stay here."

She melted into the shadows of the surrounding jungle. Behind her came a startled gasp, quickly strangled, from Keagan, but Shay didn't look back. Moving silently through the thick tree trunks, she continued north. That first early morning, calculating from the stars and consulting her map of Aquas, she'd determined they were somewhere on the western coast and not, thankfully, on one of its many uninhabited satellite islands. The nearest place with any population was to the north, hundreds of leagues away, but closer than any area to the south. They couldn't go overland to the east without becoming mired in the vast, swampy wetlands that made up most of Central Aquas. Heading north wasn't ideal, but it was the best option. Unless they came across some alternative means of travel or Shay sensed a Path, they'd have to walk. The terrain wasn't suited to riding Onyx, especially when they had to break from the beaches and head into the bush to avoid the powerful waves crashing directly against the jagged rocks at the base of looming cliffs.

As Shay crested a ridge, she became aware of the faint scent of wood smoke and an indication of a clearing below. Immediately dropping to a crouch, she looked down. Various voices were audible, though she couldn't make out exactly what was being said. Frowning, she studied the scene for several minutes before she withdrew and returned to where Keagan stood waiting.

"People ahead," she muttered as she stepped from the shadows.

Keagan started abruptly, eyes wide as she nearly dropped the dagger she'd been holding at the ready. "Aigua's balls, how do you do that?" she hissed.

"Do what?"

"Disappear and reappear like that. Do you…are you going into the Shadow Realm?"

"No, of course not." The question surprised Shay. "I just…I was trained to move quietly. Anyone could learn to do it."

"Not everyone. So what did you find?"

"Six men setting up camp." Shay paused. "And one female captive."

"Captive?" Keagan's features hardened. "Explain."

"They're just over the ridge. They look like mercenaries, and they're well-armed. The woman is tied up on the other side of the camp," Shay said. "She's around our age, well dressed. Really well dressed, not at all suitable for this terrain. I don't know why they're here, but it doesn't look like they've been in the jungle long."

"What would they be doing here in the first place?"

"No idea." Shay went to Onyx and retrieved her stars from his saddlebags, slipping the deadly little shapes into small pockets along the outside of each boot, then slid a few extra daggers into her belt as she tried to find the words for what she had to say next. "About the captive. It was hard to tell from my vantage point, but I'd swear she's a redhead. And her eyes are gold."

Keagan stared at her with a mix of surprise and dismay. "A Salamas? Captured? How are they even holding her?"

"Some kind of bracelets around her wrists," Shay told her grimly. "They don't seem all that binding. I would think she'd be able to melt them off."

"Describe them."

"Silver. Thin. Engraved with some kind of symbols."

"Like these?" Keagan drew a pair of cuffs from a pouch on her belt, dangling them in the air so Shay could see them.

Shay felt her eyebrows lift. "Exactly like those. What are they?"

"Suppression shackles," Keagan said soberly. "For Elementals."

"For Elementals?" Shay was astonished.

"What? Did you think none of us would be criminally inclined?"

Shay shook her head. "I suppose I never thought about it. Why would you? You have gold thrown at you every time you turn around."

Keagan shrugged. "Not all Elementals like to earn their money," she said. "They think it's easier to take. Others simply want more than they feel their gifts can provide. Don't forget, not all Elementals are born equal."

Shay had learned from her conversations with Keagan that the level of an individual's natural abilities varied, and that those could be greatly enhanced with training and study. But someone could study all their life, gain complete control of every aspect of their abilities, practice constantly, yet still be flattened by an uneducated child who possessed greater innate talent. That was why the Academy made a point to track down every Elemental. Not only so that they could derive every iota of potential from their abilities, but also so they were taught control before their abilities got away from them. Still, Shay had believed that once educated and exposed to a world that couldn't wait to richly reward them for what they could do, life would come easy for any Elemental. Why bother breaking the law?

It was possible she was far more naive about the world than she'd thought.

"How would mercenaries get their hands on those kinds of shackles?"

"I don't know." Keagan sighed. "But then, a lot's been going on lately that I don't understand."

Shay couldn't argue with that.

"What's the plan?" Keagan looked down, almost as if she were ashamed. "The strongest of my abilities haven't returned. Not even close."

Over the past couple of days, Keagan had recovered enough to fill Shay's canteen every morning with pure, cool drinking water, but the effort left her shaking and bent nearly double from the debilitating headache that came with it. Yet she insisted on doing it for the practice, determined to regain her strength. Keagan considered what seemed like magic to Shay, and infinitely useful, to be a far cry from the effortless way she had shaped and commanded the water prior to her encounter with the wraiths.

"And I don't have my weapons," Keagan added, somewhat querulously.

Shay wanted to comfort her, to enfold her in her arms and hug her tightly, but she contented herself with patting Keagan on the shoulder, somewhat like she did to Onyx whenever he did something good. "It's getting better every day," she reminded her gently. "Look. They don't know we're here. We can always find a way around them."

"I'm a marshal, Shay. It's my duty to protect the citizens of the Five Nations," Keagan said with such asperity that Shay felt ashamed for her suggestion. "You're right, though. We do have the element of surprise. They'll never see you coming. Once you cause a distraction, I can take out a couple of them. Plus, once I have a sword in my hands, I'll be far more effective than with this." She gestured briefly with the dagger, which she was wielding like a sword. A very short sword. That method wouldn't be very effective in a fight, Shay agreed grimly. "They do have swords, don't they?"

"Plenty of them."

Shay wasn't pleased, but she couldn't think of a better plan. She looked toward the sun that was nearing the horizon. Before this interruption, she'd been searching for a place for them to bed down for the night. "Is it possible that they're bounty hunters and not mercs? That the woman's a criminal and they've been hired to transport her somewhere?"

Keagan shook her head forcefully. "No. That's not how it works. Arresting an Elemental is major, and no one other than marshals with abilities handles it. We certainly wouldn't transport such prisoners overland, nor would we use independent contractors. Plus, those cuffs are marshal issue. Mercenaries shouldn't even know about them. No, this had to be a kidnapping, probably for ransom. Companies pay well to get their people back."

"That's what I thought." Shay tried not to sigh in resignation. "I just had to be sure before..." She squared her shoulders. "We'll get her out."

"Did the woman look..." Keagan swallowed hard. "Was she hurt?" Shay regarded her soberly, understanding what she was asking. "I don't think so," she said. "She looked pretty lively, and they seemed to be taking care of her. Restrained, and under control, but as comfortable as possible. She even spit and cursed at one of them when he got close, and he didn't retaliate. Didn't even look at her."

"Good," Keagan said, obviously relieved. She offered Shay a smile. "I will admit, I feel a lot better about this plan knowing how well you can see in the dark."

The remark warmed Shay far more than it should have. She couldn't deny the feelings that were stirring for her companion, but she knew better than to let them show. Or allow them to become any stronger, for that matter. They had no future there. Even if Keagan was open to the idea of being with a woman, it was unlikely she'd consider someone like her. Keagan was Undine, for Lady's sake. They ruled the world. The thought made Shay's next words a little curter than she intended.

"I do have the advantage in the dark. In fact, it might be better if you stay here while I take care of them."

Shay didn't think Keagan could look more offended. "Which of us here is actually the law?"

"Yeah, sorry. I shouldn't have said that." Shay dropped her head and then lifted it again when Keagan stepped close and put her hand on Shay's arm, her fingers warm against her skin.

"Look, Shay. I haven't been acting like myself the past few days," Keagan said. "The whole experience in the Shadow Realm, losing my abilities, it was traumatic. Plus, I'm far more comfortable in the city. Honestly, you've had to take care of me out here in the jungle. But this? This is my job. This is what I know how to do."

Reminded of the warrior who had been holding off five wraiths in total darkness, Shay felt awkward again. Though she was also reminded that they were trying to capture, not kill her. "I know. I just...I'm not sure how much you rely on your abilities. How well do you fight without them?"

Keagan hesitated, apparently considering that question. "Okay, that's fair. But rest assured, I can handle myself." She paused. "Do you think we can take any of them alive? For questioning?"

Shay frowned. "This isn't the city. And I've never known a merc to willingly surrender when confronted. There's always a fight. It's a point of honor."

Keagan sighed. "No. You're right. We have no backup out here. If we do this, we have to go in hard. Anything less and it could go very badly. Especially for their hostage."

"There's a ridge above the campsite," Shay said, pulling away from her touch reluctantly. "We can take up position there until it's time." She went over to Onyx and patted his neck. "Stay," she said in a low tone. "Watch." He dipped his head and nuzzled her as she rubbed his forehead lovingly. "I'll call for you." With a final pat, she left him and joined Keagan.

"He'll stay there?" Keagan whispered as they quietly worked their way through the jungle toward the ridge.

"Of course."

"I've never seen such an obedient horse. It's like he understands what you're saying."

"He does." Shay smiled. "He's Shadow-bred."

"I've seen Aether horses in Naiad. They're considered the fastest and most easily trained. Only the very wealthy can afford them."

"What you've seen are our culls," Shay said with a touch of disdain. "Those are all we allow to leave our herds to go to outsiders. Meanwhile, Riders are chosen by the best of the Shadow-touched, like Onyx." She tapped Keagan on the shoulder. "Quiet now. They're just over the hill."

Keagan nodded shortly, and they ascended the ridge in silence, settling on top in the shelter of a jutting rock formation that provided adequate concealment for them and a clear line of sight below. The camp was set up in a small clearing, a sliver of stream burbling through the rocks beyond. Three tents circled a central fire, where one of the mercenaries, a bald, hulking man with colorful tattoos tracing his forearms, was preparing food. Three other men sat some distance away, sharpening their swords, their heavy shields leaning on the log beside them. The final two men stood at opposite ends of the camp, bows at the ready, obviously keeping watch. All their armor and clothing was a varied mix of styles and nations, indicating loyalty to none. Shay noted that they were relatively well groomed, and the camp was neatly organized. Their milled-wood table and the trimmed logs scattered around for seating indicated that it had been established for much longer than a day. She also noticed wooden chests perched on small platforms, keeping them clear of the ground, undoubtedly to protect perishables from scavengers, and even an outhouse tucked away in the bushes, far away from the stream.

"They don't have horses, but they didn't get all the way out here just by walking," Keagan whispered in a barely audible tone.

"No, they didn't." Shay nodded. "We need to find out how."

"And use whatever it was to get us home."

Shay turned her attention to the captive seated on the bench by the table, on the other side of the fire from the swordsmen. Her blouse was of the finest silk, a shade of deepest blue, while her black skirt was embroidered with golden thread on the hem in a pattern of leaping stags and does. Her boots were ornately decorated with buckles glinting in the sun, laced up the front, and sporting absurdly high heels. She looked as if she'd been on her way for a night out on the town rather than tramping through the jungle. Her hair hung loose around her shoulders, a deep, rich auburn. Her cute, snub nose and rosebud lips made her pretty rather than beautiful. Though it was too far for her to be absolutely sure, Shay knew the eyes would be a burnished gold, seeming to glow around dark pupils. Once a person saw the eyes of a Salamas, they never forgot what they looked like. Assuming they survived the encounter.

Keagan made a small sound, hastily stifled.

"What?" Shay whispered.

"I know her," Keagan said. "We attended the Academy at the same time. Her name's Ashley Van Vuur."

"Ah," Shay said. "Friend?"

Keagan made a face, one Shay couldn't quite decipher. "I'm never sure."

Though curious, Shay didn't pursue the comment. Instead, she studied the movements of the men below, assessing their skill level and attentiveness, as well as how they interacted. They didn't speak a lot, didn't joke or show any interplay beyond what was necessary for communication. Strangers then, thrown together for a job, though still very professional. They only acknowledged their captive's presence and made sure she was still restrained. She could move about the confines of the camp within reason, though every time she did, they tightened their hands on their weapons and scrutinized her more carefully. Only the man cooking supper ignored her, focusing on the meat roasting on the spit, though the other men paid closer attention whenever the captive wandered within his vicinity.

"The bald guy has the key to her shackles," Keagan whispered.

"I think he's in charge."

"They're good." Keagan turned her head and looked at Shay, appearing very serious. "Very good. You're right. We definitely can't take prisoners."

Shay agreed. If they did this, they'd have to do as much damage in as short a time as possible. And they had to be thorough, with no mistakes and no faltering, or they'd be overwhelmed.

"We wait until they're asleep," she whispered. "I'll take out whatever guard there is first. Then you come down and we'll finish the rest."

Keagan nodded, jaw tight.

It wasn't the most honorable way to fight, but in a situation like this, honor wasn't a concern. Only life or death mattered. Shay exhaled slowly and settled deeper into the leaves, watching closely as she waited patiently. Beside her, Keagan did the same, and Shay tried to ignore how good the warmth of her body felt next to her.

The last of the day's light filtered away through the foliage overhead, and dusk descended, as around them, the jungle resumed its natural progression, the last cries of diurnal life fading to be replaced by the sounds of the nocturnal inhabitants.

The mercenaries didn't finish feeding their prisoner and themselves for a couple of hours, but Keagan and Shay waited quietly and patiently, still, with the skill of long practice. Shay had learned such technique while hunting. She supposed Keagan had cause to practice surveillance in her job. Below, one of the men would occasionally speak to the captive, but she would ignore him haughtily, staring at the fire. She hadn't been held captive long, Shay decided. She was still too offended, too defiant to have accepted that she was helpless.

Still too hopeful.

Finally, the camp retired for the night, the woman escorted into her own tent, the five men split between the other two. An archer remained on guard, patrolling the camp at regular intervals and sitting at the fire the rest of the time.

Shay gave him long enough to become relaxed, to settle into the routine of an uneventful night, but not long enough to think about waking his replacement. She would have preferred to take action after the mercenaries had been in the jungle for a few nights, but who knew where they had come from and where they were going. She touched Keagan on her shoulder, alerting her that it was time.

Leaving Keagan lying there, Shay slipped into hunter mode, descending the ridge with exquisite care, placing each foot carefully as she slipped through the foliage, barely disturbing the ferns littering the jungle floor. Near the camp, she paused, waiting until the archer rose to begin his next patrol. As he passed by her, unaware of her presence, she took two steps forward and reached around, covering his mouth with one hand as she slit his throat with the other.

Blood spilled hot and wet over her hand, but she didn't let go, accepting his weight as she lowered him quietly to the ground. Then she looked toward the ridge where Keagan waited and waved, unsure whether she could see her. But soon she heard her descent and winced at the noise she made moving through the jungle. Keagan wasn't loud, but she was far from silent.

No one seemed disturbed, however, and soon, Keagan joined her, looking distastefully at the body lying motionless on the ground before picking up the bow and wrestling the quiver of arrows off the corpse.

She notched an arrow and pulled experimentally, testing the stiffness of the draw. Apparently satisfied, she nodded briefly at Shay. She was ready. Returning the nod, Shay drew her other dagger and slipped toward the nearest tent. Things were about to get tricky. Five-to-two odds.

Hopefully, humans would prove less deadly than wraiths.

IV

Keagan forced herself to control her breathing as Shay slipped toward the nearest tent. Even watching her directly in the firelight, she could barely see her. Shay might think anyone could learn to move like that, but Keagan knew better. Whatever she was doing, it wasn't natural. Shay seemed to become one with any kind of shadow, merging into the darkness and appearing again only as a hint of motion, the smallest glint of flame on blade, a bit of a blur before she disappeared again.

Her abilities frightened Keagan a bit, but in a good way. Her heart rate increased, not only because she was about to engage in battle.

Lifting her bow, she tensed as Shay reached into the tent, grabbed whoever was closest, and yanked him out. Keagan had noticed before that Shay was stronger than she appeared, more physically capable than her lean form implied. Her arm rose and then plunged down once, dispatching the man she had pulled from the tent, but that was their last unopposed kill. The rest of mercenaries erupted from the tents, swords at the ready, angry voices raised.

Keagan fired steadily, her arrows bringing down the first man out of the other tent, and then the second. She was peripherally aware of Shay fighting the third of her opponents, hampering his rush by slicing through the tent ropes to drop the canvas around him. Then Keagan focused fully on the large man, the leader, who appeared with an ax in one hand and a sword in the other, roaring in clear anger and frustration. Ambidextrous, then, she thought with sinking stomach, equally deadly on either side. Not the most promising of opponents.

Keagan threw the bow at him and dove to the side, taking advantage of his momentary distraction. Rolling past him, she swept up one of the swords that had fallen on the ground. Another lunge to the side snagged her a shield, and then she was facing his rush, meeting it on more familiar terms.

Had she her abilities, she would have blinded him with a rush of water into his eyes or tried to sweep his legs with a wave. Without them, she could only catch the ax's edge on her shield and block the swing of his sword with her blade. Immediately on the defensive, she soon realized she was badly outmatched physically, and concern flickered through her.

Then he was rearing back, dropping his weapons with a shriek that penetrated to the bone as he reached up to his head. Shocked, Keagan could only stare stupidly at the metal stars that suddenly studded his face, including one in each eye. Then instinct took over, and she lunged forward, dispatching him with a swift, sure thrust through the heart. She yanked out her sword and then stood there, heaving for breath, staring wildly at Shay, who had thrown the metal stars with such pinpoint accuracy.

"Thanks," she said weakly.

Shay nodded and glanced around. Like all fights, it had seemed to take forever but had probably lasted only a few minutes.

From the middle tent, a low, throaty voice sounded. "May I come out now?"

Shay pulled back the canvas, revealing Ashley, who'd clearly been making herself as small as possible on the floor as she peered through the slit in the tent. At Keagan's nod, she rose and exited the tent with surprising grace, considering she was still shackled.

"Thank Baast," she said as she regarded Keagan. "A marshal. You've come to rescue me, I suppose. I knew you would." She looked around, frowning when she saw Shay and nobody else. "Where are the rest of you?"

"We're it." Shay came over and retrieved her stars, wiping them on the corpse's tunic before searching the rest of his clothes. She came up with a key and tossed it to Keagan, who immediately moved to remove Ashley's shackles.

As soon as she was freed, Ashley snarled, stomped over to the closest body, and lit it up with bluish flame that was so hot, Shay yelped and scuttled back. The corpse was reduced to ash in a matter of seconds, the smell harsh and pungent.

Keagan had to swallow a sudden rush of nausea. Salamas, she thought in disgust. Too much temper and never enough brains. Half of them didn't survive the onset of their abilities at puberty, and the other half usually managed to kill or hurt some innocent bystander before the Academy tracked them down. Dealing with them was pure annoyance.

"Stop!" Keagan snapped as Ashley made a move to burn the next body. "You're disturbing evidence."

The authoritative tone evidently sparked a memory, because Ashley turned and looked at her more closely this time.

"Keagan? Keagan Riley? Is that you?"

Keagan resisted a sigh. "How'd you manage all this, Ash?"

"You're a marshal?" Ashley was clearly astonished. "Why would you join the civil service? You had your pick of offers after school."

"That's an irrelevant point," Shay said. "Who were these men, and what were you doing with them?"

Ashley gave her a withering glance that raked her from head to toe, assessed her, and then, just as quickly, dismissed her as unimportant before returning her attention to Keagan.

Keagan saw the expression of anger and humiliation that swept over Shay's face before it settled into impassiveness. "I'll get Onyx," she muttered and disappeared into the darkness.

Keagan wanted to slap Ashley so hard, her head would fly from her shoulders, but it was hardly the first time she'd ever felt that way about the girl, so she damped her feeling down easily. Instead, she slipped the sword into the empty sheath on her belt. It wasn't nearly as good as the one she'd lost in the Shadow Realm, but at least it was Urodela forged, giving it a tempered quality most weapons didn't have. Then she hooked the shield over her back, fastening it to her armor harness.

"What's going on, Ash?" she asked.

Ash blinked, frowning, but she responded. "I'm not really sure. I thought they were kidnappers, but they never contacted my family." She paused. "In fact, I got the impression that they didn't take me because I'm a Van Vuur. They took me because I'm Elemental."

"Really?" Keagan was nonplussed. "That would bring the entire crown and Council down on them. I'm surprised they made it this far without getting caught."

"Wait. Isn't my kidnapping why you're here?"

Keagan resisted a grin. "No. We just happened to be in the area. When were you taken? How?" Ashley suddenly hesitated, looking a bit sheepish. Keagan was intrigued. "What happened, Ash?"

"Uh, the one I fried? He and I were...well, you know. I met him in a tavern a few days ago. We sort of hit it off."

Keagan swallowed back another smile. "How'd he get the cuffs on you?"

Ashley looked even more embarrassed. "I took him back to my room, where he brought out those cuffs. I thought it would be fun. The next thing I knew, I'm completely blocked, and he's letting his buddy in. The bald guy. Thank Baast I was still dressed. Mostly. Besides, I didn't know handcuffs could do that. Who would create something like that? To block abilities?" She seemed more offended by that loss of power than by being kidnapped.

Keagan looked around. "So if they took you because you're Elemental, why bring you here?"

Ashley shook her head. "I don't know. They're working for someone. Maybe I'm wrong. Maybe it's still ransom, but not for gold. Maybe it's some kind of power play with the company. You know Daddy would do anything to get me back."

Keagan thought about that possibility briefly, then just as quickly rejected it. The various mining companies were cutthroat in their competition, but kidnapping Elemental assets from each other wasn't standard operating procedure, no matter how much of an edge any such asset could provide. And involving family members of the owner? The fallout would be catastrophic. The crown certainly wouldn't stand for it. It would immediately dismantle any company responsible and turn over its entire assets to the injured party.

"How'd you get here?"

"Ship at first," Ashley said. "Then a skiff landed us on the beach this morning. That's where these other guys met us." She glanced at her boots, making a face at the mud clinging to them. "We've been walking all day. My feet are killing me." That fact seemed to grievously offend her as well.

"Where were you going?"

Ashley shrugged. "I don't know, but we were supposed to arrive there tomorrow. At least that's what they kept telling me every time I complained about having to walk." She brightened. "Oh, good. You have horses."

Keagan looked over her shoulder to see Shay return, leading Onyx into the light of the fire. She stoically stripped off his tack and began to groom him with painstaking care.

"We have *a* horse." Suddenly feeling exhausted, Keagan moved over to Shay, leaving Ashley at the fire. "What now?" she asked in a low tone as she joined her. Tentatively, she patted Onyx, who accepted the gesture without objection.

Shay glanced sideways at her with a bit of a sardonic grin. "What did you discover?"

"They arrived here this morning by boat," Keagan muttered. "From a larger ship. Not sure if it's still in the area. Two of the men and Ashley. The other four met them there and were leading them somewhere they planned to be tomorrow. They left the boat beached on the coast."

"Good thing you're a sailor."

"It is," Keagan told her. "Should we head there now?"

Shay lifted her brow. "I'd rather wait until it's light. We can use this camp for tonight. Get some rest, have something to eat." Shay tucked the brush back into the saddlebag and went over to the nearest body. "We should move these into the jungle, but it has to be some distance away. They'll attract animals."

"No. We just need to pile them in one place. Ash can take care of the remains, the way she did with her boyfriend."

"Boyfriend?" Shay said. "I need to hear this story."

"As soon as we eat," Keagan said. She looked over to where Ashley was standing near the fire, staring into it and undoubtedly absorbing its energy. It did seem dimmer than it should. "Ash, give us a hand."

Ashley lifted her head and strode over to them, but she addressed Shay when she reached them. "You, Rider, you'll take me home, now."

Shay regarded her evenly. "Sorry. Can't be done."

"I don't believe I was asking," Ashley said, eyes beginning to glow with golden incandescence as her right hand twitched.

"Shay is my associate. A deputy. Don't make me cuff you again." Keagan kept her voice mild but with a subtle note of deadliness in it. Shay and Ashley turned toward her with wide eyes. Keagan raised her hands casually in front and kept them there as a trickle of water flowed from the right down to her left and then back up again, slipping through and around each of her fingers, mesmerizing in its motion.

Ash blanched, flinched, and immediately put her hand behind her back as if she were a child hiding a sweet. "Sorry, Keagan," she said, with forced servility. "It won't happen again. What do you need?"

"We need help with the bodies," Keagan told her, her tone now pleasant as she clenched her fists, stopping the water. She even offered a thin smile and hoped that would be enough to cover the sudden weakness that swept through her and the headache that stabbed along her temples. Shay looked clearly concerned.

A suitably chastened Ashley helped them drag the dead off to the side, piling them on top of each other after stripping everything useful they could find, including a journal of some kind from the leader and a respectably heavy bag of gold. Then she and Shay stood back some distance as Ashley set them ablaze, blasting a steady jet of flame at them until nothing was left but a fine, gray ash in the middle of a larger, blackened circle of earth.

That unpleasant task complete, they searched the rest of the camp, piling everything they found in a stack near the fire. There, Ashley began going through it, retrieving what was clearly some of her belongings, including a large belt with various alchemy vials of colored powder that Keagan knew Ashley used for her work. Mixed together, they created explosives of varied intensity, detonated by her abilities. She also managed to find a pair of clean socks and correctly sized boots that, if they weren't hers, at least worked better than the high heels she'd been wearing. Ashley didn't often choose to show it, but she could be quite practical when she wanted to be. Brutally so, at times.

Meanwhile, Shay had placed her pot near the fire, filling it with tubers, the last of Onyx's carrots, and some leftovers from a tapir she'd brought down a couple of days earlier. After throwing in some seasoning, she glanced uncertainly at Keagan and then at Ashley, who was still sorting through the supplies. Firming her jaw, she rose and went over to the stream, where she retrieved some water to boil. Keagan was relieved. After her little display, she didn't feel up to providing the liquid part of the stew Shay was making. She was very reluctant to let Ashley know how much she had lost of her abilities. The Salamas wasn't evil, but she was spoiled, and Aigua only knew how she'd react.

"I'm going to sleep," Ashley announced, once she had finished scavenging the discard pile. She cast a disdainful look at the stew, then, again, at Shay. "I've already eaten." She rose from the log and headed to the middle tent where she'd been held, disappearing inside and tying the canvas behind her, closing it firmly.

"Gee, that's a shame," Shay muttered as she stirred the stew, making Keagan smile. She looked up. "So, not friends?"

Keagan exhaled. "Elementals can be born of anyone," she said in a low voice. "That's the truth. Even so, a lot of us think it has to do with bloodlines, that Elementals marrying other Elementals will increase the chance of producing Elemental offspring. The richest Guild family of Elementals in Urodela might produce a Salamas of great potential, but—"

"Some orphan kid raised on the street can still be her better?" Shay asked.

Keagan smiled. "Better is a relative term. Ability wise, we're evenly matched, I'd guess. Or we were at school, anyway."

"Except you're a marshal and trained to use your abilities offensively. Plus, you're Undine," Shay said, regarding her steadily. "That's just better because…"

"Water drowns fire," Keagan said. "A more powerful Salamas could boil off my water, of course, but Ashley never could. In our bouts, the best she could do was warm it a little before it doused her fire and then knocked her off her feet. Alternating jets kept her down until she tapped out."

Shay smiled faintly. "And just how many more powerful Salamas than you are there?"

Keagan paused. "I'm what's considered a high level four. Anyone I know who's a five is on the Council. Right now, though, I'm barely operating as a level one. I still know all the moves. I just can't seem to draw any amount of moisture, even though plenty's around."

"Oh." Shay stirred the stew thoughtfully, then ladled out some for Keagan and herself. "I know how much it took for you to do what you did just now. Thank you. It's obvious she doesn't think much of Riders."

"Not just Riders." Keagan tried her stew. It was true. Tapir really did taste like beef. Very lean beef. She never thought she'd ever be in a position to confirm that fact. "Ashley arrived at the Academy already thinking she was better than most Elementals, let alone those who aren't. That's how she was raised. School was a real eye-opener for her. Believe it or not, she's a lot better now than she was when I first met her."

Shay smiled. "I guess I'll have to take your word for it." She shook her head. "Although we do agree on one thing. I still can't believe you settled for the marshals."

Keagan sighed. "I don't feel I 'settled' for anything, but you're not the only one who thinks like that," she said, deciding not to pursue the subject further. Instead, she touched Shay inquiringly on the leg. "Are you all right?"

"Shouldn't I be?"

"That was a—it was a bad fight."

"Oh, that." Shay looked down at the hand on her knee. "It wasn't my first battle, Keagan. I've been a courier since I was sixteen. Now I'm responsible for the transport of sensitive diplomatic material for the crown and Council. Before this job, I carried valuables for the Merchant Guild. I'm not always in the Shadows. I have to travel the world between Paths, and I've been held up more than once. I've been trained to handle it."

"Oh, sorry." Self-conscious, Keagan withdrew her hand. "I just thought—"

But Shay captured it before Keagan could pull back entirely, entwining their fingers as she regarded her earnestly. "It was good of you to ask. To be concerned. But no, it's not the first time I've killed someone. Chances are, it won't be the last. I'm sorry if that disappoints you."

Keagan looked at their linked hands. "It doesn't. I like that you can take care of yourself." She swallowed and squeezed lightly. "That you can take care of me. You saved my life again."

"You were holding your own." Shay followed her gaze and seemed to grow a little self-conscious also, abruptly releasing her grip. "I just distracted him so you could finish him off." She picked up her dish and began to eat her stew quickly, as if wanting to concentrate on something else. "You can take the remaining tent. I'll stand watch."

"Onyx always stood watch before," Keagan said. Were the close quarters and privacy of a tent suddenly making Shay feel they couldn't sleep in proximity to each other, even though prior to this, they had bedded down side by side every night? Of course they slept fully dressed, with no hint of impropriety. Not that Keagan had thought about impropriety at all.

"Before, we didn't know mercenaries were running around," Shay said. "What's on the west coast, anyway, besides jungle and ocean? I know the Lernaean Swamps cut off most of it from the rest of the nation."

"There are countless ruins from before the Element War," Keagan said. "Mostly just rubble, but a few structures are supposedly still standing. Authorities have conducted a couple of archaeological digs in the southwest, but not many. No one seems very interested in revisiting the worst time of our history."

"History wasn't my best subject in school," Shay said. "I'm still not sure who exactly was fighting who, or why. It was so long ago."

"Nine hundred and forty-three years. Urodela and Aquas were the major combatants," Keagan said promptly. "And the reasons were complicated, though a lot of it seems to boil down to the fact that fire and water don't mix, personally or politically. Once war was declared, Arias allied itself with Urodela. The firestorms they created nearly lit up the atmosphere. Terras united with Aquas to oppose them, and finally, after a lot of destruction on both sides, the war ended."

"With the Shadow Lands caught in the middle." Shay sighed. "As always. And to the victors go the spoils. Is that why Arias and Urodela still need more crown assistance than the other two?"

"Partly," Keagan said. "Arias no longer has the resources Terras does, and Urodela is so seismically unstable that it's hard for them to maintain any continuity in their culture, though their mining and manufacturing keep them economically healthy."

"Sylphs can fly, though." Shay sounded wistful. "I always thought..."

Keagan smiled. "What? That if you'd been born Elemental, you'd want to be a Sylph?"

Shay blushed. "I guess. No offense."

"None taken," Keagan said, lightly. "I'd love to have Sylph abilities. Though they really can't fly, you know."

"They can't?" Shay looked so disappointed that Keagan felt a pang at having revealed the truth.

"They glide. The highest levels can ride wind currents that they control," she said. "But if there's no wind, or not a lot of updraft, then they can't get lift. And if the wind suddenly dies, and they're too tired or inexperienced to generate their own, they...well, they crash. It's not pretty."

Shay let out a quiet laugh. "I've learned more about Elementals in the last five days than I have in my entire life. Why don't people know more? Maybe if they did, they wouldn't look at you as..." She stopped, obviously trying to think of the right word.

"Monsters?"

Shay shook her head violently. "No, not monsters, but you're definitely seen as different than the rest of us. Either feared or fawned over. But that's not you. You're just a person, you know?"

"I know," Keagan said and took the last bite of her stew. "Believe me, I know."

V

Shay started awake, opening her eyes to realize she had dozed off by the fire that was now mere embers. There was a quiet to the jungle, not the frozen disturbed silence of the day before, but the peaceful stillness of dawn's early light. She had thrown her cloak over herself for warmth and was leaning up against the log. Yawning, she rubbed her eyes and rose, draping her cloak around her shoulders as she moved over to where Onyx dozed by the trees, his head down. She frowned as she realized how skinny he was, ribs beginning to protrude through his coat. There wasn't much fodder for him in the jungle. She needed to get him food, and soon. She'd hoped to find some in the camp but found only rice, no grain.

And even if the boat could take her and the others back to civilization, there probably wouldn't be room for Onyx. She'd have to leave him behind. Except, of course, she'd never do that. She'd take her chances in the Shadow Realm first, ride as fast as she could in a straight line until she encountered a Path and exit there. It would be incredibly dangerous, but leaving him in the jungle meant certain death for him.

He lifted his head, nickering quietly, and she fed him the last of the apples. Then she wrapped her arms around him, hugging him. "I'll get you out of here, boy," she told him. "I promise. One way or another."

He snuffled her hair, his solid bulk comforting as she leaned against him.

A sound from behind her indicated the others were waking, and she wiped her eyes unobtrusively on her sleeve before returning to the camp. Both Ashley and Keagan were standing by the fire that was now blazing merrily. Ashley's doing, no doubt.

"Rider," she said as Shay joined them.

"Sie," she replied neutrally, not knowing her title or even if she had one.

Keagan offered her a smile. "Is Onyx all right?"

Shay exhaled. "He won't last much longer. We need to find something for him." She paused. "If the boat's still there, then you need to take your friend and sail somewhere safe. I'll return to the Shadows and look for a Path."

Keagan's eyes widened. "That's too dangerous."

"I don't have a choice."

"It's just a horse." Ashley stared at Shay, obviously confused.

"Don't," Keagan said, reaching out to grab Shay by the arms, holding her in place. Shay hadn't realized she'd even made a move toward Ashley until she was being restrained. Keagan glared at Ashley over her shoulder. "Don't talk about things you don't understand."

Seeming taken aback, Ashley opened her mouth to say something, took another look at their expressions, and let out her breath in a hiss, raising her hands defensively as she backed away. Shay watched her stalk to the other side of the camp and then looked down at Keagan, who was still holding on to her.

"I wasn't going to do anything," Shay said, sullenly.

"Good, because you're not much use to anyone as a pile of ash," Keagan said quietly. "Especially to Onyx. Don't forget, I can't stop her at the moment. And she'd never be charged with anything if you struck the first blow. It'd be considered self-defense."

Shay relaxed, bowing her head. "You're right. That was stupid."

Keagan regarded her a moment, seeming to search her face. "We may just be people, Shay," she told her in a serious tone. "But we're people who walk around with the equivalent of an aimed and loaded crossbow all the time. Run into one who acts before she thinks, and bad things happen."

"I understand."

"You weren't serious about going into the Shadow Realm again?"

Shay avoided her eyes. "I won't leave him behind."

Keagan started to say something, stopped, and then squeezed Shay's arms before letting her go. "We'll figure something out," she told her, eyes warm with compassion. "Maybe the boat's big enough for him, too."

Shay doubted that, but it was nice of her to say. And it was terrible. The longer she was with Keagan, the more she liked her. And the more she liked her, the worse it would be when they had to say good-bye.

Standing some distance away, arms crossed over her chest, looking petulant, Ashley asked, "So are we going back to the beach?"

"Yeah. Let's get something to eat, and then we'll head west." Keagan went over to one of the secured chests, pulling out bread, butter, bacon, and a container of eggs. Mercenaries ate well, it seemed, even in the middle of nowhere. From the other chest, Shay discovered a skillet and some metal dishes. Leaving Keagan to make breakfast, Shay headed for the latrine to take care of some biological necessities. After washing her hands and face in the stream, she returned to the fire.

"I wish I knew where they were taking you," Keagan said to Ashley as they ate. "And why. I didn't see anything in the journal the leader was carrying. Just information about you, where you'd be and when, but nothing about where they were going. What were you doing in Terras, anyway?"

"Daddy's thinking about opening a mine there," Ashley said, her mouth full of egg. "I was scouting the Shadow Hills when I met Gerald. We were staying in a little town near the foothills. Daear, I think it's called. Boring as a box of rocks, and dry as a bone. Had to bring in my own booze. The inn was acceptable, though."

"The Shadow Hills are ours," Shay said, feeling a sudden jolt in her midsection. "There's no mining there."

"Not on Aether's side. The other side. The Terras side."

"There is no 'Terras side,'" Shay told her acidly. "All the Shadow Hills belong to the Lady."

Ashley started to say something, stopped, glanced once at Keagan, and frowned. "I don't know what to tell you," she said finally. "I was working with a Terras liaison. He seemed to think that Terras extended right up to the top of those hills."

"He was wrong."

Ashley stared at her a moment, shrugged, and turned back to Keagan. "I'm just glad I don't have to find out where they were taking me. Besides, I hate being part of a collection."

Shay exchanged a glance with Keagan, who had straightened visibly, eyes narrowed. "What do you mean?" Shay asked.

Ashley blinked. "I just had the impression there were others where we were going."

"Others. Other...what? Mercenaries?" Shay heard Keagan catch her breath. "Other Elementals?"

Ashley seemed to finally realize that Keagan was more than merely interested. "What?"

"Ashley, have they captured other Elementals?" Keagan was clearly exasperated. "Why are you telling us this only now?"

"I don't know anything for sure," Ashley said, defensively. "A couple of things I heard them say made me think that."

"Like what, specifically?"

"Nothing really." Ashley stared at them and then let out her breath in a huff. "Fine. After Gerald handcuffed me and let his buddy in, the bald guy stuck me with a needle and drugged me. They weren't good drugs either. The needle just put me to sleep. I woke up in the cabin of a ship, but they must have been standing just above me on deck. They were talking about this place, about some kind of palace belonging to a lord or something."

"A lord?" Keagan glanced at Shay. "What's a lord? Isn't that something to do with landholders in Terras?"

"Yes, particularly in the north. That's how they address the owners of the large farming estates there," Shay said. "It's a pretty important title. I've delivered messages to many of them from the crown."

"What's a northern Terras lord doing in the Echidna Wilderness?"

Shay shook her head and spread out her hands. Very little had made sense to her since she left Naiad six days earlier. She looked back at Ashley. "What else?"

"He said that I was the last thing this lord needed. That he already had water. That air and earth were finally being delivered and that fire was the last piece. I figured fire meant me. And if fire meant me, then air and earth—"

"Meant two other Elementals," Keagan said bleakly. "Maybe three, if he already has water."

"Four Elementals." Shay let out her breath. "What could someone do with that?"

"Anything he damned well wanted if the Elementals cooperated," Ashley said, with no trace of modesty. "Which we wouldn't, of course. I mean, I don't know about anybody else, but whatever they threatened me with, I'd just say I'd cooperate until he took off my cuffs, and then I'd fry everyone's ass. I don't know anyone who'd be stupid enough to come up with a plan like that. Though, if he is from Terras…" She shrugged. "Well, they aren't the brightest, are they?" She scooped up the last of her breakfast. "Are we going to the beach now?"

Shay put a hand over her face. What the hell had she done so wrong in the Lady's eyes that her life had been reduced to this? Beside her, Keagan was frantically leafing through the leader's journal until she let out a cry of triumph, obviously having found the page she'd been looking for. She held it out to Shay. "Is this a map of where we are?"

Shay looked down at the rough scrawl and sighed. "Yeah. I think it is. That symbol is probably the landing site on the beach."

Keagan pointed at one of the other markings. "And this?"

"Possibly where they were headed."

"Can you get us there?"

Shay met her gaze and held it for a long moment. "Yes," she said finally. "I can get us there."

Keagan smiled, the warmth in her brilliant blue eyes unmistakable. "Thank you."

"I'll go saddle Onyx."

Ashley was looking back and forth between them, clearly becoming agitated. "What now? What are we doing?"

"We're going to rescue the other Elementals," Keagan said.

"We're going to see if we can," Shay said as she picked up her saddle and carried it over to Onyx. "It might not be possible, but we have to check it out, at least."

"Why?" Ashley was clearly horrified.

"It's my job," Keagan said as she began to pick out things from the pile of supplies. She thrust a bow and a quiver of arrows at Ashley. "Here. I'm certain you know how to use these."

"I used to," Ashley said as she accepted them. "Back at school. I haven't fired a bow in years. I haven't needed to."

"It's not like you were all that accurate to begin with," Keagan said. "You didn't have to be. You just set them on fire and blew things up."

Ashley's face cleared. "That's true," she told Shay, who tightened the cinch around Onyx's belly. "I do like to blow things up."

"I absolutely believe that," Shay told her.

"Here," Keagan said, handing Shay supplies. She began filling saddlebags, strapping things to the saddle, everything that might prove useful. "We should carry a tent, too. Just in case." She grabbed Ashley's arm, dragging her over to take down one of the tents.

Onyx turned his head to look at Shay mournfully. "I know. You're not a pack horse," she told him sympathetically. "But for now, you're all we have."

Once they had gathered all they needed, they extinguished the fire, Ashley soaking it into herself, leaving cold, dark ashes, which both impressed and terrified Shay. They left the clearing and headed east, fording the small stream and pushing deeper into the jungle, where they quickly found a trail. Keagan had acquired a machete from the camp and seemed a little disappointed to find the way already cleared, but she began hacking her way with great enthusiasm to widen it as Ashley walked beside her. They chatted about their shared experiences at the Academy and what had happened since graduation, which made Shay feel a little left out. She lagged behind so she didn't have to listen, walking with Onyx, hand on his neck as he snatched mouthfuls of various vegetation that she knew wasn't offering him much nutrition. She was afraid he would eat something she didn't recognize and could poison him, but she didn't have the heart to prevent him from eating anything.

Every so often, she'd check the hand-drawn map and update Keagan, knowing they were going in the right direction every time she identified one of the crude landmarks. A bird-shaped boulder, a trio of trees that looked like three sisters, and then another, larger rock formation that resembled a sleeping donkey. When they reached another, wider creek, she moved to join the other two.

"We need to be quiet from here," she told them.

"We're getting close?" Keagan paused, machete lowered.

"This creek is the last landmark shown on the map, so it can't be much farther," Shay said. "We're probably expected. Or, rather, those mercenaries were. I'd like to find higher ground, get off this trail, and arrive from another direction. We should follow this creek downstream a league or so, then make our way from there."

Keagan nodded. "If you think that's best."

"Do I get a vote?" Ashley asked.

"No," Keagan and Shay said at the same time.

"Well, aren't you two just the cutest."

Ignoring Ashley, Shay took hold of the reins and began to lead Onyx downstream, pushing through the water as she picked their way through the gravel. Ashley chose to stay near the bank as much as possible, stepping from rock to rock, but Keagan joined Shay, splashing along with her. Glancing over at her, Shay thought she was looking stronger, more vibrant somehow. After making sure Ashley wasn't immediately near, she leaned over. "How are you feeling?"

Keagan, brows lowered, looked as if she didn't immediately understand what Shay was referring to. Then she relaxed. "A lot better," she murmured. She twitched her fingers, and a stream of clear liquid rose in a thin line to her hand, staying there as they walked. "No pain at all. Still not pulling anything near what I should, but I'm able to manipulate what I do pull without strain."

Shay exhaled. "Good. I'm glad."

And she honestly was, even as she felt that the more Keagan's abilities returned, the more she would pull away, mostly because she wouldn't need a Shadow Rider's help anymore. Shay didn't presume to think they were friends. What had Keagan said to Ashley? Oh, yes, that they were "associates." Shay understood that terminology. They had been thrown together in a bad situation and luckily had found an easy working relationship. But once this experience ended, assuming they survived it, they'd separate. What other outcome existed?

Surreptitiously, Shay looked over at Keagan's profile, daring to admire it even as that hurt.

"What's that?'

Startled, Shay stumbled, splashing a bit, then looked over at Ashley pointing at something up ahead. She looked, and her jaw loosened, even as Keagan made a strangled sound beside her.

"What is that?" Keagan blinked rapidly, as if trying to get a better perspective.

"A bridge of some kind?" Shay said.

Slowly, they approached the broken structure arching above them. Vines and creepers wound around it, while other vegetation sprouted from the underside through cracks in the stone. Shay looked around with new eyes, at the terrain surrounding them, at the lines of rocks and stones. None of it was natural except the foliage that had overgrown it.

"It's a ruin," she said. "We've probably been in it for a while."

She waded to the shore and knelt, brushing away centuries of dust and debris, only to discover a smooth surface a few inches down. The other two joined her, staring down at the murky, greenish depths of the uncovered material.

"It's melted," Ashley said, her voice subdued in a new way.

"Firestorm," Keagan said soberly.

Shay glanced up at them. "You've said that before. What is it?"

"Something I hope to never see in modern times," Keagan said. "When a Salamas and a Sylph join forces, they can produce a fire far hotter than any Salamas can produce on their own."

"We do it at the company all the time," Ashley said. "When I first started, I was in the metalworking department, paired with a man who fed certain gasses to my flame to make it so hot, it can melt metal. Urodela smiths use the same technique while making blades. That's why our weapons are the best in the world. None are harder, last longer, or sustain a keener edge."

Shay nodded. She had several Urodela daggers, though she had no idea how they were made.

"If Salamas and Sylphs work together, the fire they produce begins to feed on itself, becoming larger and hotter until it consumes the air itself." Keagan paused. "I mean, fire consumes air, anyway. Remove all the flammable gases in the air around, and the fire dies. That's how Sylphs battle Salamas in the Grand Tournament. They remove the air around the Salamas to prevent them generating flames. But if a group of both keep feeding a fire, it eventually becomes so large, it starts to feed on the atmosphere itself, and only a lahar can stop it."

"A lahar? What's that?"

"When a group of Undine and Chthonic combine their abilities, earth and water," Ashley said.

"Earth and water combined is…um, mud." Shay tried not to sound dismissive. Keagan must have detected her tone anyway, because her eyes glinted slightly, becoming bluer.

"Yes, mud, a gigantic, solid mass flowing at a hundred leagues an hour, crushing everything in its path."

"Oh." Shay exhaled. "That sounds terrifying."

"It is. After the war, new laws prohibited the same company from employing a certain number of Elementals or many of them even gathering in large numbers in one place."

Shay, in the company of two Elementals, chose not to say anything, just looked at them both, but Keagan seemed to read her mind, as she was doing more and more lately.

"That number being a lot more than two," Keagan said dryly, and now the glint in her eye was clearly one of amusement. "Or even fifty. In the war, thousands on either side were combining their abilities. Some historians claim it could have been tens of thousands. Entire armies."

Shay tried to imagine that much destruction and couldn't. Instead, she glanced around. "It doesn't look as if this place was buried."

"No. Just blasted," Ashley said with a casualness not reflected in her gaze, her mouth twisted slightly. "If you lift the firestorm high enough, no lahar can touch it. You can have the wind move it to where you want and then drop it."

Shay swallowed. "On a city." She looked around again. "This was a city. People lived here."

"Once," Keagan said, looking grim. She let out her breath. "Never again."

"Never again," Ashley said in a tone that sounded ritualistic, even religious, though Shay doubted either woman shared the other's beliefs. Keagan followed Aigua, obviously, while Ashley kept swearing about Baast, the Goddess of Flame. But in this area, their fervor apparently coincided completely.

"Why would mercenaries bring Elementals here?"

Returned to the current issue, both Keagan and Ashley lost that distant gaze, their expressions sharpening.

"We'd better find out," Keagan said. "How much farther should we go?"

Shay looked up at the sun overhead. Barely past noon. "Any idea when you were expected to arrive?" she asked Ashley.

"One of them said we'd be there in time for lunch. He was looking forward to it."

"So you're past due. They might give it a few hours, but eventually someone will go looking. We left a big trail to the creek."

Keagan frowned. "Why didn't you tell me?"

"Oh, I wanted a big trail," Shay said absently. "Ours wasn't big enough, frankly, for it to be six men and a prisoner, but hopefully, they won't notice." She smiled at Keagan. "Besides, you enjoyed all that hacking and slashing."

"I did," Keagan said, returning the smile. "It made up for all those days we had to struggle along without being able to cut our way through. I mean, you never seemed to have a problem, but every tree seemed to want to strangle me with its vines." She studied Shay for a few seconds. "That's why you were walking in the creek, not because—"

She stopped, glanced at Ashley and then back at Shay. *Not because you wanted me to be surrounded by water*, her unspoken gaze said.

Shay dipped her head and carefully brushed dirt back over the exposed surface, scattering detritus over it to make it look undisturbed. "And now we all walk in the water."

"I hate getting my feet wet," Ashley said, but she gingerly entered the creek with them, sloshing behind them as they resumed their journey downstream.

The farther they went, the deeper the water became until they were mid-thigh. The slowing current meant an obstruction of some kind lay ahead. The jungle thinned as well, as the ruin became more evident. Larger formations of the greenish rock were not rock at all, but the melted combination of buildings, streets, and carts. Probably of people and animals, too. She recognized other rubble, not melted, beneath the vegetation as scorched walls and foundations. Shay paused, looking ahead. The creek was flowing into a deeper pond, spreading out. "We go overland from here." She motioned at the others. "Try to follow me exactly. We don't want anyone to know we left the water here. Don't disturb anything."

VI

Following Shay was no easy task. Though she made it look effortless, it was difficult to move through the ruins without leaving an obvious trail. Frequently, Shay would drop behind as Keagan and Ashley forged ahead, undoubtedly doing her best to further obscure their passage. Then they reached a hill that turned out to be a large structure, surprisingly intact, though so covered in dirt and vegetation, it was barely visible.

"This looks like a pyramid," Keagan muttered as they wound their way upward.

"Like the Elemental Academy?"

"Yes. Before the war, they were used as military bases." Keagan paused. "Elementals gathered there."

"To launch their strikes against the other side," Shay said. She reached down and brushed aside the dirt to reveal a marble step. "I'm surprised this wasn't the main target of whatever happened here."

"It probably was," Ashley said dryly. "But they were also the most protected buildings in the cities."

Keagan was surprised Ashley remembered that much, since history had never been her strong suit. And while everyone at school had learned what had happened a millennium ago, those who weren't Elemental hadn't. Apparently, even the Shadow Riders were as ignorant as everyone else. Why was that? Keagan had always thought the average person didn't bother to learn about the war, but perhaps they were discouraged somehow.

Those who didn't learn from history were doomed to repeat it. How many times had her instructors told her that? But while Elementals were drilled incessantly at the Academy to absorb all that history, why wasn't everyone?

She'd never really thought about it. But she'd be thinking about it a lot from now on. When she reached the summit, she paused, amazed, looking out over a large valley. About a league away, an area cleared of all vegetation surrounded a central structure that boasted the same pillars of white that adorned Naiad's palace and the temple buildings. Keagan barely had time to take it all in before Shay grasped her and Ashley by the arm, drawing them into the shadow of the four square columns that topped the pyramid. Engraved with strange markings, they held up a giant slab of stone as a roof. Vines draped the area, enclosing it in cool shade, creating a room with living green walls. In the middle of the room lay a smaller slab of stone on top of a round, stubby pillar, almost like an altar of sorts, though Keagan had never heard of these buildings being used for offerings. Something should fit into a hole in the middle of it, filled with centuries of dirt, though whatever it was, it was long gone.

"Hey," Ashley said.

"If we can see them," Shay said grimly, "always assume they might be able to see us. Stay out of sight. Don't give them an easily recognized outline against the sky."

But Shay was agitated for another reason. Over the past few days, Keagan had come to know Shay's face, more easily reading each small expression and deciphering each tiny alteration in the quirk of brow and mouth. She thought she knew why that was happening, even if she wasn't sure what she should do about it. Or even if she could do anything about it. She didn't think Shay felt the same way.

"There's more," she said in a low voice. "What's wrong?"

"There's a Path here," Shay said, eyes dark. "I don't recognize it."

"Should you?" Ashley asked. "Will it get us home?"

"It's not new," Shay said, her tone sober. This was very serious. "It's old. The oldest I've ever felt."

"I don't know what you mean." Keagan touched Shay's shoulder. "Explain it to us."

Shay glanced at her, then nodded. "Some Shadow Riders, not me, but a very few, are scouts," she explained, sounding reluctant, as if unsure she should be sharing the information. "They know exactly where they are in the world all the time, even in the Shadow Realm. They discover and mark new Paths between where we are and where we want to be. The Paths that I ride, that we all ride, are easy to identify. We feel them. I can practically taste them. I even know which scout marked each one and when in our history they explored that part of the Shadows. But I can't tell which scout marked that Path down there, and I can feel that it was marked long before the oldest Path I know, the one that runs between Aether and Sombra near the Shadow Hills. I have no idea how it got there or where it goes."

"I thought the oldest Path was between Aether and Boden." Keagan was puzzled.

Boden was the crown city of Terras, and she had always believed it was the first place that Aether reached out to after the War. They were the ones that requested another Path be made to Naiad as soon as possible.

In truth, the war didn't end with a peace treaty. The war ended because barely anyone was left to fight. Elementals had almost gone extinct, and for a certain period afterward, a great many people believed they had. Perhaps even hoped they had.

"We were always taught that the Shadow Paths didn't exist until after the War," Keagan added. "That the people of Aether didn't learn this skill until everything had nearly been destroyed."

"No, the Lady of the Shadows revealed the first Path to Scout Cesareans thousands of years ago, leading him from Aether in the central plain, to the Shadow Hills in the north, the Zjarr Mountains in the west, Lost Bay in the east, and the Itzal Wilds to the south," Shay said. "Those would be our borders. They would cut us off from the other nations, protecting us from the rest of the world. After your War, the Lady told us we must help the other shattered nations recover."

Shay paused, looked at both her and Ashley, and shut up, clearly unwilling to say more.

"So Aether isn't just the name of your nation? It's also your crown city?" Ashley asked.

"You're the ones who refer to our nation as Aether," Shay said. "We know it as the Shadow Lands. Aether is only the city."

Ashley pursed her lips. "Who's the Lady of the Shadows?"

"Who's Baast?" Keagan asked quickly, before Ashley could pursue the questioning further. "Who's Aigua? We all believe as we choose. That's our right."

Ashley quickly backed down. Freedom of religion was one of the basic tenants of the Five Nations. Otherwise, more than one international war would have been fought over the years. "Of course. My apologies."

"Except the Lady is real," Shay said stubbornly. "We've seen her."

Keagan knew a change of subject was required, and immediately.

"Are those horses?" She pointed to a corral constructed near the building. Several four-legged forms grazed in the emerald grass.

Shay followed her gaze, brightening. "Yes. If they have horses—"

"They'll have fodder," Keagan said. "So even if we can't rescue the others, we still have to find a way in there to get food for Onyx."

"Well, I'd hate to think we came all this way for nothing," Ashley said dryly.

Shay crouched down and peered through the vines, studying the clearing intently. Keagan knelt beside her, doing the same. Ashley pushed at the altar, found it solid, and sat down on it, looking very bored. Minutes passed as Keagan tried to determine how many might be in the structure below. Outside, a few figures were walking around, patrolling perhaps. The afternoon was too hot for anyone to be outside otherwise.

Who knew how many were inside? The place was big enough to hold hundreds.

"You're the only one who stands a chance," she murmured, finally.

Shay looked at her, then nodded. "Tonight. I'll slip in, take a look, get out."

Keagan straightened as she saw a group of people appear at the top of the stairs leading into the structure. Four, no, five people, too far away to judge how well armed. They descended the stairs, stood a few moments talking, and then started off toward the west in a steady trot.

"Search party," Shay noted, her voice hard. "Going to find their missing people or, more likely, their prize Elemental."

"Aren't I flattered," Ashley said darkly.

"The only thing they'll find is the empty campsite," Keagan said.

"With a couple of very large scorch marks," Shay said, sounding a little more cheerful. "They'll think she did it. Freed herself of her shackles somehow and is now headed back for the boat. If they don't find her at the boat, they may even think she got lost and start looking for her in the jungle."

"Can you access that Path?" Keagan asked.

"I can. I don't know where it leads, but hopefully to another Path that's more familiar. It's protected well. Those markings are old, but they're strong. No wraith would come within leagues."

"Do you think they use it? Is that how they brought in all these horses and men?"

Shay looked surprised, then her eyes narrowed. "They shouldn't even be aware of it. Unless…" She sounded unhappy.

"Unless they have a Shadow Rider working with them." Keagan gripped Shay's shoulder, squeezing lightly.

"I can't believe a Rider would work with mercenaries," Shay said, but she sounded uncertain.

Behind them, Ashley snorted. "Anyone will do anything—if enough gold's involved."

Keagan suspected only her hand on Shay's shoulder kept her from responding, and she glared at Ashley over her shoulder.

Ashley widened her eyes and spread out her hands. *What?* she mouthed.

Keagan exhaled audibly. "We know they have someone in the marshals working with them. They wouldn't have put their hands on those shackles otherwise."

"What? Those things belong to the marshals?" Ashley was clearly aghast.

"How else would we be able to arrest you?"

"Is that why you joined? To arrest Elementals?"

"No, but on occasion, it's a bonus." Keagan grinned and glanced sideways to see a small grin from Shay, as well. Then she sobered. "Elementals who break the law give all of us a bad name. We nearly destroyed the world. People need to know it will never happen again, for any reason."

"You always did take Mistress Powell's lectures about duty and honor to heart," Ashley said in a strange tone. "I just didn't think you'd build your whole life around them."

"Someone had to." She gave Shay a little shake for support and removed her hand, leaning forward a bit as she peered at the structure. "That looks like some kind of government building. Or a temple of some kind. I wonder what this city was called."

"My map of Aquas shows this area, but no settlements are marked on it. How did they find it? And why this place? Didn't you say there were ruins all up and down the west coast? What makes this one so special?"

"I don't know, but it looks as if they've been here a while. It took a lot of man-hours to clear that much jungle, especially to make pasture for their horses." They continued to focus on the palace, assessing it for strengths and weaknesses.

"So, is it true that Elementals aren't allowed in Aether?" Ashley asked after several minutes of silence had passed. Keagan was surprised she had shut up for that long.

Keagan looked over at Shay curiously. She hadn't heard that, though she had learned more about it in the past few days than she had in her entire life.

"That's true," Shay said, almost absently. "In return for the Paths, the other nations promised to keep Elementals from our lands."

"Well, then, that's just bad negotiating from the start. You'll never have a thriving economy without the companies. They won't do business in a place where they can't send in their people," Ashley said.

"If that's the price, then we pay it." Shay looked troubled, though.

Keagan was troubled as well. If no Elemental was allowed into Aether, and Shay went back there, she'd never be able to see her again. Of course, Shay might continue to travel the nations as a courier, and Keagan still wouldn't see her, but their paths might cross again. The other option offered no hope.

Keagan didn't like that thought.

As the afternoon slowly passed, the three of them settled into the shade of the pyramid and shared some of the food they had scavenged from the mercenary campsite. Then, since she would have to be alert that night, Shay pulled her hood over her head, snuggled down on top of the altar, and dozed off.

"Looks like a little sacrificial lamb in there, doesn't she?" Ashley muttered as she joined Keagan outside the room. They remained concealed in the shade of the pillar. Keagan had been studying the engraved symbols, copying them down in the mercenary's journal as she wondered what they meant, intending to do further research once she returned home.

"What's your problem with her, Ash?" Keagan couldn't tamp down her annoyance as she tucked the journal into her uniform shirt. "She's practically the one person keeping us alive in this place."

"I have no problem with her," Ashley said, with a careless grin. "I just like seeing the expression on your face every time I poke her a little. You get madder than she does." She glanced at her slyly. "Why do you suppose that is, Keagan?"

"You don't know what you're talking about," Keagan said firmly.

"Right, because I don't understand what it's like to play with those who aren't us. You know you have nothing in common there, Keagan. A Rider will never really understand what it's like to be an Elemental, no matter how hard you try to explain it."

"I'll never know what it's like to be her," Keagan said. "That's true for everyone, Ash. I don't know what it's like to burn so hot you can melt anything. You'll never know what it's like to feel submerged all the time."

"But we're not talking about different abilities. We're talking about no abilities at all."

"But she has abilities. She can see perfectly in the dark. Did you know that? She walks through it like it's the brightest day. And the way she moves. Aigua knows neither of us will ever be able to move like that."

"So you like her moves, huh? Just how good does she move?"

Keagan closed her eyes. "Shut up, Ash. Sometimes I don't know why I bother trying to talk to you."

"Sometimes I don't know, either." Ashley paused. "Who's that?"

"What?" Keagan leaned forward and saw a single person running from the west toward the palace. "Hmm. I bet they're coming back to tell them no one's at the campsite."

They watched the figure disappear into the structure. Several minutes passed, almost a half hour, before another group of six, including the first man, rushed out and headed back into the jungle.

"At least fewer people are in there now." Ashley slapped at a bug. "Though I'm a little worried at how many they can pull together for a search team on short notice."

"We'll know more after Shay does some reconnaissance."

"If she doesn't get caught."

"Oh, she won't get caught. Trust me."

They continued to watch until the sun went down. Lights appeared at the entrance of the palace and glinted through windows at various places, tinted the unique white illumination of vapor lamps. Keagan was startled when Shay abruptly appeared beside her, placing a hand on her shoulder.

"Damn, you're quiet," Ashley muttered, having started so bad at Shay's appearance that she was left sprawled over the roof. Brushing herself off in clear irritation, she muttered something else under her breath and went back into the room, forcing her way through the vines.

Keagan caught Shay up on what they had observed. "So fewer people are in there, but I don't know what that means."

"Don't worry. I'll keep a low profile."

"If you come across any shackle keys, make sure you secure them. Each version of cuffs has a corresponding elemental key."

"I'll keep an eye out."

Keagan softened and reached for Shay's hands, gripping them. "Be careful. I wouldn't want to—" *Lose you*, she wanted to say. Instead, she said, "Have to go in after you if things go sideways." She wished she could see Shay's face, although it was so dark, she was a mere shape in the gloom, a bit of extra warmth in the humid air around them.

"I'll be careful. You be careful, too. Keep an eye on your friend. Make sure she doesn't light up anything. It'll show up on a moonless night like this as if we were in the Shadows."

"I understand."

Shay squeezed her hands once, and then she was gone.

VII

After checking on Onyx near the base of the pyramid, Shay began to make her way through the jungle, pausing as she hit the cleared area. Standing in the shadows, she spent several minutes watching the patrolling guard. He mostly seemed bored, keeping to the circle of illumination near the palace entrance. Near the corral, she could hear the shuffling of the horses moving around, soft wickers and snorts, the munching of grass, and gentle thuds of hooves. After she was convinced the guard wouldn't become any more energetic, she tensed and sprinted forward, rolling under the fence and crouching once she was inside.

A couple of horses shied briefly, but none panicked. Reaching down, she felt the grass, realizing it wasn't native to this area. After she pulled out a handful, she checked the dirt below, far darker and richer than it should be. A Chthonic had been here, either voluntarily or coerced to alter the area.

Moving quietly, she slipped through the herd. About ten animals were here, none of which were Shadow-bred, to her relief. Instead, they were small and sturdy, with long ears, intended for carrying rather than riding. Pack horses. When she reached the other side of the corral, she ran lightly along the fence until she was well beyond the view of the guard. Prowling in a wide circle, she searched for another point of entry. As she came around the back of the building, she paused in surprise. They hadn't been able to see this from their vantage point on the pyramid. This entire side had collapsed, a slope of rubble that reached all the way to the top of the structure.

It was perfect, and Shay quickly ascended to cross the roof, pleased when she found a series of openings constructed for ventilation. Slipping through one, she dropped into a dark, empty corridor, dust puffing up around her briefly as she landed. With an effort, she held back a sneeze and looked carefully at the marble floor, not seeing any tracks in the thick dust, no indication anyone had been there for centuries. Apparently, no one was using this part of the building.

A courier didn't do, or shouldn't be doing, this sort of thing, though she was thoroughly enjoying it in some strange way. She wasn't frightened. Instead, she was calm but alert, an anticipatory tingle permeating her. Did Keagan feel this way all the time? Perhaps that was why she had joined the marshals rather than work for some company after leaving the Academy. Perhaps Shay should think about joining them also. But did she even have that option? She'd been channeled into her profession since puberty. It had never occurred to her to be anything else.

That she might want to be anything else.

Drawing her daggers, she quieted her mind and began moving through the corridor, aware of leaving a visible sign of her passage to an experienced tracker, but hoping one wouldn't be checking this part of the palace soon. As she descended a wide staircase, she moved through more dank rooms until she neared a populated area, the sound and light attracting her as much as it would a wraith. Slowing her movements, she endeavored to become even less intrusive.

She constantly noted her surroundings, the place littered with statues and carvings, though the furnishings had long since rotted away. She paused beside a statue of a woman standing about three feet high. Elegant, in a flowing garment, hair piled on her head, she had a serene expression. In her right hand, she held a staff, topped with a crystal shaped very much like the one the wraith had possessed in the Shadow Realm. Shay filed that puzzle away as something to investigate in the future.

Approaching footsteps made her flatten against the wall as flickering light traversed an outer corridor. As she held her breath, two people walked by, a man and a woman, the woman carrying a vapor lamp. Intrigued, Shay waited until they passed and then slipped out after them, slinking along in their wake until they reached a grand room located near the center of the palace. It looked like it had been an important hall at one time, the high walls still draped with the rotted shreds of expansive tapestries. At one end, a dais held the remains of what had possibly been a throne. The couple paused in front of it and embraced.

Shay melted into the protection of a nearby statue, watching as they kissed, trying to take in every detail. The woman wore simple clothes: a brown tunic and trousers tucked into high boots. A long dagger was sheathed on her belt, a crossbow strapped across her back, her quiver of bolts attached to a thigh harness. Her features were plain, but strong, small chin and jaw, a pert nose, framed with dark hair held back in a braid that wrapped around her head. Brown, unremarkable eyes.

The man was dressed much better, his jacket, trousers, and boots made of high-quality leather. Odd tools dangled from his belt. His sword was in a decorated sheath on his back, beneath an engraved shield. Both it and the pommel of the sword bore the insignia of the marshals. Keagan wouldn't like that, Shay thought soberly.

His long hair, a rich chestnut brown, fell nearly to his shoulders. A neatly trimmed mustache and goatee adorned a strong jaw, the man handsome enough that even Shay, with her total disinterest in that sort of thing, could appreciate his looks.

She couldn't hear what they were saying, both murmuring in low, intimate tones, and she debated moving closer. She squelched that thought when they suddenly parted, the woman lifting the lamp higher.

"I'll await your return, my Lord."

"I'll be back tomorrow night, my Lady," he replied as he took one of the unfamiliar devices from his belt. "They need to have found the girl by then. Once the stone has absorbed her abilities and the ritual is finally complete, we'll need to deal with all of them in a way that looks accidental. It's regrettable, but necessary if we want to continue our work unnoticed."

"We'll succeed, my Lord. We've come too far not to."

Shay watched as he put the device around his head. Leather straps held two lenses that he placed over his eyes, like the goggles some wore in a high wind, but these were tinted an odd violet shade, looking black and impenetrable. She doubted he could see through them. Why would he blind himself deliberately? Once they were secure, he took another device from his belt, a tube of some kind, silver, with a handle wrapped in leather. He squeezed a trigger such as a crossbow had, aiming it across the room, thankfully away from Shay's direction.

What happened next made her double over in pain, fear, and shock. She nearly cried out, stuffing her mouth with her fist to stifle her inadvertent grunt. She barely hung on to her daggers.

Wavering in front of him, an entry had appeared, ripped open rather than naturally created, revealing the dark of the Shadow Realm and the Path beyond. He stepped through and was gone, the rip sealing behind him in a ragged line of blackness that lingered for several minutes in the air before gradually fading away.

Sweat beaded her forehead as Shay cowered by the statue, breathing shallowly as the woman, clearly oblivious to her presence, left the room. It took another few moments before Shay could stand, the violation of the Path still lingering, her joints aching, a dull pain throbbing at the base of her skull.

Whatever was going on here went against everything she thought she knew about the world. The man was no Shadow Rider. In fact, though she hadn't been close enough to be certain, she bet his eyes were green in that particular vivid shade that only the Chthonic possessed. She needed to return to civilization as soon as possible and alert someone with far more authority than she possessed.

With an effort, Shay straightened and slipped out of the hall, moving back toward the unoccupied area of the palace, taking an alternate route, wanting to see as much as possible. She came upon an area containing supplies: boxes and burlap bags stacked high, various weapons, and stores of provisions piled neatly. The sight of several sacks of grain made her stop and regard her surroundings with far more interest.

Against one wall stood a table with tools and peacekeeper cuffs scattered over it. Hanging above it she saw a heavy brass ring with several keys attached. Shay paused, thought about it, then walked toward it, all the while listening intently for any approaching footsteps. On either side of the table were two doors made of solid wood, recently added, each boasting a large, brass lock. Meant to keep something inside from being easily accessible. Or, more likely, to keep somebody inside from getting out.

She hesitated, evaluating her idea, and then, before she could talk herself out of it, she gathered all the cuffs and stuffed them into her tunic before grabbing the key ring. Moving over to the doors, she searched through the varied keys, found a likely match, and unlocked the closest one. Cracking it open, she slipped inside and quickly closed the door behind her, pausing for a moment to listen.

When she turned back into the room, she saw a young woman sitting up on the bunk, impossibly slight, a mere wisp of a girl. With golden features, she was clearly from Arias, her short shock of sunny blond hair standing straight up from her head. Her cloud-gray eyes were wide as she regarded Shay. Her mouth dropped open, but she closed it again as Shay put her finger to her lips. For a moment, they regarded each other in the light from the single vapor lamp on the wall.

"I'm Shay," she said finally, in a low tone. "Shadow Rider. I'm here with a marshal. Are you a captive?"

The girl lifted her hands, shaking them to reveal the silver cuffs binding them. Shay nodded and moved quickly to her. It took several tries before Shay noticed the identical symbols between the lock and the key, indicating the cuffs were designed to hold Sylphs. She should have paid closer attention to what Keagan had said.

"Cassius is in the next cell," the girl said in a low voice as she scrabbled for her boots, pulling them on. She wore a simple gray tunic and tight, blue leggings. An odd layer of fabric ran from her sleeves to the outside seams of her legs, unlike anything Shay had seen before. "I'm Lyria, by the way."

"Cassius?"

"A Chthonic. We've been here for days."

"Any other prisoners?"

"Only us that I know of."

"All right. We need to get out of here. Stay quiet and follow me."

"Are you taking us into the Shadows?"

Shay almost shuddered, the pain from the incident in the grand hall still lingering. "Not now. Let's get out of here first, and I'll be glad to answer all your questions once we're safe."

After checking to make sure no one had entered the outer room while she'd been busy freeing Lyria, Shay slipped out and went to the next door, searching her stock of keys before she found one that fit the door. Stepping inside, she had to duck quickly as a large woman swung at her, hands together in a fist, with a blow that would have knocked Shay flat had it connected.

"Cassius, no!" Lyria hissed from behind Shay. "She's here to rescue us."

The woman straightened. She was older, close to forty, with silver appearing in her dark-chestnut hair that was cut short and neat, practical rather than fashionable. She wore a brown doeskin vest over a green flannel shirt, tucked into trousers made of the rugged denim material that those in Terras favored. Her features square and tanned, she had a firm jaw and high cheeks, and her piercing emerald eyes swept Shay up and down with keen assessment. Unlike Ashley's scornful look upon meeting her, however, this gaze was measured, and Shay might have even described it as kind. "Sorry."

"No talking," Shay insisted as she unlocked the cuffs.

"I get that," Cassius said somberly, "but you need to know something. We can't help you. They've taken our abilities."

"With a diamond-shaped stone, by any chance?" Shay said dryly as she tucked the cuffs and keys into her belt.

The women stared at her. "You know about that?"

"I'm not sure I know anything," she said soberly. "But we'll catch up once we're safe. Any idea how many are here?"

"Fifty-three people are working for the Shadow Lord and his woman," Cassius said, her tone so precise that Shay didn't question the number. "Four of them left the day before yesterday to meet a boat."

That was the second time she'd heard the title. She filed it away, too, but her head was starting to feel crowded with all this strange new information.

"Yeah. I met them."

"A lot more left earlier today," Lyria said. "They were upset." She regarded Shay curiously. "Your doing?"

"You could say that." Shay did the math in her head. Fourteen were gone, then, fifteen including the "lord." That left plenty unaccounted for, as well as the woman with the lamp. So one Shadow Rider and two Elementals without weapons or abilities against forty. Not to mention that any of the search parties might return at any time.

"We slip out without anyone being the wiser," Shay said. "Keagan will know what to do from here."

"Who's Keagan?" Lyria asked brightly.

"The marshal," Shay said. "Quiet. Follow me."

In the outer room, Lyria and Cassius secured personal supplies, including weapons. They both took crossbows and quivers of bolts, while, additionally, Cassius grabbed a long pole from the corner. A quarterstaff, Shay thought, and eyed the familiar way Cassius handled the weapon. Clearly, she was trained, and skillful in that training. That upped the odds in their favor a bit, but Shay would still prefer to vacate the area without anyone knowing they had left, or that she had ever been there.

As Shay was about to exit the room, she paused to grab one of the sacks of grain, hefting it over her shoulder. The other women eyed her skeptically, and she made a face at them, hoping they wouldn't waste time asking questions. Fortunately, they seemed to acknowledge the urgency of the situation and followed without speaking.

When they reached the unoccupied part of the palace, Shay stopped Lyria before she could activate a hand torch. "No. No light."

"We can't see," Cassius said.

"Grab my belt," Shay said. "Lyria, you grab hers. Follow immediately behind me. Don't deviate, and you won't run into anything."

The women looked at each other, but clearly they were willing to trust her at the moment. Shay felt them take hold, and she led them through the corridors, following the very apparent trail she had left until she was in the hall where she had first entered. She looked up at the vent about twelve feet above her and eased the bag of grain off her shoulder before turning to the other two.

"Okay, there's an opening near the ceiling," she whispered. "It leads to the roof. Lyria, if I give you a boost, can you reach it?"

"I can't even see it," Lyria muttered. "It's pitch-black in here."

Shay exhaled, thinking. This part of the palace was a good distance from where the women had been held, and she couldn't hear anything. "Okay. You can light your torch now, but don't turn it too high."

She closed her eyes as Lyria thumbed the switch to set the vapor alight, adjusting her vision so it wouldn't blind her. The two women were waiting expectantly, looking up at the window.

"You came in that way?" Cassius sounded dubious.

"Yes." Shay held out her hand. "Lyria?"

Lyria exchanged a look with Cassius, then handed her the torch. "Aim it at the window."

As Cassius sent the beam of light up, Lyria ran a few strides, stepped onto Shay's linked hands, and jumped, aided by Shay's push. She was much lighter than Shay had anticipated, and for a horrified second, Shay was concerned she had catapulted her into the ceiling, but at the last second, Lyria somehow twisted in midair, grabbed the top edge of the window, and shot through onto the roof.

Shay let her breath out in a huff at the display of acrobatics and then looked at Cassius, who was regarding her keenly. "You next. I'll lift you."

Cassius shook her head. "I'm a lot heavier than I look."

Shay believed that. Chthonic were usually solid muscle, drawing on the earth beneath them, and this woman looked even fitter for her age, broad-shouldered and wide-hipped. Her thighs were like tree trunks. "That's okay," Shay told her. "I'm a lot stronger than I look."

Cassius didn't appear entirely convinced, but she put the lamp on the floor and then stepped onto Shay's offered hands. Lifting with her legs, because Cassius had not undersold how solid she was, Shay nonetheless was able to raise her high enough for her to grab the windowsill. With Lyria pulling, Cassius wiggled through, though it was touch-and-go for a minute.

Then her face appeared.

"Okay," she whispered.

"Take this," Shay said. First, she tossed up the torch, which Cassius caught easily, handing it back to Lyria. Then Shay hefted the bag of grain and threw it up toward the opening, where it caught briefly on the sill, long enough for Cassius to grab it and pull it through.

"Now you," Cassius said and reached down with her hand.

Shay nodded, backed up several steps, and then ran at the wall, taking two strides up and grabbing Cassius's arm, feeling the strong grip close around her. With minimal effort, Cassius hauled her the rest of the way up and through the vent so quickly Shay was nearly tossed across the roof.

"Douse the light," Shay whispered once she regained her bearings. Lady bless her, Cassius was *strong.*

After picking up the sack of grain, she had Cassius grasp her belt again, with Lyria behind her, and silently led them down the rubble slope to the ground.

"Steal some horses?" Cassius hissed as they neared the corral.

"They're pack animals," Shay told her. She eyed Cassius. "And too small for you, anyway."

Cassius shrugged. "Okay."

Leaving the horses undisturbed, Shay led them through the corral and out the other side, where they slipped into the jungle.

VIII

It felt like hours had passed, and Keagan could scarcely breathe. It wasn't the first time she'd had to wait for an operation to run its course while she was stuck on surveillance, but she'd never experienced such tension before. She knew it was only because it was Shay out there alone. But she wasn't ready to address what that meant to her personally in the long term.

"She'll be all right," Ashley said, suddenly. She was sitting cross-legged next to Keagan, bow resting on her lap, the quiver strapped over her back. Several of the arrows had their heads replaced, the steel tips giving way to vials of powder with a brief fuse inserted into each. Others glistened from oil that Ashley had applied to the heads, highly flammable, requiring only a spark to set them ablaze.

"I just wish I could see something," Keagan said. The only thing visible in the distance were the lights in the entrance at the top of the stairs, though Keagan doubted that Shay would try to enter through the front door. She wasn't sure there was another way in, however. "It's so quiet."

"Quiet is good," Ashley reminded her. "If things liven up, that's when you need to worry."

"I know." Keagan drew a sharpening stone along the edge of her sword, the scraping sound soothing in its familiarity. "But I should have gone with her."

"You'd have held her back." Ashley didn't mince words. "You were right. She bloody disappears when she moves. I've never seen anything like it. She should be an assassin, not a mail carrier."

"I don't think she'd like being an assassin."

"Know her that well, do you? When exactly did you meet again? A week ago?"

"What's your point?"

"Other than the obvious? None at all." It was too dark to see Ashley's expression, but Keagan suspected she was smiling smugly.

She opened her mouth to respond when—

"You need to come with me."

"Baast's tits!" Ashley started with such force, falling over onto her side, that she nearly dumped her quiver, which, considering the contents, might have been very bad.

Keagan thought her heart would thrash its way out of her chest. She managed not to squeak, but it was close. "Shay! You're back."

"And I've got friends. Look, no time to explain. We need to get out of here."

Keagan felt Shay's fingers encircle her wrist, and then she was being urged to her feet. Sheathing her sword, she followed as they moved to the stairs and stumbled down the crumbling pyramid. Keagan could barely see Shay in front of her, but it was fortunate she was there, because when Keagan tripped, Shay was able to catch her.

"Quietly," Shay said as she righted her.

"Yeah, Keagan. Quietly," Ashley muttered from behind them. "You're like a cow in a porcelain shop."

Keagan gave Ashley a poisonous look over her shoulder that she knew likely couldn't be seen and managed to make it the rest of the way down without incident. As they joined Onyx, she was surprised to see he was already saddled, a burlap sack of grain added to all the other items they had tied to it. She was even more surprised to find two strangers standing near him, one clearly Chthonic and the other with the slight, hollow-boned build of a Sylph. The Sylph was holding a torch on its lowest setting, barely illuminating their faces.

"Introductions later," Shay said before anyone could speak. "We're taking the Path and leaving here before anyone knows Cassius and Lyria are gone." She turned to them. "Look, I'm a courier, not a guide. I don't have the proper equipment to make sure you're safe. All I can do is tie you together, but if anything attacks…well, we'll all be dead anyway, so it doesn't matter."

"What?" Ashley looked incredulous as Shay wrapped a rope around her waist before moving on to Keagan.

"I'll lead Onyx. Each of you will hang onto the saddle, Keagan and Ashley, on his left. Cassius and Lyria, you're on his right."

"Wait, can't we discuss this?" Ashley looked at the two newcomers. "How about you? Any objections? You know, the rational kind?"

The Chthonic Keagan assumed was named Cassius merely shrugged. "She's gotten us this far. And Lurra knows, I want to get as far away from here as possible."

"Douse the lamp," Shay said. "We can't have any excess noise and absolutely no light once we're in the Shadows. It attracts the wrong kind of attention."

"And we don't want that attention," Keagan added somberly. "I was in there. We'll be blind. Nearly deaf. Your elemental sense will be gone, your reserves drained. There's no moisture or flame or earth to draw upon and barely enough air to breathe."

"Well, it's not like our abilities are working anyway," Lyria said.

Keagan looked at her, a multitude of questions trembling on her lips, but Shay was right. Explanations would have to wait. She could hear faint shouting from a distance.

"Don't mean to hurry you, Rider, but it appears they've discovered our absence," Cassius said.

"Everyone have hold of Onyx?"

At everyone's mutters of assent, Shay took Onyx by the bridle and lifted her hand. "Here we go."

Keagan swallowed hard as, suddenly, an entry appeared before them, darker than dark, and without hesitation, Shay led them forward. The Shadows wrapped around them like a shroud, pressing in with tangible pressure even though it was nothingness. Keagan hadn't really had time to notice how oppressive it was before, too busy fighting for her life, but now she was keenly aware of all the things she couldn't sense. She kept straining to see, and she closed her eyes, just to give them a break.

"Undine, you were wrong," Lyria said suddenly, her voice high. "Whatever we're breathing, it's not any kind of air I recognize."

"Quiet!" Shay said. "Walk. Don't try for anything more."

Obediently, they fell into step with the horse, clenching his tack. Keagan touched Shay on the back. Shay either didn't feel it through her leathers or, more hopefully, didn't mind Keagan's resting her hand on her. Time seemed to lose all meaning. They could have been walking for hours, though Keagan suspected it was only minutes. With hardly any sound, their footsteps, the rustle of clothing, the sounds of their breathing, all strangely muted, the noise seemed to come from very far away, through a fog. The atmosphere around them was cool but very dry.

So dry.

Keagan sensed the moisture in the bodies around her and steeled herself not to draw on it, not to automatically fill her reserves that suddenly seemed achingly empty. Were Cassius and Lyria forced to resist as well—Cassius with the minerals found naturally in a human and equine body, Lyria with the gases moving in and out of their lungs? Aigua only knew what urge Ashley was fighting. Such were the conditions in this Shadow Realm that the thought would even occur to Keagan.

She shuddered, horror edging her mind.

After too long, Shay paused. "The Path ends ahead. I don't sense another. These markings are very odd."

"Any idea where it comes out?" Keagan whispered.

"None."

"Any other choice?"

"Only to wander around in the Shadows and hope to find another Path."

"So we should leave here, then."

"I guess we have to."

"Are they like this all the time?" Lyria asked quietly.

"You have no idea," Ashley said.

Keagan felt the muscles in Shay's back tense, and then suddenly, she saw light, all of them objecting as they stumbled into it. Only after a few moments had passed and their vision adjusted did Keagan realize they were in the deep shadow of a high cliff, and the sun wasn't shining directly on them at all. Only the contrast to absolute darkness made it seem so painfully bright.

"Where the fuck are we?" Ashley unwrapped herself from the rope and tossed it over to Keagan, who barely got her hand up in time to catch the loop.

She untied herself and handed it to Cassius over Onyx's back, then turned to look at Shay. "How long were we walking? All night? It didn't seem like it."

The Shadow Rider was standing before a stone obelisk set into a rock-face, studying it with a strange intensity. It was constructed from the same reddish-brown stone around it, making it hard to distinguish. Around them, the vegetation was sparse, spiky, unfamiliar to Keagan, and the smells that filled her nostrils were dusty, harsh, not at all like the salt humidity she was used to. They definitely weren't in Aquas anymore. It was just as hot, however.

Across from them was another cliff, and Keagan realized they were in a small canyon, the sides towering over them. Not far away, where the canyon narrowed to a point, a steady gush of water fell into a small pool of clear water that was so sweet, she nearly wept at its purity as she drew it within herself, washing away the lingering horror of the Shadow Realm.

"I think we're in Arias," Lyria said with a note of wonder. "It smells like home. I'm not sure where, though. Maybe north?"

"Rider?" Ashley asked. "Any idea?"

Shay seemed so lost in thought that Keagan wasn't sure she had even heard the question, but then she turned. "This isn't the entry location of any Path I know."

"Do you know every Path?" Cassius asked. She had coiled the rope and tied it to Onyx's saddle. Now she was standing near his head, stroking his neck. He leaned into the caress and nudged her shoulder with his muzzle, even though she was a stranger. Keagan wondered if she should feel jealous.

"Not at all, but I should, at the very least, recognize what's written on this marker, telling me where we are." Shay touched one of the engravings, tracing it lightly as she shook her head. "This is the ancient symbol for Arias. Lyria is right. It's late afternoon, but it's not the next day. It's the same day, only ten hours earlier. We've traveled west, much farther than we should have considering the amount of time we spent on the Path."

Keagan blinked, confused. "We've traveled back through time?"

Shay shook her head. "No. The sun rises and sets ten hours later in Arias than it does in Aquas, so while it's just past midnight where we were, it's afternoon here."

While Keagan tried to wrap her head around that explanation, she noticed equal confusion on the others' faces and the beginning of anxiousness that could easily lead to panic.

"So. What now?" Lyria looked very small, shoulders hunched as if afraid of another blow.

"Figure out where we are," Keagan said, firming her tone. In situations like this it was best to sound like she knew what she was doing, even if she didn't. "Shay has maps of every nation. If we can determine the local landmarks, or take readings from the stars, we'll be able to determine where the nearest settlement is."

"Well, someone's been here," Cassius said, kneeling as she brushed at the ground. "Tracks from horses, three or four maybe."

"The Shadow Lord would have been ahead of us," Shay said. "He probably had a ride waiting. If we follow the trail, we can find out where he's going."

"The Shadow Lord?" Ashley glanced from face to face. "Who in Baast's name is that?"

Keagan caught Shay's eye. "Let's get something to eat, rest a bit, and catch up on what's going on."

As she dug out some meat and cornmeal wraps from the saddlebags, she took stock of what they had left. With two more people, it wouldn't last more than a couple of days. That fact concerned her because this area didn't look nearly as bountiful as the jungle, which had barely been bountiful at all. As everyone ate, Shay told her and Ashley what had happened when she was reconnoitering the palace, including what she saw in the throne room. She could hear the horror of that moment still lingering in Shay's voice. Then Keagan filled in Cassius and Lyria on how they had come across the mercenaries while walking through the jungle, just in time to rescue Ashley before deciding to rescue them, tactfully leaving out that it wouldn't have happened except for Ashley's slip of the tongue. Finally, Cassius and Lyria revealed how they came to be captured in the first place.

"I was working in a community just outside Zephyrus," Cassius said.

"Not large, mostly just the farming cooperative and a crossroads where the market's held every week."

"What were you doing there?" Keagan asked.

"Trying to determine if it's possible to grow certain fruit trees. The soil in Arias isn't very good, as you know, and they don't get a lot of rain. But the farming cooperative that we're working with had just hired a couple of Undine fresh out of the Academy to provide water directly from the river, and they wanted to see if they could supply some exotic fruits for the gourmet trade."

"They wanted you to enrich the soil?" Shay asked.

"Yes," Cassius said. "We were negotiating a price, and how long the contract would run."

"Is that what you do? Go to places and enrich the soil?"

"It's what my company does, yes. We work with local agriculture in all Five Nations to not only maintain their current viability, keeping the land arable, but also if they want to open new areas where the soil isn't as good." She paused and regarded Shay curiously. "Well, Four Nations, actually. What kind of soil is in Aether? I've never met anyone who's been there. Do you really have types of grass that doesn't grow anywhere else?"

Shay lifted her brows. "I'm not sure. I'm not a herdsman."

"Is that relevant to why you were kidnapped?" Ashley asked. The corner of her mouth twisted a little. "Let me guess. You met a farmer in a bar."

"No. I was surveying the new fields, taking samples," Cassius said after eyeing Ashley. Keagan suspected she wasn't the sort to suffer fools gladly, and that if Ashley tested her, she'd be brought to heel quickly. "I planned to be out there a few days. The first night, a couple dropped by the campsite. Gave the impression they were with the cooperative." She shook her head. "I let down my guard."

"The Shadow Lord?" Shay asked.

"And Olive, his, uh, partner in crime, I guess. Though I think they may be a couple."

"They are," Shay said. "Their farewell in the throne room was definitely romantic."

"Anyway, Olive offered to cook dinner. She must have put a sedative in the stew." Cassius shook her head with an expression of disgust either at them, or at herself, for being deceived. "When I woke up, I was cuffed and in a cell half a world away."

"That's a little like what happened to me," Lyria said. "My company assigned me to Vokanus. They're trying to create an airship."

"Airship?" Keagan asked. "A ship that can fly?"

"Something like that," Lyria said. "They think if they can find the right ratio of gases combined and contained in a large sack of some kind, they can achieve enough lift to transport people and cargo faster than ships or caravans. I was working with a Salamas, Zika, who's experimenting with the heat input." She shrugged. "It's decent pay, and the company provides living accommodations on the top floor of the highest building in the city."

For a Sylph fresh from the Academy, as Lyria appeared to be, that last enticement would have been the only real perk. While any Elemental could make a decent wage in their native land, only working in the nations lacking that particular elemental resource made one truly wealthy. But living so far away from the open desert of Arias at such a young age, surrounded by mountains and deep gorges, staying in a city constructed low to prevent collapse during earthquakes would have been difficult. Keagan wondered how often Lyria would have made it home.

"What happened?" she asked gently.

"I was out with some friends. There's this place up the mountain." Lyria hesitated, glancing at Cassius, who inclined her head. "It's really high. My friends had never seen anyone fly before, so I was showing them how we ride the winds. A couple of marshals showed up. A man and a woman. They said I wasn't allowed to display my abilities without authorization from the company, that it violated my contract, and that I was under arrest."

"They cuffed her, took her away from her friends, and then drugged her once they were out of sight." Cassius's brows were lowered, her gaze stormy.

"I don't think they were real marshals," Lyria said. "At least, I hope they weren't."

"Me, too," Keagan said, anger stirring sour in her stomach. She was very much afraid that at least one of them was. Perhaps the woman?

"Besides, there's no law against Elementals showing their abilities anywhere in Urodela." Ashley's eyes glowed gold. "Arias, Urodela, Terras, Aquas—this damned Shadow Lord certainly gets around, doesn't he?" She glared at Shay. "Out of Aether?"

"No. He doesn't walk the Paths as we do." She frowned. "He used some sort of device to tear open an entry. And he was wearing something over his eyes. Perhaps it allows him to see in the Shadows."

"We know he isn't from Aether," Cassius said. "He's Chthonic."

"You're sure?" Keagan kept trying to arrange all this information into a comprehensible picture. She was good at deduction, but at the moment, too many pieces still seemed to be missing.

"Very." Cassius narrowed her eyes. "Weak, though. Level point five or one at best."

"Why did he take you?" Keagan asked.

"Well, our captors weren't very generous with the details," Cassius said. "We overheard a bit from the guards when they fed us, but not much. I don't even know this guy's name. They all called him Lord, but they didn't add a clan designation."

"Then they used that crystal on us." Lyria slumped against the boulder she was leaning on, suddenly looking very small. "It knocked us out. When we woke up, our abilities were gone." Tears welled up, and Keagan realized just how frightened she was.

"I don't think it's permanent." Keagan glanced at Shay, and at her slight nod, she firmed her jaw. "The same thing happened to me." She explained her encounter with the wraiths in Naiad and what happened in the Shadow Realm, trying not to look at Ashley as she spoke. She could only imagine Ashley's expression when she realized Keagan had been bluffing. "Fortunately," she said, sending up a small stream of water that danced in the air above her hand, "I'm almost back to full strength. It took nearly a week."

"That's a relief," Cassius said. "They used it on us the night before last. It was…" She paused, obviously trying to think of the right words. "Disturbing."

"It sounds horrible." Ashley looked at Shay, eyes glowing slightly. "I guess you showed up at the right time. I didn't have to go through any of that."

Probably as close to a "thank you" as they would ever get, Keagan thought.

"Well, not getting their hands on you is really going to upset their plans," Cassius said, gesturing at Ashley. "I had the impression the rock needed to absorb all four abilities to do whatever they planned."

"They planned to kill you after some kind of 'ritual,'" Shay said. Everyone stared at her, clearly horrified. She exhaled, looking slightly bashful. "Sorry. Did I forget to mention that part?"

"Without Ashley, that means they might go looking for another Salamas," Keagan said. "We really need to get back to Naiad. The Council has to hear about this."

"We'll follow the trail," Shay said. "It must lead somewhere that can take us to a village or town. Once we catch up to this Shadow Lord, I'll kill him."

Keagan winced and noticed the expressions of the others had changed from horror to varying degrees of concern and offense. "Um, we'll take him into custody," she said calmly. "Charge him with kidnapping." She didn't add that the death of an Elemental at the hands of a Shadow Rider would have political repercussions that would echo throughout the farthest regions of the Five Nations.

"Right, because crimes against the Shadow Lands don't count, only

Elementals do," Shay said, regarding her with a hint of betrayal in her dark eyes. She rose to her feet. "I need to feed Onyx."

She strode away, anger radiating from every line, leaving the four of them sitting near the pool.

A few moments of awkward silence passed, and then Cassius exhaled audibly. "She's not wrong, you know. Man probably needs killing. Especially since he was planning to kill us. He's gone completely rogue."

"But she can't be the one to do it," Ashley said bluntly. "It's unacceptable."

"Plus, it would be useful to discover why he's doing what he's doing," Keagan pointed out. "He can't answer questions if he's dead. He also seems to have his hands on formidable resources, far more than he should at his skill level." She shook her head. "I don't know how the Council isn't aware of this."

Ashley looked at her. "What makes you think they aren't?"

Keagan was equal parts shocked and offended. "What do you mean?"

"Just that you don't hire this many mercenaries without word getting around," Ashley said. "And it's not like traveling into the Wilderness with that many people wouldn't be noticed. Supplies have to be purchased, transportation has to be arranged, people and cargo have to be moved. So either the Council is oblivious to a major operation going on in Aquas, when they normally don't miss much, or an important palm somewhere is getting greased to smooth the process. That's just how it works."

Cassius leaned back against the boulder. "I hate to admit it, but she's right. Not necessarily that the Council's aware of what's going on, just that someone in a very high place has to be actively covering it up."

Cassius's expression became very grave. "Whoever this Lord is, he's not working alone."

IX

Shay fed Onyx a handful of grain at a time, not wanting him to overindulge after going without for so long. She tried not to feel so betrayed. After all, what did she expect? Keagan was an Elemental, just like the rest. They protected their own, even those who preyed on others. It was a matter of pride that they stood apart from most of the population. Shay had no place in their world. Just because she had started to believe that Keagan might be different, might look at her as different in the same way, didn't make it so.

She wouldn't forget that fact again.

A part of her understood that what she said might have been a little inflammatory, but she didn't plan to assassinate this Chthonic. Yet if he attacked her, if he attacked her nation, she would defend herself and her people, even if it meant putting down an Elemental. She was just disappointed that Keagan didn't seem to understand that intent.

She had a right to feel disappointed. Didn't she?

"Shay?" Keagan came around Onyx, patting him briefly on the flank as she passed.

Shay pulled out another handful of grain, stubbornly keeping her attention on her mount so she didn't have to look at her. She heard Keagan sigh softly.

"You know that killing mercenaries is one thing," Keagan said finally, in a soft voice. "Most of them probably had bounties on their heads to begin with. But an Elemental?"

"Who clearly hired all those mercenaries to do his dirty work," Shay pointed out.

"I know." Keagan paused. "Shay, personally, I wouldn't blame you if you did kill him. He probably deserves it." Reluctantly, Shay lifted her eyes to meet Keagan's, seeing the compassion and warmth within the oceanic depths. "But it's not my opinion that matters here," Keagan said "What do you think would happen if you killed him? How do you think the Council would react if a Shadow Rider killed an Elemental? The crown? They'd be forced to act, not just with you, but possibly with

Aether." She paused, meeting Shay's gaze squarely, her expression open and just the slightest bit yearning. "And if anything ever happened to you, I'm not sure what I'd do."

Shay was so stunned she wasn't aware of Keagan moving closer until her body was almost pressed against her. Reaching up, Keagan placed her hand against Shay's cheek, cupping it lightly, the warmth penetrating to the bone. She regarded her for a long moment, searching Shay's face as if memorizing it, then leaned forward, her lips a mere breath away. Shay thought her heart would stop.

Suddenly they heard someone approaching, footsteps squelching on sand, and Keagan stepped back, quickly dropping her hand.

"So, are we following this trail?" Cassius stepped around Onyx, looked at them both, and hesitated as she raised both eyebrows. "Uh, sorry. Am I interrupting?"

"No. We were just deciding what to do," Keagan said smoothly.

Cassius didn't look as if she believed her but had the grace to move on as if she did. "What do we have in terms of supplies?"

"Some food," Keagan said. "It should last a couple of days. A tent, Shay's equipment, our weapons, and one horse to carry it all."

Lyria and Ashley joined them. "We should have taken some horses back in Aquas," Lyria said.

"I couldn't guide those animals through the Shadows," Shay told her, finally finding her voice again. She still felt a little light-headed about what had almost just happened, as if her brain wasn't quite connected to her body, but she had to shrug it off. "They wouldn't have trusted us without time to bond. Without that preparation, they'd panic. It was hard enough keeping you four from panicking, and you understood what was happening." She took Onyx's reins, wrapping them around her hand. "We walk from here."

"Well, then, I'm glad I changed my boots," Ashley said.

At Keagan's nod, Shay led the way from the gully, the others falling in step around her. As they went up the slight slope, away from the canyon walls, they stepped out into the desert, where they stopped as one, staring out over the blasted landscape that lay before them. Dry, arid earth, baked hard, stretched on for leagues, flat and cracked, interspersed here and there with spiked, stunted bushes that looked black, as if burnt. In the distance, reddish rocks rose, massive formations carved into odd shapes by the wind that blew harsh and dry, rippling as if in water. Not a cloud was in the sky, and sand peppered Shay's skin, thrown up by the capricious breeze. Drawing her scarf over her face, she squinted as the sun beat down, struck by how the heat penetrated, like a blacksmith's furnace. The shadowed area of the canyon had protected them, feeling almost fifteen degrees cooler. No such protection lay ahead of them.

"Sweet Sirocco, we're in the Badlands," Lyria said, sounding shocked and a little frightened.

"What are the Badlands?" Shay asked.

"Where the people of Arias once lived," Keagan said. "This is like the west coast of Aquas, where the original cities and towns were located. All destroyed in the War."

"So that Path from one ancient area in Aquas led to another in Arias," Ashley said, thoughtfully. "Did the Paths once join the old places like they do with the current cities?"

Shay felt overwhelmed with all she was learning. "Possibly," she said, with difficulty. "If you'd asked me a day ago, I would have laughed at the idea. Now I realize I may not know anything."

"This was once our best land," Lyria said soberly. "On the banks of the River Anemoi, we could grow more than enough food to feed the whole of the Five Nations. It was the source of travel, trade, and life. Now the river is polluted, filled with dangerous creatures, and the soil on the banks only allows the toughest weeds to grow. We have to live in the south along a pathetic excuse of a stream, where sandstorms kill our crops, and we have barely enough fresh water to sustain us. Only the work the Sylphs find outside keeps the nation's economy aloft."

Shay wasn't sure what to say. She now knew the east coast of Aquas was as habitable as the west, but currently, ships had to sail the Alameada Ocean by going north up the coast and around the top of the nation, before heading southwest along the Paracelsus Sea to Terras. That was why merchants were willing to pay Shadow Riders to transport certain goods in a timelier fashion. The war had done that by turning their west coast into ruins.

Terras, meanwhile, was settled mostly in the west and south, which remained incredibly fertile, while their side of the Khamsin Mountains was filled with glacial lakes and rivers that provided the whole nation with plentiful fresh water. It suddenly occurred to Shay that no settlements existed on the length of coast, even when, logically, there should be several. But only the southernmost part of the coast had a major city on it, Port Tanmen. It was Terras's single trading harbor on the Alameada Ocean, where ships from Aquas docked.

"The northeastern part of Terras," Shay asked. "On the coast. Was that originally settled before the War?"

Cassius nodded. "Yes. Several cities once thrived there, but all were laid waste during the final months. The surviving population moved inland and never went back. We call that area the Chimera Wastelands. Even today, the weather in that area is extreme. Storms occur every few weeks, and they're bad. Water surges inland for leagues, with wind so strong it can drive a piece of wood through a person's body, even if they're wearing armor. The blizzards in the winter can freeze a person solid in minutes before burying them in snow ten feet deep. It's not worth trying to make a living there. Not when the weather's much easier elsewhere."

"Your northern farms, though. They extend farther east than most."

"They do." Cassius lifted her brow. "They're not the most productive. Those who couldn't afford land in the south or west settled there, and offering land grants so far to the northeast caused a bit of a scandal. People accused the assembly of being greedy, of trying to take advantage of the poorer families, but plenty took them up on it. To own your own land? Run your own farm? Be accorded lordship? That's hard to resist, regardless of where it's located."

"I wonder if this Shadow Lord was one of those farmers," Shay said.

Cassius looked thoughtful. "That might explain the 'lord' and that he's Chthonic. Though not how he can find lost Paths."

"Maybe he liked to explore the wastelands on his days off," Shay said. "Lyria, can we walk in this? How hot does it get?"

"Brutally hot," Lyria said. "But the real problem is the lack of water. As long as we stay hydrated, we would probably survive." She looked inquiringly at Keagan.

"I'll be able to draw on the pool back there for about twenty leagues," Keagan said. "Then I'll have to find water from somewhere else. I can sense the river. It's not far from here, but you're right. It's vile and would take a lot of energy to purify it enough for drinking, maybe more than I can manage. There's a system of aquifers beneath Arias in the south. I heard that Undine working there draw on them to fill wells, but I'm not sure the system extends this far north."

"We'll return to the pool," Shay said. "We'll drink our fill until we're completely hydrated. Onyx, too. You may feel like urinating, but restrain yourselves. Once we're walking, the urge will pass, especially once we start to sweat."

"Once I reach the limit of my ability to draw from the pool, I'll refill the canteens a final time," Keagan said. "Hopefully, we'll have reached someplace a little more hospitable before we run out."

"What if we don't?" Ashley, of course, didn't feel the heat at all, perfectly comfortable even in this landscape. But while she would survive longer than the rest, even she needed to eventually hydrate.

"This lord is riding, but he can't have gone far," Shay said as they headed back to the pool. "He told the woman he would return to her by tomorrow night. With the time difference, he didn't plan to be here long."

Cassius twirled her quarterstaff. "We may even meet him on the way back." She sounded rather pleased at the prospect.

"Again, if that occurs, we arrest him," Keagan said.

"He might resist," Cassius said.

"Even so."

"Fine." Cassius sighed and winked at Shay, which surprised her.

After drinking their fill at the pool, Shay fed Onyx another handful of grain and began to lead him forward, studying the trail laid out before her. She saw tracks from four distinct sources, traveling in a straight line. The distance between strides indicated they were galloping. Wherever they were going, they were in a hurry. Still, Cassius was right. They would probably encounter this Shadow Lord and his friends on the way back.

Shay considered that possibility as they stepped out into the desert and began their journey across the barren wastes. This land made her feel painfully exposed. The canyon was rapidly falling behind them, and the pitiless sun provided few shadows. The ones that did exist wavered weakly, barely there, leaving no real darkness for her to use. She was uncomfortably aware that this lord was probably riding with three more mercenaries, undoubtedly fully armed. And he was Elemental, capable of using all this earth around them to his advantage.

Then she glanced at the others walking beside her and relaxed a little. She wasn't alone. Even without their abilities, Cassius and Lyria looked quite capable, while Keagan had almost returned to full strength, all the while being very formidable with a sword and shield.

And then there was Ashley.

Yes, if this Shadow Lord showed up, Shay would just stand back and wait for him to insult the Salamas in some fashion, possibly by looking at her the wrong way. Then it would simply be a matter of staying upwind and not getting any ash caught in her throat.

She'd take those odds any day.

X

The sun was merciless. Keagan tried to walk in the little shade provided by Onyx's comforting bulk, forcing herself not to lose any more moisture to the dry air than she could prevent. She was also keenly aware of feeling dirty. Though she and Shay had both taken time to bathe in the ocean while on the beach, once they were forced into the jungle, they'd had no opportunity for hygiene. And of course, she'd been wearing the same set of clothes for days now.

And she had tried to kiss Shay? It was a wonder the poor woman hadn't passed out from the body odor alone.

Fretting about that little moment in the canyon kept her from worrying about where they were going and what they would do when they got there. The whole situation was insane, so far above her rank that it made her dizzy. Worse, she felt as if she were going into it without all the necessary information, or that the information she did have was completely wrong.

"Riders ahead."

Lyria had taken point, her ability to see long distances an advantage. Keagan immediately drew her sword, moving away from Onyx and to the front. The others spread out just behind her. They had no cover here, no way to take the strangers by surprise. This would be a show of force.

"Beware arrows," she said, just as if they were all marshals and under her command. "Ashley, watch your flame. We'll need those horses. Take the mercs alive if we can. Otherwise, take them down."

The riders approaching had apparently spotted them, pulling up briefly before resuming their approach, spreading out into four distinct targets. When they were within hailing distance, Keagan took another step forward, lifting her left hand to hold her marshal badge aloft, making the gold emblem clearly visible.

"Halt and be recognized," she shouted. "Marshals. Discard all weapons on the ground."

The riders drew up a few yards away, two men and two women. The one who dismounted was obviously this "Shadow Lord," a tall, well-built

Chthonic. Keagan gritted her teeth when she saw he had drawn what was unmistakably a marshal sword. On closer inspection, she thought she recognized a nick in the hilt.

Aigua's mercy, it was her sword! He probably had her shield, too. She was damned well getting those back.

"Stay where you are and disarm, or we will fire," Keagan stated. "There are Elementals in my party. It will not go well for you."

To Keagan's left, Lyria hefted her crossbow and pointed it directly at the lord, though she looked frightened and the crossbow wavered slightly. Keagan doubted she'd be able to hit anything. Beyond her, Cassius twirled her quarterstaff lazily, appearing focused but calm. Keagan knew she could count on her. On Keagan's right, Ashley had not bothered to retrieve her bow from her back. Instead, she stood, eyes glowing a deep golden, fists clenched, lips drawn back from her teeth in an almost smile. Keagan didn't know where Shay was, couldn't see her in her peripheral vision.

The mercenaries, still in the saddle, looked at each other and shifted uneasily. They had their weapons drawn, but they weren't aiming them at Keagan's party. Not yet, at any rate.

"Marshals?" The proclaimed lord looked them over with a frown edging his features. "What are you doing out here?"

"Looking for you," Keagan said. "I'm placing you under arrest for kidnapping, attempted murder, and various assaults on private citizens. Oh, and theft. That sword and shield are mine."

He stopped. "You! That's impossible! You're dead! The wraiths consumed you!"

"Sorry to disappoint," Keagan said, dryly.

He didn't seem to know what to say to that. Then he finally noticed the women on Keagan's left and blanched. "You! How did you—"

"Hey, dirt digger," Ashley said, apparently wanting him to know where his attention should really be focused. "Got your invitation to dance. So let's dance."

"Identify yourself," Keagan demanded again.

The lord whirled and sprinted back to his horse. "Kill them," he said loudly. "Don't worry. Their abilities have been stripped!"

"Is that what he thinks?" Flames suddenly wreathed Ashley's hands, but she didn't unleash them, clearly conscious of Keagan's admonishment and willing to wait until the mercenaries were separated from their mounts.

As the lord reached his horse and swiftly mounted, his people seemed to take courage at the lack of elemental abilities being displayed and spurred their horses forward, firing their bows. Mounted warriors usually had the tactical advantage in a fight over those on foot, and these mercenaries were obviously intending to use it to the fullest. The hired killers spread out and began to circle them, clearly intending to flank them with their superior speed.

"Ashley!" Keagan pocketed her badge and pulled around her shield to protect her from the missiles. Meanwhile, Ashley began to pick arrows out of the air, burning them to ash before they reached Cassius and Lyria. And Shay?

Shay was suddenly right there, her daggers flashing silver in the sun as they brought down one of the female mercenaries, the woman tumbling from her mount. The horse galloped away, but Keagan knew it wouldn't go far. Herd animals, especially horses trained for fighting as these seemed to be, would remain in the vicinity, even after they escaped the immediate field of battle.

Then Keagan could no longer pay attention to what was going on around her. She focused suddenly on the lord galloping straight toward her. Really? He intended to kill her with her own sword? If she wasn't so focused on the immediate threat of being skewered, she'd be offended.

Stepping to the side, she drew on her reserves, sending a jet of water along her sword blade and out the tip, directed at the lord's center mass. Obviously unexpected, it struck him full in the chest, knocking him backward. His expression of utter shock would have made Keagan laugh were the situation less dire. The sword flew to one side and the shield to the other as he grabbed frantically at his pommel, trying to remain in the saddle. His horse, clearly disturbed by the blast of water that had just shot past its ear, shied violently, bucking to relieve itself of its burden.

Keagan glimpsed Shay and Cassius protecting Lyria as they sought to bring down the remaining female mercenary. Meanwhile, Ashley had set up a circle of flame around herself, keeping her opponent, the male mercenary, at bay. He was having more trouble controlling his horse, the animal's natural aversion to fire making it refuse all commands. Finally, he gave up and dismounted, kneeling on the ground as he drew his bow, obviously intending to shoot his arrows at Ashley through the flames.

That was a fatal mistake, because once he parted from his horse, he no longer enjoyed its protected status. Ashley lit him up so fast that his cremated corpse remained intact for several seconds, hanging in place before a sly gust of wind made it crumble into a scattered pile of ash.

Keagan approached the lord, sprawled on the ground. Belatedly, she realized he had some sort of goggles hanging around his neck, the type Sylphs occasionally wore while flying, except the eyepieces weren't clear. Tinted an odd shade, they were completely opaque. "Give it up," she ordered him, even as she remained aware that even at level one, he might draw on the tainted land around him. She kept an eye out for clods of earth shooting at her from behind. "It's over."

"On the contrary, it's only just begun." He snarled, glaring at her. Rather than draw on his abilities, he yanked a strange little tube from his belt and aimed it at her.

Keagan immediately threw up her shield and knelt behind it, but no projectile appeared, just an entry that appeared a few feet in front of her. The blackness oozed out, and every hair on the back of her neck stood up. Entering the Shadow Realm had always disturbed her, but this felt wrong in a way she couldn't identify. A shrill scream rose behind her, full of terror and pain.

"Shay?"

Keagan looked back to see Shay sprawled boneless on the hard ground. She could spare only a fleeting glance before turning forward once more to counter the lord's attack. She worried that he might somehow be bringing wraiths through, but he wasn't attacking. Instead, he lunged through the entry, which immediately sealed behind him, although a line of darkness remained hanging in the air. Angry that she'd let him get away, Keagan rose and paced around it, trying to figure out what it was and what it was doing. Reaching out with the tip of her sword, she poked at it tentatively, immediately rewarded with a jolt of some kind of energy that buzzed up her arm and made her teeth clench.

"Damn it," she said, dancing backward. The sword, smoking, dropped to the ground, and she shook her arm violently, trying to get the feeling back into it. As she did, she realized that Shay was still down. Lyria crouched over her, trying to revive her, as Cassius and Ashley gathered the riderless horses.

Bypassing the sword she'd been using, Keagan scooped up hers from where the lord had dropped it, exchanged shields as well for her old one, and then sprinted toward Shay. "What's wrong?" she asked as she fell to her knees beside Lyria.

"I don't know. Nothing hit her. She just screamed and fell as soon as he did—that thing he did with the other thing." Lyria's lower lip trembled. "Sirocco, what's happening?"

"When I figure it out, I'll let you know," Keagan said. She placed her hand against Shay's cheek and tried to remember all she'd been told about the Shadows and Paths. "She's fevered. It's possible that creating an entry like that affected her. She said the other one gave her a headache, but he created that one on a Path at night. This one was an act of desperation because he was caught. Maybe this isn't the kind of place where you should do that."

She looked around at the barren, sun-blasted wasteland and swallowed the lump in her throat. She didn't blame Lyria for wanting to cry. She wanted to join her. Instead, she rose as Cassius and Ashley approached, each leading two horses.

"Is she all right?" Cassius asked, frowning as she looked at Shay.

"She's still unconscious," Keagan said, chest tight. Onyx approached on his own and lowered his head to his mistress, nuzzling her face as if anxious. "We need to get her out of here."

"And go where?" Ashley was petting a little mare. "Back to the pool?"

"We may have to, eventually," Keagan said, "but before we do, I want to see where they were coming from. It might be important. Cassius, can you follow the trail?"

"Probably. I'm not the tracker Shay is, but they weren't trying to hide their movements."

"Check the bodies, especially for anything that might identify them." Keagan hadn't consciously decided she was in charge. She just fell back into marshal mode, and the others seemed willing to go along with that reflex, not questioning her orders.

"You want me to clean up?" Ashley asked after they had stripped the corpses of anything useful, including a lot more gold. Apparently, this "lord" paid well.

Keagan considered the situation. She'd given them every chance to surrender. She looked again at Shay, who appeared so vulnerable and helpless on the ground. "No," she said coldly. "Leave them for whatever lives here." A vicious insult no matter the religion.

The supplies that had been strapped to Onyx were redistributed among the others, and then, with the help of Cassius, she managed to lift Shay's limp body into the saddle. While Cassius held Onyx's head, Keagan mounted behind Shay, grateful when Onyx didn't object. Indeed, it was as if he seemed to understand she was helping his mistress and stood motionless until she was settled. Wrapping her arms around Shay, keeping her secure, Keagan gathered the reins and urged him forward.

The others fell in pace around her, Ashley on a brown mare, Cassius on a huge, dappled dray that appeared quite graceful for his size, long hair feathering his back hooves, and Lyria on a swift-looking desert gelding with a golden coat that gleamed almost metallic in the brutal daylight.

"I'm going to call him Sunny," Lyria said happily as she patted his neck.

The last horse, the one the lord had been riding, was Aether or, at least, was one of their culls. Now that Keagan was seeing it side by side with an actual Shadow-touched, she realized his lines weren't nearly as fine as Onyx's. Nor did he possess as good a conformation. His tail didn't arch as high, and his head didn't have the distinctive curve from forehead to muzzle. Most significantly, his big, dark eyes didn't have the silver sheen that would allow him to see in the Shadow Realm. Still, he appeared to be a fine, Shadow-bred horse, with a dark brown coat, his mane and long tail a deep black. Ashley took his reins and led him behind her mare as they continued to head east, following the trail of tracks that marked the hard ground.

After almost an hour, they approached the edge of the plateau and saw the wide, shimmering expanse of the Anemoi below them. It didn't appear polluted, looking as beautiful as any river, but Keagan could taste the heavy metals contaminating every drop. It was so large and overpowering, she couldn't sense anything else. Vegetation grew along the banks, sickly, silver and black rather than green, bristling with large thorns and sharp-edged leaves. From under it, several reptilian things slithered into the water with a splash. They were thickly scaled, with long snouts full of too many teeth and even longer tails ridged with bony spikes.

As they descended to the riverbank, Keagan tried to pick out any ruins of a city surrounding them but failed. Then she realized that any evidence of structures would be beneath them, buried under a massive layer of mud. A lahar had struck here at one time. The river was polluted because a combination of Undine and Chthonic abilities had destroyed countless thriving communities lining its banks, and contaminants from them continued to leach into the water even now.

She felt ashamed, even though she was several generations from those responsible. In her arms, Shay stirred, lifting her head.

"Easy," Keagan said as she reined in Onyx. The others, once they realized she'd stopped, did the same. "It's okay, Shay. You're okay."

"Glad to see you're awake," Cassius said, drawing up beside them. "I was beginning to worry."

"What happened?" Shay looked over her shoulder at Keagan, who was still holding her firmly, though she didn't appear to need any further aid to remain upright. She didn't try to pull away, though. "Where are we?"

While the rest filled her in, Keagan contented herself with a final, unobtrusive squeeze before slipping from Onyx's back. Retrieving the other horse from Ashley, she gathered the reins and mounted, noting the ornate decoration of the saddle, obviously expensive and far showier than the surroundings dictated. The gelding shifted uneasily beneath her, but she soothed him with some murmured words and a few pats on his neck.

After giving Shay a few minutes to regain her bearings, they started off again, Keagan bringing her mount into stride with Onyx, the two of them riding side by side along the river's edge.

"So, what happened?" she asked softly. "When he escaped into the Shadow Realm?"

Shay shook her head. "It was like being torn apart," she said. "I never felt such pain, and it wasn't mine. It was the Shadows, resonating as the entry was torn open. He must be insane. There was no Path there. Was he planning to travel through the Realm unprotected?"

"He may not need to be protected," Keagan said. "Remember, it wasn't mercenaries that took me. It was wraiths. That sword he carried? That was mine. He must have returned to where we fought them and retrieved my weapons."

Shay looked pained. "I don't know how, but this man seems to walk the Realm as if he owns it. He must have retrieved the stone from the wraiths as well, assuming the same one that took your abilities also took them from Cassius and Lyria."

Keagan shuddered. "I'd hate to think there was more than one."

Shay exhaled audibly. "Is he capable of controlling the wraiths? The more we discover, the less I understand what's going on."

"Before he pulled out the device, I told him to surrender, that it was over," Keagan said. "He told me it was just beginning."

Shay stared at her. "That doesn't reassure me."

"It wasn't supposed to."

Ashley rode up beside them. Ever since they'd rescued the other Elementals, she'd been far more subdued, less cocky, either realizing the enormity of the situation they found themselves in or cowed by the knowledge that she'd nearly had her abilities taken as well. Keagan doubted that reticence would last long.

"What happens now?"

"You've been here for most of it, Ash," Keagan said mildly. "Why would you think I suddenly have all the answers?"

"Because you're in charge," Ashley said, as if it were self-evident. "You've been making all the decisions." She lifted her chin in Shay's direction. "Oh, tall, dark, and deadly there makes one once in a while, but she always checks with you first."

Startled, Keagan looked at Shay, who lifted a brow. "She's not wrong. Don't forget that I was willing to go around those mercenaries. It definitely wasn't my idea to rescue some spoiled Salamas."

Ashley made a face at Shay but otherwise didn't react to the comment. Instead, she focused on Keagan. "Well?"

Keagan stifled a sigh. "We find out where the lord went. We'll figure out our next move from there."

"So make it up as we go along. Just like in school. Good to know some things haven't changed."

She slowed her mount so that she fell behind with Cassius and Lyria, leaving Shay and Keagan alone once more.

Shay eyed Keagan. "Are you sure you weren't friends?"

Keagan sighed. "We did become friends, I suppose, but only after a lot of confrontations, and only after finally taking the time to get to know one another. It took about two years, but we were in school together for five."

"Maybe more than friends?" Shay's tone was more careless than the expression in her eyes.

Keagan let out a laugh. "Me and Ash? Sweet Aigua, no. Fire and water don't really mix, remember?"

"Oh, I don't know. Maybe you found your way into hot water together."

"Well, we did do that, those final years," Keagan said readily. "Ash would come up with the idea, and I'd figure out how to do it without getting caught. The teachers were apoplectic. They could never prove anything, though."

"So you learned how to break the law before you decided to uphold it."

Keagan laughed again. "Something like that."

XI

With high, reddish cliffs on one side, and the shimmering expanse of river on the other, Shay picked her way carefully, trying to follow the trail. It was becoming harder and harder to track, indistinguishable on ground that had become mostly rock rather than soil. Drawing Onyx to a halt, she turned and looked back at the others. They had fallen behind and were clearly feeling the heat and exhaustion of changing time zones with little to no sleep. The sun was sinking toward the horizon, and Shay knew that while the dark didn't hinder her and Onyx, the rest weren't so gifted. Even now, they were practically dozing in the saddle, swaying back and forth with the slow plodding of the horses who walked with their heads down.

Then, even as she watched, the horses lifted their heads and quickened their pace. They had altered her course slightly, as well, though their riders had yet to notice. Shay followed the direction of their pricked ears and saw a break in the cliff ahead, a small opening, possibly to another canyon.

"Onyx?" she said, leaning forward and patting him on the neck. "Water?"

He was looking in the same direction, and his ears flicked toward the opening.

"Hold up," Shay said, loud enough to make the others stir, straightening in their saddles. They drew to a stop beside her.

"Has the trail ended?" Cassius looked down. "Frankly, I don't know how you managed this long."

"Nothing's here." Ashley looked around.

"Look at your horses," Shay said. "They're more alert, leaning into the reins, wanting to go."

Lyria blinked sleepily. "What does that mean?"

"They're close to food and water," Cassius said, managing a weary smile. "They know they're nearly home."

"I suspect we'll find both in there," Shay said, pointing at the break in the cliffs.

"Ah." Keagan inhaled deeply as she looked at them. "This isn't the best option. We're all exhausted. More mercenaries may be in there, but also food, water, and possibly shelter for all of us. We need to investigate."

Ashley shook her head, squeezing her eyelids tightly together before opening them with false wideness. "I'm ready."

Keagan exhaled and then held out her hand to Lyria. "I know you're still recovering. Enough for this?"

Lyria looked at her, brow furrowed, and then brightened. "Yeah. I think I can manage that."

Perplexed, Shay watched as Keagan and Lyria joined hands. Then steam began to rise from their joined fists. No, not steam, condensation, a sheath of white forming around their fingers. Frost, Shay thought, just before they released hands and Keagan gestured abruptly. A dash of icy water splashed into Shay's face, jolting her into a heightened sense of alertness and provoking a variety of outcries from the others.

"Was that really necessary?" Ashley sputtered, wiping her face with her hand.

"It helped," Cassius said, shaking her head, droplets splattering.

Keagan drew her sword. "Let's go," she said, riding past Shay and taking point.

Shay and the rest fell in behind, the horses picking up their pace with little urging when they saw where they were headed. They thundered through the passage, a narrow trail between the stone cliffs, barely wide enough for two to ride abreast before it abruptly opened into a large canyon. Shay was relieved when she realized no one was waiting for them and saw no cover for anyone planning an ambush.

A waterfall, much larger than the first one they had encountered, plunged into an expansive pool, and next to it was the mercenary camp, very similar to the one in the Aquas jungle. Three tents were pitched in the shadow of a southern cliff, protected from direct sun, surrounding a central fire pit. A roughly constructed picnic table and secured chests sat next to a single, crooked dwarf tree with silver bark. Nearby a ceramic sink perched on a wood frame. The latrine was constructed well away from the pool, and an outdoor shower was set up, complete with holding tank. A corral had been constructed with a trough at one end, water being fed to it by an aqueduct constructed midway up the waterfall. The pipe also fed into the sink and shower tank before reaching the corral. Several bales of hay stacked by a platform held several boxes and sacks of provisions. This was clearly a long-term base of operations, intended for future expansion.

However, the empty camp didn't command their attention. The massive carvings on the far cliff caused them to rein to a halt and stare up at it, jaws hanging.

They saw two gigantic statues of women—no, the same woman carved twice, Shay decided as she recognized the features, worn as they were from the wind and sand. They were the same as the statue she had seen in the palace—graceful, serene, each holding a staff with a diamond-shaped stone at the tip. Or rather one statue still boasted an intact staff. The other, on the right, had its arm broken off, along with most of the staff, the rubble at the base of the statue indicating its demise at the hands of time. Between the two statues, the stone wall was engraved with faded symbols, and in the very center, at the base, appeared to be a stone door. In the center of the door was a tablet shaped like a diamond, with five smaller stone shapes that looked as if they could be compressed. Each was adorned with the ancients symbols of the Five Nations: Terras on the top, Aquas to the right, Arias to the left, Urodela at the bottom, and in the center of them all, the symbol for Aether, with a small opening in the center, perhaps for a key.

"Sweet Baast, what the fuck is that?" Ashley said.

"A doorway," Keagan said, looking up in awe. "To where?"

"And how does it open?" Cassius asked, more practically.

"I don't think it does. At least not easily." Lyria tossed her reins to Ashley, who caught them automatically and slipped off her horse. She mounted the crumbling staircase until she stood before the tablet, studying it intently. She looked like a child, so small against the huge dimensions of the door. Her hands clasped behind her back, she bent forward, peering at the engravings before gazing upward and then at the ground around her.

"It's locked," she said. "There's a way to get in, but only if you know the correct sequence. I don't think they did. There's a body up here. Well…" She paused. "Bones, anyway. Charred. This doorway is trapped." She inhaled, sniffing delicately. "Ethylene. Definitely not something to mess with."

Curious, the rest of them dismounted but then quickly realized they couldn't take the horses up the stairs and looked at each other in consternation.

Shay exhaled, resigned. "I've got them." She could always examine the door later. In the meantime, the horses needed tending, which was far more important.

Leading all five animals over to the corral, she tethered the four, leaving Onyx free, and methodically began to strip off their tack, throwing the saddles over conveniently provided stands located near the hay. Only four, she noted. Whatever the camp was planned for, it hadn't yet been populated. She slung Onyx's saddle over the top rail of the fence, behind the trough, where no inquisitive teeth could reach it. Then she led the horses, one by one, into the corral, where she stripped off their bridles and let them loose. Thick, rich grass and clover grew in a field here, which meant the soil had been altered, perhaps by the Shadow Lord, since she now knew he was Chthonic. Was that the extent of his abilities—to create grazing regardless of location?

She filled another trough with hay from the bales for roughage and checked the water. The overflow, she noted, was directed toward the cliff, where it disappeared into the rocks at the base. That was the thing with water in the desert. It rarely got far. Even the waterfall and the pool didn't extend beyond its location. It must be flowing back into the cliff, perhaps into some subterranean cavern.

She looked back at the huge door. Perhaps even somewhere behind that. Sending out a tendril of sense, she detected no Path. Whatever the Shadow Lord had been doing here, it had been only for the door that he apparently couldn't open.

By the time she moved to the camp and began to explore, the others had started to wander back. Only Lyria remained behind, obviously fascinated by the puzzle before her. Keagan walked over as Shay was examining one of the large boxes that sat on some planks laid across two rocks of roughly the same height. The chest was square and solid, Urodela-made, with a thick lid. Amazingly, it was a portable cold box, designed to keep whatever it contained at a certain temperature, an energy crystal inside making it work. When she lifted the lid, she discovered a variety of meats, cheeses, bread, fruits, and vegetables from all over the Five Nations.

"I don't like this Shadow Lord," Shay said as she regarded the bounty. "But he appears to treat his people well. Good pay and great food."

"That may be why they're so loyal," Keagan said as she peered into the box. "But I doubt they're loyal enough to die for him. Something else must be involved. Most mercenaries wouldn't go against four Elementals, even if they believed us stripped of abilities. The punishment, if caught, would be execution." She carefully made her choices from the selection. "We'll eat well tonight."

Shay indicated the other chest with a tilt of her chin. "That's a portable hot box. Expensive as hell. They cooked in it. Any fire they had was just for warmth, comfort, and security from predators."

"Portable hot and cold boxes set up in the middle of nowhere," Keagan said. "Each worth more than I make in a year. Whatever the purpose behind this, I don't think gold's motivating it. He's spending freely."

"Too freely," Shay said. "He must expect a considerable payoff of some kind."

"Which would worry me more if I weren't so hungry, tired, and dirty at the moment," Keagan said with a wry grin.

"Well, we should be able to alleviate all three problems tonight." Shay glanced up to see Ashley already heading for the outdoor shower, shedding clothes along the way. Clearly, she possessed no sense of modesty, or if she did, it didn't manifest in the company of other women. Naked by the time she reached the shower, Ashley held up her hand and placed it against the underside of the tank, holding it there until it glowed red, heating the water inside.

Shay promptly forgave any lingering resentment she held toward the woman. A hot shower? That made Ashley all right in her book, to the point where she retrieved her soap and shampoo from her saddlebags and carried them over to Ashley, who took them with a smile of unspoken appreciation and acceptance.

While Shay and Keagan made supper, Ashley eventually returned to the central pit, where she sparked a generous fire. She was wearing a towel she'd found stacked inside a wicker basket near the shower stall and had gathered her clothes in a pile, where she eyed them balefully.

"You can't burn them," Keagan told her cheerfully. "They're all you have. You'll have to wash them in the sink."

"I'll find something from those female mercs," Ashley said as she tossed the skirt and blouse into the fire. "One of them was my size."

"We'll do laundry for the rest of us tomorrow," Cassius told her on the way by, clearly intent on being the next one to shower. She waited until she was actually inside the confines of the shower stall, concealed behind the tarp that was strung around the four wooden support poles, before she disrobed. After tossing her clothes over the side onto the ground, she turned on the nozzle. Shay could actually hear her groan of sheer delight as the hot water hit her.

Keagan took her turn next, as Shay finished the meal preparation, and it was all Shay could do not to whimper when she saw her return in a towel, carrying her reeking Peacekeeper uniform. She tossed it onto the pile with Cassius's clothes and then came over to where Shay was filling a plate with roast potatoes, green beans, and chicken. Shay tried not to stare at all the exposed skin on Keagan's shoulders and chest, especially not at the fascinating cleft between the firm breasts holding up the towel.

"Fantastic," Keagan said, nudging Shay with her shoulder as she accepted the plate. She lowered her voice. "Share a tent with me tonight?"

Shay managed not to choke, but it was a near thing. She was quite sure her eyes were bugging out, however. "Sure," she said with a casualness she was far from feeling.

After making a plate for herself, she carried it over to the picnic table. The other women joined her, and they consumed their meal hungrily, with little conversation. Only once their bellies were full did they settle back with some tea and discuss the day.

"It looks like they've been working on that lock for a while." Lyria said, almost vibrating in her enthusiasm. "It's an elemental design that requires all four abilities to activate it. Now, most people don't know this, but you don't necessarily have to be an Elemental to unlock these. If you're quick enough, you can spit on the Aquas symbol, toss some dirt on the Terras symbol, hold a match to the Urodela symbol, and blow air onto the Arias symbol." Lyria smiled widely. "But this one has an Aether symbol in the middle. That's not on any lock I've ever seen. Messing with that set off the trap and fried whoever was manipulating the lock."

Keagan glanced at Shay, eyebrow raised. "We have someone from Aether here. Maybe Shay can figure out the last symbol?"

Shay was doubtful. "Maybe. But let's hold off trying until tomorrow. I want my own shower, and then I could use some sleep."

"Do we require a watch?" Cassius asked.

"Do we expect the Shadow Lord and his buddies to return here?" Ashley looked utterly weary, which Shay never thought she'd see.

"He entered the Realm in an area without a Path," Shay told her. "I don't care what devices he has, or how protected they might make him, it'll take time to find his way back to Aquas, more time to gather any amount of support there, and far longer to transport that support back here. I don't think he's found a way to bring untrained horses and non-Riders through the Paths. In Aquas, it's more likely they brought all the supplies, mercenaries, and pack horses in by boat and unloaded on the same beach as Ashley, before cutting a trail through the jungle to the ruins. That's why a permanent camp was established at the halfway point. Here, they probably came up the river by boat and unloaded on the bank just below. Rivercraft carry a lot less than ocean ships. That may be why only a few people were here to work on the door."

"One of which is at the top of the stairs. One set of bones," Lyria remarked. She paused. "I do wonder why all of them were escorting the Shadow Lord back to the Path. Were they expecting to go with him to Aquas? Abandon this place entirely?"

"Maybe not entirely, considering how much equipment they left behind," Keagan said. "But they could have planned to help out with that ritual he mentioned, then return here later. Or maybe the dead person was more important, and without him, the mercs were useless."

"Whoever those bones belonged to, he owned the cull the lord was riding," Shay said thoughtfully. "He had to be wealthy. Maybe he was working with the Shadow Lord rather than for him?"

Keagan shook her head. "Too many questions and, frankly, not enough answers. I'll be glad to kick it upstairs once we discover a way home." She looked at the others. "Shay and I will take one tent. You three can divide the other two."

"We actually have four tents, remember?" Ashley pointed out, a small grin curving her lips. "We can always set up the one we brought with us."

"Some of us still have to double up in one," Keagan said, her voice even, though her eyes glinted. "Shay and I have been traveling together the longest. We don't mind sharing."

"No, we don't," Shay said, trying to keep her tone casual.

"We're all exhausted from lack of sleep and the time change. Onyx has been keeping watch for us in the jungle," Keagan said. "He's better than a dog, frankly."

"I'm sure he'll appreciate the compliment." Shay tried not to take offense. Onyx was leagues smarter than any dog.

Once Lyria had finished her shower, Ashley cheerfully reheated the tank before retiring to one of the tents, leaving Shay to shower away too many days of dirt and sweat. She was almost in tears at how good she felt as the water cascaded over her.

Leaving her shirt and underclothes with the others, she laid her leather tunic and trousers out to air, intending to clean them tomorrow, along with Onyx's tack. Wrapped in a towel surprisingly soft to the touch, she made her way across the camp, headed toward the tent where she knew Keagan was. As she walked, her stomach tightened in anticipation. The other tents still had vapor lamps glowing from inside, but even as she watched, they went out one by one, and she was left with only the light in Keagan's tent acting as a beacon.

She tried to catch her breath as she ducked inside the tent and then stopped as she saw that Keagan was snoring, sleeping so heavily it would take an explosion to wake her. Shay briefly debated having Ashley provide her with one but then smiled, dropped her towel, turned down the lamp, and slipped into the bedroll beside Keagan. Gathering her naked form in her arms, Shay snuggled into her back, delighting in the feel of warm, soft skin against her.

Then, between one breath and the next, she was asleep.

XII

Keagan woke to the sensation of a warm, naked body wrapped around her, strong, slender arms around her belly, long legs tangled within hers. The feeling was amazing and such a contrast to how she'd been waking up in the days prior, she wanted to remain there forever.

Days? Who was she kidding? It had been more than two years since she'd shared a bed with anyone, and even then, she hadn't really wanted to stay once the morning came. But this was heaven, and she snuggled back against the warmth, making a small sound of delight. Shay stirred, pulling her closer, nuzzling into Keagan's neck.

"Hi," she whispered.

"Hi yourself." Keagan wiggled, and Shay relaxed her embrace long enough for Keagan to roll over to face her. She smiled, reaching up to touch her cheek. "I'm sorry I fell asleep."

"We'd been up for days," Shay said in a matter-of-fact tone. "What else were you going to do?"

"Wait for you," Keagan said, plainly. At Shay's lifted brows, she smiled and drew her near, kissing the lips she'd been dying to taste for days.

That they would share their very first kiss stark naked in bed might be an omen of some kind, but Keagan wasn't about to worry about it. She kissed her again, desire rocketing through her as they pressed against each other, Shay kissing her back with unrestrained passion.

Then they heard Cassius and Ashley talking out by the fire pit, clearly up for the morning. Keagan wanted to weep. "We can't," she whispered, once they finally parted for breath.

Shay looked a little dazed, those dark, silvery eyes needing a few seconds to clear. "You're right, we can't," she said with deeply felt regret. "Not now. It would be…awkward."

"I really want to," Keagan said earnestly. "I have for some time. I like you a lot, Shay. I know we didn't meet under the best of circumstances, but over the past week, you've become very important to me."

Shay looked bashful and pleased and utterly adorable. "I really like you, too. I didn't dare—well, let's just say I never thought I'd ever meet anyone like you."

"Once we're back in the city, I want to spend time with you," Keagan told her. "A lot of time. Just us. Whatever you want to do."

Shay smiled that shy smile that made Keagan's heart beat faster. "Oh, I can think of a few things." They kissed again, hands wandering dangerously close to areas that really didn't require any further teasing. It would only increase the torment when they had to stop.

But, oh, what sweet torment, Keagan thought dazedly.

Shay drew away first, clearly the practical one in this relationship, and Keagan ached at the loss. She tried to control her breathing as she watched Shay carefully wrap the towel around her lean, sinewy form, covering up too much of that wonderful, dusky skin. She threw back another smile full of promise over her shoulder and slipped from the tent.

Keagan needed a few more minutes to recover, contemplating the merits of a cold shower, then rose also, wrapping herself in the towel and creeping out of the tent. Ashley eyed her sardonically as she joined them at the fire, where she gratefully accepted the tea Cassius handed her. Thankfully, Ashley didn't feel compelled to say anything untoward, which must have been a first, Keagan thought as she sipped her tea. She noticed that all the clothes had been washed and were now hanging from a rope strung from the single tree to the corner of the outhouse.

"Look what I found," Ashley said instead, holding up a thick leather-bound journal, various slips of paper protruding from between the pages. "It was in my tent, tucked under the bedroll. It says it belongs to a Professor Wilfred Tannehill."

"Tannehill?" A memory sparked. "Didn't he lecture at our school once? Something about prewar civilization not being organized along the same lines as our own. That Elementals didn't really exist then as we know them now?"

"I wouldn't have attended anything like that. It sounds tedious. I'm sure you did, though. You remember anything?"

"Not really." Keagan searched her memories. As she did, she watched Shay cleaning her leathers, her smooth arms and shoulders bare and flexing in the sun. She looked so relaxed and beyond beautiful as she spoke with Lyria, who was putting out fresh fodder for the horses. Keagan wondered if they were talking about flying. She was glad to see Shay losing some of her reticence around Elementals. With an effort, she dragged her attention back to Ashley. "It was a long time ago, and his theories were so fanciful that Headmistress Kaleath didn't bother using any of it in her class."

"You studied history?" Cassius asked, interest darkening her emerald eyes. She stirred the pot hanging over the fire. It appeared to be porridge of some kind, filled with berries and nuts. "What was that like? I thought about continuing to advanced once I left basic, but agriculture sciences seemed more suited to my abilities and what I wanted to do."

"It's probably why she's a marshal," Ashley said without rancor. "She took the history and ethics courses very seriously, to the point of still taking classes in them after basic."

"I gather that you attended at the same time." Cassius looked back and forth between them as she handed Keagan a bowl. "How long ago?"

Keagan did the math. "What, ten, no, twelve years ago? Aigua, time flies."

Ashley made a face. "Don't remind me."

"What else is in the book?" Keagan asked, her mouth full of oatmeal. Flavored with honey and cinnamon, it was surprisingly delicious. Cassius apparently knew her way around a campfire.

"Hard to read his scribbling. But there were a lot of sketches of those statues and those symbols we saw in Aquas. The ones on the door are the same, as well as the obelisk back by the Path." Ashley paused. "He dated the entries. The book begins fifteen years ago."

"What does the final entry say?" Keagan asked, curious.

Ashley let out a laugh. "Just a couple of lines. 'We open the door tomorrow. Then, I'll be vindicated.' More like vulcanized, as it turned out."

"We need to go over the journal a little closer than that," Keagan said. "Especially before we try anything with the door." She lifted her head and called over to Lyria. "Any chance you can blow our clothes dry?"

Lyria looked back, surprise on her face before growing thoughtful, as if she had never considered such a thing before. Which wouldn't be surprising. The young and powerful tended to gravitate to the splashy and exciting aspects of what they could do, like flying. Or they focused on the very limited, very precise parameters of what their company required of them. And since most went directly from the Academy to a company, both of which took care of the basics for their prized assets, Elementals never really had to learn about the more mundane uses for their gifts.

Keagan, living a more economical existence as a marshal, had been forced to learn, and she often thought of ways she could have used other elemental abilities had she possessed them. Of course, anyone who possessed all four would never deign to perform such menial tasks like washing or drying clothes.

She frowned. Tannehill had mentioned possessing all four aspects of the Elements, which would be beyond imagining. Anyone like that would be so powerful no one could prevent them from doing exactly what they wanted. And if that person turned out to be cruel or malicious? They'd be despots, tyrants. Keagan shuddered.

Once Lyria had dried their clothes, Keagan pulled on her uniform, finishing with boots, belt, and weapon harness. She left the armor aside for the moment. Even though they were in the shade of the canyon, the day was rapidly growing hot. The desert beyond the canyon mouth must already be a blast furnace. Then everyone gathered at the doorway, allowing Shay her first close look at the tablet.

She traced her finger over the symbol for Aether, and Keagan thought she detected a little sadness in her eyes, as if she were missing it. Keagan couldn't blame her. She was missing Naiad, with its sea breezes and people and noise and wonderfully chaotic city markets.

Shay bent over to look more closely at it, peering into the hole. A sudden flash of light shot directly into her eye, and she stumbled back as a loud click sounded. Beside her, Keagan swiftly threw her shield over them as the others immediately backed away. But nothing happened, and after several seconds, they all relaxed.

"What was that?" Ashley asked.

"It recognized her," Lyria said, excitement making her voice rise, almost to an uncomfortable decibel. "Or at least her eye. The eye of a Shadow Rider. The eye of one from Aether. The professor wouldn't have had that. He might have the spit, the dirt, the flame, and the breath, but no way could he provide eyes that see in the Shadow Realm."

"Does that mean Shadow Riders are the fifth Elemental?" Cassius asked. "That they've always been one of us?"

Keagan tried not to wince. She hated the "us" and "them." It was the source of most of the world's problems. Ashley opened her mouth as if to say something, caught Keagan's gaze, and promptly shut it again. Keagan frowned at her and then returned her attention to Shay. "Do we really want to attempt this? We know what happened to the last person who tried."

As one, they all looked over at the charred bones scattered at the top of the staircase, arms outstretched, legs straight back, as if he had tried to leap away. The head had detached and was somewhere down the stairs, probably having rolled beneath the vegetation by the pool.

"I can live without ever knowing," Cassius said honestly.

"Me, too," Ashley said.

"I can't," Lyria said, plainly. "I want to see what's inside. If we apply the elements all at the same time, I'm sure the lock will release, and the door will open."

"Then maybe we should come back, someday," Shay suggested. "With a lot more marshals and some scholars from your Academy."

Keagan became aware that they were all suddenly looking at her. Apparently, she held the final decision. She met Shay's gaze, regarding the depths of it, and knew that whatever she decided, Shay would support her without reservation. That knowledge was like having strong hands on her shoulder, ready to help propel her forward in her journey, or drag her back from danger, or catch her if she fell. Keagan hadn't felt anything like that since—well, had she ever? She couldn't remember her parents, who should have made her feel that way. Not even the kindest and most caring of her teachers had provided such encouragement. And she had certainly never found it from her varied lovers.

How had she discovered it in the blackest of black, surrounded by monsters, on the verge of losing it all?

"It's more important to return home," she said, finally. "Even if we do manage to open this door, it could take weeks to figure out what's significant and what isn't. I'm not an actual historian. I just have an interest. Meanwhile, the Council needs to know what's going on as soon as possible."

Shay nodded. "I'll go over my maps. With Lyria's help and her knowledge of Arias, I'll try to pinpoint our location. Once we know exactly where we are, and where we're going, we'll be able to figure out how long a journey it'll be and how long it will take. Fortunately, we'll have a lot of provisions to draw on, and we all have horses. We won't be walking."

Decision made, they went back to the camp and began to prepare. While Shay, Cassius, and Lyria reviewed the maps on the picnic table, Keagan settled by the fire and began skimming through Tannehill's journal. Ashley was right. His writing was barely legible, and a lot of it was gibberish, using terms and references that apparently only he understood. Or perhaps another historian would know what he meant. Another reason to return home as soon as possible.

She didn't lift her head as Ashley joined her, though she was very aware of her presence as she settled onto the log next to her. But Ashley didn't immediately say anything, and the anticipation was more than Keagan could handle. She finally looked over, surprised to see Ashley staring at the fire, her gaze distant.

"Hey," she said, nudging her gently. "You okay?"

Ashley made a face and sipped from her mug. Keagan wasn't sure what was in it. In the old days, it would have been spiked, but she hadn't seen any alcohol in the mercenary camps. Surprising, but hardly the only thing out of the ordinary.

"I guess...this whole experience. It feels like there's this whole world that I just stopped living in after I left school," she said. "I joined the family business right away and haven't really done anything else. Meanwhile, you're out there rescuing people, fighting mercenaries, meeting Shadow Riders..." She shook her head. "I envy you."

Keagan smiled. "Even if I'm poor?"

"You were poor when they found you on the streets. I'm sure you're not now. The marshals must pay something."

"Yeah. It's not near company rates, but the city compensates me well enough. A roof over my head, food on the table, incidentals. I work a lot, though."

"Will that change now?"

Keagan blinked. "What do you mean?"

"With her. With Shay. I see the way you look at her. That's new, isn't it?"

Keagan didn't answer right away. Ashley didn't mean the relationship. She meant that Keagan was willing to take a chance on such a relationship in the first place. Take the chance of being hurt. Take the chance of being left behind, again. She was reminded that at one time, Ashley knew her that well. "Yes," she said finally. "Yes, it is."

"Quick."

Keagan couldn't argue. "It is. But it's also been very intense."

"Maybe that intensity is unduly influenced," Ashley said delicately. Not sarcastic, just concerned.

"By the situation, you mean?" Keagan sighed. She couldn't exactly argue with that point. It was entirely possible. "Why so interested?"

Ashley patted her knee. "Because even though it's been years, and even though you and I didn't start off well, we did eventually become friends. Good friends. In fact, now that I look back, I'm starting to think that maybe you were the best friend I ever had. You never let me get away with anything. Nothing I ever did impressed you. You have no problem being completely honest with me. And until all this happened, I didn't realize how desperately I missed that. How much I need it." Ashley looked into her mug, as if she could find some answer there. "Whatever happens from here? Let's not lose touch again."

Keagan smiled. "I guess I kind of missed you, too. I promise. We'll keep in touch."

"Will you track down this Shadow Lord?"

"If I'm assigned the case. He's an Elemental. That's usually what they toss my way, elemental crime, both by and against."

"Against?"

"Not everyone likes Elementals, Ashley," Keagan said. "You may only enjoy the positive side of being one, with the added protection of your family name, and Guild membership, but an undercurrent of fear and resentment results in crime that a lot of the public doesn't hear about."

"Why not?"

"The Council doesn't want to fan any flames. You may think it's ancient history, but some do remember that we once nearly destroyed the world. That fact comes up on occasion in the form of assaults, especially against lower levels."

"I swear, Keagan, being with you again is a constant education."

"You should never stop learning," Keagan intoned in a shaky voice.

"Mistress Philomena," Ashley said with a laugh, identifying the owner of the original quote, as well as the source of Keagan's imitation. Her smile faded. "I think maybe I let her down."

Keagan patted her shoulder, utilizing another Philomena platitude. "Never too late to get better." She looked up as Shay motioned to her. "Oh, I think they've discovered where we are."

She tucked Tannehill's journal into her saddlebag and rose to join the others, putting her hand on the small of Shay's back as she looked at the map. "What have you found?"

"I think we're here," Shay said, pointing at a spot on the map.

"We think so, too," Cassius said. "I mean, neither Lyria nor I have been this far north, but among the three of us, we think we've identified all the local landmarks. If that's the case, the nearest settlement is about seventy leagues to the south. Boreas, it's called. Small town on an oasis, exports some of the best almonds and figs in the nation. It should take about a week."

"Though if we can wait until I've recovered enough, I can catch an updraft and get a bird's eye perspective," Lyria said. "That would confirm our location."

Keagan hesitated. "What do the rest of you think?"

"We have plenty of food and water here," Cassius said. "Once we head out, we can't count on finding more between here and Boreas. We should be as certain as possible that we're heading in the right direction. The desert doesn't forgive mistakes." She paused. "It also wouldn't hurt to have both Lyria and me back to full strength on a journey like that."

"What about the heat?" Ashley asked. "I don't mind it, but the rest of you can't say the same. Neither can the horses."

"We won't travel through the hottest part of the day," Shay said. "That means starting early, before the moon sets, and stopping before noon. In the hottest part of the day, we'll try to shelter in the shade of rock formations, rest the horses, and make sure they have plenty of water. We'll be dependent on them." She paused. "Regardless, it won't be pleasant." She glanced up at Keagan. "There's a Path in Boreas. I've never been there, but I know Riders who have. From there, I can get us back to Naiad within a day."

Keagan nodded. "Okay then. We have a plan. We'll give it a few more days. Then we leave."

She just hoped they had made the right decision.

XIII

Later that morning, Shay settled on a log near the corral and began to meticulously clean Onyx's tack. Before long, she was joined by Keagan, who began doing the same for the cull's saddle. It was a very ornate setup, Shay thought, as she glanced over, more suitable for riding about town than any real work. She hoped it would hold up under the conditions the upcoming journey would impose. They didn't speak, simply cleaned the equipment, sharing the occasional smile and furtive glance, as lovers were wont to do. Except they weren't lovers, Shay thought.

Not yet, anyway.

That possibility caused a hitch in her breath and another smile, wider this time, because now she believed it was simply a matter of *when*, rather than *if*.

She finally broke the companionable silence. "Are you keeping the cull?"

"I'm not sure," Keagan said. "Granted, his owner no longer needs him, but I did acquire him under questionable circumstances. Besides, won't we be leaving the horses behind once we take the Path in Boreas?"

Shay thought about it. "He's not trained, but he'd be calmer than the others, especially with Onyx nearby. I could probably lead him all the way to Naiad if you wanted." She paused. "Would the marshals have rules about you keeping him?"

"I think, because he's considered such a valuable horse, they'll attempt to get in touch with Tannehill's heirs. If no one legitimately claims him, then he'll be assigned to our stables. Assuming no one above me pulls rank, I'll claim him."

Shay nodded. "Well, if you can't, let me know. I'll get you another one."

Keagan grinned crookedly. "That easy?"

"My clan runs the best herd in Aether," Shay said with quiet pride. "Onyx is one of ours. If I ask my mother, I'm sure she can set aside one of the culls for me."

"Thank you," Keagan said, clearly touched.

"You should have a good horse," Shay said, using a serious tone. "It's important to be able to trust your mount. I don't know what the marshals provide, but I can't remember ever noticing one, so they must be of unremarkable stock."

"They're definitely not Shadow-bred." Keagan rubbed some glycerin on a rein, keeping the leather soft and supple. "What was it like? Growing up there, I mean. I know you've told me some of it while we were in the jungle, but I know so little about your nation."

"It can be hard, especially in the winter when the ice is on the water and the wind burns as it blows," Shay said. "But in the other three seasons, the plains are beautiful." She paused. "Aside from the city, we have only four towns: Umbra to the west near the mountains, Penumbra to the east near the ocean, Sombra to the north, and Tenebrous to the south. Two are empty at any given time, or, rather, mostly empty. We have locals, usually those who want to remain in one place, but nothing like it is when the clans are there."

"How does that work?"

"Every year, ten major clans move the herds to new grazing," Shay said. "Five may winter in Tenebrous one year, while the other five winter in Sombra. In spring, we'll begin the migration to Penumbra, while the others go to Umbra, leaving the plains around Tenebrous and Sombra to recover for a year. Then the next year, we migrate to Sombra while the other clans move on to Umbra." Shay smiled. "It's an exciting day when we reach the new town and find the room where we slept four years earlier. We always discover letters from the other clans tucked beneath the mattress, telling us about their year there and the best places to fish and hunt." She paused, rubbing her stirrup leather idly. "When I was sent to the city to learn the way of the Shadows, forced to remain there year after year until graduation, I had a difficult time. Even now I miss life on the plains. It could be hard, but it was also very…" She searched for the right word.

"Free," she said finally.

Keagan was looking at her, her eyes soft. "Do you see your clan often?"

"Not very often, no. I try to get home for the solstice and equinox festivals, but sometimes I can't. I would love to take—" She stopped awkwardly, embarrassed.

"Take me home for solstice?" Keagan smiled gently. "I think they have rules about that."

Shay shook her head fretfully. "Rules I never questioned before. Now I'm not sure why they exist."

"This adventure has raised a lot of questions about things we've always taken for granted. Not just for you. For all of us."

Finishing the saddle, Shay returned it to the fence rail and then grabbed the big, dappled gray's saddle. It was huge, and as she lugged it back to the log, she noticed Cassius, Lyria, and Ashley all intently conversing around the fire pit. Keeping half an eye on them as she sat down, she wasn't surprised when, after a while, they stopped talking, looked over to where she and Keagan were seated, and finally urged Cassius in their direction. She watched her approach with curiosity.

"Marshal?" Cassius hesitated slightly before taking a seat on another log.

Keagan glanced over at her inquiringly. "Yes?"

"We've been talking."

"I saw," Keagan said pleasantly. Shay was impressed. Keagan hadn't let on she'd even glanced that way. Shay reminded herself not to underestimate the woman. "I assume this has to do with my decision. I was under the impression you agreed with it."

"I did. I still do, to a certain extent, but Lyria pointed out some things that we may be forgetting."

"Such as?"

"That even though no one on that side has thought of it yet, those lenses that lord wears might mimic the eyes of Shadow Riders."

Shay lifted her brow. Could their vision be replicated artificially? Was that what allowed him to see within the Shadow Realm?

Keagan paused, then spoke. "If that's the case, they could substitute those as they substituted the other elemental abilities."

"I'm not sure how you'd feel if we made it home, alerted the authorities, and brought them back here, only to find that the whole place has been ransacked and whatever he was looking for was long gone. With no way of knowing what that ever was." Cassius shrugged slightly. "I know I wouldn't feel good about it."

"Or we might open the door, be unable to discover what he's searching for, and grant him access that he wouldn't otherwise have once we leave here."

"Lyria thinks that if we open the door properly, we'd be able to reset it once we're done," Cassius said. "Possibly even add a few traps. Ashley is convinced she could do that."

"I'll bet she can." Keagan exhaled slowly, audibly. She glanced at Shay. "What do you think?"

"Whatever you decide is fine with me." She paused. "It would be interesting to see what's inside, though."

"Fine," Keagan said after a minute. "We'll do it this afternoon. We'll probably need torches. We have no idea what we'll find in there."

Cassius grinned faintly. "There may be nothing. It could all be collapsed."

"Can't you tell?" Shay asked, curious.

"Not yet," Cassius said. "The walls may be so thick I can't sense the dimensions of any opening beyond them. I'm not able to trace the deep strata of rock, only the composition of the immediate layer. That's why I'm in agriculture rather than mining."

Shay recalled that abilities were diverse. "Um, is it rude of me to ask what you can do?" she asked, feeling awkward. "I mean, normally."

Cassius flashed another grin. "Can I throw stones, in other words?"

"It would be good to know what we have at our disposal should we find ourselves in another battle," Keagan said professionally. "You look pretty good with that staff. Is that because you don't have offensive capabilities?"

Cassius held up a finger, indicating they should wait as she went over and found the saddle from Lyria's mount. Keagan, watching her, followed her lead and took the mare's tack. After bringing them back, they joined Shay, and once they had settled, Cassius began to talk.

"I can lift about four stone and toss it a fair distance. But I can also do that with my hands, and far more accurately. Mostly I can draw on certain minerals from a deep depth and infuse them into the soil around me. I can do that for acres at a time. I can taste the earth…" She looked at Shay. "Not literally. I guess I taste it the same way you can taste Paths."

Shay nodded. "I understand."

"I can taste the soil in my vicinity and know exactly what it's comprised of and what needs to be added to make it fertile. Offensively, I can disrupt soil to a depth and width of ten feet."

"That's useful," Keagan said. "You can create pits instantly beneath the feet of a combatant."

"At full strength, yes."

"Level?"

"Four point one."

"Nice," Keagan said. "I'm a four point six. Ashley's a four point four. So long as she has direct sunlight, or is near an open flame, she's fully charged. Lyria?"

"Not sure," Cassius said. "She can fly, though. Talks about it all the time That's level three point five at minimum."

Though Keagan and Cassius delivered all these levels and points in a tone that indicated they were reliable indicators to what an Elemental could do, to Shay, it was gibberish, just another aspect of Elementals that they tended to keep to themselves, learned in their Academy that only they attended. Why did they need such secrecy?

"Which means Lyria can also propel debris, increasing the velocity exponentially," Keagan said thoughtfully. "That's why she uses a crossbow.

Not only to help her accuracy, but to increase the ballistics. She brought up a significant breeze to dry our clothes with minimum effort. At full strength, she can probably blow someone off their feet. Hurricane force, at least."

"At least," Cassius said. "Maybe a lot more. Knock down buildings maybe."

"Could be useful," Keagan said. "I'll keep it in mind."

"So you learn how to do all these things in the Academy?" Shay asked casually.

"More like we know instinctively how to do them," Cassius said. "As our abilities develop, we attempt the things we feel we can do, and the abilities work with varying degrees of success. School teaches us how to apply them in the real world, how to refine them, make them precise and focused. It takes practice and discipline. From the beginning, I could always disrupt the earth, but I usually did it under my own feet and fell into holes a lot. I always knew if the plants around me were healthy, and if they weren't, I knew some of what they needed, but I couldn't always draw the proper minerals, only the ones that 'tasted' similar, so sometimes the plants died anyway. School taught me to identify each element precisely. In my specialty, regardless of spiritual belief, the periodic table is part of our true bible."

She paused, obviously evaluating Shay's level of understanding based on her expression. "When I go to a place like southern Arias that's so lacking in the necessary nutrients, I need to bring those elements along with me. Then I can transfer them from their containers and into the soil instantly. Otherwise, I'd have to draw them from other soil leagues away, which would take more out of me physically than would be healthy. Part of the cost."

"I respect that," Shay said. "You bring life to where there is none." She paused. "Could you, I mean Elementals in general, work together to repair those areas that the war destroyed? Restore what had been destroyed? Like the river?"

Now Keagan looked surprised. "I suppose if enough of us worked together," she said thoughtfully. "It would be a massive undertaking."

"Never happen," Cassius said, with absolute certainty and a touch of cynicism. "Various companies would have to cooperate and then split the profits, if there were any, in the aftermath. In the end, such a project would truly benefit only one nation and be too much of a long-term investment. I can't see any one company being that altruistic, let alone several. Not even the nations banding together could do it. It would empty the government treasuries, and Arias certainly doesn't have enough to pay for it on its own."

Shay nodded and returned her attention to her tack, thinking about all she had learned. Eventually, Ashley and Lyria joined them, clearly impatient to find out what Keagan had decided.

"We go in this afternoon," Cassius told them as they approached.

"Yes!" Lyria punched the air in triumph.

Keagan narrowed her eyes at Ashley. "I thought you were eager to get back home?"

"I am," Ashley said. "But I'm also curious to know what this guy is so hellbent on finding here. If we discover it first and take it with us, we'll really screw him up. Maybe even figure out what his plans are. It'll also make it easier for everyone to believe our story."

A shadow ghosted over her face, and Shay wondered who Ashley might be referring to. Who hadn't believed what she said on previous occasions? That was odd, because Ashley tended to say whatever was on her mind, tact be damned. But had she always been honest about it? Shay had no way of knowing.

"We were discussing our resources," Keagan told Lyria. "Level?"

"Five point six," Lyria replied promptly. "I can generate lift from a dead stop at sea level. I don't require a high launch point, although it makes it a lot easier."

The others all paused to stare at her, and Shay recalled that level fives were apparently powerful enough to join the Council. Lyria bent her head under their sudden scrutiny, cheeks coloring.

"At least I could before I lost my abilities."

Cassius patted her on the back comfortingly. Obviously she had taken Lyria under her aegis, Shay decided. "You will again. Just give it time."

"How much can you carry?" Keagan continued her questioning.

"What I can on the ground." Lyria looked a little embarrassed. "About two stone. Maybe a little less."

"Well, you're not very big." Shay tried to encourage her.

"No Sylph is. But some can carry up to ten times their body weight." Lyria looked wistful. "I wish I could do that."

"Velocity?"

"One hundred twenty knots. With a natural wind behind me, up to one sixty."

"Baast. That makes you the fastest I've ever heard of," Ashley said, clearly astonished. "Once you're at full strength, you can make it home in a hurry. You won't have to wait for us."

"I will, though. I'll wait for you." Lyria suddenly appeared anxious. "We're in this together, right?"

"Having you with us will be a tremendous advantage," Keagan said. "You'll be able to scout for water everywhere around us and bring it back if we need it. That way, we won't have to carry so much. Or worry about running out. Altitude?"

"Twelve thousand, though at that height, I have to take my time descending, or I get sick. Any higher and I have to generate my own air to breathe. Also, the more I carry, the lower I have to fly."

"All right. I'm going to tell you something now, and I need you to absolutely obey," Keagan said in a very serious tone. Lyria's eyes grew wide, and she nodded. "If I say the word, or if anything happens to us, you go. You take to the sky, and you don't look back. As soon as you're someplace safe, you find the authorities and tell them what happened. I'll write a report that you can always carry on you. Are we clear?"

"Leave you behind? But—"

"If I tell you to go, then that means there's no hope for the rest of us. In that event, the Council must know what's happening here. Do I have your word?"

Lyria's lower lip trembled ever so slightly, but she nodded, and Cassius put her arm around her shoulders, squeezing her comfortingly. "Good," she said. "We'd be counting on you."

"That goes for everyone." Keagan glanced briefly at Shay. "If something happens and it looks as if all is lost, then take the Path and go."

"Sure," Shay said, so evenly and readily she knew that Keagan didn't believe her. For that matter, she didn't think any of them did, because Ashley grinned, and Cassius let out a snort. Only Lyria looked surprised, but as she glanced around, she seemed to catch on and smiled slightly.

"I'm serious," Keagan said, looking stern.

"I'm sure you are," Shay told her. "But I'm never going to leave you behind. You'll just have to live with that fact."

Keagan opened her mouth, paused, then closed it, brows drawn down. But Shay could see that part of Keagan liked it.

Maybe even liked it a lot.

XIV

After lunch, they assembled in front of the door, and at Keagan's count to three, they all activated their respective tablets: a splash of water from her on the Aquas symbol, a spurt of flame from Ashley's finger sizzling against the Urodela symbol, a clot of earth propelled by Cassius onto the Terras symbol, and a blast of air from Lyria's open palm onto the Arias symbol. Shay crouched in the middle, looking into the Aether symbol, the light bathing her pupil. For a few seconds, nothing happened aside from a few soft clicks. Keagan was beginning to feel rather apprehensive about the murder holes above her when a massive, grating sound erupted. With a deep groan, the door slid open, dust falling from the top to patter down onto the landing.

Keagan switched on her torch and lifted it high, shining through the dark opening. It didn't illuminate far, just enough to see a corridor stretched before her, the floor thick with dust, the high walls made of stone blocks, so finely crafted nothing separated them other than a thin, almost imperceptible line of grout. The ceiling was twenty feet above them, making the passage feel narrow, though they were all able to walk abreast.

At Keagan's nod, Shay and Ashley stepped forward with her into the corridor, the dust puffing up beneath their feet. Shay covered her face with her scarf, leaving only her dark eyes visible, deep pools of silver and black. Keagan glanced at her, inclined her head, and Shay moved away, melting into the shadows beyond the circle of lamplight.

Behind Keagan, Cassius let out an oath, the first time Keagan had heard her blaspheme the name of her earth Goddess. "Lurra!"

"How does she do that?" Lyria said, delight evident in her voice. "Where did she go?"

"Not far," said a voice from the darkness. "Just ahead."

Yet despite how much Keagan squinted, she couldn't see her, not even a hint of motion.

"That is so awesome," Lyria said. "Why didn't you do that in the palace when you were rescuing us?"

A small chuckle from ahead. "Because I didn't want you to get lost. I needed you to follow me."

"Can you see anything?" Keagan asked, using a rather sharp tone to remind them this wasn't exactly a walk in the park.

"Just corridor," Shay said, more professionally as the rest of them subsided. A few seconds passed. "Door ahead."

Shay waited there until the others had reached her, her lean form finally coming into sight. The door was made of wood, though the frame was stone, carved with more of those unfamiliar symbols. Shay reached down for the handle and opened it with some difficulty, putting her weight behind it. It creaked open, the hinges hindered by the dirt of centuries. As they entered a huge room, Keagan's breath caught as she glanced around her, the others uttering various sounds of awe and astonishment.

"Baast's tits, who is this woman?" Ashley's jaw hung open.

"This is like the hall in the Aquas palace," Shay said. "A lot bigger, but it has a similar layout."

Lined with statues of the same woman as those outside on the cliff, a carpeted walkway led to a raised dais at the far end of the hall, where a heavily engraved golden throne dominated its surroundings. The rest of the furnishings, comprised of cabinets, tables, and various seating, were set up in the adjoining space between the statues and the stone wall. They seemed intact for the most part and their quality was obvious, even covered in a deep layer of dust. But Keagan and the others spared them only a glance as they approached, their attention drawn to the throne. Lying across the ornate arms was a staff, an actual staff, with a familiar diamond-shaped crystal at the tip, sapphire-blue veins lacing through it. Keagan's stomach tightened unpleasantly.

"I think we've found what he's looking for," Ashley said with a lightness not reflected in her expression.

"So there is more than one," Keagan said, grim. "One entombed with Queen Heratherus in Naiad and one here."

"Oh, Lady."

Bemused, Keagan followed Shay's gaze and saw the large painting spread across the wall in the area immediately to the right of the dais, set above a dining table with five chairs. The colors were still visible after all the centuries, even through the layer of grime coating the smooth surface. It took her a few seconds to recognize what it represented, and when she did, she was staggered, her knees weakening. "Those are maps."

"Of the four nations, side by side," Shay said, sounding angry. "None of the Shadow Lands, of course."

"Which meant you were out of the war," Cassius said as they all walked over to inspect it closely. She put her hand on Shay's shoulder. "Be glad."

Shay slipped off her cloak and began to wipe away the dust, revealing the well-defined details, sharp and clear, unlike those of the regular hand-drawn maps Keagan was familiar with. No borders separated them, each nation displayed on its own, painted directly onto the wall. A multitude of dots with accompanying names marked areas that she knew to be uninhabited now: the Echidna Wilderness in western Aquas, the Anemoi Badlands in central Arias, the Chimera Wastelands in northeast Terras, and the lava-covered Vatra Expanse on the coast of Urodela. Several dots were placed in the middle of the Lernaean Swamps, one larger than any of the others.

For long moments, they all stood, contemplating the world that had been, ignoring the throne and staff. For the time being, none of them wanted to get near it.

"Look at it all," Cassius said in a low, sad voice. "Look at everything that's been lost."

"Are all those dots supposed to be cities?" Lyria was subdued as Keagan held the light high to illuminate the smooth surface. "Look. There's the River Anemoi. So many lived along its banks."

"Is that what I think it is?" Ashley asked, tracing a black line from the area on the Aquas west coast where Keagan and Shay had rescued the others. According to the map, it had been a city called Amane, and the crown symbol next to it identified it as the original capital. The line traversed the nation and then continued across the Alameada Ocean until it went off the side of the painting. Ashley moved over to pick it up on the other side as it crossed the ocean to intersect with Arias, ending in the general vicinity of where they were standing, in a crown city called Anemoi, like the river.

"A Path," Shay said, her voice trembling slightly. "The Path we took here. We didn't go west. We went east. That explains why we were able to go so far so quickly. We traveled in a direction no other Path takes, across the open ocean with no obstacles. Look, in Arias it's marked with the Aquas symbol, and in Aquas, with the Arias symbol, indicating it joins the nations."

Keagan hadn't known Paths didn't normally cross the Alameada Ocean. She did know that, in the past, the Transport Guild had attempted to cross the vast expanse of water to travel directly from Aquas to Arias, hoping to develop new trade routes. The very few ships who made it carried stories that made it clear it wasn't economically feasible to try it on a regular basis. Much easier to dock in Terras and transport goods through the mountain passages, away from the massive, violent storms and the rogue waves and the many and varied sea creatures large enough to swallow an entire ship with its crew in one gulp.

"There are other black lines. I don't know any of these Paths, linking places that no longer exist." Shay ran her fingers over them. "All lost."

"This was once our world," Keagan said. "All gone now, thanks to us. Thanks to Elementals."

"I need a copy of this," Shay said, stepping back and glancing around.

"Spread out," Keagan said. "See what else we can find."

The others lit their own lamps, and for the next several minutes, they gave various cries of discovery from all corners as they searched through the various cabinets. They piled a large variety of unfamiliar items, undoubtedly quite valuable to collectors, in the center of the floor, but none of them proved useful. They found a few more doors leading from the hall, but nothing but rubble was behind them, indicating that time had bested the rest of what Keagan was beginning to think of as the palace for this lost city. Then Shay yelped in triumph. She'd been rummaging through a cabinet to the left of the dais and also found a couple of desks, along with shelving, which held moldering remains of books. Possibly some kind of administrative area for the throne room.

The others joined her as she opened a long, tubular container and removed a roll of what looked like paper, though impossibly shiny and smooth, unlike anything Keagan had seen before. Unrolled, it turned out to be four separate sheets, replicating the nations on the wall.

"We'll take these with us," Shay said, eyes bright as she studied them. "Look at the detail!"

"None of those places exist anymore," Ashley said. "And the current cities aren't marked. They're useless."

"Not if these black lines represent Paths." Shay waved her away like a buzzing fly.

With her Shadow Rider happily occupied, that left the obvious problem for the rest of them. Keagan lifted her lamp and moved back to the throne, accompanied by the other Elementals. They stopped a few feet away, regarding the staff uneasily.

"As far as I could see, merely lifting it would activate it," Cassius said.

"Yeah. The wraiths did the same thing," Keagan said. "Lifted it and a light flashed red. Then I was out."

"So it absorbs abilities," Ashley said. "Like energy crystals."

Lyria blinked. "Yeah, like the ones that make cold and hot boxes work. Or the small ones in the torches. Absorbs energy and releases it slowly over time until it needs to be renewed."

"Except you have to refine the mined rock and then deliberately pour ability into the finished gem until it can't hold any more," Ashley said. "Shaped crystal like this doesn't arbitrarily suck all the ability out of you against your will."

"Maybe these did before the war," Keagan said slowly. "Maybe it's a weapon. Take your enemy's abilities away and store them until needed." She thought furiously. "An Undine would be able to take a Salamas ability and use it for their own. Absorb all four abilities…" She felt sick. Was this what Tannehill had been talking about? "You'd be unstoppable."

"Except by someone using the same kind of weapon," Ashley said. "Then it would be like a tournament, where the strongest and smartest wins."

"Take another look at the wall," Cassius said quietly. "I don't think anyone won anything."

"Do we destroy this?" Lyria asked.

"Can we?" Keagan said. "I'm not sure how. It would just absorb any energy we offer. I suppose we could physically try to smash it."

"Do we want to?" Ashley asked. "If this Shadow Lord has one, won't we need one for our side?"

"So we have sides now," Cassius said. "This doesn't bode well."

"No. It doesn't." Keagan paused. "The stone didn't affect Shay in the Shadows. It's possible she can handle it, even transport it somehow." She glanced at Cassius. "Who exactly used the stone on you? The Shadow Lord?"

"No. His woman. She's null." Cassius's square features brightened. "It didn't affect her. In fact, now that I think of it, the lord stayed well clear, though he hardly has any abilities to absorb." She paused. "Maybe that's why he wants these. For the abilities he has a taste of, but can barely generate."

"He wouldn't be the first who wanted more than he deserved," Keagan said. "And if he's somehow tracked down the locations of these stones, he could become very powerful."

"More powerful than the Council?" Lyria looked horrified.

"If the stone can absorb their abilities before they can use them," Ashley said, "yeah. In a heartbeat."

"But a good sword could still take him down," Cassius said. "Or better yet, an arrow."

"Not if you can't get close enough to use one," Keagan said. "Look. Elementals are naturally stronger than those who aren't. That's why we're valuable, that's why we find ourselves in positions of power and authority, and that's why ordinary people fear us even as they fawn over us. We make their lives easier, but everybody understands at the same time that we could make those lives a lot harder if we wanted to. Every fight is won because we go into it with more powerful weapons than they can muster, especially when we work together."

"But maybe the Shadow Lord only thinks he's in charge until some null funding him gets what he wants," Ashley said.

"Oh." Keagan absorbed that statement with discomfort, and judging from the faces of others, they hadn't thought of it either until Ashley brought it up. Would it be possible for a non-Elemental to gain all the abilities and use them at will, without the stringent ethical training received from the Academy? Was that why a "ritual" was involved? Perhaps Keagan had a blind spot regarding this situation. Perhaps an Elemental wasn't behind it at all. Perhaps just some ordinary person hiding behind him was.

Or beside him. Keagan was reminded of the woman helping him, the one she was beginning to suspect either was or had been a marshal.

"What are we discussing?"

Shay made Keagan start so badly, she caromed into Cassius, who, fortunately, absorbed the weight without pushing back, catching her effortlessly.

"Damn it. Will you stop doing that?" Ashley muttered.

Shay didn't smile, but Keagan could see the amusement in those silver eyes. She made a face at her and then looked back at the staff. "It's possible we're all wrong. Maybe this isn't what he's looking for. Maybe it doesn't do anything at all." Keagan knew that was wishful thinking even as she spoke the words.

"Are you willing to take a chance on that possibility?" Cassius spread out her hands. "Look around. Nothing else is here. It's like the whole place was designed to display it. To signify its power."

"You're right." Keagan sighed. "Shay, do you think you can take the stone and, I don't know, wrap it up in something? Keep it away from us?"

Shay contemplated the throne briefly and wrapped the corner of her cloak around the stone. Then she slammed it over the arm of the throne, broke it off from the staff, and slipped it into her tunic, out of sight. Keagan, horrified at the treatment of an ancient and valuable artifact, managed not to wince, but it was a near thing. After all, she had asked Shay to take care of it.

"Can we get out of here now?" she asked, rather plaintively.

"We'll secure the entrance," Lyria said. "But I don't think we need any traps now. We found what he was looking for."

Back at camp, by the corral, Keagan watched Shay stash the stone securely in a diplomatic pouch and put it in Onyx's saddlebag, the one normally reserved for her crown missives.

"I hate that it'll take up room better reserved for food and supplies."

"I do, too," Keagan said, "but it's probably why this camp is here, and what Professor Tannehill died for."

"Do you really think someone could use this to become Elemental?"

"So you *were* listening." Keagan stood close to her, near enough to smell the faintly spicy scent of her skin. With Cassius in her tent and the others still behind the door, Keagan pulled Shay into her arms and kissed her. Following some apparent surprise, Shay returned the embrace with enthusiasm.

After they parted for breath, Shay looked at her fondly. "That didn't answer my question."

"Do you want to use it? Have the chance to fly?"

"Lady, no!" Shay looked so horrified that Keagan was ashamed of her playful suggestion. "Do you think that woman might be the real brains behind this?"

"Possibly," Keagan said. "You saw her. I haven't. What do you think?"

Shay hesitated. "Hard to say. She looked…ordinary. Just another woman. I had the sense he was in charge, but maybe that was a preconception because I recognized him as Elemental. She called him 'my Lord,' but he called her 'my Lady.' He instructed her to make sure Ashley was found, but maybe that was just advice and not an order." Shay shook her head. "I honestly don't know. Maybe he doesn't know."

"We should leave tomorrow. The others might not be at full strength, but I don't feel comfortable staying around here with the stone in our possession." Keagan pulled her close and kissed her again. "Share my tent tonight? I promise, I'll be awake when you join me."

Shay smiled, brushing her nose against Keagan's. "I look forward to it." Tilting her head, she kissed Keagan again, and this time, it felt a little different, deeper, more caring, tender and sweet. Keagan pressed against her, tangling one hand in Shay's thick, dark hair, keeping the other firmly around Shay's waist, not wanting to let her go, lost in this moment of absolute bliss.

The unwelcome sound of someone clearing her throat behind Shay reminded Keagan exactly where she was.

"Uh, sorry," Cassius said, head bent as she peered up at them through her lashes. She seemed to be trying very hard not to laugh. "The others are on their way back."

Keagan reluctantly released Shay, who appeared amused again, sharing a look with Cassius, who returned it with a faint smile. Keagan turned to see Lyria and Ashley entering the camp, immersed in a conversion about something that required a great number of hand gestures from both of them.

"What's going on?" Keagan asked as she joined them by the fire pit. "Is the door secure?"

"It is," Ashley said. "Lyria reset the lock. That's not what took us so long."

"We were looking at that big map again." Lyria motioned at Shay. "Did you notice the black line to the east? The symbol beside it?"

Shay blinked and then reached into her tunic, pulling out the roll of maps. Flipping through them, she found the right one, studying it for a few seconds. "Yes. I see what you're saying. It's only about ten leagues from here." She paused, eyebrows rising. "That symbol is for the Shadow Lands. So it ends there?"

"What's going on?" Keagan asked.

"If the lines are Paths, as we suspect," Shay said, "this one is much closer than Boreas." She lifted her gaze to meet Keagan's. "Depending on where it exits, we could be with a clan and help in only three or four days. Sooner if we leave immediately."

"Oh." Keagan felt her heart rate increase. Was it at the thought of meeting Shay's people, including, possibly, her family? "That's a better idea than spending a week or more in the desert. But what about taking all the horses through the Shadows?"

"And what about Elementals not being allowed in Aether?" Ashley added, more practically.

"Surely they'd understand, considering the information we're bringing," Cassius said with a frown.

Shay looked at her, brow furrowed. "They'll have to. The Elders need to hear about this as soon as possible. I suppose we can blindfold the horses, keep them close to Onyx so they can sense him. It won't be ideal. They might bolt. If that happens, we'll have to let them go. It wouldn't be safe to go after them."

"They'd die." Lyria appeared stricken suddenly and looked over at the desert gelding, all golden with its snowy white mane and tail. It was clear she had grown fond of him very quickly. "We should leave them here."

"In the hopes that the Shadow Lord will come back and reclaim them?" Cassius looked uncomfortable. "What if he doesn't? Eventually, they'd starve to death." She gestured toward the pasture. "It's already starting to wither. I can renew the soil, but that will last only so long. Grass doesn't grow here naturally for a reason. And horses don't run wild in Arias."

They all looked at Keagan, and she felt the weight of those stares on her shoulders. "We'll take them if we can," she said. "We'll need them in Aether." She managed a smile for Shay. "And if anywhere will be safe for them, it'll be in your nation."

"They might not want to see us, but they might like to have some more horses."

XV

They spent dinner discussing what they should take with them, with Shay, Keagan, and Cassius on the merits of traveling light, and the others on being prepared for anything.

"We can't take the hot and cold boxes," Keagan said with forced patience. "They're far too heavy for the horses to carry. The tents will weigh enough. And we need only two among us all."

"I like having my own tent," Ashley said. "I certainly don't want to bunk with you two. Baast knows what you'll be doing."

Lyria snorted, and Shay tried not to sigh. Clearly, not just Cassius knew what was going on between her and Keagan. Would anything happen in the tent that night, located so close to the others? Who knew that adventuring could be so difficult on the love life, though she hadn't had much of a love life prior to this. Her encounters had been infrequent and mostly temporary. She was away from her home base in Naiad for long periods of time, and trying to maintain any kind of serious relationship was impossible.

She looked at Keagan, at the way her brilliant blue eyes sparkled in the firelight, how her full mouth firmed when she was being serious but was curved in a half smile the rest of the time, and knew a moment of despair. Would it be any different with her?

It was already different with her, Shay told herself, heart aching. She had never felt this way about anyone before. She would just have to find a way to make it work. Whatever it took.

Eventually, the others drifted off to bed, leaving Shay and Keagan alone at the fire. More aware of each other physically than intellectually, they found it hard to concentrate on any topic other than the one foremost in their mind. With unspoken agreement, talking about it seemed rather unnecessary.

Keagan poked the fire, sending up a shower of sparks, as Shay watched her with tenuously leashed desire. Finally, after it seemed everyone else was finally settled for the night, Keagan glanced over at her and smiled. "Ready to turn in?"

Shay nodded, not trusting herself to speak, and together, they rose. Keagan doused the flames with a burst of water and then took Shay's hand. Shay noted that her hand was already dry, warm in her own, and wondered if Keagan had simply absorbed the excess moisture without even thinking about it. Her breath quickened, and she had a pleasant sensation in the pit of her stomach, one that moved lower as they approached the tent. Keagan drew back the flap and inclined her head, inviting Shay to enter first.

Shay sank to her hands and knees, crawling inside, waiting on top of the bedroll as Keagan joined her, switching on a vapor lamp to its lowest setting.

"I know you don't need it," she said, her voice low and slightly uneven. "But I want to be able to see you."

"All right," Shay said, feeling absurdly shy and uncertain. It wasn't as if she'd never done this before. It just felt that way.

Keagan, gazing at Shay's face, began to unbutton her uniform shirt. Shay stilled her hand. "Let me," she whispered.

Keagan smiled faintly and nodded.

Shay moved closer and dipped her head, kissing Keagan on the lips as she began to unfasten the uniform, finding the buttons stiff and uncooperative. The difficulty made the anticipation rise, however, so she didn't begrudge it. As she trailed her lips over Keagan's face, nuzzling along her jaw to her earlobe, which she nibbled gently, she managed the last of the stubborn buttonholes and slipped the shirt off Keagan's arms, immediately transferring her line of kisses to the bared right shoulder, mouthing her collarbone with tender regard.

Clad in only the sleeveless undershirt, Keagan made a pleased sound in her throat and tugged at Shay's tunic, unlacing the vest and pushing it off, making another sound, deeper and hungrier, when she discovered Shay was wearing nothing beneath. Then Shay involuntarily gulped as Keagan covered her breasts, palms smoothing over her nipples, making them rise in response. Eager, Shay managed to get Keagan's undergarment off, dropping it to the side, and ran her hands over the muscular torso, fingertips tracing lines of delicate discovery. Sinking to the bedroll, they worked at each other's trousers, Keagan busy untying the leather lacing, Shay tackling the line of buttons up the front, loosening them enough to slide them down their legs, both muttering brief groans of annoyance when they realized they had yet to remove their boots.

They shared a glance and smiled as they sat up and pulled them off, finally getting rid of their trousers. They paused, regarding each other with hungry eyes, then came together once more, nothing left to hinder them, skin on skin in lovely harmony. Side by side, they spent several moments simply exploring each other, familiarizing themselves with the other's body, hands smoothing over back and hip, along flank and thigh, pressed together as they kissed and kissed until Shay thought she would pass out from sheer pleasure. Then Keagan had a strong hand on the back of Shay's leg, gripping it securely as she lifted it over her hip, affording more intimate access. Shay's breath caught, and her head went back involuntarily as the firm, warm fingers touched her, tentatively at first, a slow stroke of inquiry before a more intent foray, firm yet gentle.

"Oh," Keagan whispered. "You're so wet."

Shay chuckled. "I thought you, of all people, would appreciate that."

"Oh, I do," Keagan muttered. Her kiss was powerful, commanding. "Now, let me."

Shay surrendered, hands idly tracing patterns of sensation on Keagan's back as Keagan's fingertips moved over her, fondling her with increasing intent, bathed in the moisture, plying her with a knowing touch before slipping inside, probing deeply. Shay lost herself in the softness of Keagan's skin, the warm, salty scent of her body, the way her lips seemed to drink the very essence of her soul. The pleasure built with easy intensity, growing ever more delightful until, abruptly, she was there, cast over the edge to utter bliss. Burying her face in Keagan's neck, she stifled her outcry, throbbing around the long fingers inside.

"You are beautiful," Keagan murmured. Shay relaxed in her arms, allowing herself to be held as the trembling subsided, feeling safe and secure, cossetted by the muscular embrace.

But only for a short period of time. Then she was pressing Keagan down against the bedroll, covering her with her body as she kissed her with open demand and desire. Keagan didn't resist, smiling against her lips and then lifting her head as Shay kissed down the line of her throat, lips brushing over the steady throbbing in her neck, quick and heavy, before trailing down her chest, moving over the firm swells to cover one firm point, tonguing it delicately.

Keagan made another sound and immediately muffled it by putting her fist against her mouth, making Shay smile as she looked up at the smoldering expression of need. Moving ever downward, she nuzzled along the firm ridges of abdominal muscles, then lower, ever lower, until she was urging Keagan's thighs apart to settle between them.

Keagan tasted of the sea and the wild, free places that Shay now knew she needed in the very core of her being. She felt like she was home once more, riding the plains where nothing stood between her and the horizon. When had she lost that feeling? And how had she managed to find it here, not in a place, but in the arms of a person she'd known for only a week?

Keagan shuddered beneath her, like a wind through the long grass, and Shay intensified her caress, mouth moving over her, teasing, taunting, before finally focusing. She felt Keagan's desire building, concentrated on lifting her that final bit, holding her firmly in place as she would an unbroken filly, keeping her steady as she rode the waves of pleasure.

Afterward, she moved up to deliver several deep, loving kisses before settling into Keagan's compelling embrace. Head pillowed on her shoulder, she rested her hand on the toned belly, feeling it rise and fall beneath her palm with easy strength.

"That was…amazing," Keagan said, and Shay felt her lips brush over her hair.

"It was," Shay said. She paused. "I hope we didn't disturb the others."

"We were quiet," Keagan whispered. "If not, then they just need to mind their own business." She paused, fingertips light on Shay's back, tracing a teasing line along her spine. "Sleepy?"

Shay lifted her head to meet the hopeful gaze. "Not at all."

Reaching over, Shay switched off the vapor lamp and watched Keagan's pupils grow large as Shay moved over her again. "I can't see you," Keagan said softly.

"That's all right. I can see for both of us." Shay bent her head and captured her mouth in a soft kiss. "You won't get lost."

And loved her again.

When she woke the next morning, she and Keagan were so entwined, it was difficult to tell where she left off and Keagan began. Shay smiled, feeling such a sense of belonging that she never wanted to move. But the sounds from outside let her know that they had slept long enough. She made a move away, only to feel Keagan stir, protest quietly, and tighten her embrace, pulling Shay back into her.

"We need to leave soon," Shay said, though she didn't really resist. "We don't want to travel in the heat of the day."

"I know," Keagan muttered. "But we have time for a kiss good morning, don't we?"

Shay smiled. "Of course." Several minutes later, she drew back for breath. "Only a kiss?"

"I can skip breakfast," Keagan told her.

Shay laughed. "I can't. And you shouldn't." She kissed her a final time. "Come on."

Wrapping the blanket around her, Shay carried her clothes out of the tent, aware of varied glances sent in her direction as she headed for the shower. She dared not look over, afraid of what she might see in their expressions.

"The water should still be hot," Ashley said helpfully.

Shay was pleased that was the extent of it, but as she soaped up, basking in the hot water cascading over her, she could see Keagan join the others at the fire pit. The rising redness of her face as she sipped her morning tea indicated they were cheerfully making life difficult with their comments.

When she joined them, giving way to Keagan to head for the shower, Shay accepted the mug offered by Cassius and sipped it. No untoward comments were directed her way, which relieved her on one level but discomfited her on another. Would they ever feel comfortable enough with her to be as casual as they were with Keagan and each other? She doubted it. Even if the Elemental women hadn't known each other before this, they had an unspoken bond that others simply weren't privy to, born of shared history at the Academy and their lives of assumed privilege.

"We break camp after breakfast?" Cassius asked.

"Yes. We're getting a late start as it is," Shay said.

"And whose fault is that?" Ashley asked, but her eyes were, Shay thought, unusually kind, and it struck her that perhaps Ashley was happy for her and Keagan. Then Ashley abruptly sucked up all the fire, leaving cold, dead embers and making Shay nearly spill her tea.

They left the canyon, riding east along the river for a few hours, though well away from the reptiles sunning on the bank. Keagan rode at Shay's side, not speaking often, simply enjoying each other's company, sharing the occasional sideways glance and seductive smile. Behind them, Ashley and Lyria chattered about a multitude of things, mostly clubs and work and things that Shay didn't really relate to. Cassius rode midway between them, part of neither pairing, and Shay wondered if she felt she couldn't intrude on either group, the new lovers in front, or the new friends in the rear.

Or maybe she just appreciated the ride and the solitude. Cassius really seemed to like her horse, patting his dappled neck often, and was obviously an accomplished equestrian. Shay thought Cassius would enjoy the Shadow Lands greatly, especially once she saw their herds. Then, reminded she was about to bring four Elementals into her nation, she felt a sharp qualm. Showing up without warning would ruffle more than a few feathers. Of course, what they had to tell the Clan Elders would be a bigger shock.

But first they had to get there. Shay felt the first stirrings within her, the sense of a Path located ahead, confirming the map's accuracy. "We're close," she said, glancing at Keagan.

Keagan nodded briefly and straightened in her saddle. Immediately, her expression changed, becoming impassive, harder, far more authoritative. Shay tingled all over, finding the expression incredibly sexy, though she readily recognized that before all this, it would have put her on guard and maybe even scared her a bit.

They came upon another break in the cliffs, leading into a dark little gully. The obelisk here was crumbling, almost gone, only the base remaining to mark the entry. Shay could taste the time layered upon it, the sense of no one accessing it for centuries, the markings eroded and faint.

"This is small," she said as she reined Onyx to a halt.

Keagan looked at her. "I don't know what that means," she said in that level, opaque tone. Her marshal voice, Shay had dubbed it.

"It'll take more effort to enter," Shay said, searching for the proper terms. Did the Elementals have equal difficulty explaining their own processes? "The markings have faded. It won't be as safe. It isn't as protected."

"But you can still ride it?" Cassius asked. "Still follow it?"

"Of course," Shay said. "It just won't keep things away from it as well as the present Paths do."

"Well, we were already relying on you to get us through," Keagan said, sounding patient "Are you recommending we don't try?"

"No, but we'll have to be extra vigilant." Shay glanced back at them, looking over their clothing and gear. "You'll need to remove all reflective surfaces." She drew some bits of charcoal from her tunic, burnt wood she'd retrieved from the fire pit. "Smudge any buckles and shiny bits on your tack and clothing, make it dark." She glanced at Ashley. "Remove your jewelry, tuck it away. Just keep it simple."

After helping them prepare as well as possible, with Cassius's help, she covered the horses' eyes with several strips of cloth sliced from a merc's cloak. Some tossed their heads, but with each of them attending to her own mount, soothing it, they soon quieted.

"Keep one hand on your horse and one on the rope," Shay told them. "Remember, the calmer you are, the calmer they'll be. If the horse starts to panic, release the bridle, but keep hold of that rope. It's your lifeline. If I tell you something, obey without question. You won't get a second warning. We won't have time." She shared a final glance with Keagan. "Ready?"

"As we'll ever be," Keagan said.

Shay centered herself and, with a focused effort, eased open the entry, slipping through onto the Path, Onyx striding easily beside her. The rest moved behind her, so far without any stumbles, and she wondered if it would help if they had the goggles that the Shadow Lord possessed. She wished they had found more of them in Anemoi.

As she walked, she was conscious of the Shadows beyond the Path more than she normally was. Maybe that was because the glyphs were so faded. She could still see them, but they were far from the clear and distinctive markings she normally followed. The muted sounds of the four behind her reminded her how much she was responsible for, which made her head ache. She'd never become a guide, that was certain. It was too nerve-racking.

Then she felt it.

"Stop!" she hissed, thankful when the others instantly obeyed. For long moments, they stood there, and while it was hard for Shay to remain still, peering through the murk, she could only imagine how much harder it was for the rest, who had no idea what was going on.

Then she saw it, something moving up ahead, something massive. She held her breath as it crossed the Path, ignoring the markings as if they weren't there, an unnatural displacement of shadow and darkness. Behind her, she was aware of the others freezing, like prey trapped in the malevolent gaze of a predator, and as her heart thudded, Shay knew that was exactly what they all were—prey. Any second, she expected the horses to bolt, but even they seemed paralyzed, unable to move. Did they sense what passed before them?

She held her breath, terrified that any sound would draw its attention. Her lungs began to ache, and then, finally, it was gone, beyond her sensing. She let out her breath, and that was when she realized they had all stopped breathing, the expulsion of collective exhalation unbelievably loud in the silence.

"Is it gone?" Keagan whispered, her voice barely carrying.

"Yes," Shay said. So they had sensed it then, somehow knowing something had been there.

"What was it?" Lyria asked, hushed.

"Queeb," Shay said, shortly.

"What's that?"

"You don't want to know. Let's go."

It took a bit to get the horses moving again, all of them trembling and sweat-soaked, hides foaming. Shay was beyond impressed with how well the others had kept them calm, though perhaps they all had somehow known instinctively that they were safer in their little human/equine herd than by going off into the Shadows on their own.

Time passed without measure, and then Shay could feel the end ahead. And the beginning. Several beginnings, Paths converging to a single point, overlapping, layer upon layer, and she felt pulled in ten different directions. With an effort that reverberated to her very bones, she opened an entry, stumbling through into the world.

They abruptly stood in a grassy clearing, as above them, the sliver of moon was on the rise and stars were appearing. Shay was used to adjusting to the time differences between nations, but all the others looked considerably discombobulated when they discovered it was night. Cassius and Lyria immediately dug out some torches from their saddlebags and turned them high to illuminate the immediate area.

"What is this place?" Ashley asked as they all looked around. Massive standing stones rose in a circle around them, constructed rather than naturally formed, crudely carved pillars with heavy capstones resting on top, making it seem like some sort of ritualistic, ancient gathering site. Beyond them, the dark shadows of the forest rustled in the night wind. It was late spring, not particularly cold this evening, but after the heat of Aquas and Arias, a considerable drop in temperature. Ashley had her arms wrapped across her chest, hugging herself, and even Cassius seemed uncomfortable. Only Lyria didn't react, immune to the cold.

"Some kind of central hub of Paths," Shay said, voice thick and uneven. She was vibrating from the proximity of so many located so close together, all activated by their arrival, and had never felt anything like it. How did the clans not know this was here? "I need to leave." Her legs crumpled, and she fell to her hands and knees. "It hurts."

Keagan immediately went to her side, appearing concerned as she slipped an arm around her waist, helping her back to her feet. "Mount up," she ordered the others. In a lower tone, she pulled Shay to her. "Direction?"

Shay looked up and, with an effort, took better note of her surroundings. "Oh," she said, heart sinking. "Oh, no. We're in the Shadow Hills."

"What does that mean?"

"That we need to get out of here as soon as possible." She looked up, squinting at the stars, searching for something familiar. "There. That way's southwest."

"I understand." Keagan helped her mount, then mounted herself after removing the cull's blindfold. Cassius handed her a lamp, and once they were ready, she took point and led them from the stone ring into the forest.

Shay swayed in her saddle, allowing Onyx to follow without her providing direction, wanting only to put some distance between her and the Paths that cried out to be ridden, lost and so very, very lonely.

XVI

Keagan found a game trail, hoping it didn't belong to anything dangerous, and led the others through the forest until Shay appeared less likely to collapse at any minute. Keagan didn't know what to think when she looked at her, noting the dark shadows beneath her eyes, how very ashen she appeared in the vapor lamp, but mostly how she swayed uncertainly in her saddle. That was disconcerting. Shay normally rode Onyx as if they were one creature. Even while unconscious in Arias, she'd moved with him, making it easy for Keagan to keep her upright until she woke up. Now she looked as if she were merely along for the ride, like the sack of grain thrown across his withers.

Coming upon a stream, Keagan drew up, raising a fist to halt the others. She peered at Shay. "Are we far enough away?"

Shay looked at her, hunched into herself as she nodded slowly. "I'm okay."

She wasn't, but Keagan didn't want to continue riding through an unfamiliar forest at night. The horses might step wrong, and they might lose one altogether. She nodded at Cassius. "We'll make camp here."

Cassius returned the nod and dismounted. While Ashley and Lyria set up a camp much rougher than the one they'd been enjoying in the desert, Keagan helped Shay off Onyx and led her over to a rock. "Sit," she said.

Leaving Shay there, she helped Cassius settle the horses, tying the four and leaving Onyx loose to move as he pleased. He wouldn't go far. Then she returned to where Shay sat, head down, fingers massaging her temple.

"Talk to me," she requested gently.

"So many Paths, all in one spot," Shay said. "All untraveled for centuries." She paused. "When I say I sense Paths, I mean that they call out to me. I'm drawn to them. They want me to ride them. But I've never had them converge like that. Even in the crown cities that have more than one Path leading from them, the entry points are held in separate locations a few leagues apart. Not here. Here, they were all together, entries layered upon entries." She exhaled. "I felt like I was being yanked in ten different directions."

"Sounds unpleasant."

Shay laughed shakily. "It was." She winced. "It is."

"I'm sorry," Keagan said, rubbing her back lightly. "I wish I could do something."

"I'll survive." Shay glanced over to where Ashley had started a fire. "I know it won't get out of control, she'd prevent that, but can we make that a little smaller? It can attract as well as repel."

"I'll take care of it," Keagan said. "Rest. I'll get you something to eat."

After advising Ashley to bring it down a few levels, she and Lyria prepared supper, though it felt like lunch. "This is weird," Lyria said as they made wraps with chicken, leafy greens, peppers, and cheese. "First Arias, and now Aether. I've never traveled through the Shadows before. I know time differences exist between nations because I've been told of them, but you never notice them when traveling by caravan or ship. You just adjust as you go."

"I don't know how the Riders do it," Keagan said. "They must experience the changes all the time."

"Maybe that's part of their abilities," Lyria said. "Not feeling them. Not feeling like it should be day when it's night."

They carried the food over to the fire and handed the wraps to Ashley and Cassius. Shay had made her way over from the rock to perch uneasily on a log, the firelight making her face appear even more drawn. Keagan sat beside her and offered her a wrap, putting a canteen on the ground between them. Shay accepted it and took a bite, chewing without enthusiasm, clearly eating because she knew she had to.

Keagan did have an appetite, and she tore into her meal avidly. "It's so quiet here," she said between bites. "Is it because of our presence?"

"No. It's always quiet here," Shay said. "The predators in this forest hunt swiftly and silently. Few see them coming, but even then, it's difficult to survive an attack."

"Well, that's disturbing." Keagan peered at her. "Do they move the way you do?"

"Possibly," Shay said. "Though, to be honest, until I worked with you, I was unaware I was so difficult to see."

"Are all Shadow Riders like that?"

Shay shrugged. "I don't know. It's never come up." She managed a weak smile. "I can always see them."

"You must have your own marshals," Keagan said. "All nations do."

"None of them are Riders. In the city, a small unit keeps the peace. But on the plains, the clans take care of their own. If someone does something wrong, they're brought before the Elder. Each clan has its own, and together they form the local council. They determine guilt or innocence, if necessary."

"In the case of wrongdoing, who tracks down the culprit?" Keagan asked, keenly curious.

"It's difficult to do something wrong without someone else in the clan knowing or finding out about it," Shay said. "It all gets reported to their Elder sooner or later. *The clan comes first.*"

"What's the punishment for a guilty verdict?"

"It varies according to the crime. The most serious infractions warrant death or, worse, banishment."

Keagan inhaled slowly, noting how Shay thought the latter superseded the former. "What's the punishment for smuggling in four Elementals?"

Shay lifted her brows. "The information we bring is beyond the clans or even the Shadow Lands. It involves all the nations." She looked away. "I hope that fact will outweigh the infraction."

"If it doesn't?"

"Then I pay the price," Shay said simply. "And hope it isn't too severe."

Keagan spent a few seconds wrapping her head around that statement. "You talk about the city and the plains with its towns as separate and distinct entities. Who actually lives in the city?"

"Those who are no longer only of the clan. Like the Riders, or others who aren't suited for life on the plains and find purpose in other professions. The rest are from other nations who prefer a life without Elementals. Some find their place with the clans, but most live and work in the city."

"Do that many people dislike being around Elementals?" Keagan had never really thought about it before. Some were resentful, of course, afraid, but to want to be completely away from her kind?

Shay hesitated, obviously trying to find an answer. "More than perhaps you realize," she said after a bit. "Aether doesn't enjoy all the wealth and benefits of the other nations, but some individuals want to do everything on their own, without elemental input. It's understood, though unspoken, that if anyone requests asylum of a Rider, that person or family will be taken to Aether without question. I've never done it, but I know plenty of others who have."

"And how does everyday life work? With no elemental input?"

"It doesn't, always," Shay said. "Sometimes it's harder than it has to be, but in the end, it's our choice." She paused, her brows rising. "I never really understood that point before. I've always felt that the other nations—that the Elementals—were holding us back. But no, it's us, and it's deliberate."

"Why, do you suppose?"

Shay shrugged. "I'm not sure. I've never bothered to find out how and why. Maybe it's time I did."

"Maybe it's time we all did." Keagan took Shay's hand, linking their fingers. "I won't let anything happen to you."

Shay squeezed gently, her eyes dark. "You wouldn't have a say. And, in the clan's eyes, no right to say it."

"Even if I lo—care about you?"

Shay regarded her for a long moment. "Not even then," she said, and thankfully she didn't pursue what had almost slipped from Keagan's lips.

Disconcerted, Keagan offered a weak smile, then stood up, moving over to where Ashley sat at the edge of the camp, staring out into the dark forest. "Do you see something?"

"No, and that's the problem," Ashley said. "I don't see anything, or hear it. No night creatures, nothing moving in the brush. It's almost like the Realm. I thought Aether's penchant for putting the word 'Shadow' with everything was…" She hesitated briefly. "Stupid, frankly, but maybe there's a reason. Maybe it's not unimaginative. Maybe it's literal."

"As if the Shadows bleed over into these lands?" Keagan asked, following her gaze, straining to see beyond the first line of trees. "Affects the animals?"

"And maybe the people, too? Is that possible?"

"I don't know," Keagan said. "Who's ever researched Aether? How much did we really learn about it at the Academy? It was an afterthought, like it was barely a nation, the least important of us all. But they rebuilt the world after the war, they brought everyone together, found a way to begin the recovery. Then, they just…stepped back."

"Into the shadows?" Ashley asked dryly.

"Something like that. They could have established local governments with laws and rules that left them in complete charge. United with the people to eliminate Elementals as soon as abilities manifested rather than protect us."

"Eliminate us?" Ashley sounded horrified.

"After the war? Easily. We caused it. Why wouldn't everyone hate and fear us? Only the very young or very weak would have been left. They couldn't have defended themselves. And those who came into their abilities in the years following? There's a big difference, Ashley, between being reviled, rejected by family, alone, and hunted down to be killed, rather than actively sought out for a life of wealth, privilege, and power."

Ashley looked shaken. "I hadn't thought of it that way."

"I don't think many of us do. We're not educated about the alternative."

"We're educated to serve," Ashley said.

"Yes, and well compensated for that service." Keagan shook her head. "They and those who followed could have easily kept us from all we now enjoy, but they didn't. At the very least, they could have made it servitude rather than service. Slavery rather than financial independence. Does that sound like any nation you know?"

Ashley shook her head. "No, it doesn't."

Keagan knew that despite her flighty demeanor, Ashley was quite intelligent, especially when it came to business. Once something was pointed out to her, it wouldn't take long for her to see the ramifications. But it didn't really make sense, not knowing people as they both did in their respective fields—law enforcement and the ultra-competitive Mining Guild. Why would an entire nation choose anonymity over authority?

So much they didn't understand. Worse, they didn't know where that ignorance began, or why. Keagan felt adrift, uncertain, very much as she had in those early days in the jungle, without her water sense, when she could hold on to only Shay's protection of her. Was that why she felt as she did toward Shay? Was it dependence rather than actual emotion?

"What's wrong with you?" Ashley was looking at her now, rather than at the forest. "You have the oddest expression."

Keagan shook her head. "It's nothing."

"Oh, it's about her," Ashley said. "How is she, anyway?"

Keagan glanced over at Shay, her heart aching when she noticed how she sat, hunched over herself, arms across her chest, so slender, with no indication of the strength she possessed. "She's hurting. This close to that…what did she call it? Hub of Paths? A station that must have been a thriving center of transportation before the war, taking people and goods all over the old world."

Ashley looked around. "That would have required facilities beyond a circle of stones."

"Maybe, but if a city or town was here, it's long gone."

"If they built with wood rather than stone, little would remain. A few foundations maybe, hidden under layers of vegetation. You'd have to know what you were looking for and then search for it." Ashley looked back at Shay. "She seems done in. I know the rest of us aren't sleepy at all. It still feels like the afternoon. We can take first watch. You should take shadow girl and get some sleep if you can."

Keagan hesitated and then nodded. "All right," she said. "Wake me when you finally do get tired. I'll take second watch."

Returning to Shay, Keagan helped her into one of the tents that had been set up, nodding briefly at Lyria and Cassius seated by the fire as they passed. She got Shay out of her boots and tunic, though she left her shirt and trousers on. Then Keagan removed her armor and boots, lying down next to Shay, behind her, wrapping her up protectively in her arms.

"Thank you," Shay whispered. "For keeping me safe."

"Always," Keagan said. "I'm just returning the favor, anyway. Remember when we were first in the jungle? I didn't know what was dangerous, couldn't stop running into vines and snakes and ants and spiderwebs. It's a wonder I didn't break my neck falling into quicksand or the hundred other ways I could have died."

"Losing your abilities distracted you," Shay said sleepily. "It made it hard to concentrate on what was right in front of you."

"Well, I know what's in front of me now." Keagan nuzzled into her neck, hugging her close.

And she did, she realized. The feelings were only becoming stronger, not weaker, the longer they were together. Wouldn't the opposite have been the case had her attraction been based only on dependence? Once she recovered her water sense and didn't need Shay's assistance any longer, wouldn't this deep desire and adoration diminish? Perhaps Keagan should just accept that she had felt an instant connection to Shay, regardless of what else was going on around them. She'd just have to see where it took her.

Where it took them.

Shay sighed softly and snuggled back into Keagan, seeking out her sheltering embrace. Her breathing altered, smoothed out, and Keagan knew she had drifted off. How much of a physical toll had riding the Shadows taken on Shay? Maybe it was similar to Keagan using her abilities for several hours without interruption. However, because she lived in Naiad, on the water, she'd never really felt deprived, nor was using her abilities there nearly as debilitating as it would be if she lived in a place like Arias or Urodela. Was that why she had stayed where she was born, so she'd never feel weak like she had as a child?

Keagan closed her eyes, thinking that all this adventuring to other places was forcing her to reassess so many things, not only about how things were in the world, but about her place in it and who she really was. It was exhausting. She slipped into a deep sleep, only to be awakened hours later by Ashley's panicked shout.

"Marshal! Rider! We need you right now!"

Jolted awake, Keagan was already slipping on her boots and grabbing her armor and weapons before she was consciously aware of what she was doing. Shay was right beside her, tugging on her boots and shrugging on her tunic with its multitude of concealed stars and knives.

Sweeping up her sword and shield, Keagan stumbled from the tent to see the fire blazing high and the other three women in a defensive circle around it, weapons held out.

At first, Keagan didn't understand why, but then a dark shape darted in and snapped at Cassius, only to receive a rap over its snout from her quarterstaff, making it yelp and retreat.

"Shadow wolves," Shay said, taking up position next to Lyria.

"Why call them that? How are they different from other wolves?" Keagan asked as she stood next to Cassius, so she and Ashley, the two strongest Elementals, were on opposite sides of the fire. As she watched, one of the wolves scampered past the shadow of the tent, blurred, disappeared, only to reappear seconds later next to the other tent. She blinked. "Oh, never mind."

"Aren't they scared of fire? Normal wolves are." Ashley spat a bluish flame at the nearest wolf, who nimbly dodged it, disappearing into the shadow of a tree that combusted in an instant, lighting the area to reveal no sign of the animal.

"Not really," Shay said. "They're too fast to be hit. And it doesn't really counteract their camouflage." She glared at Ashley. "Try not to burn down the forest."

"Fine," Ashley said. She pulled around her bow and drew an arrow from her quiver. "Let's see them avoid this."

She fired directly at another wolf. Again, it sidestepped her shot with contemptuous ease, but when the arrow hit the ground only a couple of feet away, it exploded, shredding the animal into a bloody mist and causing a thundering boom to echo through the forest for leagues. After a frozen pause, the other ten wolves around them suddenly became visible in the firelight, dark coats with darker markings, tufted ears up, gleaming silver eyes wide. Then, as one, the surviving pack scattered into the woods, not looking back.

"Huh. Should have done that in the first place." Ashley grinned widely at Keagan. "Maybe you're right. Abilities aren't always the answer."

"Put out the tree," Keagan said, taking a few steps toward the forest. "Shay?"

"I think they're gone. As is every other living thing within range." She turned and looked at Keagan. "Never thought of explosives as a deterrent."

"Few people do." Keagan resisted a shudder as she remembered how the wolf had died, though it had been quick. It wouldn't have known what hit it. "Anything else specifically we need to know about? Are all the animals here like that?"

"Pretty much." Shay looked considerably better after her sleep, alert and aware, her shimmering eyes bright, almost as if the night was restoring her. "The largest are the dark bears. They don't really need to walk silent, though I understand that they can. I've never encountered one." She lifted her shoulder in a half shrug. "As you can tell since I'm still alive."

"Are they why your people stay out of the Shadow Hills?" Lyria asked.

"That and the fact that we have no real reason to be here," Shay said. "It's difficult to ride in the forest. Our horses do better on the plains."

"And perhaps after the war, it was considered off-limits," Cassius said. "It wasn't destroyed, but the Paths no longer went anywhere safe."

"Possibly," Shay said.

"Well, I'm awake now," Keagan said, nerves still thrumming after the fight. "I can take watch."

"We both can," Shay said. "I'm feeling much better. The adrenaline seems to have wiped away the hangover from the Paths."

"Like I can sleep after that?" Lyria said in a high-pitched tone that grated slightly. She hadn't gotten a shot off, her crossbow still shaking a little in her hands.

"Come on. I'll tell you the story of Lurra and the mud people," Cassius said, putting a hand on her bow and pushing it down gently. "It always helped you sleep in the cells."

Lyria frowned. "I'm not a child, needing a bedtime story to soothe me."

"Hey. Who says you're the only one who needs soothing?" Cassius said as she led her away. "Telling it always puts me to sleep, too."

"It's a boring story."

XVII

Shay glanced at Keagan, who was seated across the fire, enjoying the play of flickering light over the steady features. "What do you feel here?"

For a second, Keagan looked at her blankly. Then her gaze softened, irises expanding across pupils and whites into solid blue orbs that glowed in the firelight. "Plenty of water—fresh, clear, full of life. A lake's some five leagues from here, and another to the north. Rivers and streams and a few marshes." Her gaze cleared, became normal again. "Aside from the dangerous animals, it's very habitable. Maybe Cassius is right. Settlement is discouraged for some reason."

"Possibly." Shay poked the fire with a stick, sending up a trail of sparks. "Sombra is the closest town to the Shadow Hills. My clan is wintering there, and they won't have begun the migration yet. They'll be able to help us."

"Do you know how far it is to Sombra from here?"

Shay looked up at the stars, lifted her hands to make a rough sextant, and did some mental calculations. "Maybe a day to the edge of the forest. Another few to reach the town, but it'll be much faster to ride on the plains, away from the trees."

"You're looking forward to it," Keagan said, a smile edging her lips. "I can see how much in your expression."

"It will be good to be home again," Shay said. "Regardless of how they react."

"Home, meaning the clan and not the town."

"Yes," Shay said. "I miss them."

"Do you have to be a Shadow Rider? Couldn't you return and be a—what did you call it—a herdsman?"

"I could, I suppose. I never really thought about it." Shay looked down at the knife she was sharpening, at the edge of it, considering the suggestion. "I'd miss the travel," she said after a minute.

"I thought that's all you did." Keagan had a hint of humor in her tone. "Travel from one grazing land to another each year."

"No. I meant to other nations. To the rest of the world. Getting to know other people." She met Keagan's gaze squarely, allowing the longing in her eyes to show. "Meeting someone like you never would have happened if I'd stayed in the Shadow Lands."

Keagan's face softened, and her smile grew wider. "Then I'm glad you became a Rider." She tilted her head. "What are wraiths? Exactly?"

Shay paused. "I don't know," she admitted finally. "I never really bothered to find out anything other than that they're deadly and how to defend against them. But there must be more to them than what I've learned. Otherwise, they wouldn't be able to exist outside the Shadows, and they wouldn't be at the Shadow Lord's beck and call." Her jaw firmed, and a bad taste filled her mouth. "Honestly, you're right. We need a better name for him."

"Well, hopefully, we'll find one soon. Once we're back in civilization, we can begin a real investigation into all this. Track down names and places and clues as to why he's doing this."

"Will you do that alone?" Shay thought about what that meant, that Keagan's work would separate them as quickly as her own duties would. Her stomach hurt.

"I'm sure I won't be alone," Keagan said. "Assuming I'm assigned the case, I'll also be assigned a team."

"You have a team here," Shay said.

"Yes, but none of you are marshals," Keagan said gently. "If it were up to me, then yes, I'd love to have you along. But I'm sure Ashley will want to go home as quickly as possible, and both Cassius and Lyria will return to their own jobs and lives. Won't the Shadow Riders have more work for you once you return?"

"Yes," Shay said, glumly aware that she was right. Somehow, riding the Paths as a glorified mail carrier didn't have the same appeal. But what were her options? That was, assuming she wasn't punished for being in the Shadow Lands with four Elementals. Maybe she'd be lucky if she just returned to courier duty.

Keagan took Shay's hand. "We'll figure it out," she said quietly. "Somehow, we'll be together."

Keagan's reassurance warmed Shay. "Yes," she said, wanting to be that positive. "We will." She nuzzled Keagan gently, and then, with more intent, gave her a long, slow, deeply felt kiss that went on for some time. When she finally drew back, Keagan nestled her head into Shay's shoulder, and they sat in warm silence as the sky lightened above them, the surrounding trees preventing them from watching the actual sunrise.

Cassius woke first, stepping out of the tent into the light, where she stretched and yawned, her large frame even more impressive clad in only a sleeveless shirt and undergarment. Her musculature was supremely defined, rippling beneath her skin. Shay eyed her as she carried over the morning tea and wondered how she had ever managed to lift her that night in the Amane palace.

"Good morning." Cassius blew gently on her tea. "Feeling better?"

"Yes," Shay said. "We'll head out after breakfast."

"I'll wake the others."

After breaking camp, they mounted, and with Onyx in the lead, they set out in single file, the sure-footed Shadow-bred picking his way through the forest, avoiding the worst of the branches and the underbrush. Other than the wind rustling the leaves above and the creak of saddle leather, they detected no sound. It wasn't as bad as the Shadows, Shay knew, but it was not like other forests. Even Ashley seemed subdued, and when she spoke to Lyria, it was in the quietest of tones.

The air was full of the scent of pine and resin, and the musty wood rot from downed trees. They rode for hours, eating in the saddle rather than stopping for lunch, and Shay realized why this had been called the Shadow Hills. They were either climbing up the damned things or climbing down them, hard on both horse and rider. It was a relief when the terrain finally began to level out and the trees began to thin, allowing more and more sunlight to reach the ground. Ferns and moss began giving way to grasses, and when they finally crested the last hill, she drew Onyx to a stop, looking out over the plains at the long grass rippling in the wind, while her heart soared. To the west, the Zjarr Mountains loomed to snowcapped peaks, while the horizon east and south was a thin line blurring palely into blue sky.

"It goes on for leagues," Keagan said in seeming wonder, as she pulled up beside her. "I've never seen such wide, open space other than on the ocean."

"Wait till the stars come out," Shay told her, smiling. She glanced back at the other women. "Welcome to the Shadow Lands."

"There's certainly a lot of it," Ashley said.

"Wow. What kind of speed would I get here?" Lyria said, eyes wide. "I certainly wouldn't have to worry about running into anything or losing uplift no matter how low I flew."

Cassius dismounted and pulled up a tuft of grass to reveal the soil, dark and rich beneath. She examined it carefully, then took a sample, putting it in one of her glass tubes. Shay thought about stopping her and then decided it hardly mattered. It wasn't as if learning more about the soil would invite other Chthonic in to alter it.

To the west, the sun was already touching the mountains, and Shay looked around, spotting a stream winding through the grassy plain as it flowed from within the Shadow Hills. A few willows, cottonwood, and cedar lined its banks, in complete contrast to the pines and dark oaks they were leaving behind. She pointed. "There. We'll make camp for the night and ride for Sombra in the morning."

Ashley pointed at some brown dots far off in the distance. "What are those?"

"Bison," Shay told her. "Grazers. Harmless unless they stampede. They're a long way away. We needn't worry about them."

"Anything else to worry about?" Keagan asked.

"Sometimes bad thunderstorms birth twisters," Shay said. "But you can spot a storm forming for leagues." She waved her hand at the cloudless sky. "As you can see, no weather coming in."

"What's a twister?" Lyria asked. "Is that like a dust devil? We have those in Arias."

"Yes, only a lot bigger and more powerful. They can wipe out an entire herd. I've never seen it happen, but I've heard of it." Shay felt Onyx trembling beneath her, and she smiled. "I'm going to ride. Meet me at the campsite."

She leaned forward, touching her heels gently to Onyx's side, and he sprang forward. Even after a day of climbing hills, he obviously still felt the need to stretch his legs. They so rarely got home to do this, and within seconds, they left the others and their startled cries behind. He galloped, head up, ears swept forward, running for the sheer joy of it, thundering across the prairie as if he owned it.

She finally drew him up near the stream, and he fought the bit briefly, clearly still wanting to run. "We'll go tomorrow," she promised him, patting his neck. "They won't be able to keep up with you, but we'll double back occasionally to make sure they're still following."

She had him cooled down and his tack removed by the time the others reached the spot near the creek where she planned to make camp. Cassius regarded Onyx with a hint of awe as she dismounted from her dray. "I've never seen a horse run like that," she said. "I've heard that Aether bred were fast, but that was unreal."

Shay smiled, accepting a compliment for her horse in a way she could never accept one about herself. "He likes to run," she said, modestly. "He doesn't get the chance often. We're usually in cities or in the Shadows, where it isn't safe to draw attention by moving fast. But it's good to know if we have to, he can get us out of trouble in a hurry."

Keagan patted her cull's neck. "How fast is this guy?"

Shay glanced at him. "He'll be much faster than the others," she told her, forcing herself not to sound dismissive. "But he won't keep up with Onyx for very long. Besides, he doesn't seem conditioned for it. I think he was a city horse."

Keagan stroked his nose. "Well, I still like you," she told him in a comforting tone.

Rather than tying them, they left the horses free to graze. Shay knew Onyx wouldn't stray, and the rest wouldn't wander far from him. While the others set up camp, Cassius grabbed her crossbow. She and Shay went off for a quick hunt and didn't have to go far to bring down some grouse for supper.

"You're good," Shay said as they walked back to camp. "Why the quarterstaff and not a bow?"

"I don't like to kill unless it's absolutely necessary," Cassius said. "Less chance of accidents happening with a stick than with a blade or a bow, unless I crack a skull just right." She looked over at Shay. "Why the blades?"

"Courier is up-close work," Shay said. "Slash and go. You don't really want to fight in the Shadows. Escape is always the preferred option." She shrugged. "Never really been good with swords, anyway."

"Our leader is," Cassius said. "Really good from what I can see, though, granted, our fights haven't lasted long."

"Do they ever against Elementals?" Shay asked, somewhat rhetorically.

Cassius laughed. "No. Not usually."

Back at camp, they cleaned and dressed the grouse, placing them on spits and roasting them over the fire. With the accompanying vegetables, cheese, and bread left over from the Anemoi camp, it made for a fine meal. As they sat around the fire, eating, Shay realized she would miss all of them. She'd never thought that would happen, that she would make friends with Elementals, but now it hurt to think she might never see them again.

Afterward, their conversation wandered until they began to share more personal things about themselves. Shay discovered that Lyria had grown up in Zephyrus, the capital city of Arias, with younger twin sisters, and a mother that she clearly adored, though her face darkened when she spoke of her father. He had died a few years earlier, and his loss apparently still had a significant impact. Cassius told them about being the oldest of a large brood who all still resided in the area where she grew up, a farming village called Aarde. Surprisingly, her parents were still alive. Despite being the only Elemental out of seven offspring, she had obviously never cut ties and still considered herself the one the family reached out to for advice. Conversely, when Ashley spoke of her family in Surya, Urodela's capital city—of her domineering mother, her distant father, and her two older siblings—her detached coolness seemed to explain a lot about who these Elementals were as people.

None of them lingered on what would happen once they returned, almost as if they didn't want to think about it either. But when they reached Sombra, they were a Path away from Aether, and from there,

they could reach any crown city in a few hours. Return to lives and jobs
so abruptly interrupted. Shay shared a look with Keagan, seeing the way
her eyes darkened. Was she thinking the same thing?

"So how will this work?" Ashley asked, finally. "We'll reach your
town and then what?"

Shay exhaled slowly. "I speak with my Elders. I imagine the rest of
you will be escorted to Aether and then guided back to your respective
homes."

"Just like that?" Cassius frowned. "Won't they want to speak to us,
as well?"

"It's possible we'll all be going to Naiad," Keagan said. "Speak with
the Queen and Council there. Then you'll be sent home."

Lyria looked down. "I'll be sad when it's done," she said. "I mean, I
was scared a lot, but now that I look back, some of it was fun." She stared
at them all. "This, I mean. Spending time with all of you. Exploring
badlands and lost places. Sitting around a fire and sleeping under the
stars. This was really enjoyable. Not like what I normally do."

Cassius threw a gnawed bone into the fire. "It was. I like my work,
and it takes me a lot of places, but sometimes, I'm sure any Chthonic
could do what I do. But taking on a bad guy? Screwing up his plans?
Fighting mercenaries? It makes me feel like it matters. Like I matter.
I'm beginning to see why you chose this path, Keagan, rather than join a
company. It's…" She paused. "Satisfying."

Ashley sat with her arms wrapped around herself, as if giving herself
a hug when no one else would. She obviously felt the cooler temperatures
more than the rest. Shay slipped off her cloak and offered it to her
wordlessly. Just as wordlessly, she accepted, though she looked honestly
grateful. "Well, I know my job is important," she said after wrapping
herself up in it. "And I can live without tents and a hard ground to sleep
on." She paused and looked at Keagan. "But I will miss trying new things
and working with people who aren't impressed with my job title."

"What is your job title, anyway?" Shay asked.

"Vice president in charge of acquisitions," Ashley said pompously.

"Well, you're not acquiring anything in the Shadow Hills," Shay
told her. "Neither in Terras. The Elders will want to know about that,
as well."

Ashley shrugged. "We don't want to set up a mine where creatures
can come in silent and deadly and wipe out all our miners anyway." She
looked at Shay. "I'm including the two-legged creatures, too."

"You would do well in thinking that," Shay told her cheerfully.

"I'm sure we can come up with a better topic," Keagan said firmly
at that point.

The rest exchanged smiles but obediently moved on to other things.

No one seemed eager to go to bed, lingering by the fire and discussing all that had happened, knowing that this would be one of their final evenings together. When the others finally did drift off to their tents, Shay took Keagan by the hand, scooped up her bedroll with the other arm, and led her away from the camp and into the prairie. Overhead, stars spread out over the night sky in a tapestry as old as time, and in the east, a sliver of moon hung in the sky. They walked without speaking until Shay was certain they were out of earshot. She had no idea what would happen to her once they reached Sombra. Banishment was one thing. Being placed under clan arrest, forced to remain in the Shadow Lands for the foreseeable future as Keagan went back to her life in Aquas seemed just as bad, if not worse, at the moment.

"Are we walking to Sombra?" Keagan asked dryly after a time.

Shay smiled and stopped, turning to face her. "This is good. I just wanted to be alone with you."

"Well, I can't even see the camp." Keagan's brows lowered. "Are you sure they're safe?"

"Onyx will raise an alarm if anything approaches," Shay said as she unrolled the bedding and spread it on the ground. "Either of us. He knows where we are, as well."

Keagan's lips curled in a half grin. "Well, now that you have me to yourself, what do you plan to do with me?"

"Many things," Shay told her as she began to unbuckle Keagan's armor. "Many, many things." Then she kissed her, long and deep and slow as the night wind wafted capriciously around them. The long grass welcomed them down onto a soft cushion of bluestem and sideoats. Making love beneath the stars was magical, the soft breeze bringing the scent of the prairie, wild and free. And so far from camp, they felt uninhibited, able to express their appreciation in sounds both urgent and joyful. In the days and weeks to come, Shay would often think back to their encounter, finding comfort and renewed strength in it.

The night she fell completely and irrevocably in love with Keagan Riley.

XVIII

They came upon the Aether herds long before they reached the town, hundreds of beautiful, graceful horses, their coats glossy, with long, flowing manes and elegant, arched tails. Their colors spanned the range from a brilliant white to bright sorrel to the deepest of blacks, but all had the distinctive slope to their muzzle and excellent conformation. As they passed, Keagan patted her horse on the neck, wanting to reassure him that while he might not be as fine, he was still a very good boy.

She and Cassius rode side by side, the large dray dwarfing the cull, and Cassius's greater height making them even more mismatched. Behind them, Ashley and Lyria chatted amiably about all they saw. Shay was off in the distance, Onyx far too fast for them to keep up as they rode across the prairie. Shay would double back occasionally to check in with them before she was off again, galloping across the grasslands like she'd been freed from a long incarceration.

"Do you think they know we'll be coming?" Cassius asked.

Keagan shifted in her saddle. She wasn't used to this much riding, but fortunately, it seemed her muscles were adjusting. "Probably. I thought I saw other riders in the distance. Herdsmen. It would make sense for them to ride on ahead and let the town know we're on our way."

"What kind of reception do you think we'll get?"

"Hard to say." Keagan had affixed her marshal badge prominently on her breast, in the hopes it might help mitigate any upcoming situation. "They're not fond of Elementals. We know that."

"So many horses," Cassius said as she watched the play of young colts nearby. "They could supply armies. If they let only their castoffs be sold to other nations, why maintain such large herds for themselves?"

"Perhaps in the knowledge that they might need to mount an army," Keagan said. "With invisible spies that can transport messages in minutes and get behind enemy lines without ever being spotted."

Cassius looked at her, features troubled. "That's a hell of a thought."

"It is, but were the other nations to renew old antagonisms and start another war? Maybe the Shadow Lands are the ones who are called upon to finish it."

"Called on by who?"

Keagan shook her head. "Maybe by their Lady. Or maybe by our own gods who despair at our foolishness."

Cassius opened her mouth to say something, seemed to reconsider, and lapsed into a thoughtful silence. Keagan lifted her head as she saw Shay riding back toward them, Onyx's long legs covering the ground in a hurry. She drew up, Onyx twirling prettily in place until they had fallen in neatly beside Keagan and Cassius.

"Sombra's just ahead. Down in the valley by the river," Shay told them.

"We're expected?" Keagan eyed her keenly.

"I expect so. Herdsmen spotted us days ago. We even have several flanking us." She offered a wry grin as Keagan and Cassius looked around wildly. "Sorry. You won't see them unless they want you to. They're probably holding back because they've identified me as a Shadow Rider and think I'm escorting civilians, even if they wouldn't understand why I'd be coming from this direction or why civilians like you would be heading for Sombra rather than Aether."

"Good to know." Keagan felt uneasy. They'd been escorted for days? She prided herself on being observant. It was her job. But this wasn't her natural habitat. She hadn't enjoyed that comfort for weeks.

They crested the hill, and Keagan blinked as the town spread out below her. Situated by a wide, slow-moving river, the outskirts were comprised of a multitude of corrals and paddocks, along with many long, thin buildings. Keagan identified them as stables, constructed to house the herds during the worst of winter weather. Farther in was the town itself, constructed of single-dwelling homes, low and mostly sand colored. A few taller buildings, none more than three stories high, surrounded a single obelisk that towered five stories over a central square.

Then they descended the gradual slope, and she lost her vantage point, suddenly surrounded by fences and pastures. The road beneath them was dirt, packed hard and firm, well-trodden by years of countless hooves. They wound through the stables until they came to the houses, the street they rode on wider than the radiating side roads, allowing them to ride five abreast as they entered the town proper. People stopped and stared, either at their foreign mounts or at what they recognized as Elementals. Keagan suspected the latter. Dogs barked and horses neighed greetings, far more friendly toward their cousins than their riders appeared to be. Children, running around, stopped to chatter excitedly and point, obviously unafraid to appear rude.

Keagan glanced over at Shay, who seemed relaxed, though the

corners of her eyes were a little tight. Those eyes, Keagan thought, wistfully. Now that she was among these people, she could easily tell Shay was born of them, boasting the same similar lanky build and dusky looks, but the eyes of the others were different. They were mundane, mostly browns and a few hazels, none possessing that odd silvery sheen or the reflective qualities of Shay's. Of course Shadow Riders were the fifth Elemental. How could anyone have missed that?

Then they were riding into the town square. Keagan glanced around quickly as they dismounted near one of the larger buildings. The town hall, she decided, the tallest structure in town after the obelisk. Wide stairs led to an entrance offering a small crowd of people clearly waiting for them. She took in what could be a general store of sorts on the right side of the square, flanked by a healer's office on one side and what looked like a library on the other. Opposite the town hall, across the small park, was a low, squat building that had carvings in front of it, abstract, flowing sculptures. Their temple, Keagan decided, dedicated to Stygia, their Lady of Shadows. Its entrance was full of robed people gaping at them. Jarringly, next door stood a tavern, large enough to include an inn above it.

"Carry your saddlebags." Shay nodded as a few youngsters moved toward them. "They'll take care of the horses."

"I don't suppose we can do a little shopping first?" Ashley said, looking longingly in the direction of the general store that had items displayed in the large windows, including some mannequins sporting simple, rustic outfits. She'd found pants and a shirt to replace her destroyed outfit, but neither fit well, and they were of low quality. "I want new clothes so very badly."

"Later," Keagan said in a low voice as the group from the town hall descended the stairs. "Keep it tight. No need to show off."

"Unless we have to," Cassius said, but her tone was amiable, and her eyes glinted slightly in amusement.

Keagan squared her shoulders and took up position next to Shay. She immediately picked out a couple in the crowd that was approaching. The man was tall, wearing a beaded vest over a brown shirt, his denim trousers half concealed beneath worn leather chaps. He had high-boned features, with deep eyes and long black hair tied back in a braid that hung midway down his back, feathers intertwined within the dark and silver strands. He was staring at Shay as if he'd never look away. Beside him walked a woman dressed in similar style—tall, elegant, with shorter hair than her partner but features achingly familiar to Keagan. An older version of Shay's. Tears glimmered in her large, dark eyes.

"Parents," Ashley said in a quiet voice.

Keagan had already figured that out. Wordlessly, as if stricken dumb,

Shay was moving forward, her saddlebag slipping from her shoulders to fall on the ground. Keagan hastily scooped it up, throwing it over her other shoulder, her right already bearing the cull's. She didn't dare let the stone out of her sight, though holding both saddlebags left her without any hands free, and its proximity made her skin crawl. She tried not to feel nervous about the stone as they were surrounded by curious—and armed—clans folk. No weapons were directed at them, but she was aware they were there. She hoped the others would remain calm and not make any sudden moves, inciting an unfortunate incident.

"Shay." The man had his daughter's face cupped in his hands as he looked down at her. "When you failed to show up in Zephyrus, Riders in all the nations were dispatched to search. It's been weeks. We thought you were gone forever, victim to wraiths."

"I know, Father," Shay said, holding on to his forearms and smiling. "I got a little lost. It took us a while to find our way home."

"Our?" The woman was looking at Keagan and the others intently. Her gaze wasn't unfriendly, but it wasn't open, either.

"Yes. These are my friends," Shay said, turning to lift a hand, indicating them. "Marshal Keagan Riley of Aquas, Sie Ashley Van Vuur of Urodela, Sie Cassius Suolo of Terras, and Sie Lyria Hawke of Arias. These are my parents, Diana of Kendrith Clan, and Calvin of Rylak Clan." She offered a warm look at Keagan before she turned back to her parents. "I ask that they be allowed to clean up and eat before we meet with the Elders. It's been a long ride."

"You bring Elementals here?" another man interjected. He was a stocky man, older, more gray than dark in his thinning hair.

"I rescued them, Elder Donovan," Shay said firmly. "Much has happened, and all the Elders need to know. More than the Elders. The Queen and Council must be informed. The Shadows are under attack, and so are Elementals."

Diana looked concerned. "We have heard of Elementals going missing in the other nations. Such is the concern of the Queen and Council that news of it has reached all the way here."

"There is a great deal that needs to be said," Keagan said, stepping forward. "We encountered a man who not only walks the Shadows unafraid but has mercenaries and wraiths working with him."

"Wraiths? That's impossible." The querulous man looked at Keagan with obvious dislike.

"You know nothing of the Shadows," Shay said, her face growing still, though her eyes sparked anger. "The Paths we've had to ride have been lost for centuries, and this man, who calls himself the Shadow Lord, can violate the Realm at will. He's not a Rider. He's from Terras and has some device that tears open the entry."

"The rips in the Realm have been felt," Calvin said, appearing troubled. "I've heard that Scout Atlas has been dispatched to investigate." "He should be called back," Keagan said. "He could be walking into a trap."

Shay's mother held up her hands, stilling the murmuring of the crowd and the rising tension. "Enough," she said, and that's when Keagan realized she was also an Elder, the authority in her voice commanding instant quiet. "It's obvious there is much to learn. Messages must be dispatched to Aether, and to Naiad, informing them that our missing Rider has been found, along with some of their missing Elementals."

"Some?" Cassius asked, seizing on the word.

Diana regarded her somberly. "Only four of you are here. The last we heard, at least twenty have disappeared over the past few years."

"Twenty?" Keagan was staggered. "Why am I only hearing of this now, Sie Kendrith?"

"From what I understand, the Council didn't wish to cause a panic. But now, marshals are dead in Aquas, an heiress is missing in Terras, and companies in both Urodela and Arias are complaining of lost high-level assets."

"That'd be Cassius and me," Lyria said dryly. "That last part."

"And I think I'm the missing heiress," Ashley said, sounding greatly satisfied. "Knowing Daddy, he'll be putting up a big fuss. Everyone in the Five Nations will be getting an earful."

"A great deal of concern is rising in the capital. No doubt, you can fill in some of the missing pieces." The Elder raised her hand. "Shay calls you friends. That's enough for us. Be welcome here and safe in the shelter of the clans. You look both worn and hungry. Lodging and food will be provided, as well as"—she paused only briefly and didn't wrinkle her nose at all, though Keagan knew exactly what she was really referring to—"new clothing while yours are cleaned and mended."

"Thank you for your hospitality, Sie Kendrith," Keagan said, truly grateful. This all could have gone much worse.

"Diana, please," Shay's mother said. She gestured at another woman, younger than Shay, though similar in looks. Another relative, Keagan thought. "This is my assistant, Merrill. She will take you to the inn and arrange rooms for you."

Keagan looked over at Shay, deep in conversation with her father. She hoped to catch her eye, but Shay didn't look her way as she accompanied the Elders back inside the town hall. Without any other option, Keagan and the rest followed Merrill across the street to the tavern, where adjoining rooms were secured above. They weren't luxurious, but they were clean and comfortable enough. Each room—Keagan and Ashley assigned to one, Cassius and Lyria in the other—contained two beds, a dresser, a sofa, a table, and some chairs. Each had a lavatory attached, and Ashley didn't wait, shedding her clothes as she headed toward it.

Merrill watched her, amusement in her dark eyes.

"Are you related to Shay?" Keagan asked as she dumped the saddlebags in an upholstered chair by the window.

"Cousins. Her mother and mine are sisters," Merrill said, eyes lightening. "I haven't seen Shay since the Fall Equinox. She missed Winter Solstice. I know her parents were disappointed. She had promised to come to the New Year Equinox in a couple of weeks, and the beginning of the migration, but I'm not sure how that will work, now."

"She told me she returns whenever she can," Keagan said. "She misses you all, as well."

Merrill seemed to draw back into herself, as if reminded of who she was dealing with. Her tone became more formal. "Food and clothing will be sent up. I hope you find the accommodations acceptable."

"After how we've been sleeping? It's a resort," Keagan said.

"Please remain in the inn until someone comes for you."

Keagan knew what she meant and met her gaze squarely. "I understand."

After she left, Keagan went across the hall to the other room, where Cassius stood at the window, looking down on the town square. From inside the lavatory, Keagan could hear the rush of water, undoubtedly Lyria taking advantage of the shower. It had been a few days since they'd enjoyed the outdoor setup in Anemoi.

"Watch this," Cassius said, sounding fascinated. Keagan joined her, peering over her shoulder to see three dark-clad Riders approaching the obelisk. As they entered the shadow cast by its height on the eastern side, they simply disappeared, one moment there, the next, both Riders and horses gone. No abrupt tear, no ragged rip lingering in the air.

"Wow, that's…something," Keagan said. "I've never had a chance to watch that before. I'm usually too busy being terrified to concentrate on how it looks when Shay does it."

"Isn't that the truth." Cassius frowned. "That's twelve gone in the last few minutes. I wonder how long before they start coming back?"

"I'm sure it will take some time to pass on the news and receive what information needs to be returned," Keagan said. "Bureaucracy." She rested a hand on Cassius's shoulder. "While we're here, it might be a good idea not to display any abilities."

"Well, it's not like we have the full range, anyway," Cassius said. "Lyria still can't get liftoff. But you might want to tell Ashley. She's really looking forward to burning her clothes once she has new ones."

"I'll see to it," Keagan said. "Food's being sent up. We're to remain here."

Cassius's dark brows went up. "House arrest?"

Keagan hesitated. "I think they just want to know where we are, and not out in public."

"Best to keep us under wraps as much as possible." Cassius looked thoughtful. "I kind of get that. Especially since they have rules against us even being here in the first place."

"I'm sure Shay will check in as soon as she can."

She heard a knock on the door and opened it to find the innkeeper with trays of food. Behind him stood a young girl, his daughter, Keagan thought, laden with bulging sacks.

"In here," Keagan said, gesturing to the bed, where the girl deposited the sacks, offered Keagan a shy smile, and scampered out. She pressed a gold coin into the man's hands after he put the trays on the table. "Thank you."

"This is far too much," he said mildly as he tried to hand it back. "And the Elders are taking care of it all, anyway."

"Consider it a tip, then," she said. "From people who have been sleeping on the ground for too long."

He hesitated, then nodded, leaving. Keagan went next door to discover Ashley in a towel, on the verge of burning her clothes. "Stop," she said. "We don't need to damage the inn with scorch marks. Come on. Food's been delivered and so have the new clothes."

"Fine." Ashley left her tattered outfit scattered across the floor as she joined Keagan in the other room, where Cassius and a freshly showered Lyria were busy serving the food on actual china plates with silverware. Mashed potatoes and gravy, steak, and some kind of multicolored corn filled the room with a savory aroma.

"The water in the shower was hot," Ashley said as she sat down. "Not as hot as I like, so I had to heat it a little as it left the nozzle, but where does it come from? I didn't see any tank, and I don't sense any crystals here."

"No. Just some kind of large cisterns beneath another building," Keagan said, reaching out without thinking, tracing the flow of liquid. "Pipes run from one that's being heated by an outside source. A furnace of some kind?"

"A gas furnace," Lyria said, head tilted as she probed curiously, eyes becoming a solid white. "Brought up by more pipes from deep below. Ingenious, really. Is that how it works here in Aether? All mechanical and built by hand?"

"The houses are," Cassius said, doing her own probe, eyes glowing green. "Wood frames surrounded by clay. Adobe, I think it's called. It's good. Thick. Warm in winter, cool in summer."

"We know so little about their culture." Keagan savored a bit of steak, unbelievably tender. "I'm beginning to wonder if it's on purpose." She shook her head. "Enough about plumbing. We have far more important issues to discuss."

"Yeah," Lyria said. "It seems we weren't the only Elementals being messed with."

"Twenty missing?" Cassius sounded dismayed. "Why wasn't there an outcry before now?"

"Maybe they weren't important enough," Ashley said, and at their collective look of condemnation, she put up her hands defensively. "I don't mean it like that. I meant that maybe only low-level Elementals were taken at first. Immediate family and friends might miss them, assuming they remained in touch after the Academy, but a lot of level ones and twos quit their jobs and move on to other opportunities all the time, always looking for a bigger payday. That would be a great way to lure them in, in fact, pretend to be a new company recruiting employees. But maybe the low-level abilities weren't enough for the Shadow Lord and his plan with the stone. Then he had to start going after more powerful Elementals, the sort that don't leave their jobs for anything less than a considerable promotion."

Keagan exhaled. "Ashley's right," she said, and, at Ashley's vindicated expression, added, "Surprising as that is. The higher the abilities, the more such Elementals are valued and protected by the companies that employ them. That loss is noticed, especially when they discover those employees haven't been lured away by a competitor and they can't recruit them back. The more they're missed, the louder the companies complain to the Guild authorities, which moves it up from the local level. The more complaints from the Guilds, the more attention is paid, and patterns are detected. The more patterns marshals detect, the quicker the disappearances become a big deal, reaching the highest level of government."

"Whether he wants to or not, this lord won't be able to stay in the shadows much longer."

XIX

Shay was hoarse. She'd gone over the story at least a half dozen times, interrupted frequently by outbursts by the other clan Elders, though her mother seemed content to let them spout off. But then, that was her way: let the others talk, listen, form an opinion, and then speak in a measured, calm fashion. As head of the Kendrith Clan, she'd been an Elder for decades, and her voice mattered more than most. Shay's father, Elder of the Rylak Clan, was more forceful in speaking out, and right now he was arguing with Donovan, the Elder of the Hoeg Clan. He was the one who had eyed Keagan with such antagonism outside. Shay had never liked him.

Debai of the Pettipas Clan, a solid woman with years of experience and one of Diana's closest friends, along with newly appointed Benvie, of the Detmers Clan, looking too young to be known as an "Elder," were arguing about the kidnapping of the Elementals and what it might mean.

"And what is this stone this lord has?" Debai asked. "How soon before he has more?"

"Oh, we have the one from Anemoi." Shay thought she had mentioned taking it from the temple. With so much to remember, and while she'd described the palace and the staff on the throne, it was possible she hadn't told them they'd brought it with them to the Shadow Lands.

Silence filled the room as the five elders stared at her. So she hadn't mentioned it, she thought sheepishly.

"Where is it now?" Diana asked in a cool voice. Shay knew that tone and tried not to fidget.

"In my saddlebags." Shay tried to remember where she'd left them. Hadn't Keagan picked them up after Shay had dropped them on seeing her parents? "I think Keagan has it."

Diana nodded. "It's time we spoke with them, anyway. I'm sure they've eaten and cleaned up by now."

"Speaking of which," Shay said, "I'd like to clean up a little, too."

Shay's father leaned toward Diana. "We should break for the day," he said. "Not only do we need to bring in the other Clan leaders from

Tenebrous, but we've also discussed this as much as we can with Shay. Until we receive some kind of word from the crown, we can't proceed with the others. They're not of Aether, and jurisdictional issues exist. Not to mention one's a marshal." He lifted his head and looked at the others in the council room, the assistants who'd been busy taking notes at the back of the room. "Have any of the Riders returned?"

"I'll check." His adjunct, a young, handsome man, sprang to his feet. When they were younger, he had displayed an uncommon interest in Shay before she made it clear she'd never return that interest for inherent reasons. As he rushed out the door, Shay tried not to roll her eyes. He still hadn't outgrown that puppy-like eagerness to please her father.

"In the meantime, you should join your friends and clean up," Diana said. "When we send for you in the morning, make sure you bring the stone."

Shay dipped her head in acknowledgment, offered a gesture of respect, and hastily made her way out of the town hall. It had grown dark while she'd been in there, which surprised her. She hadn't realized she'd been in there so long. As she crossed the square toward the inn, she took note of clan archers standing patrol on the surrounding rooftops, a decidedly uncommon occurrence. She also realized she'd never seen so many Riders in town other than at festivals. Had the clans called them home because she'd gone missing? Inside the tavern, two Riders stood guard by the stairs, and the taproom was empty of all but the most dedicated drinkers. Shay nodded briefly at the innkeeper behind the bar, who looked a little glum at the lack of patronage.

"Your room has been prepared," he told her. "Top floor. End of the hall. Near your friends."

"Thank you," she said, then paused. "The bed. Large?"

"The largest. Best room in the house."

She swallowed back her smile, walked past the Riders who exchanged nods of acknowledgment with her, and ascended the stairs. Were they there to keep the Elementals in or the rest of the world out? The whole atmosphere was tense, unlike the freewheeling, boisterous feel the town normally had during the late spring, with the avalanche of new foals and everyone preparing for the migration in the upcoming month.

She took the next set of stairs and stopped at the top, realizing she didn't know where the others were located. End of which hall? She looked around. Ten rooms on this floor, and ten below on the second. There weren't a lot of visitors at the best of times, of course, but the town did get some over the course of the year: traveling merchants, a few wayward tourists, entertainers, and occasional repair technicians from the city, which is why an inn existed. Somehow, she suspected that with four Elementals on the premises, other accommodations had been made for anyone else who might have been staying there.

Tentatively, she knocked on the nearest door. "Keagan?" she called out.

A door much farther down the hall flew open, and Keagan poked her snowy head out. "Shay?"

As she joined her, Shay pointed at the door at the far end of the hall. "I'm down there. I need to clean up, and then I'll join you?"

"How about we'll join you in a little while?" Keagan said. "Have you eaten?"

Shay was suddenly aware of the growl in her belly. "Not yet."

"I'll have the innkeeper bring you up something." Keagan put her hand on Shay's arm. "How did it go?"

"It went," Shay said, not wanting to get into specifics now. Her clothes seemed ready to walk off by themselves. She looked at Keagan and realized she was dressed in a new herdsman outfit: simple denim blue trousers and shirt, along with a colorful poncho, designed for warmth and protection against the rain, thrown over her shoulders. "I don't suppose they provided any Rider leathers?" she asked hopefully.

"They did," Keagan said. "I'll bring them in for you."

In her room, quite spacious and with a very large, very comfortable-looking bed, Shay stripped off her clothes and left them piled on a chair as she went into the lavatory. She took a long, hot shower in the gleaming silver-and-white-tile stall, not thinking about how it worked at all. She was too used to such things and didn't distinguish between it and how the plumbing was set up in other nations. She heard a tap on the door as she was toweling herself off and opened it to find Keagan holding an armful of leathers.

"Put them on the dresser," Shay asked. "I'll be heading to bed soon." She leaned closer. "Join me?"

Keagan flashed a smile. "Of course I'll join you. That bed's much larger than the one they gave me."

Then Shay heard a noise at the door and lifted her head to see the other three enter the room. She hid behind the lavatory door. "I'll be out in a minute."

Wrapped in a large bath sheet provided by the inn, she joined the others at the table. Her mouth watered when she saw the juicy steak taking up most of the plate. As she ate, she filled them in on what she'd told the Elders.

"Are they planning to do anything in particular?" Cassius asked. "About us, I mean?"

"They want to speak with you in the morning, and they want to see the stone. But they need to contact the other clans in the south. They also plan to wait until they get word back from Aether, and perhaps Naiad. Something about jurisdictional issues."

"Meaning they have none over us," Ashley noted dryly.

Shay looked at her, then at the other two, realizing that all their clothes matched, right down to the color, a rugged blue, even for Cassius and Lyria, the two most contrasting in size. Their ponchos had the same exact pattern of brown, green, and gold. Shay grinned broadly. "You look like a singing group. The Elementals, live and in person, one night only."

Keagan made a face at her. "The outfit's clean. That's all that matters," she said. "Anyway, they've picked up our old clothes and promised to have them back by tomorrow. I'll be back in uniform as soon as possible."

"Not me," Ashley said, with a disdainful shudder. "I never want to see those clothes again. I'll check out the store, see what they've got, and if it's not much different than this, I'll wait until I'm back home. Until then, I'm wearing this, as rustic as it is." She eyed Shay. "Or maybe I'll get some of those Rider leathers. They look useful."

"They do stand up to a lot," Shay said, not responding to the provocation. It wasn't as if it was a uniform. It was just what most Riders preferred to wear. "But you have to clean them the same way you clean a saddle. It means carrying the proper oils and soaps to make sure the material doesn't dry out, and you have to do it all by hand."

"I hire people to do that," Ashley told her.

"I'm sure you do. Anyway, once the Elders finish speaking with you, they'll probably dispatch Riders to take you home."

"Well, we have one more night together," Lyria said, smiling. "That's good, right?"

It occurred to Shay that Lyria might not have had many Elemental friends. Or any real friends at all. Though she'd said she was with some when she'd been kidnapped, now Shay wondered if they were actually the sort that were only hanging out with Lyria because of what she was. The fawners. Certainly, it seemed as if they were more interested in her ability to fly than anything else. Perhaps it was like that for all Elementals.

"Agreed." Cassius smiled gently at Lyria, then paused. "You know, there *is* a tavern below us."

They glanced at each other. "A drink before we turn in?" Ashley asked.

Shay shared a look with Keagan. "Guess I'll get dressed after all."

Down in the tavern, they took a table by the window that looked out onto the obelisk. "I see archers on the roof over there," Lyria said, peering out at the general store.

"Archers are on all the roofs," Keagan said, calmly. "No doubt to keep an eye on us. So are they." She nodded at the Riders now seated at a table rather than standing by the stairs. "I saw more out by the alley."

Shay lifted her brows. She hadn't noticed those groups before, though now that Keagan mentioned it, she could see them lurking in the shadows between the general store and the healer's, with a direct line of sight into the inn's front windows. There were probably more to the rear of the building. If Keagan wasn't particularly sharp out in the wild, within the confines of a town or city, she could easily pinpoint all the areas of seclusion. In Naiad she probably knew every inch of the city and what all its denizens were up to.

The barkeep came over. "Ladies?"

"Whiskey, neat," Ashley said.

"The same," Cassius said.

"Wine." Lyria clearly tried to look very serious, as if afraid she'd be refused service because of her age. As if it had happened before. "White, if you have it."

"Ale," Shay said, trying not to smile.

"The same," Keagan said.

Once they had their drinks, Cassius lifted hers to the middle of the table. "To our little team. It was fun while it lasted. Let's not lose touch."

"Agreed," Ashley said, clinking her glass against Cassius's as the rest followed suit.

Shay saw a flicker out the window, harder to detect because of the reflection of the lights in the tap room, but still visible to her. She frowned. "Some Riders have arrived."

They watched as two Shadow Riders drew up just outside the tavern. They dismounted, and one Rider took both horses, leading them away as the other headed for the front door.

"That's William Isaac," Shay said, bemused. "Headmaster of the Rider school in Aether. He's also the Aether representative on the Ruling Council. What's he doing here?"

The man, solidly built, with gray hair held back by a decorative band, stepped into the taproom. He paused when he saw them, met Shay's gaze with silver eyes, nodded in acknowledgment, and then went to the innkeeper. After a few minutes' discussion, he ascended the stairs, clearly intending to stay for the night. The innkeeper began directing his staff in a flurry of activity as they also went up the stairs.

"Who is—" Keagan realized everyone was staring out the window at the obelisk as other Shadow Riders began appearing, all bearing passengers riding pillion behind them. "That's Dean Perrin from the Academy!"

Shay had never seen Shadow Riders carry people like this. Not even the guides rode with someone on the back of their horses while traveling the Paths. They usually pulled clients and any precious bulk cargo in light, armored chariots designed to be detached in seconds if necessary. They provided a protective shell while leaving the Rider and mount free to quickly counter any attack. Single riders that she recognized as the clan leaders from those currently wintering in the south were also arriving, apparently able to ride the Paths without any assistance from guides or scouts. She'd never suspected they could navigate the Realm while wearing eyepieces, similar to the ones the Shadow Lord possessed. Again, she felt a yawning sense in the pit of her stomach of not knowing her own home—her own people—as well as she thought she did.

"Oh, Lurra," Cassius said, eyes wide as a squarely built woman with graying hair slipped awkwardly off the back of a Shadow Rider's horse. "That's Leanna Dewitt, the Terras representative to the Ruling Council."

"And Fiona Ralston, the Arias representative," Lyria said, pointing out a thin, hawk-nosed woman who spoke briefly with Dewitt after dismounting. "The Ruling Council is coming here?"

Shay blinked. More Elementals being brought into the Shadow Lands? And not even to Aether, but to a clan town? This was unprecedented. She saw her parents out by the obelisk, greeting them, along with the rest of the Elders. She would never have suspected such familiarity and ease between all of them. What in Lady's name did that mean?

"That's Nigel Dunbar, the rep from Urodela," Ashley said. "He's a friend of my dad. And isn't that Damian Lynch? The null rep from Aquas?"

Keagan's eyes were wide. "And that's Abraham. He's captain of the marshals. These are the most powerful people in the government. The only one missing is the…" Her jaw fell open. More Riders came through with four heavily armed crown guards and a statuesque, white-haired woman riding in the middle on her very own Shadow mount.

"That's Queen Chiesa!" Shay could hardly believe her eyes. She had met her on brief occasions in the past because of her duties to the crown but had no opportunity to interact beyond that. Where the hell did she get the horse? She squinted. She had seen it before—a showy, white stallion—in the Rider stables in Naiad. She thought it had belonged to another Rider. It was the Queen's? After she dismounted, Chiesa patted him and bent her head against his briefly, before a groom took him away. Definitely hers, then. Lady, what was going on?

"Oh, do you think we should be drinking?" Lyria asked, trying to hide her glass under the table.

Keagan shook her head. "Are they here for us? What does this mean?"

"And where the hell are they staying tonight?" Cassius asked, more practically. "They can't put Queen Chiesa and the Ruling Council in an inn!"

"Hey." The innkeeper who had come over to watch with them gave Cassius a wounded look. "I run a nice place here." He paused and glanced at Shay. "You have to give up your room, though. I put a cot in with your friends."

Cassius took a long sip from her glass and glanced at Ashley. "Well, I don't think you're getting much sleep tonight."

"Yuck," Ashley said, succinctly.

"Where's the stone?" Shay muttered to Keagan, leaning over to speak directly in her ear.

Keagan glanced at her. "Still in Onyx's saddlebags. Under the bed upstairs."

"Good, because I think that's the part of the story that got them here, and once they discover we have one of our own? It's going be really interesting then."

"You didn't tell them?"

Shay was embarrassed. "I did, but not until after they dispatched the Riders. I was so busy explaining how we found it in the temple, I forgot to add that we brought it back with us."

"What about your maps?" Ashley asked, dryly. "Did you tell them about those?"

"I told them about the big one on the wall," Shay said, evasively.

Cassius snorted. "That's why you forgot to tell them we took the stone. You were too busy trying to avoid telling them about the maps you have tucked in your tunic."

"I want to study them further," Shay said. "They'll take them, and then I'd never see them again."

"They're coming in," Keagan said.

They put down their glasses and rose from the table, waiting as the innkeeper scurried over to greet the contingent as they entered the tavern. A lot of people were milling around, and it took more than a few minutes for everyone to be sorted out and led upstairs. No one seemed to notice them by the window, and after a while, they exchanged wry looks and resumed their seats.

"Guess they aren't here for us," Keagan said, dryly. "Maybe they just happened to be in the neighborhood."

"That's unlikely," Shay said, though she knew Keagan was joking. "Any visit by a Council member takes a lot of pomp and circumstance. And only Lynch has ever visited Aether. I've never heard of any of them other than Isaac visiting the Shadow Lands."

"Maybe they just want a good night's sleep before they roast us over the coals tomorrow," Ashley said.

"It's late," Shay said. "Especially for those coming from Aquas. They're six hours ahead."

"I keep forgetting that," Keagan said. "Until this little adventure, I'd never really thought about the difference in time between nations."

"Visitor," Ashley said.

A royal guard crossed the room. "Marshal?" The question in his voice and the way he scanned all of them indicated he didn't know which of them was Keagan. And, Shay noted, she wasn't wearing her badge on her poncho as she had on her uniform.

"I'm Riley." Keagan stood up.

"Captain Abraham would like to speak with you in his room."

"I'm on my way." Keagan shared a look with Shay and then followed the guard up the stairs.

Shay watched her leave, a sick sense rising within her. Was this the beginning of their inevitable good-bye?

XX

"Riley, it's damned good to see you," Abraham said after the guard deposited Keagan in the captain's room. "We feared the worst after what we found in the tomb."

"Did anyone..." Keagan swallowed hard. "Did anyone else make it?"

Soberly, he shook his head. "I'm sorry, no." He gestured to a chair. "Please. I have a bare-bones report from the Shadow Riders. I'll like one directly from you."

"Of course, Chief." Keagan passed him the journals she'd recovered from the mercenary camps and the combined bag of gold confiscated from the various bodies, along with the Elemental shackles Shay had recovered. Then she sat down on the chair, back straight, shoulders squared, head up as she told him all that had happened as concisely as possible. After she finished, he looked very troubled. He was a small, burly man, with a gleaming bald head and furious eyebrows complementing a pugnacious nose. She'd heard stories that he'd come up through the ranks from the very bottom. Not a political appointment at all, simply a man who'd been on the streets and knew what it was about. Keagan had always respected him greatly, and he didn't disappoint now, zeroing in on what she already suspected.

"You think one of them was a marshal."

"They managed to get their hands on those cuffs. Not standard issue at all. You need to know they even exist in the first place, and to access them requires a certain level of authority."

"Well, it can't be him." Abraham stood up and began to pace around the room. "I can count the number of Elementals currently in the marshals on one hand, and none of them are Chthonic."

"So it may be the woman," Keagan said. "We have so little information. I wasn't able to get into the palace at Amane. The mercenary camps had little evidence of what's behind all this." She shivered. "And the Shadow Realm is a little out of my purview."

He ran his hand over his scalp. "This whole thing is bigger than a bunch of thieves, Riley, or even a group of kidnappers. There's a pattern that hasn't been brought to our attention until now."

"You believe someone in the Council could be involved?"

He met her gaze squarely. His eyes were a pale blue, normal, not the sharp, penetrating brilliance of an Undine. Some people looked down on her choice of profession, Keagan believed, because she took orders from nulls. Even those teachers at the Academy she had considered more progressive than most had voiced their concerns when she applied to the marshals. Elementals owned and operated the largest and most successful companies. Freshly graduated Elementals, particularly those rated high level, generally refused to work under ordinary humans. Any company that didn't employ numerous Elementals couldn't compete with those that did and quickly went out of business. It was a vicious circle she didn't think could be broken.

"It's possible," he said. "In which case, we're already in trouble. However, it's also possible that it's someone below them. Administering to a nation takes a certain amount of bureaucracy, and people can lose oversight along the chain of command. Certainly, we've been just as guilty of that on occasion."

Reminded of past instances of corruption in the ranks, Keagan nodded. "What now, Chief? I'd like to be assigned to the case. I don't know exactly how this 'shadow lord' is connected to the wraiths, but he is, and they killed my squad. I want him to answer for it."

"You'll get your chance," he said in a grim tone. "The Queen has already dispatched members of her royal guard, with the help of the Shadow Riders, to secure the sites in Aquas and Arias. We'll assemble a task force as soon as possible, and I want you to head it up. Once we finish the debrief with the Council tomorrow, we'll return to Naiad and get started."

Keagan felt a qualm. So quickly? But of course, it made sense, even though Shay would probably have to remain in Aether for a few more days. Unfortunately, by the time she returned to Naiad, Keagan might be gone. This sort of case wouldn't be local. She'd have to travel to various nations, beginning with northern Terras, tracking down any leads there.

"I look forward to it, Chief," she told him, hoping her lack of enthusiasm didn't show. She was torn. She really wanted to bring him in. But she wanted to remain with Shay with equal intensity. An impossible quandary.

She took her leave and made her way back to her room. Ashley and Shay were already there, Ashley tucked in one of the beds and Shay stretched out on the portable cot. It didn't seem fair that she had been forced to go from the promise of a large double bed to this rickety thing, but such was the case when royalty was involved. After stripping down to her undergarments, she leaned over Shay and brushed her lips over her temple. Shay stirred, rolling over to look up at her.

"Sorry," Keagan whispered. "Didn't mean to wake you."

"I wasn't asleep." Shay's eyes were luminous in the low illumination from the vapor lamp. "What did your boss have to say?"

"I've been given the case," Keagan told her. "Once I'm back in Naiad, I'll be assigned a squad, and we'll begin the investigation."

Shay didn't reply, though her expression spoke volumes. Keagan nudged her shoulder. "Come on," she said. "Sleep with me. The bed's small, but it's better than that cot."

Shay didn't resist, rising from the cot and joining Keagan in her bed, the two of them curling up in the center. It was just big enough if they didn't try to move too much. "You'll be leaving tomorrow," Shay said, her voice quiet in the darkness.

"I'll always come back to you," Keagan said.

"Are you two going to talk all night?" Ashley's voice floated from the other bed. "Although I suppose that's better than the alternative."

"What? Sleeping?"

"You know what I mean."

Keagan smiled as she snuggled closer to Shay and let herself relax. The bed was far more comfortable than the thin sleeping pads of their bedrolls, and she soon drifted off.

After a flurry of activity in the morning that included showering and dressing in the clothes that had been laundered, mended, and returned to them, they went down for breakfast in the tavern where many others were also eating. Keagan was aware of the scrutiny leveled at them as they gathered around the table, but no one approached them other than a clearly overworked barmaid.

They ate breakfast quickly, with little conversation, and made their way outside before anyone else. "Suddenly, I'm feeling crowded," Ashley said. "Hard to believe. Maybe I just got used to hanging out with you four."

"Probably going to get worse before it gets better," Keagan said. "They'll want to speak with us soon."

"Well, before that, I'm off to do some shopping," Ashley said as she headed toward the general store. Keagan was about to stop her when she realized she didn't really have any real reason to do so. Cassius and Lyria decided to go with her, leaving Keagan and Shay standing by the obelisk.

Keagan looked at it closely. "I've never really studied one of these," she said. "You're right. The symbols are much different on this than they were on the others."

"Except for the insignia of the nations," Shay said, tracing some engravings. "Those haven't changed all that much."

"Shay?" Both of them turned to see Merrill approaching.

"Cousin," Shay said. "Do they want us in the hall?"

"Not yet," Merrill said. "I just wanted to track you down for when they're ready. They're doing a bit of setup."

"I'll bet, with the Queen being here," Shay said. "Though I doubt we have any thrones lying around. Has anyone from the royal family ever been in the Shadow Lands?"

Merrill shook her head. "Not to my knowledge. We're too unimportant."

"She was probably honoring the pact between our nations, respecting Aether's ban," Keagan said. "All the heads of state are Elemental. I'm just not sure why they came here rather than have us travel to Naiad."

"Above my pay grade, that's for sure," Merrill said, wryly. She eyed Keagan for a second. "What's it like? Being Elemental, I mean."

"Merrill!" Shay was appalled.

Keagan laughed. "Not so different," she said. "It's just another skill, like being able to ride a horse or fire a bow. Some have more talent with it than others, but it still takes practice and study to do it well."

"You're Undine, right?"

"I am."

"Is it true you can suck the water right out of a person, leaving behind only a husk?"

"Merrill! For Lady's sake!" Shay looked as if she wanted to strangle her cousin.

"I've heard of it," Keagan said, less amused, but trying to remain diplomatic.

"Merrill, go wait over there," Shay said sternly, pointing at a bench on the other side of the park. "And learn some manners. I can't believe Mother chose you as her assistant."

Merrill made a face at Shay but obligingly did as requested. "Sorry," Shay said, turning back to Keagan. "We don't know much about Elementals."

"That's the case everywhere," Keagan said, though ordinary people rarely asked questions of Elementals, especially about how they used their abilities. Too afraid of the answers, perhaps.

"So can you?" Shay asked.

"Can I what?" Keagan frowned.

"Suck the water out of a person."

Keagan exhaled. "It's been done," she said. "A human body is mostly water. Removed, the only thing left is dried-up skin and muscle draped loosely over a brittle pile of bones."

"You've never done it?"

"What? Never!" Keagan tried not to shudder. "It's illegal under any circumstances. Take a life that way? To use it to power abilities? To knowingly take the moisture from another living creature is evil and pathetic and sick."

Shay was silent for several minutes. "I'm sorry," she said finally. "I didn't mean to upset you."

Keagan sighed. "I caught a case once," she said. "The victims were as I described. The Undine responsible was completely mad, but clever. It took us a while to catch up with him."

Shay hesitated. "What level would you have to be?"

Keagan met her gaze. "Only a one. That's why he did it. He believed it would somehow increase his level. It didn't."

"Oh."

Keagan bent her head, sadness echoing through her as she felt Shay recoil a bit. "That fear and fawning response to us? There's a good reason for the former. And perhaps even the latter behavior is based in fear, as well."

Shay put her hand on Keagan's shoulder, squeezing lightly. "I overstepped. I shouldn't have pursued such a topic."

"No, Shay. You can ask me anything at all," Keagan said. "I'll always tell you the truth. It's just that you might not like what that truth implies." She was about to say more when she saw the others returning. Ashley was still dressed in her herdsmen outfit. "They didn't have anything?"

"Oh, I'm having some leathers tailored for me," Ashley said. "They took my measurements and said they'd be ready by tomorrow morning."

"That quickly?" Keagan was astonished.

"They won't make them from scratch," Shay said. "They'll alter some existing leathers. It would be different if she was asking for an entirely new outfit like the one she had on when she was kidnapped."

"I'm having some made, too," Cassius said.

Keagan wondered what use either of them would have for Rider leathers, though Cassius was obviously an equestrian. She might feel a greater connection to Aether than others would.

"Shay?" Merrill was motioning at them. "They're ready for you."

As they entered the foyer of the town hall, Keagan noted the beaded decorations on the wall, scenes of bison and wolves and bears and horses. So many horses. The meeting room where they were led had a large table with chairs on one side. Queen Chiesa was seated in the center, the crown guards standing at attention behind her, backs against the wall. To the Queen's left was Diana and the rest of the Clan Elders. To her right, the Ruling Council was seated in order of the nations from east to west: Aquas, Terras, Aether, Urodela, and Arias. Such details were necessary, Keagan knew, to maintain political delicacy.

Captain Abraham sat in the front row, with Perrin. Merrill led

Keagan and Shay to seats next to them, while the other three settled in the row behind. Then Merrill retreated to the back of the room, where she and four other young members of the clans were set up to take notes at small desks. Keagan shared a glance with Shay.

"Is this where you spent yesterday?"

"Most of it," Shay said. "Guess it's your turn."

"Marshal Keagan Riley? Please step forward," Diana said.

Keagan squared her shoulders and rose from her chair, taking a position in front of Chiesa. "Your Grace," she said, kneeling briefly, head bowed, before rising again. She stood at attention, hands linked behind her back, chin up, gaze set above the Queen's head as she waited to be addressed.

"Marshal," Chiesa said, with royal authority, "please tell Us everything that happened, beginning with the attack in the tomb."

Using the same detached tone she had used to fill in Captain Abraham, Keagan recited her story from beginning to end. Once she had finished, she gave way to Shay, who repeated her story from the day before. Keagan noted, fighting back a smile, that again Shay didn't mention the maps in her tunic. However, she did bring forth the stone. As she began to set it on the table in front of the Queen, the guards all drew their swords and stepped toward her. Shay froze.

"Sorry," she said, looking around, holding it out before her very carefully with both hands. "What would you have me do with it?"

"Put it here, Shay," Diana said gently, clearing a space on the table in front of her.

The other Elementals in the room leaned away from it, Keagan noticed, including herself. Her back was pressed so hard against her chair that it was a wonder it wasn't collapsing. The stone remained there for the duration, an uncomfortable presence as Ashley told her story, then Cassius, and finally, Lyria.

When the Sylph had finished, the questions began, including a flurry of demands and vague accusations that mostly couldn't be answered. Keagan noticed that Abraham stayed out of it for the most part, as did the northern Elders, who undoubtedly had asked all their questions the day before with Shay. By the time everyone had begun to repeat themselves, even the Queen, who was undoubtedly used to this sort of foolishness, Keagan was ready to run from the room screaming.

"Enough," Chiesa said finally, raising her hand. "We have thoroughly discussed what has happened. Now We must determine Our course of action moving forward."

"If I may, Your Grace," Abraham said, rising, "I've assigned Riley to this case. We'll be returning to Naiad immediately to assemble a task force. We'll bring this Shadow Lord to justice."

"With all due respect, Captain," Chiesa said, frowning, "it's obvious your organization has been compromised on some level. The presence of Elemental cuffs in these kidnappings proves that suspicion. While We grant that it might be as simple as intercepting a box between manufacturing and delivery, it may also indicate a deep-seated conspiracy within your ranks. That would imperil any task force you might assemble." She raised her chin imperiously. "This is no longer a marshal issue. It is a matter for the crown and, as such, will be dealt with by the crown. We shall create Our Own task force." Her expression softened. "But an experienced investigator will be required. If you wish to provide the services of Marshal Riley, We would be most grateful." Not really a request, Keagan knew, but an imperial demand offered in the most polite of manners.

Abraham and Keagan exchanged looks, and at his nod, she stood up. "Of course, Your Grace."

"Very good. Squadrons of the Guard have been dispatched to the Amane and Anemoi ruins to secure the sites and deal with these mercenaries," Chiesa said. "It will be up to you, Marshal Riley, to track down and secure the leaders. Whatever you require to carry out this task shall be provided."

"I understand," Keagan said, even as she felt the weight of the task settle on her shoulders.

Isaac leaned forward in his seat. "She'll need a better mode of travel than ship or caravan," he pointed out. "If you want this resolved as quickly as possible, you'll need a Rider to guide her and anyone else involved along the Paths."

The words were barely out of his mouth before Shay was on her feet. "I volunteer," she said. "The marshal and I have already established a functional working relationship."

"Is that what they're calling it now?" Keagan heard Ashley mutter behind her.

Isaac regarded Shay evenly. "You're a courier, not a guide."

"No, Headmaster," Shay said, gaze intent on his. "But I've successfully walked Paths no current scout or guide has, and I remember the map on the wall. I know where the other lost Paths are located. They may be needed."

Isaac held her gaze a few beats longer and then nodded. He turned to the Queen. "She's an experienced Rider, one of our best. If she's willing to ride these lost Paths, and the marshal accepts her service, then I see no reason why she wouldn't be a satisfactory option."

"I accept her service," Keagan said quickly. She was thrilled to be able to work with Shay on this mission, yet worried about the potential danger she would have to face at her side.

Chiesa nodded. "Very well. Rider Kendrith, as you have ridden for Us as a courier, now ride for Us as Aether's representative to Our task force."

"We must all have representatives," Dewitt said. "Terras stands ready to serve."

"Can we trust anyone from Terras?" Dunbar asked, somewhat spitefully. "Considering they can't keep track of their landowners."

"Then allow me to represent my nation," Cassius suddenly said. Keagan looked back to see her rise to her feet, head raised proudly. "As one of his victims, I have the right to hold this Shadow Lord accountable."

"An agricultural specialist?" Ralston said. "Really?"

"I can handle myself in a fight," Cassius said, evenly.

"I can vouch for that," Keagan said, wanting to show her support. At this point, since it had been wrenched out of marshal hands, she wanted this royal task force to be assigned people she could trust. "Besides, we have no idea if all twenty missing Elementals were taken or if a few may have joined him willingly. I'm comfortable with Cassius."

Perrin stood up. "If we wish to keep this as quiet as possible, I would point out that these Elementals already know the situation. They won't need to be brought up to speed, and there'll be less chance of this getting out to the general public. I remember Sie Suolo from the Academy. She's one of the most sensible and capable we've graduated."

The Queen hesitated briefly and then nodded. "Sie Suolo, your service is greatly appreciated."

"If Terras and Aquas are represented, then Urodela must have a representative as well," Dunbar said. "I can have a list of candidates brou—"

"Oh, I'm going with them," Ashley said lazily from the back. "Someone needs to keep them sharp."

They all stared at her. Chiesa looked uncomfortable. Keagan supposed that was because of the influence the family's company wielded, even on the crown. "Sie Van Vuur, I don't believe your father would approve."

"Ashley, Her Majesty is correct," Dunbar said, frowning at her. "Cecil would have been here if he could. He wouldn't want you involved in any of this."

"I'm already involved," Ashley said, evenly. "And I intend to go whether you send someone else from Urodela or not. I won't let my friends do this alone." Her voice hardened as she leaned forward. "This asshole interfered with a Van Vuur. A Van Vuur will most certainly be part of his reckoning."

Despite herself, Keagan was quite impressed. She'd never seen this side of Ashley. Determined and resolved rather than vindictive and petty.

"Well, if they're all going, I'm going, too." Lyria stood up. As everyone looked at her, she quailed a bit, and then, straightening visibly, chin up, she looked the Queen dead in the eye. "Your Grace, I'm level five, and no one in Arias can fly faster. Whatever else a representative from Arias can offer, in that area, at least, I'm the best you can find."

"You're rather young, child," Chiesa said, not unkindly. "You may be the fastest, but this will be a dangerous mission, and as such, other qualifications will be required."

Keagan saw Lyria's face fall, and she felt a pang even as she agreed with the Queen. She was considerably surprised when Shay stood up again to speak.

"Your Grace, if I may," Shay said. "I admit Lyria requires more skill with her weapon, and she doesn't have a great deal of experience in battle situations, but in every conflict we've faced to date, she's stood her ground with unfailing courage. The rest of us know her. More importantly, we trust her. Finally, if time is truly of the essence, then she's already here and ready to serve."

Chiesa frowned and looked at Keagan. "Marshal, would this be acceptable to you?"

Keagan glanced once at Lyria and saw the determination in her young features. She was surprised to find herself changing her mind. "She *is* young, but I have to agree with the Rider. Lyria is courageous, in every sense of the word, and as level five, she has formidable abilities. Furthermore, and most important, she's displayed a willingness to quickly adapt those skills as required by the situation. Very few Elementals are that flexible. Such flexibility in all of us may be crucial to the mission's success."

Chiesa didn't look completely convinced, but she nodded. "Very well, Sie Hawke. You fly for the crown."

Keagan was relieved when Lyria limited her enthusiasm to a bright smile that lit up her entire face, rather than do that whole fist-pump gesture. She noticed that Ralston, as the Arias representative, didn't appear happy with the choice, but she didn't offer any objection. Lyria looked gratefully at Keagan and Shay as they all sat down once more.

"And what of us?" Lynch leaned over, his ruddy features sour. "Is this to be only a matter for Elementals and Aether? Isn't that the real reason you've taken this from the marshals?"

"The Guard is securing the sites in Amane and Anemoi," Dunbar told him, lip curled in an almost sneer. "They're practically all nulls. What more do you want?"

Chiesa raised her hand, quelling any further argument. Her face tightened as she glanced over at the stone in front of Diana. "We require a historian for research," she said. "Someone not only well versed in the history of the war, but also one who can handle herself in any potential conflict. And handle what would be incredibly dangerous to an Elemental." She eyed Lynch. "I believe you know someone who would be suitable?"

Lynch looked at her blankly for a moment, before his face cleared, and he grudgingly nodded. "Yes, I do know someone. She's in southern Aquas at the moment, on a dig." He looked over at Keagan. "Marshal, a Rider can be dispatched to bring her here within a day."

So they were to work with a stranger, after all. Keagan couldn't object, especially since the requirements for the position were rather stringent. If Lynch knew someone, who was she to argue?

"Of course, Councillor," she said, as graciously as she could manage.

XXI

"Are you all sure about this?"

After the rest of the details had been worked out with the Queen and Council, Shay and the others had left the town hall and gathered in the tavern. It was past midday, and after ordering lunch, they wanted to discuss what had just occurred.

"Positive." Shay smiled at Keagan. "Frankly, I didn't think we'd be allowed to help. I was afraid I'd have to go back to being a courier and spend all my time worrying about what was happening to you. Now we can stay together."

"It could be very dangerous," Keagan said, her brilliant blue eyes serious as they searched Shay's face. "For all of you."

"It's already been dangerous," Ashley said. "Shay's job as a courier is dangerous. Just being an Elemental is apparently quite dangerous now, with some idiot running around kidnapping us."

"She's right," Cassius said. "We're already in it. Up to this point, though, we've been on the defensive. Now it's time to go on the offensive and find this bastard."

Keagan looked at Lyria, who reddened. "I won't let you down," Lyria said earnestly.

"I just don't want anything to happen to you," Keagan said gently.

"Something's already happened to me," Lyria said, "I don't want to be the sort of person who just walks away from that." She glanced at Shay. "I know I'm not the best fighter, but I'll learn everything you want to teach me. I did learn all the basics at the Academy. I just haven't been practicing since graduation." She shook her head. "I don't know why you and Keagan called me courageous, though. Most of the time, I'm scared to death."

"You're the bravest of us all." Shay laid her hand on Lyria's shoulder, squeezing slightly. "The rest of us have experience. You don't, yet you stay. Courage doesn't mean being without fear. It means standing your ground, even when you want to run."

"Though if I tell you to fly, you fly," Keagan said. "Knowing when to fight another day is also part of courage."

Ashley crossed her arms over her chest. "Give it up, Keagan. You're stuck with us, like it or not. So, where do we begin?"

"Fine." Keagan appeared stern, but Shay suspected she was happier about having them as her squad than she was willing to let on. She was just concerned about their safety and a little worried about being responsible for them. Shay could understand her trepidation.

"Cassius, I'm placing you in charge of the supplies." Keagan's voice fell into a professional calm. "You'll meet with the town's quartermaster this afternoon. He runs the general store. Anything you need, he'll provide or dispatch Riders to retrieve it."

"Got it," Cassius said. "Any requests?"

Keagan slid a piece of paper across the table. "The items on this list will have to be retrieved from the nearest unit, probably from the office in Aether."

Cassius took it, glanced once at it, her eyebrows rising a little, before folding it neatly and slipping it into her tunic. She glanced at the others. "Anything you want?"

"I'm already having clothes made," Ashley said. "The general store should provide anything else I might require."

"I'd like some proper flight suits," Lyria said, somewhat timidly. "What I'm wearing is fine for short flights, but if I'm required to soar for long periods of time, I'll want every advantage." She hesitated. "They're really, *really* expensive, though."

"It's on the crown," Shay reminded her gently. "If you need it, we'll get it. Give Cassius your measurements. Get her a few."

"Tell me something," Keagan said to Ashley. "You had traveling leathers made up before we ever went in there. Did you think this could happen?"

Ashley smiled. "When everyone showed up last night, I suspected they wanted to keep a lid on the situation. Otherwise, they would have waited for us to come to them in Naiad. And if we hadn't volunteered to serve on the crown's task force, I'm certain our respective companies would have reassigned us to some isolated, backwater, make-work project once we went home, just so we couldn't discuss what happened with others."

"Even you?" Cassius asked, obviously curious.

"Worse, they would have talked Daddy into keeping me home with Mother." Ashley shuddered. "Which would mean constant discussion about why I haven't chosen a suitable Elemental husband from the list of possible matches they've provided, and why I haven't started popping out

Elemental heirs. I'd rather hunt down someone who wants to suck me dry and then kill me. It'll be less stressful."

"Why do you suppose they want to keep this so quiet?" Cassius asked.

"Between Elementals getting kidnapped and artifacts that can strip away abilities, I think they're afraid of causing a panic," Keagan said. "They may also be afraid of stirring up tension, especially if the person behind this isn't actually the Chthonic we think it is, but someone else who wants abilities for themselves." She shook her head. "Right now, we have only theories. From here on out, we operate on facts. We need to head to Terras, track down names of northern landowners, and find out if any of them know our man. We'll have some renderings made from our descriptions of him. You and Lyria will be key in that search. You saw more of him than Shay and I did. Also of his partner. Chances are, if she's a marshal, then she and this lord met there."

"Where will that happen?"

"The marshal office in Boden will have an artist. Then we can ride north to the farming communities there, see if anyone knows him."

"So, we're heading to Terras first," Shay said. "I know the Paths well. With Shadow-touched horses under you, it should be easy enough to take you through."

Diana had offered to outfit the entire task force with the best of the Kendrith herd. Lyria had wanted to keep her gelding, but when she learned that the special Shadow-touched could see in the Realm where ordinary horses couldn't, she grudgingly agreed. Shay suspected she'd get over it quick enough once she met her new mount.

"So, what do you think this historian will be like?" Lyria asked with a certain amount of trepidation.

Shay supposed she was worried about someone else joining their group and upsetting their bond of friendship, disrupting it somehow, especially her place in it. She patted Lyria on the back. "I'm sure she'll be fine. Though I'm surprised the councillor would know a historian so well suited to the task."

"That was a fortunate coincidence," Keagan said, brow furrowed.

"Not so much coincidence as nepotism," Ashley said, somewhat cynically. "If it's who I'm thinking of."

The others stared at her. "Go on," Keagan said.

"You know Daddy's company works with the crown directly," Ashley said. "That means I've attended a lot of functions with Council members and their families. Lynch's niece, Torva, is one of those scholarly types. Glasses, uptight, head in the books all the time, or ass deep in a bunch of pot shards. No sense of fashion or business." She paused. "Even if she wasn't a null, she and I didn't have anything in common, at all."

"I like her already," Shay said, dryly.

"She doesn't sound particularly adept in martial arts," Keagan said, more practically. "At least Lyria has basic combat training from the Academy. What would this girl have?"

"Well, she's always conducting archaeological digs in southwestern Aquas," Ashley said. "Out in the Wilderness, which, you have to admit, would require a certain amount of survival skills. She certainly couldn't stop talking about what she was discovering there."

"Prewar sites? What did she have to say?"

"To be honest, I didn't hang around to listen," Ashley said. "Once she started lecturing, I hit the bar."

"Hopefully, in that case, she'll be able to decipher Tannehill's journal," Keagan said. "And discover more information on the stones." She seemed to shiver a bit, and Shay pulled her closer, comfortingly. "I hope we won't have to carry that thing along with us."

"Oh, I bet we will," Ashley said. "Chiesa and the Council certainly don't want it around them, and I don't know that they'd trust it to a null."

"I suspect the Elders will be placed in charge of it," Shay said. "The Shadow Lord wouldn't dare come here."

The innkeeper brought over their meals. "So, it seems the inn will be clearing out this afternoon," he said as he distributed the plates from his tray. "You're welcome to the big room, again."

"Thanks," Shay said. "I thought after the Queen slept there, you'd put up a plaque or something. Issue tickets to allow people to see the bed."

"I'm considering it," he told her, sounding serious. "In the meantime, I got paid twice, once from the Elders and once from the crown. It's been a very good couple of days."

Keagan laughed. "At least someone's benefiting from this." Then she paused. "Please move my belongings in there as well."

He hesitated, glanced between her and Shay for a second, and then nodded. "At once, sie." His tone was completely even, without indication of approval or disapproval.

Shay was a little rocked. This request publicly confirmed their relationship and announced that it was more than merely friendship. Between a Rider and an Elemental. That it was intimate enough to share a bed, which meant it wouldn't take long for word to spread across town and reach the ears of her parents. She swallowed hard. Keagan apparently noticed the expression, because she leaned over.

"Did I overstep?"

"No," Shay said. "I'm very flattered in a way. But I'm absolutely terrified in another."

"Terrified? Why?"

Ashley snorted. "A tavern is the source of most gossip," she said before Shay could. "You just announced to the whole town that you're screwing the daughter of two Clan Elders, Elders who, by the way, have made rules against Elementals ever being inside this nation."

She was deriving entirely too much glee from this situation, Shay thought.

"Just imagine how they'll react," Ashley said, "when they find out you've probably been inside her!"

XXII

Keagan woke in the early hours before dawn. Outside the window of the inn, the sky was paling to gray, the first twitter of birdsong wafting into the room. In her arms, Shay slumbered peacefully, a long, lean warmth that Keagan wanted to wrap herself around forever. She smiled as she brushed her lips over the soft skin of Shay's shoulder, not wanting to wake her but also wishing she would wake up. The exotic scent of her skin, a mix of spice and wind, filled Keagan's senses as she trailed kisses along Shay's collarbone and up her neck.

Shay made a soft sound, a whimper of pleasure and delight, pressing back into Keagan's embrace. Nuzzling her ear, Keagan drew her fingertips down the slope of Shay's small breast, toying deliberately with the soft tip. "Good morning," she murmured.

"So far." Shay agreed readily.

Keagan chuckled and kissed her again. Shay made a move to roll over, but Keagan tightened her grip. "Let me," she whispered. "Please."

Shay resisted briefly, then acquiesced, relaxing as she put her hand back on Keagan's hip, the only part she could reach to caress.

Keagan caught Shay's earlobe between her teeth, nibbling as she ran her palm down over Shay's flat stomach, raking her fingers through the soft patch of hair. "Please," she murmured again, pleading.

Shay laughed low in her throat and shifted slightly, parting her legs to grant access. Keagan's breath caught as she slipped her fingers between them, wetness bathing them as she fondled Shay with gentle intensity.

Shay moaned, head going back against Keagan's shoulder, trembling as her pleasure built. Keagan loved the low, guttural sound she incited, the way Shay shuddered uncontrollably at her peak. She held her as Shay melted into her arms, feeling such a combination of adoration, tenderness, and caring that tears came to her eyes.

"I love you," she murmured, overwhelmed by the emotion choking her throat. And then she froze as Shay stilled and rolled over to face her. "Sorry," she said, feeling awkward as hell. "Way too soon."

"No." Shay put her fingers beneath Keagan's chin and lifted her head so she could look into her eyes. "I love you, too. And maybe you're right. Maybe this is all happening way too quickly, and it'll burn so hot and fast, nothing will be left at the end, but I know how I feel right now. And I've never felt this way with anyone else."

Relieved, Keagan drew her close and kissed her, trying to pour all her devotion into her kiss so Shay would know that she hadn't spoken lightly, and that this didn't happen to her often. Or ever. And as Shay pressed her down onto the sheets, hands and mouth roaming over her with delicious intent, Keagan surrendered to her and to the depth of her emotion, feeling as if she'd finally found a home. Growing up on the streets, and then being placed in the Academy before going on to the marshals, she'd never known this feeling, but it was the only way she could describe it. With Shay, she was exactly where she belonged.

Afterward, showered and dressed, Keagan settled her shield on her back weapon harness and gazed at Shay as she slipped several knives into her laced, leather tunic. "I'm a little surprised I didn't get a visit from a clan member last night," she said. "I'm sorry I let the cat out of the bag like that." She shrugged awkwardly. "I'm not used to dealing with families in situations like this, or even thinking about them."

Shay offered her soft, shy smile, dark eyes shimmering. "It's fine. Besides, Mother wouldn't react so soon. She absorbs a situation in its entirety and then moves in after she has as much information as she can get. And no one else in the clan will do anything until she decides how to handle it."

Something to look forward to, Keagan thought somberly. "So you consider yourself part of your mother's clan? What about your father and his clan. Rylak?"

"Oh, I'm part of the Rylak Clan as well. When you come of age, you can choose which Clan you wish to identify with, even if it's one you're not related to. Since I have the Sight and became a Shadow Rider, that didn't really apply to me, so I just kept the name I already had."

"Just like that?"

"Just like that." Shay peered at Keagan from beneath her lashes. "Riley was the name of your parents?"

Keagan didn't flinch, the wound so old, it didn't affect her so much anymore. "The name comes from the two marshals who found me, Keagan and Riley. They were foot patrol on the streets of Naiad. They looked out for us kids and tried to protect us as best they could."

Shay regarded her without pity but with clear compassion. "So you don't know the names of your parents."

"Not a clue," Keagan said. "On the street, I was mostly called Spud, because I once got away from some pervert by throwing potatoes at him.

I didn't have a name before that, other than what others chose to call me. If I was given one at birth, I never knew what it was." Shay moved over and wrapped her arms around her, holding her tight. Keagan allowed the embrace. "It doesn't matter anymore," she told her quietly. "I left that life behind a long time ago."

"I know, but I can be sad for the little girl you were," Shay said. "A remarkable little girl who grew up to be an amazing woman."

Keagan sighed. "Because I'm Elemental," she said, "I was given a lot more opportunities than the rest of the kids. I was lucky that's how it turned out. Otherwise, I might be a completely different person now. A person you might not even want to know."

"I think you would still have been clever, brave, and strong." Shay kissed her cheek. "You just would have been the smartest crook in Naiad."

Despite herself, Keagan laughed. "Maybe." Though in reality, life wasn't nearly so kind.

Downstairs, they met the others in the tavern for breakfast. Ashley eyed them sardonically. "Surprised you made it down so early."

"I want to meet this historian when she arrives."

"She's already here," Cassius said, sounding rather amused. "Arrived in the middle of the night and holed up in the town hall with the stone and the journals she got from Abraham."

Keagan absorbed that information. "She sounds rather keen."

"Very," Ashley said, smirking as she forked up her eggs. "Seriously, Keagan, you're gonna love this girl. I can't wait for you to meet her."

Keagan began to feel apprehensive, considering how gleeful Ashley sounded. Sharing a glance with Shay, Keagan tried to focus on her breakfast and not the upcoming meeting with her historian. And it was *her* historian. She was responsible for this team. Considering the last one had been killed, having a new one just added more pressure. Shay's thigh nudged against her own then, and her shoulder leaned into hers a little, just enough to let her know she was there, and always planned to be there, and Keagan worried a bit less.

After breakfast, she and Shay went over to the town hall. They weren't holding hands or anything so blatant, but Keagan was aware of all eyes on them as they walked side by side. No sense of threat, of course, but definitely the feeling of being the center of acute interest. Heat rose in her cheeks, and she looked surreptitiously at Shay to discover her glancing back with a sardonic expression.

As they entered the town hall, Keagan quailed to discover Shay's parents standing in the foyer, speaking with each other. Both looked at her as she entered, and she devoutly wished she had Shay's ability to jump into the Shadow Realm for a quick escape.

"Marshal," Calvin said, tone formal, though his eyes glinted. Was it from humor or imminent threat? "Your historian has arrived."

"We heard," Shay said. "Impression?"

Diana smiled faintly. "Different, even for someone of Aquas." Then that dark gaze centered on Keagan. "You grew up there, didn't you?"

"I, ah, yes, I did," Keagan said.

"I spoke with your Captain Abraham before he left," Diana said, her gaze steady. "He speaks very highly of you."

"I'm honored," Keagan said, even as she wondered why Diana would be speaking to the head of the marshals. Then she mentally slapped herself. She would want to know more about the Elemental sleeping with her daughter, of course. "He's taught me a lot."

"Chiesa also spoke well of you," Diana said. "She told us you've had a remarkable career. She's quite confident you're the only one who could have commanded her task force."

Keagan wasn't sure what to think. First, she hadn't been aware Queen Chiesa knew that much about a lowly Undine marshal. Second, the casual way Diana spoke of the Queen, including the warm use of her name without title, implied a more casual relationship between royalty and Aether Elders than Keagan would have ever imagined. Third, Shay's mother actually spoke to the Queen about her? Aigua, what the hell was going on?

"Mother, please," Shay said gently.

"Merely passing on the fact that her superiors think well of her," Diana said blandly.

"Why are you even interested?"

Diana fixed Shay with a sudden sharp look. "Please, don't insult my intelligence." She looked back at Keagan. "I expect you and Shay to have dinner with us this evening. Your friends, as well." Not so much an invitation as a regal demand, as forceful as any Chiesa might make.

"Yes, ma'am," Keagan said, a cold sweat breaking out.

Calvin and Diana inclined their heads in farewell and left. Shay patted Keagan on the shoulder. "It's not that bad."

"If you say so," Keagan said. "I suppose that means we won't be leaving today."

"We need to be fully supplied with proper mounts," Shay said. "That would have taken a day or so, anyway."

Out of her purview, Keagan thought. Best to leave it to Shay and her people when it came to traveling the Paths. They'd also know how to best supply them. Inhaling deeply, she pushed through the doors leading to the meeting room. The woman at the table at the far end of the room—stacks of paper, books, the two journals and the stone piled around her—clearly didn't notice them. Keagan took the opportunity to observe her.

She appeared athletic enough, sleeves of her shirt rolled up to reveal deeply tanned and well-defined forearms. Horn-rimmed glasses perched precariously on the tip of her nose as she peered at the stone through a magnifying glass. Her hair was dirty blond, gathered sloppily in a bun from which several strands escaped to dangle around narrow, intense features covered with freckles. Her eyes were deep brown, normal, with no hint of Elemental gleam.

"Professor Torva Lynch?" Keagan said finally, stepping forward.

"I'm busy," she said in a distracted tone. "What is it?" She didn't look up.

Beside Keagan, Shay made a small sound of amusement.

"I'm Marshal Keagan Riley," Keagan said, schooling her voice to patience. "This is Shadow Rider Shay Kendrith. You'll be assisting us in apprehending a suspect in several Elemental kidnappings."

"What?" Torva's head jerked upward. "I'm a historian, not a marshal. I'm here to decipher this journal and the markings on this stone."

"Both parts of our investigation," Keagan said. "I trust you can ride?"

Her eyes brightened. "We're going to the sites in Amane and Anemoi?"

"No. We're heading to Terras," Keagan said. "We'll meet for lunch at the tavern. I expect you to present an update on what you've discovered so far."

She nodded briefly at Shay, turned around, and left before Torva could say anything else. She must have caught Shay by surprise, because she didn't follow right away. Outside, in the park, Keagan let out her breath in a huff as she waited. When Shay finally came through the door, she chuckled, probably at her expression. "She's definitely focused."

"To the point of distraction," Keagan said. "I worry about her ability in a fight, because we're more apt to discover one of those than another prewar site."

"Give her a chance," Shay said.

"I will, but we also have to know whether we can count on her or if we have to carry her."

"I'm sure she'll be fine." Shay gestured down the street. "Shall we go meet your new horse? I told the others we'd join them at the stables after we were through with Torva."

Keagan smiled, though she suspected she was less thrilled at the prospect than Shay was. She liked horses well enough, and certainly they were a better form of transportation than walking, but she wasn't besotted with them the way Shay and Cassius were. Or even Lyria, for that matter. Still, it would be worth seeing the others be matched with their mounts.

"What about our historian?"

Shay's brows drew down. "I asked her after you left. She told me she trusted my judgment in selecting 'appropriate transportation.' I don't think she likes horses much. They're objects to her, not living creatures."

"That must have gone over well," Keagan said as they headed toward the town's outskirts.

Shay glanced over at her. "Horses are more than just animals to us," she said. "But I realize that not everyone feels that way, especially outside the Shadow Lands. So long as she doesn't mistreat her mount and does her part in its care, I'll try not to have a problem with her."

"As long as you try," Keagan said wryly, hoping not to see what Shay considered a "problem," remembering how ready she had been to attack a level-four Salamas over a perceived slight to Onyx.

They approached one of the larger stables, an insignia painted by the sliding doors. Studying it, Keagan realized Shay had the same insignia stamped discreetly on her leathers and weapons, alongside the crown courier symbol. She suspected it was the clan's coat of arms, or whatever the Shadow Lands equivalent was.

Cassius, Lyria, and Ashley were at the corral outside, leaning against the fence as they watched the horses inside. Keagan and Shay joined them, Keagan propping her arms along the top rail. She recognized Onyx as he nickered and trotted over to greet Shay, nuzzling her hair and clearly expecting treats, which she promptly produced from within her tunic.

"Are we all here?" Calvin came out of the stables, his lanky stride covering the ground quickly.

"I'm choosing for the historian," Shay explained. "She's not that interested." She paused. "And she probably won't be able to tell the difference." Shay sounded so disgusted that Keagan was hard pressed not to smile. "We'll need an Academy mount."

Wondering where the horses they'd confiscated in Arias had ended up, Keagan spotted them in another paddock across the yard, looking healthy enough and well-tended. While the rest were grazing, oblivious to them, the cull stood by the fence, head up, looking in their direction. She offered him a little nod before she could stop herself and turned back to the paddock containing the specially trained Shadow-bred. Or the "Shadow-touched," as Shay had called them, those individual mounts that could see in the Shadow Realm.

"So what do we do?" Ashley asked. "Just point out the one we want?"

"You're not the one doing the choosing," Shay said. "The horse will choose you."

Ashley stared at her with open skepticism. "Really?"

Shay returned the look blandly. "Trust me."

"Well, I'll give it a try," Lyria said, climbing over the fence agilely. "Just walk in?"

"Be still within yourself," Calvin said. "Calm. Let them get to know you."

"Okay." Lyria strode gracefully across the ground scuffed by countless hoofs until she was within ten feet of the herd. Then she stood and waited. After they had finished their initial shift away from her approach and settled down, it seemed as if they might ignore her. But then, from seemingly nowhere, a snowy white mare stepped daintily from the herd and trotted toward Lyria. She stood still as the mare snuffled over her, nuzzling her hair. Keagan thought she had never seen such a delighted and happy expression on anyone before.

Tentatively, Lyria raised her hand and stroked the mare lovingly on the neck, running her hand over the long, flowing mane. When she turned back to the others, she had the widest smile, and as she walked back toward them, the mare followed immediately, without halter or rope.

"Well," Keagan said, when she realized they had all been staring silently for several minutes. "That was something."

"Bring her along," Calvin told Lyria as he opened the gate. "We'll fit out her tack."

"I'm going to call her Vindur," Lyria announced happily as she and the mare followed him into the stables.

"Isn't that coat going to stand out?" Ashley asked in a practical tone after they had disappeared inside. "That's the whitest horse I've ever seen."

"Their coats darken in the Realm," Shay said. "You wouldn't have noticed it with Onyx because he's naturally dark, but they all become non-reflective once they enter. It's not a concern."

Keagan just shook her head. The more she learned about Shay and her people, the more she realized how little she knew.

"My turn," Cassius said, smiling eagerly. She didn't vault the fence, choosing to enter by the gate, but every move told Keagan just how much she was looking forward to the experience. Again she stood there waiting, and it occurred to Keagan that perhaps these horses were too small to comfortably carry the heavy Chthonic.

But then a big black stallion lunged from between two horses, snorting and tossing his head. He rushed at Cassius, who didn't move, even when he reared onto his hind legs before her, and Keagan's hand closed convulsively over the hilt of her sword, tensing in anticipation. But before Keagan could do anything, he dropped to all fours and snorted at Cassius.

Cassius appeared delighted. "Oh, aren't you the feisty one," she said, touching his muzzle, pushing at it playfully.

He pushed back, nipping at her sleeve, though he didn't actually catch it and then allowed her to stroke his head and neck.

"That's a scout horse," Shay called to Cassius as she fussed over him. "Trained for battle and the unknown. You'll have your hands full."

"Oh, we'll get along just fine," Cassius said, actually cooing as she walked with him through the gate and toward the stable. "I'm calling him Gault."

Ashley stared at Cassius and her horse with a perplexed expression. "I don't mean to criticize or anything, but does anyone else think this is a little weird?"

Shay blinked. "It's always been done this way."

"Of course it has," Ashley said, obviously not convinced. Letting out her breath in a huff, she climbed up the fence, threw her leg over it, and jumped down on the other side, walking out to the middle of the corral and standing there. Flames suddenly wreathed her hands, and Keagan didn't understand why, especially as the herd shied violently away, remaining agitated in their motion.

Shay nodded, however. "Horses are afraid of fire," she said in a low tone. "Ashley will need one who will trust her with it."

They couldn't possibly be that intelligent, Keagan thought, though she didn't want to say such a thing and insult Shay. But even as most of the horses crowded down at the far end of the corral, as far from Ashley as they could get, a single mare, with a haughty snort, remained behind, staring at Ashley with almost a challenge in the dark eyes, head up, ears pricked forward. She was a deep sorrel, with a lighter mane and tail, her coat almost pure red in the sunlight.

A smile spread over Ashley's face, the type that Keagan wasn't used to seeing. It wasn't sarcastic or wry or guarded. It was pure and simple and joyful as the sorrel mare approached Ashley in an almost playful manner, trotting sideways, waiting until she had extinguished the flame before prancing the last few feet. Ashley didn't hesitate, stepping forward and wrapping her arms around the mare's neck, pressing her cheek against the warm coat, eyes closed in obvious contentment. "I'm going to call her Fuoco."

Keagan was surprised to find tears pricking at the back of her eyes, and she blinked rapidly.

"Not a word, Riley," Ashley muttered as she walked past with the mare, one hand on her neck, through the gate and into the stables.

Shay snorted, looking down briefly to hide her smile before meeting Keagan's gaze. "Your turn."

Keagan entered by the gate and took up a position in the center of the corral. The horses shifted and moved around her, intent on grazing and, very pointedly, ignoring her. A few minutes passed, and Keagan began to feel suitably rejected.

Then, from across the yard, she heard a loud, penetrating neighing, the high shriek of a horse in distress. Surprised, Keagan moved back to the gate and saw the cull running up and down the fence of his paddock, whinnying so hard, his entire body was trembling. He clearly wanted to get out, to leap the fence and gallop across the yard. Only the sheer height of the rails prevented it.

All to get to her.

"Seriously?" Shay was staring at him in awe. "I've never seen that in a cull."

The others appeared in the doorway of the stable, drawn by the commotion. Keagan ducked under the gate and went across the yard, reaching out to soothe him.

"Easy, boy." She patted him on the neck, soothing down his muzzle. "It's okay." She put her forehead against his, suddenly understanding what Ashley and the others had been feeling. To be chosen by her mount rather than simply being his burden, her partner rather than master and servant. "I've got you."

"Father, he won't be able to see," Shay said as Calvin handed Keagan a halter. She slipped it over his head, then took him from the paddock and led him toward the stables with the others. "And he's not trained for the Shadows."

"He chose her," Calvin said with a shrug. "In the end, that's all that matters. He'll trust her to get him through."

"And I'll trust you to get me through," Keagan told Shay as they walked by, heading in to outfit her new mount. "By the way, his name is Vesi."

She understood finally that the horse informed the rider of the name and not the other way around, though how it happened, she still wasn't sure. The name had just appeared in her mind, along with a rush of certainty that this horse was hers and she was his Rider.

For as long as they lived.

XXIII

They were seated around the table in the tavern, waiting impatiently for their historian to join them before ordering. "You did tell her to meet us here?" Ashley asked.

"Yes, I told her," Keagan said in an even tone. "Guess we'll see how well that goes. Best to find out early if she can follow basic instructions."

Shay swallowed a smile and looked out the window, across the park. At the top of the stairs of town hall, a figure appeared, all elbows and knees as she scurried down the stairs. Wondering how she managed to make simple walking look so awkward, Shay turned to the others.

"Here she comes."

"This should be good," Ashley muttered.

Torva entered the tavern, blinking in the sudden dimness after the bright sunshine outside. Spotting them at the corner table, she made her way over to them. A heavy leather bag was slung over her shoulder, tattered and worn, filled with papers. Shay realized belatedly that she also had the stone in it, glimpsing it through the gap at the top as Torva dumped it under the table at her feet. She suspected she was the only one to have spotted it because, otherwise, the Elementals would be doing that thing they did whenever they were in its presence, leaning away while trying not to appear they were, as if their skin were going in one direction while they wanted to go in the other.

"Am I late?"

"A few minutes," Keagan said in her hard, professional voice. "Is that a habit? I need to know."

Torva looked at her for a few seconds. "Ah, sometimes, when I'm researching, I lose track of time. I'm not trying to be disrespectful."

Keagan nodded. "Noted. We'll make sure you're outfitted with a proper timekeeper with an alarm." She lifted her hand, gesturing to the barmaid. "We're ready."

After they placed their order, Torva looked around at them. "I've never worked with Elementals," she said. "Or Shadow Riders. My profession doesn't attract you, I guess."

"Doesn't pay enough," Ashley said readily. "And it's boring."

Keagan exhaled audibly. "You've met Ashley, I understand. This is Cassius. She's in charge of supplies. If you require anything, let her know. She'll either acquire it or let you know why you can't have it. Our funding is from the crown, so we have a lot of leeway."

Torva nodded at Cassius, who gave her an amiable smile.

"This is Lyria," Keagan said. She hesitated briefly. "She's our scout."

Lyria visibly straightened, eyes lighting up, and Shay swallowed another smile.

"So, you've been brought up to speed on the situation so far. I know you haven't had it long, but were you able to get anything out of Tannehill's journal?"

Torva frowned, linking her hands on the table in front of her. "I knew Professor Tannehill. He was one of my teachers at college, and I'm quite familiar with his theories." Her mouth tightened. "I've always considered him a good man. I was quite distressed to hear of his involvement in criminal activity and, even more, of his demise."

Keagan appeared taken aback. "I'm sorry. I didn't realize."

"No reason you should," Torva said. "In any event, ours is an exceedingly small community. Historians all know each other, regardless of specialization, and those of us who pursue prewar research are even fewer in number."

"But you were able to decipher his journal?" Shay asked, bringing the discussion back on track. "It looked to be in code."

"Not code. It's shorthand," Torva said. "I read all of it. You should know, before I begin, that I haven't agreed with many of his theories over the years. Some were what I considered extremely controversial, but I have to say, the more I hear about recent events, the more I think he may have been on the right track in certain areas."

Keagan eyed her. "You seem to be beating around the bush a little bit, Professor," she said. "Why is that?"

Torva appeared to be choosing her next words very carefully. "What Tannehill writes about, and what I've discovered in the field, doesn't necessarily jibe with a certain history currently taught at the Elemental Academy. It also doesn't necessarily jibe with certain religious doctrine."

"What does it 'necessarily jibe' with?" Ashley asked brightly.

Torva looked down. "I don't know how devoted any of you are," she said. "Before I begin, it's important you realize that I do not mean to insult any of your beliefs."

"Oh, I can't wait to hear this," Ashley said, propping her chin on her hand.

Cassius leaned forward. "Please, while I consider myself a faithful follower of Lurra, I respect all beliefs, even if I don't agree with some of their precepts."

"This isn't so much a matter of religion, as it is historical speculation and the physical evidence that backs up such speculation, thereby making it fact."

"Nonetheless, we need to know," Keagan said with a touch of sharpness.

"All right," Torva said, sounding resigned. "This is what my discoveries, and Tannehill's theories, postulate that occurred a thousand years ago. Please save any questions for the end."

Shay suspected she lectured her classes like that. She settled back to hear the story.

"Armies of Elementals never fought a war between nations. Instead, a thousand years ago, the Cerastes Empire encompassed the entire known world from the east coast of Aquas to the west coast of Arias, ruled over by a series of imperial emperors. Far fewer Elementals existed than today, and any that were known were enslaved, considered property, bought and sold at a premium. The only way to escape such a fate was to conceal any abilities once they developed. A woman, named Alameada, began to accumulate power after her lover, a scientist named Paracelsus, discovered the Element Stones, a special type of crystal that could absorb the life force of those Elemental slaves and release the accumulated energy in a single burst. Four such weaponized stones existed in total: the Undine Stone that created floods, the Chthonic Stone that created earth disruption, the Salamas Stone that created explosions and intense heat, and the Sylph Stone, which generated wind, lightning, and intense cold."

Torva seemed to take in the varied expressions of skepticism and disbelief directed her way and gamely soldiered on. "Alameada placed each of these stones in the hands of her trusted generals, granting her armies an incredible advantage, crushing all opposition in her rise to power. Once she became Empress, she dispatched the stones to the four corners of her empire, locating them in the capital cities: Amane in Aquas, Anemoi in Arias, Lurrera in Terras, and Vatra in Urodela. A fifth stone, the Primal Stone, placed on a staff that never left her side, controlled the four stones. She ruled for three centuries, maintaining control with ruthless efficiency and the constant deterrent of the stones. Some say the stones made her and those around her immortal. I can't vouch for the accuracy of that statement, but our finds do tend to indicate that she and her followers seemed to live an extended period of time. Or they had a habit of appointing their successors with the same exact titles and names."

Shay swallowed hard, painfully reminded of discovering too

many statues of the same woman in recent days. Of a sacrificial altar in a pyramid with a hole just the right size for a diamond-shaped stone. This theory was starting to sound more plausible with every statement. Having her entire belief system systematically shattered was quite an interesting sensation.

"A young woman named Stygia lived in the capital city of Elfenol in Central Aquas," Torva said, making Shay start involuntarily. "She wasn't an Elemental, but she did possess the ability to slip in and out of shadows, making her an extremely adept assassin, hired by the wealthiest of the citizens, including the Empress on occasion, though no one knew exactly who she was or what she looked like. She kept her identity secret from everyone until she was gifted an Elemental concubine in payment for a job. Falling in love with Baast, Stygia grew sickened at the mistreatment of the Elementals, as well as the cruelty imposed on the general population, and came to believe the only way to change things was to overthrow the empire. Along with the region's biggest crime boss, an Undine named Aigua, a merchant Sylph named Sirocco, and the city's most notorious brothel owner, a Chthonic named Lurra, they began to formulate a rebellion among the hidden Elementals. It was also easy to gather human followers in a population growing resentful of Alameada's iron grip."

Cassius made a small sound then, a little whimper of protest, though she didn't speak, clearly struggling to honor Torva's request of no questions. Keagan, Ashley, and Lyria all had matching expressions of bemused dismay. Shay suspected her own expression was very similar.

"Tensions rose, revolution was in the air, and as Alameada felt her power slip away, she was determined to crush any support for the rebels once and for all. Ordering her generals to charge the stones, sacrificing dozens of valuable Elemental slaves to power them, she used the Primal Stone to activate them simultaneously. But she had never before utilized all the stones at the same time over such a distance. Before she could stop the situation, the stones somehow became linked, feeding upon each other. The Sylph Stone linked to the Undine Stone, creating a massive hurricane in Lurrera that spread over the entire northeast and remained stationary for weeks. The Chthonic Stone, linked to the Salamas Stone, triggered a spontaneous volcanic eruption along a mountain chain that spread lava and ash over the coast of Urodela. The Undine Stone, linked to the Chthonic Stone, sent an unstoppable lahar along the entire length of the River Anemoi, and finally, the Salamas Stone, linked with the Sylph Stone, caused firestorms up and down the western coast of Aquas.

"Stygia, along with her companions, attacked the royal palace to stop Alameada from destroying everything. It required all of them to get past her royal guards, kill Alameada, who had been driven insane at this point, and finally, using their abilities as one, they shattered the Primal Stone, sacrificing their own lives in the process. The backlash of the stone's destruction leveled the area, even sinking it in places. Over the centuries, it eventually filled with water and became the Lernaean Swamps. The Element Stones, nullified by the destruction of the Primal Stone, were left behind in the ruins of the crown cities."

Torva fixed her gaze on Keagan. "There's also a recent discovery in Tannehill's journal that five centuries later, the first queen of the Five Nations, Heratherus, fought her way through the Echidna Wilderness and recovered one of the stones, intending to use it to defend her new capital of Naiad against any possible invasion, but apparently she couldn't make it work. Perhaps because she didn't know what it needed, or more plausibly, she wasn't willing to sacrifice Elementals in order to power it. It may or may not have been entombed with her upon her death, but it could be why the Shadow Lord sent the wraiths there."

For several minutes, silence reigned as Torva sat nervously, and the others absorbed what they had heard.

"Do you believe any of this?" Cassius finally asked in a very small voice.

"If you had asked me a day ago, I'd have said that some of the artifacts I've uncovered in my digs might substantiate some tiny portions of Tannehill's theory, while the rest was just wild speculation," Torva said carefully. "But I've just spent the past few hours studying what I believe to be the Undine Stone, so let's just say I'm becoming more open to the possibility of more truth than myth existing here." She glanced at Keagan. "You say the stone used on you was laced with ruby and glowed red? That had to be the Salamas stone."

"How could we not know any of this?" Keagan burst out. She seemed on the edge of tears. Shay slipped her arm around her waist, beneath the level of the table, hidden from view, offering what physical comfort she could. "It's completely different from everything we've been taught."

"Actually, that part makes total sense," Ashley said, seeming thoughtful. Of them all, she seemed the least affected. "Imagine the aftermath of all that. You either escaped a massive disaster by some kind of luck, good or ill, or you lived so far away, you had no clue what was going on. The entire ruling government was wiped out in a single day, along with all the major cities and most of the surrounding area. Who's left to tell what actually happened? All you can do is try to pick up the pieces, and as time goes by, you make up stories to explain how the civilization that once heavily populated large areas of your nation had been completely destroyed. The victors write history. Or, in this case, the survivors. And people in shock tend to make shit up. Explains the five separate religions that developed, as well. Why would a null worship a Goddess of Flame, after all, or a God of Water? It probably started out as just honoring their sacrifice and became more complex over time."

"So we didn't nearly destroy the world." Keagan sounded lost. Shay remembered that she had made many of her life decisions based on the history she had learned at the Academy.

"But we did, in a way," Ashley said. "Elemental abilities fueled the disasters. But in our version, we're in control—misguided villains on one side, great heroes on the other, waging righteous war rather than helpless victims fed to the stones at the whim of some mad woman. At the whim of a *null*."

"Even if most of your story is true, none of it explains us in the Shadow Lands or the Paths," Shay said quietly. "Stygia...our Stygia... certainly didn't die in Aquas. Assuming it referred to the same being, the Lady is the one who requested that we in the Shadow Lands help the Elementals rebuild the world. That's recorded in our historical chronicles, and they date back millennia. She's existed far longer than your timeline, long before this Empress or any of these events."

Torva appeared completely avaricious. "Do you think I could see those chronicles?"

"You'll have to ask the Elders," Shay said. "We're having dinner with two of them tonight. You're welcome to come along."

"Lurra couldn't be a brothel owner," Cassius said, brokenly. "How would such a person become a Goddess?"

"A brothel owner wouldn't," Ashley said with unexpected gentleness. "But a courageous woman who sacrificed herself to save the world? That's someone worthy of building a faith around. They all were, however humble their origins might have been." When had Ashley become the voice of reason for them? Things had truly turned on their head now.

Cassius put her face in her hands, obviously not comforted. Of all of them, she was the most devout, Shay knew. Always taking time to pray before going to bed or murmuring grace before eating. This theory would shake her the deepest. She might even decide not to believe any of it. Shay herself wasn't sure how much to accept, except that a lot of it fit together, especially considering all they'd discovered during their adventures to this point.

"Was there much mention of the Shadow Lord in there?" Keagan said. "Any clue to his identity?"

Torva reached down to her bag and pulled out Tannehill's journal, flipping through it until she found the page she wanted. "About six years ago, a patron began to appear, offering gold for prewar research.

Suddenly, Tannehill's speculation and personal observations began to solidify into one singular theory, the one I just related to you, as if he was discovering more tangible evidence to support it, which he could do only if he was conducting actual digs." She lifted her eyes to meet Keagan's. "The patron was referred to as Lord Darvus."

"Darvus?" Cassius took her hands away from her face, her expression clearing as if she were surfacing from a deep fog. "I know the name." As everyone looked at her, she seemed to shake herself slightly. "I mean, the Darvus I know is a prominent landowner in the south, along with his two eldest sons, who also have holdings. It's possible his other offspring had to go north at some point just to have holdings themselves."

Torva nodded. "The term Shadow Lord began to appear two years ago, with lots of references to Lurrera, as if Tannehill had been supervising a dig there." She shook her head. "But word usually gets around the community as to who's digging where. I've never heard of any sites in the Chimera Wastelands. I don't know how you'd conduct one anyway, with all the storms that hit there."

"We think all of this is deliberately being kept quiet," Keagan said. "Particularly since it involves missing people." She paused, swallowed visibly. "Any mention of Elementals being sacrificed?"

"Just in the past tense," Torva said somberly. "A thousand years ago. As I said, Professor Tannehill was a good man. I don't think he would tolerate anything like that."

"He might not have been aware of it," Ashley said. "It's amazing what we don't see when we don't want to."

"Well, at least we have a name now," Keagan said. "It's a start."

"There's something else," Lyria said. It was the first time she had spoken in a while, and the rest of them turned to her. She appeared unusually grave, and Shay felt a qualm in the pit of her stomach.

"What?" Keagan asked, her tone sharp. It seemed she realized it immediately and gestured apologetically toward her.

Lyria acknowledged her with a nod and then looked at Cassius. "The stone used on us in Amane wasn't laced with ruby crystal, and it didn't give off a red light. It was laced with agate, and the light it gave off was a brilliant white. I remember that."

Cassius's breath caught audibly. "Oh," she said in a small voice. "She's right. It was."

"So he already had the Sylph Stone." Torva looked thoughtful. "Was it recovered from Lurrera? The warrior queen had to have retrieved the Salamas Stone from the Wilderness. The wraiths must have taken it from her tomb. Though how would they know how to use it?" She looked at Keagan. "You say these objects absorbed your abilities only temporarily?"

"They returned after almost a week. I'm not sure what that means for the stone, and how long it would store the energy."

"Permanent absorption must mean taking it all, the life force as well. They may not have figured out how to do that."

"Yet," Shay said, her tone cold and hard. "They don't know how to do it *yet*."

XXIV

The moon in the western sky had not yet set when they gathered near the obelisk a few days later. The air was fresh and cool, damp with dew. Keagan sat easily on Vesi, as she checked to see everyone was settled with their new mounts. The big black stallion danced under Cassius, seeming eager to get started, while Torva looked about as comfortable on the dappled gray mare as she would probably ever be. The horse Shay had chosen for her was very phlegmatic, slow to react and bore her burden with little notice. That wouldn't necessarily be an advantage in a fight, but at least Keagan knew it wouldn't take off with the historian. She was less sure about Ashley's sorrel. She was prancing in place as excitedly as Cassius's horse, eager to run.

Shay stood by Onyx, fussing over a bit of tack, last-minute preparation before mounting. Despite her apprehension at the upcoming mission, Keagan felt a small smile crease her lips as she looked at her, emotion getting the better of her professionalism.

The dinner with Shay's parents had turned out to be as awkward and disturbing and wonderful as she could have hoped and dreaded. Awkward due to the stories that Ashley insisted on telling Diana and Calvin in great detail about Keagan's days in the Academy. Disturbing because Keagan had been constantly aware of Shay's parents watching her every move, undoubtedly judging her suitability, or lack thereof, for their daughter.

And wonderful, because aside from her self-consciousness, they had been unfailingly kind, giving her a glimpse of what being part of a family might be like. Diana had even confided at one point, as they were in the kitchen getting dessert, that Shay had never brought someone home to meet them before tonight. Keagan didn't bother to volunteer that her presence in Sombra hadn't been entirely voluntary. That they had all simply ended up in the Shadow Lands because it was the most convenient path to take.

Literal as well as figurative path, of course. They were about to take a new Path to Aether. From there, they would immediately be on the

Path leading to Boden. There would be no time lag to Aether and only four hours' difference in Boden. Hardly noticeable.

"Why are we starting so damned early?" Ashley asked.

She was dressed in her new leathers, a deep chocolate brown, rather than Rider black, tight trousers in knee-high boots, laced up the front, and a sleeveless tunic cut low at the breast over a long-sleeved turquoise shirt. She also had a heavy leather jacket with a fur collar for colder temperatures. Even though Keagan didn't find it all that cool, Ashley was huddled in it against the early morning damp. Cassius wore similar clothes in a lighter shade of brown, doe colored, while her shirt was a rich, forest green, with chaps over her denim pants. She wasn't wearing a cloak, but one was tucked in her saddlebags as required.

"Because it's easier to open an entry large enough for all of us while it's still dark," Shay explained dryly as she gracefully mounted Onyx. "It would be a lot harder to find a big enough shadow for all of us in broad daylight."

"The Shadow Lord didn't need any darkness or shadows in Arias when he escaped," Lyria said.

"Yeah. I don't make entries that way," Shay said, coolly enough that Lyria gave an apologetic gesture. "All right, if we're ready, you can put on your shades."

Keagan had no idea where the Elders had come up with goggles similar to what the Shadow Lord had possessed, tinted purple lenses in a leather strap that wrapped around the head, allowing them to see while in the Shadows. Apparently they had been stored in a cabinet in some dusty corner of the library, along with other artifacts. Shay had asked about them several times and never quite got a straight answer about their origin, other than they had always been there and simply not needed until now. What other items might exist within other libraries in the Shadow Lands? Hopefully, the Undine Stone would be kept in a more secure location.

"I can't see a thing," Ashley said after she slipped hers on.

"Out here, you're not supposed to," Shay said. "According to the Elders, they'll activate once we're in the Shadows. Remember, even though you can now see and you're on Shadow mounts, you need to ride as quietly as possible. This is a well-trodden Path, and its markings are strong, but wraiths can appear anywhere, especially if Darvus is somehow directing them." Keagan, blinded by the goggles, sensed rather than heard Shay move up beside her. "Unlike the others, your cull won't be able to see," she added in a low tone that only Keagan could hear. "You'll be the one guiding him. Be calm and confident in your directions, and he will be, too."

"I understand," Keagan said. "Let's go."

As they entered the Shadow Realm, Keagan's vision returned, though there wasn't a great deal to see. Only an impossibly flat plain without a horizon, disappearing into the greenish murk that surrounded them. She could see the markings to either side of them, glowing with an eerie radiance, symbols carved into the hard stone pavement every hundred yards or so. Protective glyphs, Shay had called them, repelling the creatures of the Shadows from the Path.

The ride to Aether barely took any time at all, and before Keagan had time to be bothered by her surroundings, they were exiting by the obelisk located in the northwest part of Aether. Hastily, Keagan pulled off her shades, looking around eagerly at a city she had known only in legends and stories. It didn't seem much different than the Clan town, she decided after a few minutes, slightly disappointed. Much larger, of course, but the important buildings were only a few stories higher, and several more obelisks were visible, one a league or so away to the north, towering over the surrounding structures, another to the east, one to the south, and then a fourth to the west. All led to the crown cities of the four Elemental nations. At the other points of the compass—northeast, southeast, and southwest—stood three smaller obelisks exactly like the one they were next to, undoubtedly leading to the other clan towns.

"Well, that's disappointing," Ashley muttered. "I expected...more."

Keagan didn't respond, but she agreed. Though, had some wraiths shown up while they were riding the Path, it would have become more than exciting enough.

"We're not far," Shay said, pointing. "The Terras marker is over there."

"No chance for sightseeing?" Cassius asked. She kept Gault tightly reined as he snorted and pawed the ground.

"I think the Elders would appreciate you not staying in the Shadow Lands any longer than necessary," Shay told her, not unkindly.

"Can we see the Shadow School, at least?" Lyria asked.

"It's in the southern part of the city," Shay said. "It'd be an hour out of our way. Maybe next time."

If there was a next time, Keagan thought as they rode through the quiet, early morning streets to the Terras obelisk. They entered without a fuss, and while the ride to Boden took a little longer, it seemed as if they were exiting the Shadows by the crown city's southern obelisk in a manner of minutes. The other trips had seemed to take so much longer, and Keagan wondered if it was because they'd been on ancient Paths, or because her impaired senses had distorted her sense of time.

Or maybe it was just much faster when you could ride at a full canter rather than stumble blindly on foot beside equally blind horses, she reminded herself.

"Do you know where the marshal office is?" she asked.

"Not a clue." Shay shrugged. "Never needed it."

"I know," Cassius said. "This way. Downtown."

Following her, they wound through the increasing traffic of people starting their day. The thrum of the crown city surrounded Keagan, almost like a living thing, and she began to feel more comfortable in her skin. As they rode, she was aware of bemused looks directed their way. The sight of four Elementals, one human, and a Shadow Rider, all mounted on what were clearly purebred Aether horses and displaying prominent badges on their chests, would probably be unusual enough to attract attention anywhere in the Five Nations.

Their new badges, supplied by Queen Chiesa, were comprised of a gold marshal symbol etched against the backdrop of the silver royal insignia, indicating they rode for both the law and the crown. Keagan had never experienced the power it implied. Would it be honored in the more remote parts of the world?

The marshal office in Boden was located on a side street, away from the main thoroughfare, a tiny building with a rather shabby facing, worn brick stained by dust and dirt. They left the horses untied out front, as per Shay's instruction, even though it made Keagan uneasy, and went in, disturbing the officer on duty at the front desk, who looked as if he'd been dozing. It wasn't long before the shift change, Keagan knew, and clearly quiet at this early hour, but such a thing never would have happened in Aquas. His rank insignia was that of a constable, and she eyed him unfavorably as she presented her badge.

"Is your chief in yet?"

The officer, a redheaded young man with freckles and sleepy eyes, blinked at her badge, clearly befuddled. "What's that?" he asked.

"Badge of the crown," Keagan said, shortly. "I need to speak with your superior."

The door at the end of the room abruptly opened, and an older woman stepped out, stocky but fit, with sharp dark eyes and gray liberally streaking her short dark hair. An emblem on the left side of her vest identified her as the one in charge. Keagan swept past the constable at the front desk before he could object.

"Chief, I'm Keagan Riley," she said, reaching into her tunic to pull out an envelope. "The crown has dispatched my team and me on an important investigation. Here's my letter of authorization."

The woman looked taken aback, but she accepted the envelope and opened it, unfolding the sheet of paper inside and reading it silently. The letters had been written in Sombra and signed by Chief Abraham, Queen Chiesa, and the entire Ruling Council. It accorded Keagan complete authority in her investigation, along with the unmistakable implication that any hint of noncooperation would go very badly for the participants involved. All of them, including Torva, had a copy, granting them deputy status even though they weren't marshals.

The woman returned the letter. "What's all this about?" she asked, stepping back and gesturing to her office.

"The kidnapping and possible murder of Elementals," Keagan said as they entered. She glanced at the nameplate on the desk. "Chief Wallace, we'll require the services of your sketch artist. We need renderings of the suspects by end of day."

Wallace took a seat behind her desk, looking at her with interest. "You have suspects?" She folded her hands and rested them on the desk. "I've heard about the kidnappings. Sounds like a mess, but why take it out of marshal hands?" That she was displeased with the latter was evident.

Keagan's jaw tightened. "There may be marshal involvement, however tangential."

"How so?" Keagan detected a decided edge in the woman's tone.

"We'll know more after the renderings." Keagan gestured toward her team, who had crowded into the tiny office behind her. "Shadow Rider Shay Kendrith, Quartermaster Cassius Suolo, and Scout Lyria Hawke. They're witnesses. They'll be sitting with your artist."

Wallace looked sour. "Apparently, we don't have a choice."

"Listen, we're not interested in taking credit for any arrests so much as we are in results," Keagan said. "Think of it this way. Your office will have a few days' jump on all the rest. It'll take time for copies of the suspect's faces to be distributed throughout the Five Nations."

Wallace blinked. "All five?"

"It crosses borders and involves us all," Keagan told her. She paused. "The artist?"

Wallace stared at her a moment and then nodded. "Packer!" she bellowed.

The officer from the front desk scrambled into the office. "Yes, ma'am."

"Go find Darnell," she said. "Get him in here."

He hesitated. "Ma'am?"

"Is there a problem?" Keagan said, putting some weight in her tone.

Packer looked uneasily between Keagan and his boss. "It's just that he's usually not up so early."

"You mean he's still drunk," Ashley said dryly from where she was leaning against the wall, doing her best to look dangerous and official.

The facial expression of both Boden marshals verified the accuracy of Ashley's presumption. Keagan let out her breath in a huff. "Just get him here," she said, annoyed. "Sober him up."

"The day shift will arrive in a couple of hours," Wallace said. "Do I need to call any in early?"

"No. Just the artist," Keagan said. "Until we can show you what these people look like, there's no point." She looked at Ashley. "You and Torva take the horses and find stables and lodging. We're here for the night."

Shay held up her hand. "Take this," she said, handing Ashley some Aether-marked tokens. "You'll find stables by the river that cater to Rider mounts and an inn not far from that. Also check with the local Rider office. Any messages for us would have been left there."

"After the horses are settled, go to city hall and get a list of all the landowners in the northeast," Keagan said. "Check to see if a Darvus is on it."

Ashley accepted the tokens, nodded at Keagan, and took Torva with her. Keagan was pleased by her willingness to follow instructions without arguing every three minutes. She really had grown up in the years since the Academy.

It took an hour before the artist showed up, stumbling in beside Packer, a scruffy, unshaven scarecrow who wasn't a marshal, of course, just someone very good at drawing what was described. While Shay, Cassius, and Lyria spent the rest of the morning huddled in a room with him, trying to come up with reasonable facsimiles of the people involved, Keagan went over the details of the case with Wallace and her officers, including the entire night shift that had returned from patrol and all the newly arrived day crew.

Keagan decided she shouldn't be surprised at the limited number of officers. Although a crown city, Boden represented a nation of farmers. Those who followed other professions like mining, or looked for more exciting lifestyles, tended to migrate to cities in Aquas or Urodela. There was little unemployment here. Even the most unskilled could find some form of labor on the massive farms that fed the world, especially here in the south, where it remained warm all year round, producing a wide range of vegetables and fruits, while cattle still needed to be tended and milked. The nightlife was practically nonexistent, and more temples than taverns lined the streets. Crime was minimal, even the low end of theft and disorderly conduct.

It occurred to Keagan that if Lurra had indeed been a brothel owner, as speculated by Tannehill, she was probably rolling her eyes at the conservative and stringently moral society that had sprung up around her legend. Of course, if Tannehill had been correct, that also meant the god Aigua was some kind of crime boss. Keagan wasn't sure how she felt about that possibility. In truth, she was still wrapping her mind around the whole story, believing some of it, rejecting other parts, but unsure how she would make the determination in either case.

Keagan considered herself religious in the sense that it comforted her to believe Aigua was indeed a god who looked out for the Undine and the people of Aquas, but she'd never really considered that he might have been an actual historical figure. That he might have existed as a person who had all the small joys and hurts of anyone. She didn't know if that possibility should make her less faithful or more so. Shay, on the other hand, had always considered her Lady to be real, to be someone who actively looked out for the people of the Shadow Lands. Who looked out for the whole world and helped in a tangible way for people to recover from horrible disaster. This whole situation probably solidified her beliefs, in a way. They hadn't really talked about it. Maybe they were afraid to.

When the others finally exited the room with several sketches depicting their suspects, Keagan was more than ready for lunch. She glanced over the renderings, judging them to be remarkably accurate, at least as far as the Shadow Lord was concerned. She'd had a pretty good look at him during the fight in Arias and chosen not to work with the artist because she wanted to judge the final product objectively. Whatever the artist's personal failings, he was pretty good at his job.

"Do you recognize either of these?" Keagan asked, handing copies of the sketches to Wallace, who frowned as she studied them.

"Maybe," she said. "The woman in particular. Feels like I met her somewhere. It'll come to me."

Keagan nodded. "We're headed north in the morning," she said. "Until then, if any new information comes in, please contact us at the inn."

Outside, Keagan fell into step with Shay as they walked toward the river. "I think we should begin as close to the Chimera Wastelands as we can," she said. "If Darvus has holdings near there, we can surmise that he may have habitually explored the ruins between storms."

"I'll see which Path runs the closest," Shay said.

They discovered Torva and Ashley in a tavern beside the inn Shay had recommended. They had already eaten lunch and were sipping tea as they waited for them. The other four of them ordered their own lunch and caught each other up as they waited for the food to arrive.

"A couple of messages were waiting for you at the Rider office," Torva said, passing Keagan two envelopes addressed to her—one small, the other large and thick.

Keagan ripped open the first and skimmed the contents of the letter.

"Abraham reports that the Amane site was deserted. According to the supplies that remained, they must have left in a hurry, though they didn't leave a trail, which is odd. The crown has brought in more historians to further research both sites, along with marshal forensic teams to search the surrounding area for..." She was uncomfortably reminded that several Elementals were still missing. "To search for bodies."

"Which historians?" Torva asked, looking positively envious.

"Doesn't say." Keagan tried not to wince. "In their initial report to the crown, the historians were considerably upset at how the ruins had been treated. Something about improper excavation technique. Apparently, at the Anemoi site, multiple artifacts were disturbed, with no record of where they'd originally been found."

"These people are animals," Torva said.

Keagan exchanged a look with the others, knowing full well they were the "animals" responsible for the disturbance in Arias. But then, who knew digging through cabinets and piling their finds in the middle of the floor in front of the throne wasn't displaying "proper excavation techniques"? She noticed Shay put her hand up to her chest unconsciously, no doubt on the maps she'd confiscated that were tucked in her tunic. She made a mental note to tell her later that it was a very obvious tell and she should try to curtail it. She opened the second envelope, flipping through the contents quickly, recognizing the official documents.

"I thought they wanted to keep this quiet," Cassius said. "That won't happen with this many people involved."

"The crown will release some kind of cover story," Ashley said. "Something about new archaeological finds, and make it boring enough that the average person won't care." She nodded at Keagan. "What's in that envelope?"

Keagan cleared her throat. "Personal files on the Darvus family." She paused. "And files on all of you. Abraham making sure I know who I'm working with."

While the rest looked vaguely offended, Lyria perked up. "I have a file?"

"Just your Academy records," Keagan told her and tried not to smile as her face fell. "Employment records. Also, there are seven arrest reports." She looked at Ashley. "Really?"

"Misunderstandings," Ashley said haughtily. "Years ago."

"All seven times?"

Ashley lifted her chin and didn't deign to answer.

"And you were never cuffed?"

"They wouldn't have dared." Ashley's eyes narrowed. "I am a Van Vuur."

Keagan sighed. "Of course you are."

XXV

The next day, they took a Path to Mustus, the most northeastern settlement in Terras that could afford to pay a Shadow scout to link them directly to Boden. From there, they rode toward the next town, Sporco. The rolling hills and extensive farmland were shaded a bright spring green, a cool breeze flowing through the trees bordering the well-traveled roads linking the settlements. They encountered several caravans traveling south, carrying hothouse produce to Boden, trains of several heavy wagons pulled by huge dray horses, the fruits, grains, and vegetables kept fresh in cold containers powered by charged energy crystals. Protected by armed riders that flanked the long trains, the drivers eyed them suspiciously as they rode past, particularly at the Rider leathers. Shay was used to such scrutiny, even if the others weren't.

Was this method of transporting goods how it had been done in the old Empire? For that matter, when had such things been discovered? Shay knew the crystals were mined mostly in Urodela. When had someone decided the otherwise unremarkable chunks of rock could be polished, refined, and then charged by Elementals to power everyday items? As slaves, had Elementals used their abilities in a similar fashion at the direction of their owners? An enforced task rather than a menial job that today's low-level Elementals often complained about even as they readily spent gold that the caravan drivers and loaders could never hope to see in their hardworking professions. And how the hell did it work in the Shadow Lands, where no Elementals lived?

This whole experience forced Shay to think about so many things that she had simply taken for granted until now. Her head hurt.

She glanced over at Keagan riding beside her. She had on her marshal expression, serious and focused, and Shay let herself wonder what life for them would be like once this mission ended. Even if they did find a way to stay together, could she go back to being a courier? It had its share of excitement, but nothing like this. Successfully delivering a diplomatic pouch or a bag of jewels certainly didn't provide her with the same sense of accomplishment that protecting people and riding for justice did. Shay promised herself that she would apply to the marshals. Maybe she wouldn't get in, but at least she had other options. She also suspected she'd be the first Rider to ever do so and wondered what kind of ripples she would cause.

They reached Sporco two days later. It was a sleepy hamlet next to a lazy river, a gathering point for all the farms in the area. The market had all sorts of fresh food available, including incredible breads and cheeses. While Keagan checked in with the local marshal office, Shay and the others topped off their supplies with some fresh fruit. By the time Keagan had returned, they had eaten half of the strawberries, standing beneath a tree, savoring the big, sweet fruit, hands stained with juice, which caused Keagan to eye them skeptically.

"Want some?" Ashley asked, holding out a few. "I don't think I've ever had such fresh ones. Picked this morning."

"Did the marshals have anything to say?" Shay looked at Keagan fondly as she accepted the berries and showed her own pleased surprise when she bit into them.

"Actually, yes. They identified both suspects," Keagan said casually.

Everyone stared at her. She appeared to be swallowing a smile along with the berries, and her eyes glinted as she spoke. "As soon as I showed them the sketches, they identified this 'Shadow Lord' as the youngest son of the Darvus landholder here in the north. Apparently, after graduating the Academy, Arthur went on to college in Naiad, where he was a student of Tannehill."

"So that's how they met," Shay said. "But how did he go from student to walking the Shadows?"

"Perhaps something he learned as a student," Torva said.

"And the woman? Olive?" Cassius asked.

Keagan looked somber. "Constable Olive Magnum, a local marshal," she said. "Believed to have interrupted a robbery at a warehouse, been taken by thieves, and presumed killed by them about five years ago, though no body was ever found, just a great deal of blood at the scene."

"Thieves?"

"An entire case of Elemental cuffs was taken, along with several valuables," Keagan said. "They kept the incident under wraps, mostly because we don't want it known that we can remove Elemental abilities when we arrest them, but had it been kicked upstairs, we might be further ahead in the investigation at this point. Or maybe it had, and after five years with nothing surfacing, the last investigating officer could have thought it irrelevant. That the thieves had made a mistake and grabbed something useless to them."

"Why would a marshal steal those cuffs unless a plan was already in place?" Ashley asked. "Which means this woman knew either Tannehill or Darvus prior to five years ago. Has this been going on for that long?"

"A connection to track down, in any case," Keagan said. "In the meantime, we're headed east. The son was given land by his father for his own homestead. It's possible our suspects fled there after abandoning Amane."

"Us against all of them?" Ashley smiled without humor. "I'll take those odds."

"How far?" Shay said.

"A few days from here," Keagan said. "Near the border of the Wastelands."

"Well, that explains how he might have discovered Lurrera," Cassius said. "Are we leaving immediately?"

"The sooner we're on the road, the sooner we're there," Keagan said, then looked at Torva, their historian. "Expect to rough it for the next few nights. There's not much between here and there."

She appeared a trifle apprehensive. "It's not the roughing it," she said. "I do that all the time. I just don't think I'll be much good in a fight if it comes to it."

"Lyria needs to refresh her training," Keagan said. "We'll take measure of your skills at the same time. If they're not up to a certain standard, we'll hold you back in any fight. If it doesn't go well, we'll need someone to tell the Council, anyway."

"That used to be my job," Lyria said, proudly. "Now I'm the scout."

"Speaking of which, are you up to try flying this afternoon?" Keagan asked. "We'll need you to transport any important messages."

Lyria's eyes lit up. "I'll be ready."

"We'll see," Keagan said, not promising anything. She'd been keeping Lyria on the ground until she was more certain her and Cassius's abilities had returned. She hadn't wanted to take the chance of Lyria possibly losing form in midair, and it was a measure of Lyria's regard and admiration for Keagan that she'd obeyed. But it had been a week, and both she and Cassius should be at full strength by now.

"We can find a camp a little early tonight, spend some time training before sundown," Shay suggested.

As they rode out of Sporco, Shay slipped to the rear of the group so that she was riding with Torva, wanting to see how she and her new mount were getting along. Torva rode competently enough, but without that special sort of connection that true riders enjoyed with their horses. Not that her mount seemed to mind. The old gray mare was even slower than Keagan's cull, and so long as she had her share of fodder at the end of the day, she apparently didn't care what she was carrying.

"Rider." Torva nodded formally as Onyx fell into step with her. He tossed his head at the laggard pace, mouthing the bit.

"Sie Lynch." Shay responded in an equally formal manner, amused. Torva winced. "Uh, sorry. Torva is fine. You're Shay, right?"

"I am."

"So this whole thing is crazy. Or am I wrong?"

"You're not wrong," Shay said, laughing a little. "To think, only a few weeks ago, I was going about my business, with no idea about how things really worked in the world."

"That's a little like being a historian. You have to give up any preconceptions because you're always learning things that turn them upside down. Otherwise, you keep trying to force discoveries to fit what you think you know and perpetuate the myth."

"So why become an archaeologist as well?"

"Because while we think we know what happened in the past, history often gets blurred, distorted in the telling. Only by digging do we discover what really happened. What's actually true."

"And you want to know what's true."

"It's the most important thing."

"I suppose so." Shay glanced over at her. "Speaking of which, this stone Darvus is using to absorb abilities. He mentioned something about a 'ritual.' Any information in Tannehill's journal about that?"

"Ritual?" Torva asked, looking baffled. "No. I found no mention of that. It sounds fanciful. Like magic or something."

"Yeah," Shay said. "Maybe he thinks he can somehow transfer the abilities to himself."

"I don't see how," Torva said. "But then, I'm not entirely sure how they were able to take away Elemental abilities in the first place."

Shay grew sober. "If they try to use the tactic in any battle, you and I will be the only ones unaffected. Have you any training with weapons at all?"

"I know how to use a crossbow," Torva said. "But mostly for hunting food. I've only used it against people on two occasions, bandits and petty thieves, and honestly, it only scared them away rather than hurt any of them. I've certainly never tried to fight a trained mercenary or, worse, an actual Elemental."

"Well, apparently, this Elemental is pretty weak," Shay said, then remembered her conversation with Keagan in Sombra about what a level-one Undine could still do to a person. What could a corrupt level-one Chthonic do to someone's body if they put their mind to it? Turn the calcium in the bones to dust? "Still, we'll get you a crossbow and set up some practice time for you. Stick to cover. You could distract someone, at least, should the need arise."

"Do you think we'll be going into the Wastelands to their original dig site?"

"I don't know," Shay said, aware that Torva couldn't wait to see an actual historical ruin. It was probably the only reason she'd agreed to accompany them. That, and whatever pressure her uncle and the Council had brought to bear on her. "I hope not. The storms there sound very unpleasant."

"They found a way."

"Yeah," Shay said. "Unfortunately, they did."

The sun was still high in the sky when Keagan called for a halt, choosing a meadow next to a small creek. While Shay and Cassius tended to the horses and Torva and Ashley set up their tents, Keagan and Lyria ascended the nearby hill. As Shay finished watering Onyx, she looked up to see a small figure soaring above the crest, the sight catching her breath in her throat. She didn't care if it was gliding rather than flying. The sheer freedom of it filled her with longing. To ride the winds so easily, she thought with envy. What was that like?

When Lyria and Keagan finally returned to the camp, Lyria was flushed, grinning widely, while Keagan looked satisfied. Obviously, Lyria was back to where she should be. Then it was Cassius's turn to show how quickly she could excavate pits. If one was paying attention and realized what she was doing, Shay noted, she could get out of range before it opened under her, but the way Cassius did it, going from the bottom up, her opponent tended to drop six feet down into a narrow pit before realizing they were in trouble. It was impressive. And not a little frustrating. It took both Cassius and Keagan to haul Shay out of a hole she hadn't avoided, and in the meantime, she had been completely helpless, stuck awkwardly in the earth like a cork in a bottle, elbows clamped to her sides, impotent and fuming. She had to bathe in the creek afterward to get rid of all the dirt, and at this time of year, this far north, it was bloody cold.

After setting up some targets, Lyria and Torva worked on improving their accuracy with their crossbows. They weren't bad, but then, most people weren't. Theoretically, anyone could pick up a crossbow and use it, firing from greater distances than the average archer. That's what made them superior to mere bows when it came to outfitting an army. But they were slower. A skilled archer could notch and fire three arrows in the time it took to crank in a bolt. Plus, the mechanical, moving metal parts sometimes broke or seized, and they required replacement not always readily available. The ammo was somewhat specialized as well, short stubby bolts with metal tips, a supply limited to what could be carried in a belt quiver. A bow required only line secured in a pouch and a nearby tree to make a new one, along with its replacement ammunition.

Torva tended to shoot low, but with Cassius's patient teaching, she was improving with every lesson. Lyria, on the other hand, seemed to get worse the longer she participated. Meanwhile, Ashley had regained a certain amount of form with her bow, hitting close to the center of the target on eight of her ten shots, looking disgusted at the two near misses. By the end of their session, Keagan professed satisfaction, though she had a little furrow between her brows that Shay recognized as concern.

As they shared a meal around the campfire, the last of the sun's rays glinting off the meadows around them, Shay tried to show support without being obvious, pressing her knee against Keagan's. She wasn't entirely sure Keagan understood the intent, but the return pressure was steady and comforting. Later, lying snuggled together in their tent, Shay ran her fingertips along Keagan's forehead, smoothing out the lines.

"Worried?"

Keagan managed a wan smile. "I'd feel better with a month's more practice for both Lyria and Torva. Maybe we won't run into trouble before then."

"One can always hope." Shay kissed her, lingering over her lips, basking in her warm breath wafting over her own. "It'll be all right."

"Promise?"

"Always."

Slipping her hand along her flank, Shay pulled her closer, deepening the kiss. She felt Keagan's fingers twine in her hair, holding her head.

"I'm so glad you're with me," Keagan whispered.

"I wouldn't be anywhere else," Shay said.

And as she lost herself in Keagan, she knew that statement was profoundly true. She wouldn't go back to being a courier or take any job that would keep her away from Keagan again.

XXVI

The farm appeared empty, at least from their vantage point on the ridge overlooking the small valley containing the homestead. They didn't even see any sign of animals, domestic or wild. Keagan felt a frisson of anxiety as she brushed back the strands of hair that whipped into her face. The wind had steadily increased over the past few days, and she wondered if it blew all the time here. To the east, a dark, foreboding cloud bank loomed, a constant presence that made the hair stand up on the back of her neck.

Standing beside her, Cassius released a huff. "I've never seen a farm like this. The buildings are so odd."

"It appears the house and barn are built right into the hill over there," Keagan said. "They must extend back into the earth. Like bunkers."

"Smart, I suppose. Means they won't blow away, which is good, because that storm doesn't look promising." Cassius regarded the approaching clouds with an uneasy expression.

"No. It doesn't." Keagan glanced over her shoulder. "Anyone sensing anything?"

Lyria raised her hand, testing the steady current of air, eyes going white. "Strong," she said. "Heavy."

"Heavy how?"

Lyria squinted, shaking her head slightly. "A storm building, but not just what we can see. It's like something more's coming behind it. A lot more."

"This area will have more storms than the rest of the nation," Cassius said. "Not as strong as in the Wilderness, but they hit here all the time." She shook her head, looking perplexed. "You'd have to be desperate to want to stake claim to this land."

"I don't think Darvus is worried about still claiming this," Ashley said. "It doesn't look like anyone's been here in a while. Half those sheds are falling down. And was that a barn? Though it looks like it burned down rather than blew down. Lightning strike, maybe?"

"We still have to check it out," Keagan said, resting her hand on the hilt of her sword. "Lyria, give us an overview. Torva, you wait here and keep an eye out from the high ground. The rest of us will sweep the area. Two groups. Shay, you're with Ash. Search the outbuildings. Cassius, you and I will take the barn. We'll meet at the house." She caught Shay's eye and received a minuscule nod, though the slight quirk of her lips indicated she wasn't entirely pleased to be paired with Ashley, or perhaps it was just that they weren't staying together. Shay liked fighting side by side with her.

Lyria crouched slightly and then launched herself into the air. The blast of wind propelling her made the rest of them stagger back before they were able to catch themselves. It was an impressive sight, and Keagan swallowed a smile even as she thought the young woman was showing off a bit. As Shay and Ashley started down the right side of the hill toward the farm, Keagan drew her sword and moved to the left with Cassius.

Insects exploded into the air from the withered strands of old grain as they crossed the field laying fallow. It was hard to tell how long it had been since any crops had been tended, but it had to be more than a year. Cassius frowned as she reached down and touched the ground, eyes glowing green.

"If this guy's strength is in restoring soil, it hasn't been done here for ages," she said. "It's very poor. Depleted."

"Maybe farming's not in his blood," Keagan said. "After all, he went to a null school for another four years right after the Academy. Delaying the family's legacy perhaps? Resentful of the fact his abilities were perfect for growing crops and not much else?" As they neared the barn, she felt a certain trepidation that she had experienced before when she'd entered a homicide scene. She didn't know why she felt that way, but it was unmistakable, even though she had yet to determine anything had happened here beyond simple abandonment.

"Oh, Lurra," she heard Cassius murmur, and she stopped, looking over at her. Cassius's face had paled, and she was staring at the nearby corral.

"What?"

"Look at the pasture. How the grass grows better in some patches."

Keagan followed her gaze, her stomach tightening. In several rectangular areas in the pasture the turf was decidedly more lush than the rest of the grazing around them.

"The earth's been disturbed and replaced," Cassius said tightly. "Those areas have a lot more nutrients."

"Something's been buried," Keagan said.

"Or someone," Cassius said. "Ten someones."

"Can you tell if…" Keagan tried to imagine how Cassius's earth sense would work in this instance.

"No," Cassius said. "It might be animals. But the carbon and sulfur are within the parameters. And definitely the phosphorus. It's not really my specialty, but what's under there is organic and not a result of those particular patches being richer in natural nutrients."

"So, he may have buried ten sheep there. Or several family pets."

Cassius's mouth twisted. "Always the optimist."

"And if I asked you to excavate one?"

Exhaling with a huff, Cassius nodded. "I'll take the oldest. Hopefully, that will be less…" She paused. "Fleshy. More skeletal." She glanced back up the hill. "I'll get Torva to help me. She's used to digging things up."

"Lovely." Keagan left her to it, secure that however unpleasant the task, Cassius was up to it, and continued to the barn. It did extend some distance into the hill, a complete stable capable of holding several animals, but she discovered only moldering fodder and old manure, the air musty and still, unused for some time. There were tools but no weapons, and no indication of when the area might have been abandoned. Unsettled, she exited and saw Ashley just leaving an outbuilding. When she spotted Keagan, a shake of her head indicated she had found nothing of note inside. They both moved into the small courtyard that fronted the house where Shay was examining the front door. She glanced back to see the others crossing the yard and waited for them to join her before testing the doorknob.

"Cassius?"

"Checking out something in the corral," Keagan said shortly. She felt a whoosh of air and turned to see Lyria landing lightly in the middle of the yard. "Report," she said.

Lyria blinked at the brisk tone but responded promptly. "A trail heads off to the east. None of the fields or pastures appear to have been attended to recently. I saw herds of cattle and sheep to the northwest. They don't appear to belong to anyone. I think they've gone feral. The nearest farmstead is several leagues south. Really large, but built like this, structures set into the hillsides."

Shay wiggled the knob. "The door's locked. Do we break it down?"

"We have the authorization to do what we need," Keagan said. "Should I get Cassius? That's a pretty solid door."

"I could blast it open," Ashley suggested.

"And possibly bring down the interior?" Keagan glanced at her. "We can be more subtle than that, I hope."

Lyria stepped forward. "May I?"

Keagan was surprised and slightly amused when Lyria drew some small tools from her belt pouch and proceeded to jimmy the lock. "Now, where did you learn to do that?"

Lyria shrugged. "I like puzzles. A lock is just a puzzle."

"I bet that's what all the burglars say," Ashley said.

Lyria blushed, and Keagan fought back a smile. "With me," she said, entering the home. A staircase stood in front of her, indicating an upper level, with archways to the right and left, one to a kitchen and the other to what had been a dining area. Light from the large windows filtered through the motes of dust in the air. "Ash, you and Lyria take the upstairs. Shay and I will look down here."

Shay glanced around. "This is awfully small for a lord's house. The few I've been in have been huge, three or four stories, at least, ten or fifteen rooms per story, and with a lot more outbuildings and barns." She shrugged. "Of course, those were prosperous landholdings. This is literally just a hole in the ground."

"Which makes you wonder how he could be footing the bill for all this," Ashley said. "Of course, it might go back a ways. Could be a whole damn palace in here."

While Lyria and Ashley took the upper level, Keagan and Shay searched the main floor but didn't find much. The kitchen was neat but dusty, while the pantries were empty. The crystals powering the appliances and lamps were dull, requiring recharge. There were no more windows besides the few looking out at the courtyard, making the rest of the rooms almost as dark as the Shadow Realm. Their handheld torches flashed beams of light over rugged furnishings, simple and handmade. The living area held a couple of battered sofas and chairs and a large fireplace. By the bath at the rear, a single servant quarters was devoid of any furnishings at all. The library, containing a large desk and several full bookcases, appeared more promising. As Shay checked out the books, Keagan eagerly searched through the desk but found nothing beyond some paper clips and writing utensils. Even checking under the drawers yielded no hidden files or paperwork. Keagan lifted her head to meet Shay's disappointed gaze.

"He's cleaned out everything. You wouldn't even know he lived here."

They met the others back in the foyer. "Nothing upstairs," Ashley said. "Three bedrooms and two baths. All the crystals for the plumbing and heat are drained."

The front of the home creaked suddenly, shuddering as the wind moaned. Lyria glanced up, looking worried. "The storm's getting closer. Are we staying here or trying to outrun it west?"

"We need to check out that trail leading east," Keagan said. "We'll take shelter here until it passes."

"Beats tents in this weather." Ashley glanced out the nearest window. "What did you say Cassius was up to?"

Keagan managed not to wince, but it was a near thing. "Oh, yes, that. We better go see what she and Torva have discovered."

It was definitely human, as it turned out. Shay's face went grim, while Lyria looked rather green as they peered down into the open grave Cassius had excavated. Torva, showing little sign of disgust, gingerly prodded the body which, unfortunately, had yet to become completely skeletal, probably due to the tarp wrapped around it. Ashley made a muffled sound, putting her hand over her mouth.

"Been dead more than two years, possibly three," Torva said in a cool, level tone. Keagan appreciated the professionalism. She hadn't thought Torva's work would have required much recent grave digging.

Ashley cleared her throat, seeming to have difficulty doing so. "The emblem on the tunic. It's from the Hatteras mining company." She found something interesting to look at somewhere over to her left. "The insignia indicates he was a low-level Salamas." Her eyes suddenly narrowed. "Baast. There are more graves around us, aren't there?"

"Considering this disrupted earth held a body, I suspect the others do, as well." Cassius swallowed convulsively. "There are nine more. I hope you don't want me to dig those up, too?"

Keagan shook her head. "No, and we'll refill this one now that we know for sure what it is. A fully equipped forensic team needs to inspect this entire farm. Lyria, how close is that storm?"

Lyria, who had taken up position some distance from the grave after her initial look at its contents, lifted her head. "It will reach us tonight. Late, I think."

"Okay. I need to fill out a report. Can you make it back to Sporco before sunset?"

"As long I'm heading west, I'll stay well ahead of the storm. And frankly, the tail winds here will increase my speed. It'll take a lot longer to make it back, though."

"That's fine. I don't want you coming back until after this storm has passed," Keagan told her.

Lyria's face fell. "You're going on without me?"

"We'll probably be stuck here for a while. I think you can catch up soon enough. We'll leave a well-marked trail." Keagan paused. "I can trust you to do this? Take the report back to the marshal office and remain there until it's safe to come after us?"

Lyria's shoulders straightened. "Of course."

"Good. While I fill out the report, you and Ashley should replenish the crystals in the house." Keagan motioned to the grave. "Torva, anything else of note? Cause of death, maybe?"

Torva shook her head as she climbed out of the hole, aided by Cassius's not inconsiderable assistance, pulled up as easily as if she were a feather. She paused to give Cassius an odd look before responding to Keagan. "Well, it's not really my area of expertise. But there's no obvious sign. No open wounds in the flesh, no nicks or breaks to indicate stabbing or blunt force to the bones. I'd need to really study it to determine if it were disease."

"Fine," Keagan said. "Cassius?"

Cassius's eyes went solid green, and she waved her hands in a circular motion, the dirt that had been deposited to the side beginning to slide back into the hole, filling the grave until only a brown rectangular shape indicated what was there. After she finished, they all stood there a moment in unspoken unity, silent with heads bowed in acknowledgment of the Elemental's demise as well as for the others who might or might not be in the various patches of earth.

The wind was increasing considerably as they strode back to the house, and Keagan could feel the rush of moisture, heavy and dark, headed their way. She shivered and set her jaw against the uncomfortable feeling as she used the desk in the library to fill out three reports recounting what they had found and requesting further backup at the farm. By the time she finished, the lights had been restored, and she could hear the hum from the appliances in the kitchen. Keagan was vaguely surprised that Ashley hadn't balked at performing such a low-level task as recharging a crystal, but she supposed that even the very privileged needed to know how. After she finished, she met her squad in the courtyard, where she handed Lyria a pouch containing the reports. "One is for the office in Sporco, suitably edited for discretion. Dispatch the other two to Mustus with instructions that they must be passed on to the Queen as soon as possible." She paused and stared at Lyria intently. "Do *not* mix them up."

"Use the Shadow Riders," Shay told Lyria as she handed her several Aether-marked tokens. "Tell them it's crown expense and priority one."

"I will," Lyria said with a firmness that Keagan was glad to see. The young woman had come a long way from the timid girl she had met in the Aquas jungle. "I'll catch up as soon as I can."

"Safely," Keagan said.

"Yes. I promise." A huge gust of wind propelled her into the air, and before long, she had disappeared into the western sky. The others went back inside, but Keagan stood a while longer, staring after her as the clouds scudded overhead, finally blocking out the sun. Eventually, she made her way to the kitchen, where Cassius and Torva were preparing supper from their supplies, chopping vegetables and marinating some beef. At the small table in the corner, Ashley and Shay had her maps spread across the surface, studying them.

"So we're about here," Shay said, tapping a portion of the Terras map. "Still hundreds of leagues from the coast. And from Lurra, the ancient capital. I think we're close to a city called Marl."

"We'd never make it to the actual coast," Cassius said as she stirred the stew in the large pot on the stove. "The storms would stop us long before."

"Where did you get those maps?" Torva asked as she glanced over and saw them. Her voice went up as she took a second, longer look. "Are they from Aether? How do you have those?"

Shay lowered her head, clearly uncomfortable. "Uh, picked them up somewhere," she mumbled.

"May I see?" Torva leaned over the maps, avidly tracing the lines shown there. "These are prewar!"

"I thought you said there wasn't any war," Ashley said dryly. "Just a misstep by an empress."

"Pre-cataclysm, then," Torva said absently. She sat down, and clearly Cassius would receive no further help from her in preparing supper.

Swallowing a smile, Keagan went over to fill her spot, hoping that perhaps Torva would spot something the others hadn't because, so far, this trip to the Darvus farm had yielded nothing but bodies.

XXVII

The storm hit just before midnight, the wind and rain creating a deep, penetrating roar that surpassed anything Shay had ever heard before. She caught her breath and snuggled closer to Keagan in the master bedroom, which was at the front of the bunker and boasted the only windows on the upper level. The driving drops against the thick glass made it hard to sleep, and she wondered if the others in the blacked-out back bedrooms were finding it easier. It would surely be quieter.

"Disturbing, isn't it?" Keagan's voice was soft in the night.

"Strongest storm I've ever heard. You think the place will hold up?"

"It's clearly held so far."

"Yes, but maybe its time has come."

"I love your optimism." Keagan laughed quietly and shifted, rolling over so she was facing Shay. "Can you imagine living here? I know we have the occasional big storm in Aquas, but that's once every five or ten years. Here, they're supposed to hit every couple of months."

"Not much wonder he couldn't make it as a farmer."

"Agreed, but it doesn't explain how he went from here to what he became."

"Maybe that trail will lead us to those answers." Another, particularly strong, gust of wind rattled the windows. "Assuming we actually get out of here." She quivered as Keagan's hands began to roam. "On the other hand, maybe being stuck here isn't so bad."

That comment proved less true as the storm continued through the night and most of the next day. They could only marvel at its ferocity as it passed through. Fortunately, Cassius found a tunnel linking the house to the barn, which allowed her and Shay to tend to the horses without going outside in the wind. The animals, for the most part, didn't seem too disturbed, sticking near the rear of the stable, munching on the little bit of usable hay Shay was able to find. It was old but had no mold.

Back in the house, they huddled in the living area, a blaze crackling merrily in the fireplace, more for comfort than heat. They had little to do except talk, read something from the limited selection in the library, and listen to the storm.

"We should have packed board games," Ashley said at one point. "It must be infinitely worse in the winter, stuck inside like this, possibly for weeks at a time."

"It's not pleasant," Keagan said in an absent tone, not looking up.

"Do you think this guy had a family living here?"

"He wasn't married," Keagan said, reading the Darvus file over for what felt like, to Shay, the hundredth time. "No children. Not even any record of a partner when he was younger."

"Those other bedrooms have been used in the past. Not just the master."

"His farmhands maybe," Cassius said from where she sat leaning back in a chair, reading a book. "It's not like they could stay in an outbuilding. It wouldn't be safe. A farm this size would need only a couple, plus maybe one to keep up the house."

Ashley snorted. "That must have gone over well. Farmhands living with the Lord Elemental in his private estate rather than in a bunkhouse."

"And what happened to them?" Torva said, uneasily. She sat in one of the other armchairs behind a low table, studying the maps Shay had lent her.

"Either they left, signed up to whatever craziness he went on to," Keagan said, "or it's not just Elementals out there in the corral."

"That's a lovely thought." Cassius shook her head and returned to her book.

Shay was curled up next to Keagan, enjoying the play of firelight on her face as she worked, but even that, as delightful as it was, had its limits. She hated inaction and was as bored as Ashley undoubtedly was, while choosing not to show it. As she wondered how much longer this would go on, her experience with bad weather told her it had already far outlasted what was normal. But she didn't want to keep asking. Keagan could detect the amount of moisture around them, but unlike Lyria, she couldn't judge the storm's duration. Shay just hoped Lyria had made it to Sporco safely and was enjoying the tavern, but knowing her as she did, she suspected Lyria was in a state about not being with them and very anxious to get back.

"Do you hear that?" Shay lifted her head, eager, like a dog hearing the rattle of food in a dish.

"What?" Ashley stood up. "I don't hear anything."

"Exactly." Shay jumped to her feet and headed for the front of the home. As she reached the windows, she could see that the wind had eased and eagerly opened the door, stepping out into the courtyard. It was still overcast, but the rain had stopped, leaving massive puddles about. They stepped outside, breathing deeply in the damp air, so fresh after the stale atmosphere inside. Shay wondered how much such living conditions had contributed to Darvus becoming what he had.

"We can still get in a few hours' ride before sundown," she said, not tempering her excitement. She looked over at Keagan, expecting to see the same excitement, but she was frowning, looking upward, her eyes a solid blue. Shay's heart fell. "What's wrong?"

"It's not over," Keagan told her soberly. "There's always a break in a storm this size. I hear it's called an 'eye.' It'll last only an hour, maybe, and then the storm returns. Sometimes the wind is worse on the back side."

"Worse?" Ashley said. "Oh, for fuck's sake."

Shay agreed wholeheartedly. She didn't want to go back inside to those dank, closed little rooms. She lingered in the courtyard as the others glumly left, soaking in as much of the outdoors as she could before her time was up. Even as the wind began to gust and the rain to resume, hard drops that stung as they hit, she didn't move. Finally, Keagan appeared in the doorway.

"Shay?"

"I hate this," she said, voice breaking. "I didn't know how much until now."

Keagan's expression altered to concern. "Hate what?"

"Being inside. Being stuck in that small, dark hole."

"You're claustrophobic? How is that possible?"

Shay blinked. "What do you mean?"

"I meant you ride the Shadow Realm, and that's far worse." Keagan moved to her side, ignoring the rain as she grasped her arms. "Completely black and so closed in."

"What?" Shay said, astonished. "The Shadows are endless. They go on forever."

"It doesn't feel that way."

"It does for me."

"A matter of perspective, I guess." Keagan shook her gently. "You can't stay out here. It's too dangerous." A tree branch skidded across the courtyard, propelled by a particularly strong gust, as if to punctuate her point.

"I know," Shay said, resigned. She looked around again, taking a few deep breaths and inhaling as much fresh air as possible. Then, shoulders slumped, feeling world weary, she followed Keagan back inside.

"We'll stay out here," Keagan said, leading her to the large dining table. "Windows will help."

Shay was touched by how Keagan was trying to accommodate her. It wasn't entirely safe to be by the windows, and she knew Keagan would prefer that they were all deeper in the structure. As they sat there, watching the storm, though nothing was really visible through the thick, rain-coated glass, the others eventually joined them. First Ashley, then Cassius and Torva.

"Look what I found at the back of a drawer," Ashley announced triumphantly, waving a pack of cards. "Anyone up for some golden-flame?"

"Perhaps something a little less provocative," Keagan suggested.

"Meaning?"

"We don't need the hard feelings when someone loses their money. And someone always ends up doing just that."

Ashley made a face. "Spoilsport."

"Unless it's Ashley losing her fortune," Cassius said.

"That would never happen." Ashley spoke with such certainty that Shay knew she was right to stay away from gambling. Besides, it wasn't as if she and Torva could afford to match gold with Elementals. She would hate the idea of owing Ashley, or even Cassius, for that matter.

"How about Battle," Torva suggested. It was a child's game, but they all knew how to play, the four suits—blue waves, red flames, green leaves, and golden whirlwinds determining the elemental abilities—with the number declaring the power, while the royal cards, king, queen and successor, were wild.

"Fine." Ashley plopped down into a chair at the head of the table and began dealing out the cards, seven each. "Let the battle begin."

Surprisingly, at least to herself, Shay was quite good at this game compared to the others, and as the cards flew back and forth, she found herself forgetting her sense of confinement. Soon, only she and Ashley were left, and she remembered to hold back her blues as much as possible, saving them for key moments, defeating Ashley's four matching flames with five sequential waves in the last hand. The disgusted expression on Ashley's face was priceless and so much better than Shay imagined it would be. The memory of how dismissive and haughty Ashley had been when they first met still lingered, and even though they got along much better now, it still stung when she thought about it. Which was more frequently than she wanted to admit, even to herself.

"Damn, a card sharp," Ashley muttered. "Maybe it's good we didn't gamble."

Which made it even better. Shay leaned back in her chair, realizing only now that it was dark. "How long have we been playing?"

"You missed dinner," Keagan said, returning to the room with a tray containing two plates. "We kept it warm for you."

"You could have called us," Ashley said.

"Oh, you two were having far too much fun." Keagan leaned down and kissed Shay on the forehead. "And it changed your focus," she added in a murmur that only Shay could hear.

"It did." Shay tucked into her meal in a considerably better frame of mind. "Where are the others?" She hadn't even noticed them drifting away once the game had come down to her and Ashley battling one on one.

Settling into the chair next to her, Keagan inclined her head to the arch leading to the rest of the bunker. "Torva's still going over your maps on the kitchen table. I think she's getting more out of them than you did. Cassius is reading by the fire."

"How do you think Lyr is doing?" Ashley asked in such a casual tone that Shay lifted her head to look at her. The inflection there piqued her interest. Not to mention the nickname flavored with perceptible fondness.

"Probably wishing she was with us," Keagan said, not seeming to notice. "But hopefully staying put and out of trouble."

"Yeah," Ashley mumbled, looking back at her supper.

Shay stared at her. She hadn't thought Ashley would be so inclined. Of course, she could be just missing a friend. There was no question they had become close in the past week, but Shay didn't think it warranted the level of melancholy touching Ashley's expression.

Interesting. Something to keep an eye on, at any rate.

Later, in bed that night, Shay nuzzled into Keagan's ear. "Is Ashley into women?"

"What?" Keagan drew back to look at her with a quizzical smile. "Where did that come from?"

"I was just wondering," Shay said, rolling over onto her back. Keagan took the opportunity to snuggle against her side, head on her shoulder. "I think she misses Lyria." She paused. "A lot."

"Ash and Lyria?" Keagan exhaled softly into the darkness. "There were a few girls in school, but nothing serious. Just her playing around, I thought. Every relationship that lasted past a month was with a guy, though two months seemed to be her limit, regardless of who it was." She drummed her fingertips lightly on Shay's breastbone. "She does like to keep her options open."

"I don't know if I like the idea of her playing around with Lyria." Shay felt her mouth twist, anger coiling in the pit of her stomach.

Keagan seemed to sense her reaction. "No. I think she likes Lyria too much to play with her. I wouldn't worry about it. Lyria can take care of herself."

"She's so young."

"No younger than we were when we were out on our own for the first time." Keagan lifted her head, though Shay doubted she could see anything. "And how would you have reacted if one of your friends told you not to get involved with someone?"

"I'd have listened," Shay said immediately, then winced. "Well, maybe not. Maybe I would have dropped the friend first, depending on how I felt about the someone. Or at least resented them for interfering."

"Exactly." Keagan kissed her gently. "I love you for caring so much. But the most we can do is just be there regardless of how it turns out. For both of them. That's what friends are for. Besides, you might be imagining things."

"Yeah." Shay looked up toward the ceiling as Keagan settled back down against her. "I might."

But as she listened to the wind and rain rattle the window, she really didn't think she was.

XXVIII

The storm must have ended sometime in the night because when Keagan woke the next morning, sun was filtering weakly into the master bedroom, a square of light falling across the foot of the bed. She stretched out her hands, running them over the cool sheet, disappointed to find herself alone, but not especially surprised. Shay would have taken the first opportunity to go outside again. Stretching and yawning, Keagan allowed herself a few more indulgent moments, relaxing as she probed with her senses, feeling only clarity and none of the oppressive moisture that had come with the storm. It had been especially difficult by the windows, though she didn't think she had let on to Shay. As an Undine, she didn't feel the drops hitting the glass so much as she felt the hard surface brutally stop the water from progressing. A totally difference sensation than perhaps anyone else would experience. It had been an effort to block it from her mind.

As she entered the kitchen, she realized she was the last one up, an unusual occurrence. Everyone else was out in the courtyard, tending to the horses. Bemused, she found some eggs, bread, and bacon and made herself brunch. By the time she had finished, Ashley and Cassius had rejoined her. Shay remained outside with the horses. Again, not all that surprising.

"I gather you're all eager to leave," Keagan said with amusement.

"We've been stuck long enough," Ashley said. "I know we won't have a full day's travel, but we'll get away from here. What needs to be done here before we go?"

"Not much," Keagan said. "Clean up, leave the crystals charged for the forensic team, write a note, and then we'll be on our way."

Barely an hour later, they were riding across the eastern field toward the break in the forest that indicated a trail. Behind them, Ashley had burnt a note into the side of the barn door, letting Lyria know which direction they were headed and when they had left. It would also serve to inform the forensics team, though Keagan suspected the marshals would be well behind Lyria.

As she drew Vesi up next to Onyx, she was relieved to see that Shay was much more relaxed now, no longer tight across the shoulders. Nor did she display that narrow look around her eyes. In fact, the change was so noticeable, Keagan realized just how uncomfortable Shay had been in that farmhouse. Something to keep in mind the next time they were in close quarters, though she still couldn't figure out how Shay considered the Shadow Realm to be open and free. It was the most oppressive place Keagan had ever been.

They rode in comfortable silence, something Keagan was learning to appreciate. Shay never seemed to feel the need to talk much, which made when she did speak more significant somehow. It wasn't that she didn't share her feelings. If asked, she would express herself plainly and with complete honesty. But Keagan was beginning to realize it was up to her to ask.

As they followed the trail, she took note of the trees around her, how they had seemed to have adapted to the constant wind and regular storms. They seemed far more flexible than the vegetation she had seen in other places, bending easily. Meanwhile, the lower bushes and plants were squat and low to the ground. Yet, for all the flexibility, there were still many uprooted trees in places, almost as if after growing to a certain height, they could no longer withstand the elements. It made the forest they were riding through quite low compared to the rest of the nations', and with a sense of being young, as if never having had the chance to become old.

"I'm going ahead," Shay said, suddenly. "Without Lyria, we need a scout."

Without waiting for a response, she touched her heels to Onyx's sides and slipped into a canter, quickly disappearing into the forest ahead. Keagan let her go without objection, understanding the need her lover had for feeling unfettered, even from people she cared about. Glancing back, she saw Ashley and Cassius riding together, talking amiably. She was glad. Ashley, more than most, needed friends. True friends. She was a much better person with others around her who weren't afraid to challenge her. Keagan had been surprised at how much Ash had regressed when meeting up with her after twelve years, almost to the point of being that spoiled, arrogant, and cruel teenager she'd been when they had first met at the Academy. Fortunately, it seemed to take only a week or so to mature her again. The white mare, Vindur, wandered in their wake, exploring idly to each side of the trail, snatching mouthfuls of grass and catching up whenever she felt like it. Keagan wasn't entirely comfortable with the horse being loose, but Shay had insisted none of the horses, outside of Vesi, needed to be led, so Keagan didn't say anything.

Behind them, bringing up the rear on her old gray mare, Torva looked very preoccupied with her own thoughts, a small frown touching her lips and furrowing her brow. Was this experience becoming too much for her? Would the whole situation crush her under its weight? Keagan had seen it before in new officers, rookies who couldn't handle what was required of them as law keepers, and this group was a far cry from a standard batch of rookies. She'd need to keep an eye on each of them as they attempted to fill their role as deputy marshals.

Turning forward once more, she brushed a few loose strands of hair from her face, the wind making it impossible to keep everything pulled back in her normal plait. The breeze, though not particularly strong, was still somewhat irritating, riding as they were, directly into it. And its unrelenting, constant presence in this part of the world made it seem less than natural and more like a steady obstacle to overcome.

Of course, that made it all the more noticeable when the wind abruptly ceased that afternoon. By that time, Shay had completed her foray up ahead and returned to riding at Keagan's side. They both responded immediately as the air grew still, Keagan drawing her sword, while Shay pulled two daggers from her belt. Keagan was pleased to see that Cassius and Ashley lagged only a few seconds behind in their reaction, with Cassius slipping from her mount to stand ready, staff before her, while Ashley had her bow drawn, blast arrow notched as she looked around wildly. Only Torva seemed oblivious and needed Cassius to intercept and urge her off the trail and into the woods.

They gave a collective sigh of relief a moment later as a slender figure dropped from the sky in front of them and the wind resumed its constant push.

"Lyria!" Ashley's cry seemed the loudest and most welcoming. Perhaps Shay hadn't been imagining things, after all. They dismounted to greet their friend, and Lyria looked both pleased and surprised at the force of their reunion.

"We missed you," Cassius said, hugging her. "You caught up so quickly."

"It would have been quicker without the damned wind," Lyria said with a smile. "I had to have a constant arrow of counter push ahead of me to get any lift."

"That's why we felt you coming," Shay said coolly. "You stopped the wind ahead of you."

"Not stopped it," Lyria said. "Angled it to both sides so it blew around where I was flying. It took a while to figure that out, but once I did, everything became much smoother."

Again, Keagan was reminded that she was dealing with a level-five Sylph who'd probably be on the Ruling Council in a decade or so. Such ability was very rare indeed. Keagan noticed the pinched look around

Lyria's eyes and mouth, though, and realized she had pushed herself hard to catch up with them. She was nearly drained. Something else Keagan needed to keep an eye on, as she taught Lyria the importance of how to pace herself.

"Scout," she said in her official tone, silencing the reunion. "Report."

Ashley glared at her, but Keagan ignored her, while Lyria straightened and sobered. "I delivered both messages as requested. The royal response is here." She drew out an envelope and handed it over. "The forensic team has been assembled, but it hadn't fully arrived in Sporco before I left. They intend to depart as soon as possible."

"I see." Keagan opened the envelope and read its contents silently.

"Well?" Cassius queried. "Anything new?"

"Not really," Keagan told them. "Some encouragement from the Queen, and some more personal information on the marshal's record. She was apparently a good officer, but something had to be there for her to go along with all this. Chief Anderson is on his way to Sporco to keep digging into her personal life. I'm not sure if she was born there or just assigned to the office. He'll find out."

"No expense being spared for this one," Ashley said. "The chief himself."

"Well, that's how it'll be kept under wraps a little longer," Keagan said, with a touch of wryness. "Assigning officers to do it just spreads the need to know."

They reclaimed their mounts and started off once more, continuing east along the trail. As the hours wore on and the sun sank lower, Keagan began to wonder if perhaps they were wasting their time. She was about to send Lyria aloft again, regardless of her weariness, when they crested a hill and saw signs of a campsite below, similar to the one that had been located in western Aquas. However, this one had clearly suffered the effects of a storm or two. There were no tents, just a small, battered cabin made of thin logs that no longer sported a roof. Around it, the cleared area was littered with broken branches and the splintered remains of a table next to an old fire pit.

"Seems we're headed in the right direction, anyway," Shay said. "Here's hoping this is the halfway point rather than the first in a series of flattened campsites."

Keagan agreed. She wanted to get wherever this was leading before another storm hit. Even a semi-permanent campsite like this would be less than useless in one of those. They needed to be dug into the ground, like back at the farm. Stifling a sigh, she dismounted, indicating they would stop here for the night. Shay took Vesi and led him away with Onyx to where the others were settling their horses, unsaddling them.

"Marshal?"

Keagan turned to Torva, who approached, leading her mare. "Yes?"
"We're in ruins," she said. "We're surrounded by them."

Keagan blinked and looked into the forest around them. It looked exactly the same as the one they'd been riding in all day. "Really?" she said doubtfully. "How can you tell?"

"I've seen foundations all around in the underbrush. They began appearing about an hour ago. I think we're in what used to be a town, and if I read the map correctly, it was possibly a town called Kaolin."

"Why didn't you say anything?"

Torva shrugged. "They're unremarkable. I encounter them all the time. I just thought you should know. This looked to be a small settlement."

"Huh." Keagan nodded, struck by the fact that they were standing where people used to live. How sad should she feel about it, or did she not feel anything at all? "Well, let me know if it becomes anything more significant."

"I will," Torva said. "Perhaps we'll find more as we progress farther. Or the ruins may simply peter out as we reach the town limits. It's hard to say at this point."

"Here," Shay said, appearing suddenly to take the reins from Torva, making her and Keagan start. "I'll take care of your horse while you speak with Keagan."

"Uh, thank you," Torva said, seeming bemused and looking after them as Shay led the mare away before turning back to Keagan. "Is that something a Shadow Rider does? I didn't see her walk over here or sense her approach at all, and I think I'm that observant, at least."

Keagan sighed, torn between amusement and annoyance. "It's one of her less appealing qualities," she said. "Or one of her most. I'm not sure yet."

"I see." Torva was silent for a few seconds and then shrugged. "I just wanted to say, if your suspect is a historian of some kind, this may be what first piqued his interest. A small town I found when I was eight began my interest in the subject."

Keagan nodded. "Thank you. That may turn out to be an interesting insight. Can you tell if anyone's been exploring here, even if it's been a few years ago?"

"I can recognize excavations, even old ones," Torva said. She gestured, waving her hand in their general vicinity. "You could say this whole camp is one. It may be where he started, and once he moved on, he just turned it into a way station."

"Oh, that makes sense. It takes time to build a cabin. It meant he stayed for a while, longer than a simple tent required."

"Plus, it's annoying to sleep in a tent with the canvas flapping in the wind all the time," Torva said. "Solid walls are much better." She peered over at the ruined structure. "Pity about the roof."

"Yeah, well, it's clear he hasn't been using this place for a while. Let's hope there's more to find, farther ahead."

Like where he had discovered his ability to walk in the Shadows, she thought but didn't add.

XXIX

Shay patted the gray mare on the neck and stroked her muzzle, wanting to show her some affection even if her rider didn't. "So what's your name?" she murmured, knowing she wouldn't get an answer so long as she hadn't been chosen. Some Shadow-touched were like that, choosing no one, but very quick to learn, and willing to carry anyone on their backs without protest. They were used while training at the Academy, initial forays into the Realm before each Rider was permanently matched with their own horse. Were they also the type of horses the other Clan Leaders had been riding when they came to Sombra? There must have been a reason for their evolution.

Or perhaps she was overthinking it. Perhaps any Shadow-touched could be ridden by anyone should the horse permit it. She glanced over at Onyx, munching happily on some grass nearby. Would he let anyone ride him? She had difficulty believing it, but then, a great deal had been going on lately that she was having difficulty believing. Keagan had ridden him, back in Arias, though, granted, Shay had also been on his back. Would he let Keagan ride him now? On her own?

She leaned toward him and told him in a low voice, "Look after Keagan. Whatever she needs." He flicked an ear but didn't stop grazing.

Not far away, Cassius groomed Gault with meticulous care. The big stallion was a mere foal under her hands, leaning eagerly into her every touch. Now, there was a horse that wouldn't let just anyone ride him, Shay decided. Or get within nipping distance, for that matter. "What do you think we'll find up ahead?" Cassius asked suddenly.

"Honestly, I have no idea," Shay said "But it might be important. This whole thing may have started here. Him heading east, looking for whatever and somehow finding it."

"What do you think about all of it?" Cassius looked troubled. "The whole story Torva told us."

Shay paused. "It's like she explained. Some parts might be true, yet some might not. History is often what people want it to be rather than what it is. Someone says this happened, someone else passes it on and may or may not get it right, and sometimes, things get lost as it goes. Only when there's evidence can we be sure. I mean, we saw those statues of that woman, and they were the same in both Aquas and Arias. Will we find more here? If so, then we know that, for some reason, she was significant enough for statues to be made of her in at least three nations. Was she a cruel empress who exploited Elementals? We know the elemental stones exist. Did they actually cause the catastrophe that devastated the world?" Shay shook her head. "I guess we just keep digging. Regardless, something happened a long time ago, and someone's decided to use it to their advantage in the present. People are suffering for it, and that's got to stop. We have to stop it. Maybe in the end, that's all that's important."

"Maybe you're right."

"Are you concerned about the story she told about the rebels who fought against the empress? About who they were?"

"Do you think that part is true?"

Shay suspected she knew what Cassius was really asking about. "Maybe," she said finally. "Or maybe the gods always existed, and those names were just used to describe the individuals involved because they were the heroes in the story. Though I'm not sure, if everyone involved supposedly died and all the cities were destroyed, how anyone knew exactly what happened, anyway."

"Yeah." Cassius brightened. "I hadn't thought of that."

"Unless Stygia entered the Shadow Realm, somehow escaped the destruction, and her telling the story later is how it was passed on at all." Shay immediately regretted adding the last part when she saw how Cassius's face fell. "Look. I can't speak to Lurra and to who she may or may not have been, but I believe Stygia existed, and does exist. It comes down to faith."

"Yes. I suppose you're right," Cassius said slowly. "Either I believe in Lurra and Her teachings, or I don't. But I do believe, and I believe because Her tenets enrich my life, make it better, and subsequently make me strive to be a better person and to treat others as I would wish to be treated. Nothing else that I might learn along the way should change that fact."

Shay thought that Cassius, and people like her, might be the whole reason religion should exist at all. The rest of it was just people bringing their horseshit into it. Giving the gray mare a final pat on the neck, she headed back to the camp set up next to the ruined cabin. Keagan, Lyria, and Ashley were seated next to the fire, eating their supper, while Torva had a couple of the maps out, studying them side by side. Shay wondered what she was seeing in them that she hadn't and thought it was time to retrieve them, if only to determine where the nearest ancient Path was located.

After grabbing her stew, she took a seat next to Torva on the log and peered over to see that the two maps were of Urodela and Arias. Torva kept placing them side by side and then at various positions around each other, frowning.

"What are you doing?" she asked finally.

Torva started so badly, she fell backward off the log, dropping the maps and causing the others to look up as Ashley burst into laughter. "I'm glad to know we're not the only ones you do that to."

Shay put down her stew and hastily helped Torva up, apologizing. She honestly didn't know why people weren't aware of her approach. It wasn't like she was trying to be quiet. How had Torva really not noticed her retrieving her supper and sitting down next to her? Had it always been that way? She'd never noticed startling people before. At least not out of the ordinary. But what was the ordinary?

"It's probably my fault," Torva said, once she was situated. "I was totally absorbed in trying to make sense of this."

"Make sense of what?" Cassius had joined them just in time to see Torva's accident. She settled on the ground next to Lyria with a bowl of stew.

Torva looked around, as if suddenly aware she was the center of attention, and blushed. "Uh, I was trying to see how the nations connect. Put them in a complete world view. It's hard to do without a map of Aether, but even so, things don't make sense."

"How so?" Keagan frowned slightly.

"Have any of you taken a passage?"

"The tunnels through the mountains?" Lyria perked up. "I've taken both—the one in the Ajror Mesa from Arias to Urodela, and then from Urodela to Terras before boarding a ship to Aquas to go to the Academy. Then another passage back to Urodela for work." She sighed. "It's a lot of work traveling from one nation to another. Riding in the Shadow Realm is so much easier."

"Too many times for my company," Ashley said. "They're tedious as hell. Caravans take a week to get through, and there's nothing to see but a curved gray hole the entire time. The little way stations don't even have taverns, which you'd think would be an obvious marketing opportunity. Still, it's good they exist, because otherwise, you'd be going over those mountains, and that would take forever, not to mention the threat of bad weather or attacks from dangerous animals."

"I've also used both to travel from Terras to Arias, passing through Urodela," Cassius said. "Thank Lurra that bit of ancient engineering remained untouched in the war." She began to look thoughtful. "Not sure why, though. You'd think that Terras would have destroyed its end in the beginning to prevent any army from Urodela from invading. The nations do have garrisons now on both departure points, manned by royal guards."

Keagan looked a little embarrassed. "Before now, I haven't traveled far from Aquas. My few trips to Terras were by ship. I've never been in a passage."

Shay shrugged. "Never needed one, obviously. None of the Paths go near the garrison towns where the passages are located, and I've never had a courier run to any, so I've never seen one." She looked at Torva. "Why?"

"Because they're not marked on these maps. It's as if they didn't exist then. The garrisons certainly didn't," Torva said. "But I can't believe that any nation's society, in the aftermath of that destruction, could build them. I've been in both passages, and the engineering that would be required to bore through solid rock so perfectly and directly is far beyond us now. How is that possible? Also, I don't know if anyone's noticed, but regardless of which passage is used, it takes exactly one week to travel through it. I've asked, and no one knows who built them or when. There's no real information on them at all. They were just 'discovered soon after the war,' and because they were there, no one's ever really explored the mountains bordering the nations. They didn't need to when they had a much safer and more direct route."

"So what does that mean?"

Torva paused, assuming a look that Shay recognized. Torva was about to blow up basic preconceptions they'd all lived with their entire lives.

"I can't see where the nations fit together, especially when I'm trying to put Aether in the middle." She looked over at Shay. "There are no passages in and out of your nation, are there? Just Paths. You can't even sail to your eastern town on the coast from Terras or Urodela. It's too far, right? Too dangerous, even though it should be well within reach if you're just southwest of Terras and east of Urodela."

"Yes. No. I mean…I think so?" Shay had become a little lost.

"I don't think what you call the Shadow Hills make up the same geological feature that Terras calls the Shadow Hills. Terras can't be north of you when Urodela is supposed to be west of you. How can a passage go from Terras to Urodela without passing through the Shadow Lands? Does it go under it? It's impossible, especially when you consider the time differences in each nation, when the sun rises and sets. It just doesn't work."

"So the Shadow Lands don't exist? That's funny, because I'm almost sure I was there," Ashley said. "So were you."

"No. I just don't think the nations are located where we think they are. Or, rather, there are missing areas that we don't know about. I'm not sure if it's all mountains or ocean or what, but too much is unaccounted for."

Silent, Shay and obviously the others tried to wrap their heads around what Torva was trying to say.

"But Aquas and Terras are exactly where they're supposed to be?" Keagan asked finally.

"Sailing is tangible," Torva said. "Sailors read the stars to navigate from Aquas to Terras. Ships also sail from Urodela to Arias around the Vatra Expanse and up the coast from Vokanus to Lucht. They sail directly, not through any passages or by any unusual routes. Plus, the weather matches up in the four nations. It's much warmer overall in Aquas than in Terras, though Terras is still mild in the south. I can locate those nations in conjunction with each other, along with the time difference. That said, Aquas should geographically be in line with Aether, but the weather is completely different. Aquas doesn't have a winter, just a rainy season, but I was told that Aether does have four distinct seasons, with a lot of snow and cold in the winter, even on their eastern ocean border, which is supposedly on the Alameada Ocean, unless it's much farther north or south than we thought. Again, it doesn't make sense."

Again, several minutes passed. Finally, Ashley, characteristically, broke the silence. "Does it really matter?"

Torva blinked. "What?"

Ashley lifted her shoulder in a half shrug. "Well, if it all works, and this is how we get from one nation to the other, and it's been peaceful for almost a thousand years, outside of a few internal skirmishes, what does it matter overall? Cargo and people still get to where they're going. It doesn't change my travel plans at all."

"But...what if there are other nations and people that we know nothing about?" Torva sounded stunned. "What if all we know of the world is just a very small part of it?"

"If no one's shown up by now, I doubt they will in the next few hours," Ashley said. "And if they do, then we'll deal with it. In any event, I'm getting out of this wind and going to bed. I'm tired, and I've got last watch."

That seemed to be the consensus, and without further discussion, they retired to their tents for the evening, leaving Cassius on first watch. But sleep didn't come easy. Lying in the darkness, Shay felt Keagan toss and turn beside her for what seemed like hours.

"Damn it, Torva was right. Trying to sleep in a tent with it flapping in the wind is impossible," Keagan muttered finally, in a sharp, irritated tone.

"Just as long as all it does is flap," Shay said, calmly. "I'd hate to see it suddenly fly away altogether." She nuzzled into the warm skin of Keagan's shoulder. "So it's the wind keeping you awake and not what Torva said?"

There was a long pause. "She just keeps throwing spanners into the works, doesn't she?"

"She doesn't think like everyone else, that's for sure." Shay waited until a particularly strong gust and the subsequent sound of canvas rippling in the wind had subsided. "She thinks…um, larger. Big picture. How society works as a whole, how the world is physically put together, why it all is, and most importantly, how it became all that. Most people, including us, tend to just go about our lives in the world, taking a lot for granted. It works this way because it works and always has, so there's no need to question it. If it doesn't work, then it's because of some huge war long ago. Religion and school teach us what is. If they don't tell us what isn't, why would we even think about it, as long as it's not bothering anything?"

"You think bigger." Keagan turned to look at her in the darkness. "You question."

"Now," Shay said. "Because I discovered you. Before then, I didn't really know any Elementals. I just accepted you were in charge of things and tried to stay well clear of you. I carried my parcels and didn't think about what was inside, or how it might affect the world as I knew it. I had food on the table, a roof over my head, a steady living, and a chance to see all the nations, which most people never do. Most don't even leave their immediate village or town. But I never wondered why things were the way they were or, rather, never wondered for long. Now I'm wondering all the time." She sighed. "It's damned exhausting."

Keagan laughed. "It is, isn't it?"

"So she's wondered like this since she was a kid, been in her head all the time," Shay said. "Maybe that's why she sometimes seems scattered. She just has too much on her mind to pay attention to the here and now."

Keagan made a small sound of discontent and snuggled closer. "Maybe we should pay attention to the here and now. It might help me sleep." Her hands began to wander suggestively.

"That's the best idea I've heard tonight," Shay said. And she hoped the tent didn't blow away while they having too much fun to stop.

XXX

The next two days saw them riding through more insignificant ruins and more campsites that would be semi-permanent in other parts of the world but, here, were quickly being erased by the ever-increasing wind. As they rode east, Keagan began to wonder if they would need to turn back, constantly worrying about the approach of another big storm. Then, on the third day, the ruins grew so apparent that everyone could see them, skeletal structures that bespoke of grand buildings in what was once a thriving city. Both Shay and Torva believed this might be Marl, though who knew how important it was in ancient times.

Pretty important to those who had once lived there, Keagan reminded herself.

As the day progressed, she sent Lyria aloft once more to see if she could spot an end to the trail or, at least, the next cleared area and probable campsite. Lyria descended again in only a few minutes, startling the others.

"People are ahead," she said, her voice rising to an uncomfortable note.

Keagan drew her sword. "How far?"

Lyria paused. "About an hour and a half, maybe two. The trail winds through the ruins. There's no direct route."

Keagan let out her breath, remembering how far Lyria could see, and sheathed her sword. "What else?"

"Two men were sitting by a campfire," Lyria said. "They had their heads down, and I didn't want them to spot me, so I came back. They were near a building, though. There may be more inside."

"A building is still standing?" Shay sounded amazed.

"It's only one story." Lyria held out a flattened palm to indicate how short. "But the opening is large. It was too dark to see inside, and I didn't have a good angle." She looked back at Keagan. "I didn't spot any other trails branching off from that area. It has to be where this one is leading."

Keagan agreed. Wherever else Darvus had explored over the years, this particular trail had been used for a long period of time. It still hadn't grown over.

"Okay," she said. "Lyria, I want you to find a high spot where you won't be seen and study as much as possible about what's ahead. We'll continue for exactly an hour and reassess at that point."

"Understood." A blast of wind swirled around them, and she was gone again, flinging herself into the air. The horses snorted and threw up their heads, but they were clearly becoming used to the unpleasant side effect of Lyria's takeoffs. Keagan wondered if she ever would.

"What do you think?" Ashley asked as they remounted. "Just more of his goons? Or will he be there?"

"Not sure," Keagan said. "We'll simply have to be ready. Hopefully, Lyria will discover more."

In a darkly serious mood, they rode east. After exactly an hour, according to Torva's pocket watch, they drew up in a small clearing that must have been an intersection or park in ancient times. In the shadow of four structures that were probably huge in their day, the largest at least ten stories, they dismounted to wait for Lyria. It must be dark in this particular spot all the time, Keagan thought as she petted Vesi, but at least the buildings cut the wind somewhat.

Or perhaps Lyria's descent was directing the breeze away. Keagan motioned her over, and without prompting, Lyria gave her report, something Keagan was glad to see. She wasn't sure how things would play out once this mission ended, but perhaps some of her team would decide to pursue this vocation, and she would have recruited some very valuable assets to the marshals and the crown. Always a good thing.

"I didn't see any others, but if they work in shifts, more may be inside resting. No signs of anyone patrolling the perimeter."

"Very good," Keagan said, before turning to the others. "We're on foot from here. We'll go in quietly and handle things quickly. With luck, they'll surrender. If not, give no quarter."

"If they do surrender, what do you plan to do with them?" Cassius asked, in her calm, rational tone. "We'll have to find a way to imprison them and then stay with them until someone else shows up. Or take them back to the farm. Either way, it will take a while."

Keagan cursed Cassius's pragmatism even as she kicked herself for not thinking that far ahead. She was too used to having marshal backup close at hand, even after all she'd been through. "We need to question them. I hope they have inside facilities of some kind," she said. "If not, we'll figure something out."

Something that, hopefully, didn't include cold-blooded execution. The new crown badge offered a lot of leeway, but killing for convenience would weigh heavy on her, as she was sure it would on the others. She glanced over at Ashley. Well, most of them, anyway, though she didn't think even Ashley was that callous.

Keagan noticed an odd expression on Shay's face as she looked to the east. "Shay?"

She didn't respond right away, requiring a second prompting, which meant, at that point, they were all looking at her.

"What is it?" Cassius asked.

"I'm not sure," Shay said, evidently confused. "It feels almost like there's a Path, but not quite. I've never experienced anything like it."

"So there might be a Path there?"

"Maybe." Shay shook her head. "If so, perhaps it's so old, it's faded away to nothing, somehow. I've never heard of such a thing, or even considered it possible, but that's the best explanation I can come up with." She glanced at Torva. "Can I see the Terras map?"

Torva produced it, and for a few minutes, they looked over it, before Shay shook her head. "There are no black lines near here at all, as best as I can tell. I'm not sure what's going on."

"We'll find out when we get there," Ashley said, a gleam in her eyes.

Keagan nodded. "Torva, you stay with the horses," she said. "If you haven't heard anything from us by end of day, head west, and don't look back. Find the nearest marshal office and tell them what happened. Don't try to come after us."

Torva appeared both relieved and shamed, head dipping. Cassius, Keagan noticed, patted her on the shoulder, silently reassuring her, and Torva's expression cleared to one of gratitude. Keagan was pleased. They were really starting to work like a team, even with the non-Elemental.

They started off, and Ashley moved up beside her. "Good call, leaving the null behind."

Keagan snorted. "I didn't leave her because she has no abilities," she said. "If Torva knew how to fight, I would have left Lyria with the horses. She's the scout." Keagan fell back to where Lyria and Cassius were walking. "Lyria, remember your duty."

Lyria looked blank for a second, then very rebellious, and finally, after exchanging a look with Cassius, nodded slightly. "I understand," she said, her reluctance evident in her tone. "If you give the word, I fly." She paused. "Did you want me to stay with Torva in that case?"

"No. Just let her know what's happened, get her on her way, and then go for backup. She'll have to make it on her own, but the sooner help is on the way, the sooner she'll encounter it."

"Okay." But it was clear that Lyria didn't like it. Keagan didn't care. She didn't have to like it. She just had to do it.

Keagan moved back to Ashley's side. Shay had melted into the ruins around them, disappearing as she scouted ahead. As they walked along the trail, Keagan was conscious that beneath the rush of the wind, there was no other sound in the vicinity—no bird cry, no buzz of insects—even though there had been plenty up until now. Whatever they were headed toward, the other living creatures in the vicinity obviously wanted no part of it.

As the trail grew wider, they slowed, spreading out into flanking positions—Cassius and Lyria to the right, Ashley to her left. Keagan managed not to start when Shay suddenly appeared next to her, but it was close.

"What did you see?"

"Not a Path," Shay said, a furrow between her dark eyebrows. "But definitely something like it."

"I meant, did you see how many?"

"No. Like Lyria said, just the two by the fire, and completely relaxed, not alert at all. I could see a little farther into the building, but not far. Enough to know they're using it as a shelter, but otherwise, there's a central point where it suddenly drops off, like a hole in the floor. Whatever they're guarding must be underground."

"Great." Keagan hated fighting underground. It made drawing moisture so much harder than through air, as if the earth hated giving it up, not at all like fighting in the city and its uncaring, man-made concrete and brick. Sharply reminded of how helpless she had been in the tomb of Heratherus, cut into bedrock, she immediately checked for nearby sources, relieved to find several small streams running through the ruins. Water found a way, she told herself comfortingly. Through everything, eventually.

As they grew close enough to hear voices, she held up the palm of her hand, happy to see everyone immediately stop. Using only gestures, she sent Cassius and Lyria to the nearby shadows of an overhanging slab of concrete, and Ashley over to a growth of trees, indicating they should remain there for the time being. Then, with a nod to Shay, the two of them strode forward, Keagan pulling out her badge and holding it before her.

As they came into sight, the two men jumped up with oaths of surprise. One made a move toward a nearby bow resting against a rock, abruptly aborted when Keagan drew her sword. Beside her, Shay lifted her daggers, making them clearly visible.

"Marshals. Elemental. Stand and be recognized."

The two men exchanged an uneasy look. Keagan took in their appearance without conscious thought, assessing what she was facing. Clothing worn, but neat and well made, rugged but not cheap. The one on the right, solid, muscular but not very tall, with dark hair and eyes, had a dagger on his belt. The other, slender, older, receding brown hair and blue eyes, scar down the right cheek. They didn't stand like mercenaries but looked like they knew their way around a bar brawl.

Not any kind of threat to an Elemental, in other words. What lay inside might be a different thing.

"If anyone's within, come out, hands where I can see them."

Keagan waited, exchanging a glance with Shay, who had moved a few feet away from her, allowing for multiple angles of attack if necessary. No one appeared, and after a few minutes, Keagan relaxed ever so slightly. Shay, she knew, would have detected any hint of motion in the shadows of the building entrance and acted accordingly.

"We weren't doing anything," the younger man said, sounding sullen. The cry of many a malefactor, well and truly caught.

"What are you doing out here?" Keagan asked.

"What are *you* doing out here?" the other asked, somewhat reasonably, Keagan thought.

"Asking the questions," Keagan told him, pegging him as the leader of the two. "Let's start with your names."

"I'm Herodotus." From Aquas then, Keagan decided, a common name in the nation.

"Kracus."

Probably from Terras, then, Keagan thought. He looked it. She inclined her head toward his waist. "Slowly. On the ground."

He hesitated and then carefully removed the dagger with forefinger and thumb, tossing it a few feet away. "Thank you," Keagan said. She had no reason to be rude, after all. They were cooperating.

So far.

"So, tell me of your association with Lord Arthur Darvus. Is he in charge of this site?"

The change in them was immediate and unexpectedly disturbing in its intensity. Face twisted in fury, Herodotus leaped toward her, ignoring the sword, while Kracus went for his dagger. Shay immediately dropped him with two stars to the throat. Keagan, meanwhile, retreated, not because Herodotus was a particular threat, but because she wanted to question him further, trying to figure out a way to bring him down without harm. She didn't like what such a reaction implied, however. These people were clearly not only willing to fight for Darvus, but they were zealots, willing to die, but for what exact cause? She really needed to understand it.

Readying her abilities, she prepared to surround his head in water, knowing he'd be a lot more cooperative half-drowned, when suddenly, he pulled up short and drew something from within his pocket. An eerily calm and peaceful expression settled on his face. Keagan paused, confused, when she identified it as a device of some kind as opposed to a weapon, small, shaped in a fat oval. He used his thumb to flick a switch on the side, and Keagan was baffled when nothing in particular happened. She honestly couldn't figure out what was going on.

Then, from the building entrance, huge black tentacles erupted, smashing Herodotus aside into a mound of rubble with brutal efficiency, crushing him into a misshapen mass of gory flesh and splintered bone before reaching out for her with deadly intent.

XXXI

Shay had a few seconds of horrified disbelief before her instincts kicked in and she lunged for Keagan, knocking her aside as she flung daggers at the thick tentacle reaching for her.

"Baast's tits. What the fuck is that?" Ashley appeared from behind them, firing arrows that had the disturbing and disappointing tendency to fly right through the tentacles. They went on to explode in the far side of the clearing.

"It's a squib," Shay yelled, dodging to the side as another tentacle flew toward her. "They shouldn't exist out here!"

"Does it know that?"

Keagan leaped forward, bringing down her sword in a savage slash and overbalancing as it encountered no resistance. She turned it into a somersault out of the way. "How do we fight it?"

"I don't know," Shay told her, perturbed. "Steel works on it in the Shadow Realm!"

A tentacle, moving too quickly, wrapped around her. It certainly felt solid enough in that moment, squeezing brutally as it picked her up and flung her across the clearing. She barely avoided smashing into a wall and managed to tuck and roll across the ground, though the endeavor knocked the wind out of her.

With an effort, she staggered to her feet and looked to see that Cassius and Lyria had joined the fray. Cassius bravely darted forward to smash a tentacle with her staff, only to have the same thing happen to her as happened to Keagan, though she was less graceful about her recovery, staggering to the side as she barely missed being picked up.

From the entrance of the building, the rest of the creature appeared, a solid black mass of smaller, wiggling tendrils, and glaring red eyes that blinked uncertainly in the sun. Keagan and the others reverted to what they knew. Ashley hit it with a blue blast of flame, hot enough to melt metal, while, on the other side, Keagan narrowed her jets of water to punishing streams thin enough to puncture, while Cassius began firing slabs of rock at it. Those attacks, at least, seemed to impact it in a way their weapons had not, making the tentacles recoil. The squib was so big, however, that they didn't seem to be doing much damage overall, and they frequently had to dodge the ten huge limbs flailing dangerously about the clearing.

Ashley's flame grew larger, blasting the creature's torso on one side, and while that seemed to bother it, it also didn't appear to wound it mortally. It burned, but her flame wasn't consuming the squib as it did with everything else.

Above, Lyria swooped and darted, shooting her crossbow that missed more often than not, though again, those bolts that did intersect the creature had no effect. Her blasts of wind tended to hamper the others more than the squib, so she quickly stopped trying and briefly hovered, looking helpless.

Pausing was a mistake because a tentacle shot out and wrapped around her, drawing her toward the center mass of the creature, where a gaping, fanged mouth opened to receive her.

"Lyria!" Shay staggered forward, flinging more daggers that she knew were having no impact, but not knowing what else to do.

That was when Lyria shrieked.

A scream of terror and desperation, it was also so much more than that. It reverberated around the clearing, causing Shay to stagger and fall to her knees, hands over her ears in a futile attempt to block out the sound. The others were also affected, expressions of pain on their faces as they fell, arms covering their heads.

The effect on the creature was far more impressive. It reared back, tentacles retreating into its body as it flung Lyria away, though she quickly caught herself and hovered as the creature crawled briefly toward the building entrance in a futile attempt to escape. Then it abruptly shivered, pulsated, and finally melted into a rancid pile of black goo.

Ears still ringing uncomfortably, Shay managed to get to her feet. She stumbled to Keagan first, helping her up, before looking for the others. Lyria slowly descended, an expression of confused pride on her face.

"Did you see that?" she asked.

"We did." Cassius looked a little shaken as she picked herself up. "I wasn't aware you could do that."

"I wasn't either. People always said it was uncomfortable to listen to me speak. I thought it was because I didn't have much to talk about."

"People are idiots," Ashley said, brushing herself off. "You're a siren. I don't know why we're surprised. You're a level five, after all."

Keagan frowned. "They didn't detect it at the Academy?"

"I guess I've never needed to do it before. How would they know when I didn't?"

"Still should have tested for it. It's possible it developed late."

"Or desperation unlocked something latent," Cassius said.

"Well, I was certainly desperate." Lyria started to laugh, the sound tinged with just the slightest hint of hysteria, and Ashley dashed over and put her arm around her shoulders, hugging her tight and calming her. Shay was impressed and shared a look with Keagan, a sort of "See, what did I tell you" glance that Keagan made a face at.

Cassius took a step toward the building, then stopped, staring at it, an uneasy tension in her broad shoulders. "What else is in there?"

"I hate to say it, but we'd better find out," Keagan said, jaw firm.

Shay didn't like it either, confused by what she was sensing, so odd and disjointed, difficult to put a finger on.

"Lyria, go get Torva and the horses," Keagan said abruptly. "Bring them here."

Shay realized that by setting a task for Lyria, Keagan clearly expected a certain standard of behavior from her, which would help Lyria recover from her fear faster than if she dwelt on it. She greatly admired that thoughtful aspect of leadership in Keagan.

Lyria hesitated briefly, then nodded, drawing away from Ashley with a final, grateful look at her before launching herself into the air. Ashley evidently noticed the others regarding her with interest and visibly straightened, a haughty expression appearing as if to imply they would see nothing there.

Shay would have smiled were the situation less dire. Joining Cassius, she stared at the entrance. The building itself was barely standing up, covered in vegetation where it hadn't been cleared away. How had Darvus found it in the first place? It looked no different than the rest of the ruins around them.

Perhaps a squib had come out and waved a welcoming tentacle at him. She swallowed hard, still finding it hard to believe that Realm creatures could inhabit the world. First the wraiths and now a squib. Could something larger emerge? A queeb? Dear Lady, what would happen then?

Keagan appeared next to them, expression grim. "Cassius, I want you to stay here and wait for Lyria and Torva. Secure the perimeter. Ashley, Shay, and I will make a preliminary foray into the structure. If we're not back by sunset, you're in charge. Don't come after us. Get the rest home safely."

Cassius frowned. "You might need me in there."

"I need you out here," Keagan said, firmly. "Ash, Shay, with me."

Shay nodded. "Let me find my daggers first."

After taking some time to search the clearing, she finally retrieved the blades that had proved so useless against the squib. Then, returning to Keagan and Ashley, both of whom had their weapons ready, Shay took point as they entered the building. Glancing around didn't provide much insight on this level. Sun filtered weakly through the vine-covered openings that had once been windows, sparking off motes drifting in the air. Just inside the door was the indication of living quarters, bedrolls for dozens of people, along with cooking and bathing areas.

People had been living here for a long time, Shay thought. There were a few rooms, most of which contained the remains of office-type furniture, while two were obviously some kind of restroom facilities, though not for bathing. They had been excavated for reuse, with charged plumbing crystals installed on the lavatories, along with a large water tank tucked in the corner.

"I think this was for a business," she said. "People worked here."

"It looks like some kind of transport depot," Ashley said, eyeing everything keenly. "Only for people instead of cargo."

In the center of the room stood a large staircase that descended into unknown depths, wide enough to accommodate at least five people standing shoulder to shoulder. The three of them paused at the top, gazing down with unease.

"See anything?" Keagan asked tersely.

"Just a landing and more stairs," Shay told her. "Lots of footprints leading farther in, including hoof prints. Somehow, they managed to move several horses down there. It's been used recently by a large group of people. Or by a small group of people a lot of times."

"Is it safe?"

"After what we just fought, I would highly doubt it."

"But no more creatures?"

"They may be farther back, out of sight."

"Do you sense anything?"

"Nothing moving."

"Can we just go?" Ashley asked impatiently as she started down the stairs.

Shay and Keagan exchanged a long-suffering look and hurried after her. The stairs descended at least three floors, with a landing on each flight. When they finally reached the bottom, they discovered a large space with moldering remains of benches and waiting areas. It was dominated by a large hole in the center of the far wall, a huge pit of inky blackness. Rubble nearby indicated that this area had been dug out, recovered from the ravages of time. Torva should be able to tell them exactly how and when.

"Should we wait for the others?" Ashley asked as she peered at the tunnel.

Keagan paused. "Let's see what's inside, at least for a short distance."

Not far from the opening, Keagan found a stack of vapor lamps next to a pillar and picked up two, lighting one and handing the other to Ashley. Shay, of course, did not require one and was glad of it, since she had both hands free for her daggers. Ashley had to sling her bow back over her shoulder as she lifted the lamp with her left hand, leaving her right one to glow red, ready to fire at will. Shay dearly hoped she wouldn't have to.

With trepidation, they entered the huge tunnel, and Shay was immediately struck by the odd sense of familiarity that remained just different enough to leave her off-kilter. It raised the hair on the back of her neck and made her shoulders tighten. She didn't know why, because she could see absolutely nothing but a round, incredibly well-constructed tunnel that went off into an unimaginable distance, with walls smoother than anything she had ever seen. The floor beneath her feet was also smooth, polished with a strange, translucent covering over the stone. A large, distinct trail had been laid down from countless footprints, leading away from her into the distance, though the dust of centuries, thick and heavy, still gathered on the sides where the floor met the curved wall.

At regular intervals, small recesses contained glass coverings over what appeared to be devices of some kind, though they were dark and dead. Reaching out with all her awareness, she probed the blackness ahead, trying to figure out what she felt. Something should be there but just wasn't.

Shay's heart stuttered as she realized what she was finally sensing, an echo of what had once been, but no longer, a direction that would cry out no more.

XXXII

Keagan suddenly realized that Shay had stopped and fallen silent, more so than usual. Concerned, she quickened her steps to catch up with her, and when she did, her shocked and bewildered expression made Keagan's heart race. "Shay?"

"This is a Path."

"What?"

"But it's not a Path any longer. It's out here in the world." Shay looked at her as if Keagan somehow had the answers. "How can this be?"

"I don't know."

"What is this?"

"I don't know." Keagan was beginning to feel somewhat stupid.

"Well, we were talking about passages, earlier," Ashley suddenly said.

"This is a passage? A...dead Path?" From her expression, Keagan knew Shay couldn't find a better description for what she was sensing. "And the other two passages? They're also dead Paths?"

Ashley blinked. "I don't know. I guess so. They're just passages to the rest of us."

"Great Lady, do you encounter squibs there?" Shay appeared both horrified and impressed. "Anything like them? Wraiths? Shades? Ments? Lazuers?" She paused, silver eyes wide. "Queebs?"

"First off, I don't know what most of those are, so I'll have to say no," Ashley said. "I told you, we don't encounter anything. They're boring as hell to travel through." She paused, snapped her fingers. "Baast, you know, now that I think of it, those markings we saw on the Paths, the ones that glowed?"

"Yes?"

"I think there are larger versions etched into the walls at various points," she said. "Usually near the way stations. In fact, that's how you know you're getting close to one. You starting seeing the symbols. They don't glow, though. Wow. I never knew those were from Aether. Did your people build the passages?"

"Not to my knowledge," Shay said grimly. "Is this why Riders were told to stay away from the garrison towns? I thought it was because they were crown property, managed by the Transport Guild, and it was far from where the Paths lay anyway. No business being there." She moved over to the near wall and reached out, running her hand over the smooth, dusty surface. "But the symbols would definitely keep the Shadow creatures away. That's their purpose." She looked around. "I don't see any here."

"Well, this isn't a way station. It's a departure point."

"Or maybe they've worn away from disuse," Keagan said. "In any event, this may be how the Shadow Realm creatures come into the world, through an old passage. Darvus found a way to take advantage of it." She winced as a bruise from the fight made itself felt. "Herodotus had some kind of device that called it. And it wasn't for it to obey him. It was like he knew that calling it meant his death. It was a last resort."

"Like Lyria's scream was for us." Shay brightened. "Sound. They say there are levels to it that we can't hear, but that dogs and birds and other animals can. Maybe so can creatures in the Realm. I know that you must always move quietly, even on Paths. Any noise will bring something eventually, quicker when you're away from one. Scouts even put sound-deadening bootlets on their horse's hooves. The creatures there clearly have much better hearing than we do. Maybe that's how Lyria killed the squib. Not with what we heard, but the levels in her scream that we can't."

"So, do we go farther?" Ashley peered toward the darkness, holding up her lamp and squinting a little as if that would somehow allow her to see an end.

"We follow it all the way," Keagan said. "Just as Darvus did. I think this was the discovery that got him and this whole thing started. But, for now, we need to regroup with Cassius."

Returning to the surface, they discovered the others were all together, anxiously awaiting their return. Clearly, they'd been gone a lot longer than Keagan thought. The sun was definitely farther along in the sky, and the relief in Cassius's features was particularly notable.

"So what's in there?" she asked.

"A passage," Ashley said cheerfully. "Leading Baast knows where, but we're going to find out."

"Is that a good idea?" Torva asked, standing between the gray mare and Vesi, holding their bridles.

"Well, we can't stay here," Lyria said. As they looked at her, she pointed east to where the sky was darkening with large, ominous clouds. "Another storm's coming." She looked at Keagan with a pleading expression. "Please don't make me go back with a report."

Keagan let out a rueful snort. "I think after what you did with the squib, we're definitely going to need you along. You may be our only way of fighting any shadow creatures we encounter."

Lyria suddenly didn't look as pleased at being included.

"Did you know that passages are apparently dead Paths?" Ashley asked.

"What?" Cassius regarded Shay, studying her intently as if to determine how she felt about it. "Is that possible?"

Shay shook her head "I don't know. I don't even know if it's accurate. It's just the only way I can explain it. I think that's why Riders don't go near the other passages. It hurts a little to be in one."

Keagan frowned. "You didn't tell me that."

Shay lifted a hand, indicating she was reluctant to talk about it. "It's all right. It's not painful, just uncomfortable."

"We may be inside it for a while," Keagan said. "A week, according to Torva."

"I'll be fine." Shay's tone was such that Keagan decided not to pursue it any further. She just made a mental note to keep an eye on her Rider.

"All right, a storm's coming, but we should be all right in the passage as far as the weather's concerned," Keagan said, turning to the others. "Darvus and his people have obviously been using it for some time, and I doubt they would if they were regularly attacked by creatures."

"On the other hand, he clearly has a way to control them," Ashley said. "We don't."

"Did he originally?" Torva asked. "Perhaps we should search the immediate area. There may be some evidence of another place where he could have gathered such technology."

"It also explains how they could move a lot of people and supplies without anyone noticing," Cassius said, catching Keagan's attention. "Bring everything to the farm and then transport it through this unknown passage to…where? Do you think it leads to Amane?"

"Possibly," Keagan said, and nodded respectfully at Cassius. "Maybe even probably. Good catch. You have a real knack for deduction. It's like you're an actual marshal." Cassius just smiled and Keagan motioned at Lyria. "Scout, when will that storm hit?"

"Late tonight, early morning. It's not as big as the last one."

"So, we'll search until sunset. Pair up, spread out, cover as much ground as you can. Wherever it looks like it's been disturbed, check it out. Shay, you're with me."

"Torva, you and me?" Cassius asked, offering her a smile. "I definitely want the historian with me when I don't know what I'm searching for."

Torva colored a little, dipping her head, but she looked pleased as she moved to Cassius's side. In the meantime, Shay had paused to pat Onyx. "Watch," she said. "Guard."

Cassius stared at her and then at her big stallion. "You do the same," she said, sternly.

Gault tossed his head, almost as if nodding. Keagan wasn't sure that was actually happening, but she wasn't worried about leaving the horses temporarily on their own. She'd come to trust that they would follow Onyx's lead, and he was remarkably obedient and clever. They left them saddled in case they needed a quick escape, even if it was only into the passage that lay below.

The structures around the area showed signs of past excavation, though clearly it had been some time ago, since vegetation was reclaiming it at a rapid pace. It was difficult to tell if anything valuable had been found, since it was almost impossible to know what the structures had been. Shay was quiet as she and Keagan explored, and Keagan took a moment to pull her aside, hand gentle on her arm.

"Talk to me. What are you feeling? Do you think it'll get worse?" Shay hesitated, clearly not wanting to get into it. Keagan let out her breath, keeping a rein on her temper. "I need to know, in the event it makes you less effective as a fighter."

Shay abruptly looked a little embarrassed. "I'm sorry. I didn't consider that possibility. I don't think it'll affect me. It's like an ache, but not a pain. Like an old bruise. I doubt it'll become any worse."

"All right. You'll let me know if it does."

"I will," Shay said.

Keagan regarded her intently and then pulled her close for a kiss. "And I worry about you," she murmured against her lips. "Just because."

"I worry about you, too." Shay tightened her hug and kissed her back. "Even when I know you can take care of yourself."

Keagan permitted herself to take a few extra minutes, nuzzling into Shay's neck and resting her head on her shoulder, simply absorbing the comfort and security of her embrace, before reluctantly pulling away. "Let's check over there. It looks like it's been dug out a little."

Cautiously, they entered the shadows of a ruined structure, stepping around rubble. The ceiling had large, gaping holes where vines had penetrated, and they could see four stories above them to the sky. The air was filled with motes of pollen, drifting idly in the rays of sunshine that managed to penetrate this far. It was difficult to see what made this spot worth working on while other structures seemed completely untouched.

They found the remains of a counter, almost as if this had possibly been a shop, with what might have been shelving behind. Keagan saw nothing to indicate what kind until her boot crunched on something on the floor. She lifted her foot and peered down, intrigued when she saw dark shards of glass. Kneeling, she picked up one and held it up, noting how opaque it was. To be sure, she drew her shadow realm goggles from within her tunic to compare the two. They seemed identical.

"Oh." Shay's voice was small when she saw what Keagan had found.

"It might not be what we think," Keagan said weakly.

"I think that in ancient times, people purchased these freely from merchants to walk the Shadows." Shay appeared grim.

"Maybe it was just while they traveled the passage. It was pretty dark there, and rather than use lamps the whole time, they used these."

"Your goggles don't work out in the world."

"Maybe these do."

Shay exhaled audibly. "I'm getting tired of having everything I thought I knew turn out to be completely wrong."

"You're not alone," Keagan said. "We're all adjusting."

She turned to head back outside when she felt a shift beneath her feet, then a cracking sound, and suddenly, she was falling. Not far. Somehow, impossibly, Shay had managed to lunge across the rubble-strewn floor and grab her by the arm.

For a few seconds, they tried to catch their breath, Keagan dangling in midair, Shay splayed over the floor above her, head and shoulders extended over the gaping hole.

"Thank you," Keagan managed to say, reaching up with her other hand to take Shay's forearm, trying to ease the weight a little.

Those silver eyes glimmered as they looked down at her. "I'll always catch you," Shay said.

Despite the situation, Keagan smiled widely.

"I'm not anchored," Shay said. "I can't pull you up. If I try, we'll both go down."

Keagan glanced down, unable to see anything. "How far? Maybe you should drop me."

"It's not far. You'd survive. But I can see gaps in the surface farther in. I doubt it's stable. No one's down there to catch you if it all goes."

"Good point."

They looked at each other and, in one breath, called out.

"Help!"

Lyria and Ashley were the first to respond to their cries, and with surprising foresight, Ashley stopped Lyria from rushing to their side. From the doorway, they assessed the situation. "How sturdy?"

"Not sure," Shay said. "The whole thing could go at any moment. There's another floor below, but just stepping on it could collapse it. Depending on how many floors exist below that, we could all end up buried when the whole building comes down."

Keagan marveled at how composed Shay was, considering things she hadn't even thought about. It was another trait she admired greatly about her. The more dire the situation, the calmer Shay seemed to become. Keagan also knew that Shay had to be having trouble keeping hold of her. Not only did Keagan pride herself on her muscle tone, making her solid, but she was in full armor and weaponry. She'd offer to drop her sword and shield, but she didn't think it would lighten the load that much, and the gyrations required in order to unhook her harness and belt would probably do more harm than good. Likewise, she couldn't try to climb up, or she'd pull Shay into the hole with her.

"What do we do?" Lyria asked, sounding anxious. "I could create an updraft—"

"No!" Keagan, Ashley, and Shay all said as one.

In a gentler tone, Ashley said, "That could bring the whole building down, too. Any updraft would have to push from below."

"Sorry," Lyria said.

"No. It was a good thought, just not the right one for this situation. If she were dumb enough to fall off a cliff instead of through a floor, an updraft would be great."

"We need to hurry this up a little." The corners of Shay's eyes were wrinkled, and the set of her jaw was very firm. She had both hands around Keagan's wrist, but even she could hold on for only so long. They might have to test the stability of the floor below regardless, Keagan thought. She looked down, but it was so dark and dusty, she couldn't see what lay beneath her.

"Whoa. This isn't great," Cassius said from above.

"Yeah. Keagan not watching where she was going again."

"Not helpful, Ash." Keagan gritted her teeth.

"Hang on," Torva called out. "I have an idea."

There was a bit of a discussion that Keagan couldn't quite make out, dangling out of sight as she was. Little bits of cement tumbled past her, and she could hear an ominous creaking in the floor joints.

"Shay, you need to let go," she said. "Get to safety. I'll take my chance below."

"I'm not letting you go," Shay said, her tone ice. "Don't even think about it."

"That's an order."

"You're not my boss."

"Technically, I am," Keagan said. "Please, Shay."

"Not happening."

"Damn it, Shay!"

"Be still and let us figure this out."

Definitely not the deputy marshals she was used to, Keagan thought, dismayed.

XXXIII

Shay tightened her grip even though she felt herself weakening, her toes digging into the unyielding floor, scrabbling for purchase. She pondered every possibility. Could she create an entry, put them both in the Shadow Realm? She had no idea how the physics of that would work. Keagan might end up embedded in what passed as ground in there. She could feel the floor crumbling where she lay, shoulders trembling as she tried to maintain her hold. Keagan was looking at her, anger and fear mingling in those brilliant eyes, but Shay knew the fear wasn't for herself.

"Don't you dare," she said, reading the calculations going on behind that blue gaze. "You try to wiggle free, I'm coming down after you."

"Please, Shay." Keagan was pleading now, her voice low and throaty, no longer that firm whip of command. "Let me go."

"Never."

"Okay, Shay, we're tossing in a rope," Torva said. "It has a hook at the end. We'll try to get it through the hole, and then you can hook it onto Keagan."

"Good," Shay said shortly. "Hurry."

The first toss was not accurate, falling short. Shay could have tried to hold Keagan with one hand and reach it, but that would be risky, and before she could even consider the move fully, Torva had already dragged it back for a second try. The next throw was more accurate, past her shoulder and into the hole. Her gaze met Keagan's.

"Do it," Shay said. "I've got you."

Keagan let go of Shay's forearm with her free hand and reached for the hook, grabbing it and pulling it down to fasten it onto her belt. "All right. I'm tied."

With Cassius pulling steadily, taking the weight, Shay was able to maneuver Keagan back up through the opening. "Stay low," she said. "As if we're on ice."

"Never been on ice," Keagan muttered, but together, they crawled back to the doorway until waiting hands pulled them through and they were once more on solid ground. Once there, Keagan turned to Shay. Her eyes were faintly glowing in anger. "You should have let me go."

"Didn't need to, as it turned out," Shay said, calmly, though her temper was rising. She was aware of Cassius motioning to the others to clear the area, which they did quickly. "There are certain things that you can order me to do, and I'll do them. But you don't own me, nor do the marshals. I make my own choices, whether ordered or not. You either accept that fact, or you don't. Better decide now."

Keagan opened her mouth, seemed to think better of it, and settled for glaring at her. "You scared me," she said finally.

"You scared me," Shay said, knowing this was the root of the anger. "You were the one in the hole."

"If you won't follow my lead, how can I expect any of the others to? How can I expect Lyria to fly away when she needs to?"

"You can't," Shay said, honestly. "She makes her own decisions. We all do. It will really come down to, in that moment, if she really believes all is lost and needs to go for help." She shrugged. "And if you insist on trying to sacrifice yourself over a mere fall, she might not believe you now, if you give that order." She allowed her own anger to show. "You have to fight for your life and believe that we can help in tricky situations. You can't just give up because you decide it's a noble thing."

"It had nothing to do with nobility," Keagan said. "It had to do with—"

"With my safety," Shay said. "Which is not your responsibility. You can't control everything, Keagan. Stop trying."

"To be a leader—"

"Means trusting in the abilities of the people working with you, and that includes our decision-making. We won't always be right. Neither will you. But hopefully, working together, we'll find a solution." Shay exhaled, trying to figure out a better way to explain her point. "We don't follow you because you're Undine or a marshal or because the crown tells us to, Keagan. We follow you because you're worthy. Because we believe in you. You need to believe in us."

"I do believe in you," Keagan said, weakly. "But there's a chain of command."

Shay managed not to openly scoff. "Chain of command only works when everyone has honestly earned their respective spot in it. When that isn't the case, it becomes the weak link. It might be why someone like Darvus has been able to operate freely before now. Somewhere, someone in a position of authority, someone with no integrity, has decided to help cover things up." She turned her back, done with the conversation. "You didn't give that order because it was the right call. You did it to protect me because of personal reasons. Don't do it again."

She stomped away, though she had learned it was unlikely anyone could hear her leaving, and went in search of Onyx. She found him with the others, grazing the sparse grass peppered about the ruins. He lifted his head at her approach, nickering inquiringly.

"We'll feed you all later," she told him, thumping his neck lightly. "We're going underground. I doubt it'll be pleasant." Did he feel the same sense of unease near the dead Path that she did?

As she patted him, she fretted over the conversation with Keagan. Or, rather, their first real fight. It had left her with a sick feeling inside, deeper than any disquiet she had felt before. She would never obey an order to let Keagan die, of course, but perhaps she could have framed her words better in the aftermath.

Around her, the wind had picked up, gusting in that familiar way, and the first drops of rain started to fall. The main storm was still hours away. She was becoming entirely weary of the weather in this part of Terras. The southwest part of the nation was so much nicer in comparison, with long, hot summers, very mild winters, and beautiful, bountiful springs and autumns. She was beginning to think that someone in Terras truly had been greedy, issuing land grants this far northeast. If only they hadn't, perhaps none of this would be happening.

But then, she reminded herself, she would never have met Keagan. And that alone was worth anything she'd faced since then and would encounter in the future.

Cassius appeared next to her, fiddling with a bit of Gault's tack. "You two okay?" she asked in a low voice.

Shay shrugged. "A difference of opinion." She glanced over her shoulder, saw Keagan speaking with Ashley and Lyria, and wondered if they were talking about her before she shook off the immature notion. Instead, she checked Onyx's girth, making sure he felt no irritation. "Did you and Torva find anything?"

"Could be. We discovered a building to the north that Torva said looked like an old military or marshal station. It had been cleared out of anything significant, but that in itself was worth noting. Whatever had been in there must have been valuable for them to strip it clean. We saw an Aether symbol on the wall, like it had once belonged to your nation."

"Perhaps that's where he found all the items he's been using to violate the Shadow Realm." Shay's anger bubbled up, again. "Or perhaps he's just doing what they did in the old times. Whatever they wanted."

"Well, if non-Elementals ruled and we were just an enslaved minority, they still wouldn't have any abilities. They'd need something to give them the advantage." Cassius shook her head. "Maybe we have it all wrong. Maybe it wasn't one person making a mistake in using the stones. Maybe there really was a war, only it wasn't between nations, but between

Elementals and those who weren't. Natural ability verses the technology of the stones."

Shay absorbed that suggestion, feeling it settle into her bones. "That's...interesting."

"Torva said that sometimes historians become enamored with a theory and start using the facts to fit the idea rather than the other way around. Maybe that's what this Professor Tannehill did. Maybe that's what the Academy did." Cassius let out a laugh. "Or maybe it's exactly what I'm doing right now. Maybe we'll never know what really happened, and we just have to pick up the pieces a millennium later."

"This situation is hurting my head," Shay said. "Sometimes, I just want a definite goal and to go from there."

"Well, getting through this passage is a definite goal." Cassius paused. "Do you think we'll run into more Shadow creatures?"

"No idea. I'm still trying to figure out why steel works on them in the Shadow Realm and doesn't out here. Meanwhile, elemental powers seem to affect them in the world, while they can't be used in there. It's as if all the rules I've learned are being broken, and I have no idea what the new ones should be."

The others joined them, leading their horses. "All right," Keagan said, gesturing toward the building, "I've been going over whether to spend the night here and tackle the passage tomorrow, or go in immediately. But the storm is forcing our hand. We'll have to camp somewhere in there."

"Maybe the passage isn't as long as the others are," Lyria suggested. "We could be out before sunset."

"I don't think distance plays into it," Torva said.

"It does on Paths," Shay said. "The longer you've been riding a Path, the farther you've traveled."

"Are we sure about that?" Ashley asked, with a wry expression. "If the nations aren't where we thought they were?"

Stymied, Shay resolved to speak to a scout as soon as possible and determine exactly how they created Paths. If anyone knew where everything was actually located, they would. Clearly, the education she had received at the Shadow School was severely lacking. Or was she simply suffering the consequences of having no curiosity about how things worked in her own nation and profession? Maybe her teachers had known all along, and she had never bothered to pursue anything beyond her own specialty. Then she remembered her parents' evasiveness when asked about the dark goggles the others were wearing and decided that perhaps certain things weren't spoken of. But why? Did they not know and were reluctant to admit it?

Her head was starting to hurt again.

Shaking off her discomfort, she took Onyx firmly by the bridle and led him into the building. He hesitated at the top of the stairs, and she waited until he'd had a good look at the situation before allowing her to lead him down, picking his way carefully as if on a mountain path. The others followed, more or less taking a cue from their riders. Ashley and Fuoco descended with confidence, as did Cassius and Gault. Lyria seemed less so, and Vindur's ears were laid back, eyes wide as she descended, but she obeyed Lyria's gentle urging. Torva, of course, didn't know what she was doing, and the gray mare made the trip on her own, unperturbed, practically leading Torva down.

But Vesi balked, head up, refusing to budge at the top of the stairs. Shay had been afraid of just this situation, where the Shadow-touched would obey their rider but the cull would not, being just an ordinary horse, after all. Leaving Onyx with the others, Shay went back upstairs, sighing as she heard Keagan pleading quietly with him. She doubted he understood.

"I'll take him." She resisted the urge to sigh again when both Keagan and Vesi looked surprised to see her, not noticing her approach. But after several minutes, no matter what she tried, she had no more luck in shifting him. It would be no good to try to blindfold him. He'd be sure to trip on the stairs and possibly break a leg. She'd suggest they leave him behind, but not only would Keagan object, he probably lacked the ability to take care of himself long enough to make it back to the Shadow Lands as the others would. Finally, frustrated, Shay looked at Keagan. "This isn't going to happen. He won't go down."

Keagan, who hadn't said anything, looked crushed. "What can we do?" she finally asked.

"We'll take a very short walk into the Realm," Shay said as she used her scarf to blindfold him.

"Will that work?"

"I don't know. If I'm lucky, the passage is right there, and I'll be able to access it from the Realm, but even if it does, we'll come out several leagues ahead of you, possibly more than one or two days' travel. We'll stay put until you catch up. Take Onyx."

"Are you sure?"

"I won't close the entry on this side immediately," Shay said. "We'll step in, and then I'll open another. Either we'll be able to exit into the passage or we won't. If not, I'll back us out. It won't take long, and if the entry closes behind me, you'll know it worked."

"All right," Keagan said, sounding uncertain.

"Like I said, it won't take long." Shay lifted her hand to make an entry, but Keagan caught it, pulling her to her in a rough embrace.

"I'm sorry," Keagan whispered as she hugged her. "I'll do better."

"I'm sorry, too." Shay gentled her voice. "I do trust you, Keagan. With everything." It was the only thing she could think to say, but it seemed sufficient, since Keagan kissed her as if never wanting to let her go. Happily, Shay returned the kiss enthusiastically, holding her for a long moment before finally, reluctantly, stepping back.

"Be careful."

"Always."

Shay eased open an entry, not wishing any disturbance to be felt on the other side, then led Vesi inside, counting her paces, three of them, until the bulk of the horse was completely within the Realm. Then she looked around and her mouth dropped open.

This was a passage? Or at least what it looked like from within the Realm?

She was standing inside a sort of cave, surrounded by jagged, black crystal, like the rock Onyx was named for, the angular surfaces smooth, as if polished. She had seen these formations before on her travels, from a great distance, what she thought had passed for rock outcroppings in the Realm. She had been taught to steer well clear of them. They were hollow inside? She looked around, noting that the geological feature extended into the distance, though only half a step to either side and behind her. Squinting, she realized she could see through it to the outside in a blurred sort of way and, more disturbingly, noticed the litter of bones stretching along the outer edges of it, as if a multitude of creatures had perished at once and had not been touched by anything since, which didn't happen in the Realm to her knowledge.

Of course, she was beginning to realize she knew next to nothing about the Shadow Realm. She reached out, suitably disturbed when her hand passed through, as if the rock didn't exist. She inhaled quietly. Perhaps it didn't, she thought. Perhaps it was out in the world and only an echo of it remained here in the Realm. Carefully, she opened another entry in front of her and peered through, relieved to see the smooth walls and dusty floor of what was clearly the passage, but confused as hell over what it all meant.

Swallowing hard, she closed the entry behind her and stepped through the one in front of her, closing it immediately once she and Vesi were through. The tunnel stretched on for leagues in front and behind her and several yards to each side. Shaking her head, she began to tend to Vesi and make camp.

She had a lot to think about before the others caught up.

XXXIV

Keagan watched the entry disappear, closing to a line of darkness, then fading quickly away. She had tried to look inside but could see only an inky blackness that immediately swallowed up both horse and Rider. But apparently, the idea had worked. Making her way down the stairs, she saw the others huddled near the entrance of the passage.

"Where's Shay?" Lyria asked.

"Hopefully, far ahead of us." Keagan took Onyx's reins from Cassius, realizing how much Shay trusted her to have left him with her, instead of taking both horses through the Realm. "We couldn't get Vesi down the stairs. She took a couple of steps through the Realm and hopefully back out into the passage."

"Hopefully?" Ashley gave her a skeptical look.

"We won't know exactly how it worked until we catch up with her." Keagan patted Onyx on his neck. "I'm going to ride you, now," she said, not knowing if she had to explain but wanting his permission if she did. He didn't pull away or balk as she carefully mounted, and she assumed that meant everything was all right.

"Let's go." She nudged Onyx with her heels, starting off into the passage, holding a vapor light high to see the road ahead. The others quickly fell in behind her and, soon, had created a steady pace, trotting along the trail cut through the dust.

Debris occasionally littered the floor, items tossed aside by the people who had come before them, clear indication of present-day use. Keagan saw packaging from a popular brand of trail mix used in Aquas. She wondered if people were as messy in the other passages. Perhaps they had staff who regularly went through cleaning up. She had no idea and realized she should.

"Torva, Ashley, can you join me? I want to know everything available about passages."

Torva urged her mount forward until she was riding on Keagan's right. Ashley was quicker in moving up to Keagan's left.

"What exactly do you want to know?" Torva said.

"Any detail, no matter how small," Keagan said. "I know nothing. Start from there. The whole process."

"First, you make arrangements with the Travel Guild," Torva said, "indicating when you want to go. I hear it's possible to just show up, but even then, it's not as if you're allowed to travel the passage on your own. You have to be part of a caravan, and they go through only once a week. You have to show up on a Firstday morning. I hear that sometimes they let people catch up on Seconday if they hire a guide to escort them in, but not after. Show up on Thirday, and you have to wait until the next week."

"My secretary takes care of those details," Ashley said, less than helpfully. At Keagan's expression, she sighed and continued. "Passengers and cargo travel on large wagons pulled by oxen. The train can be thirty or forty carts long, led by a wagon master and a few outriders. You travel exactly twelve hours from way station to way station, from six in the morning until six in the evening. The way stations have a place to eat and beds for everyone. No one has to sleep in the wagon."

Torva looked a little ashamed. "I don't know if the people manning them work in month-long shifts or if they're on the caravan with us and I've never noticed," she said. "I never really thought about the cooks and cleaners the Travel Guild employs. They might actually live there. It must be awful to stay underground for such long periods of time."

"Let's hope this place has way stations," Ashley said in a more practical tone. "Not that we'll reach one tonight. We left around two and missed lunch, by the way. We'll either be camping or keep riding until two tomorrow morning. Is that the schedule you want to keep?"

Keagan held up her hand, indicating they should all pause. Once they were together, she put it to a vote. "Ashley says we won't find a way station, assuming there is one, for another ten hours. We can try to make it or set up camp after a few more hours riding. What do you all think?"

"We have the gear," Cassius said. "It's not as if we haven't camped before, and at least we're out of the weather."

Conscious of the storm that was undoubtedly raging outside, Keagan was grateful for that fact as well.

"I think we should keep riding as far as we can," Lyria said. "I'm not that tired, and Vindur's still eager. Why not decide later? We may feel the way station's in reach if we push a little. We must be traveling faster than a caravan. They just plod along. It takes forever."

The others were nodding. "All right. That's the plan, then," Keagan said. "But don't overextend. If you're tired or ready to stop, let me know, any of you. We have no idea what's in here. We shouldn't exhaust ourselves and the horses when we don't have to. In the meantime, we'll eat as we go. Trail food only."

Ashley didn't look thrilled, but she dug into her saddlebags as they started off again and found herself an apple and some trail mix. Keagan helped herself to the trail rations in Onyx's saddlebag, not feeling particularly hungry but knowing she had to eat. As she rode, she was struck by the sheer monotony of the passage. The same rounded walls, the same dusty floor, the same still, stale air, hour after hour. If it wasn't for the occasional different type of litter marking the trail, it would be hard to believe they were making any progress at all. Hooves thumped loudly on the hard, flat surface, and the conversation between the others carried easily. A wagon train had to be exponentially noisier, Keagan thought. A complete circus, in fact. Not at all like a Path, where every small sound induced terror at the thought of what it might attract.

She was grateful for the huge size of the tunnel, however. She didn't feel at all closed in. She hoped Shay, wherever she was, didn't either. The strength of her constant ache at Shay's absence, like a dull pain settling in under her breast, surprised her. No wonder they called it heartache when you missed the one you loved. It was literal.

"Look, markings," Ashley called out suddenly. "Though they're really faint." She gestured at the thin lines engraved on the nearby wall, barely visible in their lamplight. "A way station has to be just ahead. Lyria was right. We're traveling a lot faster than a caravan would, almost twice as fast, I'd say. It only took six hours."

Keagan drew her sword. "Arms," she called out. "It might be manned like the entrance."

Weapons drawn, they increased their pace, cantering up the tunnel, and in the distance, Keagan spotted a light. They reached it quickly, a large hollow carved into the side of one wall, filled with three structures. She saw no sign of anyone, just the steady light from the vapor lamps set in the doorways, illuminating the surroundings.

With an exchanged glance, Keagan, Ashley, and Cassius slipped from their mounts, spreading out to search the area. It didn't take long, and Keagan wasn't sure if she was relieved or annoyed to find it empty. A part of her hoped to discover more answers, which was hard to do when there wasn't anyone to question.

After letting the others know it was clear, Keagan and Cassius tended to the horses, while Torva and Ashley looked around. Afterward, they gathered in the largest structure, in a cafeteria filled with long tables surrounded by metal chairs. At one end was a counter with a small kitchen behind, which Darvus and his people had apparently used. Had they brought in this equipment, or had it always been there? A bit of food was left in the cupboards, and the packaging was modern, made in Terras. The appliances didn't have any energy crystals, and Keagan couldn't figure out how they worked, but Cassius had no problem activating the stove to heat some soup for their supper.

"It's exactly like in the other passages," Torva said as they settled at one end of a table to eat. "A place to stay for the passengers and stables for the caravan. I never went into the third building, of course, but from what I can see, it contains offices and living quarters for the employees. How is it possible for these facilities to have existed unchanged for so long yet no one has ever questioned their origin? Are we really that uninterested in knowing why things are?"

"I'm not interested at all," Ashley said as she pulled some bread from the loaf and spread butter on it. "If it works, why rock the boat?"

"It's like time," Lyria said. "Who invented it?" She lifted her hands in a gesture of bafflement. "Who decided a day was twenty-four hours long and that a week had six days?"

"Well, that's astrological," Cassius said in her gentle tone. "Someone, a long time ago, discovered how long it takes for the sun to travel the sky. You can do that with a stick in the ground, reading its shadow. You can read the stars and see how they travel across the sky. Then someone discovered that it takes three hundred and sixty days for our world to go around the sun, which can be broken down into twelve months, three months in each season, five weeks in a month, a season spanning from solstice to equinox, the first of each year starting in spring. It's really just math, isn't it?"

"But how did they figure it out?" Lyria was wide-eyed, as if considering the question for the first time. Keagan had to admit that she was as well. Who worried about how time worked, after all? Other than it did and if one was late for an appointment.

"Someone did it for economic reasons," Ashley said. "How long does this take, and how much can we charge for it? If it takes longer, can we charge more? How many days in a row can we reasonably make someone work for us, and how much do we have to pay them so they'll keep working for us? Will giving them Fifthday and Faithday be enough of a break between four-day work weeks. It all comes down to gold."

"Sadly, that's true," Torva said. "In its essence, anyway. Only when a culture achieves a certain level of advancement can its citizens afford to think about things beyond food on the table each day and a place to shelter at night. Only when I and my tribe, whatever that includes, can eat and sleep safely in one area for an extended period of time can I think about why things are the way they are, and how I can make them better for us." She paused. "Or correspondingly worse for someone else."

"Civilization at its core," Ashley said with a small laugh.

"After whatever...let's say, disaster? War?...happened, only certain inherent things, like the knowledge of how time works, remained. Everything else was probably lost in the immediate need for survival. Even if you lived in an area far away, you were probably isolated, cut off from items and services that were taken for granted. Simple things, like certain tools or even spices, were no longer accessible, or possible to create, so you passed on to your children what they needed to know, and if they were lucky, they were able to improve things a little. And only after time passed and generations came into the world, and small communities grew into towns and towns grew into cities, was a person like me able to pursue a career as a historian. Being able to study history, to find out what really happened, is a luxury. It doesn't put food on the table or a roof over a head in any real, tangible sense."

"You said it," Ashley pointed out.

"No. She's right," Lyria said. "My job isn't crucial for society to survive. My company is trying to create an airship. Is it really necessary? I'm paid a lot, but who decides that?"

"I guess it's profit, after all," Cassius said. "My recent assignments have also been for the sake of indulgence, as far as that goes. It's nice for a farming co-op in Arias to try to grow trees that require a lot of water, but is it necessary? They want to do it only to expand their market into luxury goods and because they can, but wouldn't that energy be better spent in trying to expand the fields for basic foodstuffs for their own nation instead of leaving Arias dependent on other nations?"

"We don't even live where we once did," Keagan said, thoughtfully, sopping up the last of her soup with some bread. "We don't surround ourselves with reminders of what once was. It's as if it never happened."

"That may be true in Aquas, but in Arias, we're always aware of what we've lost," Lyria said. "Having no access to the river affects our society, even now."

After cleaning up, they went upstairs to rooms that contained two single beds, solid bases with sturdy cushioning that wasn't as thick as a mattress but more comfortable than their sleeping pads. Keagan thought about their conversation as she drew her blanket over her shoulders, at how much she was learning about the other nations and somewhat ashamed at how limited her world view had been before now. But that wasn't the only thing keeping her up as she tossed and turned. It astonished her at how quickly and easily she had become used to having Shay in bed beside her. Now, not having her there made it impossible to sleep. No matter how hard she tried, she just couldn't doze off, and she was actually grateful when Cassius slipped in to wake her for her watch duty a few hours later.

"All quiet," she said, as Keagan dressed. She slipped into the other bed, yawning widely. "No sign of anything. And silent. I don't think I've ever heard true silence before now."

Once Cassius had pointed it out, Keagan couldn't avoid it as she patrolled the area. The silence was oppressive. There wasn't even any of the normal, constant dripping of condensation that was usual in underground tunnels. And, as she reached out with her senses, she realized she felt very little moisture at all, almost as little as in the Shadow Realm. A holding tank of some kind lay beneath them, filled with clear, clean water, but it was very protected, layered with more than concrete. She had no idea what kept it full and doubted she'd be able to draw on it from any distance. She made a mental note to check with the others in the morning, find out how limited their abilities might be in here between way stations.

As she took a seat at the top of the ramp leading back to the tunnel, sword laid across her lap, she wondered how Shay was doing, and if she might be thinking of her, too. As the moments passed with agonizing slowness, she contemplated a future beyond this mission, assuming everyone survived. How would they proceed with their relationship? Would Shay remain with the Shadow Riders, or could Keagan convince her to join the marshals? Was it too soon to think about sharing lodgings? Would Shay move in with Keagan, or would Keagan move in with her? Or, more logically, would they find a place together, one they could share fully without causing any sense of intrusion? Would they live in Naiad? Would Keagan be able to accompany Shay back to Aether during the holidays? Would Diane and Calvin ever visit Aquas?

So much to consider.

But thinking about it did pass the time more pleasantly than contemplating the darkness that lay beyond the illumination of the way station. She did wonder if the small, periodic recesses in the walls had originally contained lights, long since extinguished because of time and degradation. If so, they weren't powered by crystals. They seemed to be more like the lamps she had experienced in the Aether inn, possessing a strange sort of transparent globe containing some sort of metal filaments within that glowed when switched on. Not the slow-burning vapor created by Sylph and Salamas abilities she was far more familiar with. Which lasted longer—the Aether bulbs fed by whatever it was, or the elemental cylinders powered by crystals?

"Keagan?"

The sound didn't startle her as badly as Shay was wont to do, but it did make her heart speed up a little. "What are you doing up? You aren't assigned watch tonight."

Ashley settled onto the step next to her. "Couldn't sleep," she said, running her fingers through her thick, auburn hair, clearly tired but alert. "Too quiet."

"Isn't it quiet in the other passages?"

"Are you kidding? With a few hundred people all traveling together? You're lucky if you get a moment's peace." Ashley smiled, probably in fond remembrance. "But with so many stuck together in close quarters like that, you can meet some interesting personalities. I've had some of my best times in passages."

"How often do you use them?"

"Baast, at least five or six times a year, so a lot of trips in total. And from what I understand, all the nations constantly use both passages. The Travel Guild makes a killing. Whoever discovered these things, they were smart to set up a monopoly on them. Of course, it's clear now that no infrastructure had to be constructed, since the way stations were already in place. They just had to build the garrison towns at either end. Or, rather, they built the towns, and the crown installed the garrisons."

"Do those work?" Keagan gestured at a nearby recess in the wall.

"What? Those?" Ashley peered closer. "Do you think those were lights?"

"I do."

"That would make things a lot brighter," Ashley said. "The caravans have their own lamps, of course, but there aren't any permanent ones along the way." She glanced at Keagan. "That could be to keep anyone from trying to use the passage on their own. Even with the five of us using our lamps, it's still damned dark in here. I wouldn't want to travel this alone."

"Do you think that the presence of so many people, in between where the glyphs are, is what keeps the shadow creatures away?"

"I hope not."

"Why?"

"Because if numbers are the reason, then Shay's all alone. And if she's not near a way station with glyphs, things could get very bad for her."

XXXV

Shay settled down against the wall of the passage, back resting against the smooth surface. Vesi stayed near, well within the small circle of illumination her rarely utilized vapor lamp gave off. She would have liked a fire, but there was absolutely nothing to burn around here, except a few pieces of litter left behind by Darvus and his people. She could see the tunnel without the lamp, of course, but she had it on more for comfort than anything. It amused her that after a life of traveling the world on her own, she was now very aware of not having the others around. And not liking it one bit. She would have even settled for Ashley as a companion, if only to have someone to talk to.

Of course, she was really missing Keagan. That dull, sick sensation in the pit of her stomach only added to her headache from being in this tunnel that echoed from its connection to the Shadow Realm. Was really a dead Path? It felt like it had once been alive but now wasn't quite completely expired. It was disturbing as hell.

She had considered trying to find one of these way stations the others had talked about, but looking up and down the disorienting and long tunnel, she didn't know which direction was which. Picking one could send her in Keagan's direction, but picking the other could take her farther away. Her promise to stay in place was proving to be a prudent decision, though she cursed herself for not noticing which direction she'd been facing when she left the entry.

Vesi was standing uncomfortably close and hopefully wouldn't inadvertently step on her. She hadn't ridden a cull since she was a child. Granted, he was still Shadow-bred as opposed to one of the ordinary horses that populated the rest of the world, but would she have to guide him every second?

In here, where he probably couldn't see any better than on a Path? Probably. At least they had replaced the dilettante saddle with a more rugged clan version. Something flickered in her peripheral vision, distracting her from her trivial musing, and she turned her head to see a wraith oozing through the wall some distance down the tunnel.

"Okay, that's not good," she muttered under her breath as she rose, drawing her daggers.

For a few moments, it seemed as if the creature didn't notice her, drifting across the tunnel away from her. It was as if it was still in the Shadow Realm and didn't realize it was out in the real world at all. Was it in the real world? Was she? Then Vesi either spotted or simply sensed it and reared, neighing loudly.

"Oh, for Lady's sake."

Onyx wouldn't have made a sound, she thought, disgusted. She darted in between the wraith and the horse, slicing at the shadow. It veered away, though Shay wasn't completely sure her blades would have been effective, considering how they hadn't worked on the squib out in the world. While it clearly recognized the weapons and did its best to avoid them, she couldn't stand there swiping at it indefinitely in the hopes of scaring it off. Then, one of her daggers intersected the wraith's midsection and, as feared, did absolutely nothing, while its responding slash of claws scoured bloody marks across her arm. For a few stunned seconds, she and the wraith regarded each other, and she would swear the fanged opening in the general area of its face turned up in a wicked smile. Then it shrieked.

She swore a particularly vile oath as she dodged backward, one involving Stygia's anatomy, which she was not usually wont to do. Scooping up the vapor lamp, she dashed over and mounted Vesi, who was less than cooperative, scrambling into the saddle as he skittered sideways. "Damn it, come on."

She wrenched his head around and dug her heels into his sides. "Go, idiot."

They thundered down the passage, and in a glance back she saw two more wraiths joining the first, and then, horror upon horror, a banthra appeared, its eight spidery legs carrying the bulbous body with disturbing speed. Bent over his neck, she pressed Vesi onward, relieved that he apparently understood the need for urgency. He was just so slow, compared to Onyx, and the surroundings made it difficult to judge how fast they were going.

Or if they were actually going at all or simply galloping in place.

Another glance back showed that wasn't the case, but the wraiths and banthra were gaining ground with every stride. Looking forward, heart in her throat, she saw a tiny pinprick of light in the distance and wasn't sure whether to be relieved or more worried. Then she was impressed at the sheer speed at which it was approaching and spared her mount an astonished pat on the neck. Before she could react further, the light streaked by overhead, and she heard a cry that blasted her ears, along with a mighty gust of wind that nearly knocked over both her and her horse. She drew up, Vesi's sides heaving beneath her legs, and looked back to see the creatures shrivel into four separate spots of goo.

"Am I glad to see you," she said as Lyria dropped to the floor a few feet away. "How'd you find me?"

"Just followed the passage and hoped for the best," Lyria told her. "Apparently Ashley said something that put Keagan in a lather, and the next thing we knew, the rest of us were being hauled out of bed and ordered to go as fast as we can. She sent me on ahead. I've been flying for a few hours." She looked back over her shoulder. "Those were...wraiths?"

"Yeah, and a banthra." Shay dismounted and began to walk Vesi, cooling him down. "I'm glad I headed in the right direction."

"So am I," Lyria said as she fell into step with her. "Though I would have caught up."

"Maybe not in time," Shay said, swallowing hard at the thought. "Have you been encountering anything?"

"Nope. That's the first." Lyria inclined her head at the vapor lamps they were carrying. "You think the light attracted them?"

Shay considered the possibility. "No. I think it was wrong place, wrong time. A wraith was just passing through. I don't even think it could see us until this imbecile caught its attention by spooking. Then it called the others." She thumped the horse gently on the neck, thinking that while he hadn't exactly covered himself in glory, at least he hadn't tried to buck her off. "Thank you for the save."

"I'd say, anytime, but I'm hoping we don't have to do that too often." Lyria paused, her mouth twisting a little. "I wasn't sure it would work again. The screaming, I mean. I'm not really sure how I managed it in the first place." She swallowed, the muscles in her neck clearly visible. "Now my throat hurts."

"Anything I can do?" Shay retrieved the flask of water from the pouch on the saddle and offered it.

Lyria shook her head as she drank thirstily. "This helped." She handed the flask back, and Shay stored it away. "Honey would be better."

"I know Cassius likes it in her tea," Shay said. "Maybe you can raid her supply. If not, once we're back outside, I know of a few plants I can make into a drink that should ease the soreness. Or we might be able to find a hive, depending on where we end up and if there's any honey this time of year."

"Good." Lyria pointed in the direction they were walking. "I passed a way station on my trip that was all lit up. I hope I was too quick and high for anyone to notice. Assuming anyone's there. No one was in the first one we found, and it had lights, too."

"Good to know." Shay eyed her, a little embarrassed to ask. "What does a way station look like?"

"It's a hollow in the wall and usually has three buildings. One for passengers, stables for the caravan, and barracks for the staff."

"Buildings?" Shay was stunned. "In here? People live in passages?"

"No. I think way stations have always been a sort of stopping point for travelers, a place to rest and eat after a day's journey."

"But someone had to build them."

Lyria shrugged. "Someone built the passages."

Did they? Shay wasn't sure, thinking of what she'd discovered in the Shadow Realm, but honestly, what did she know? Very little, apparently.

"Well, if anyone's there, hopefully we'll take them unawares."

"Yeah." But Lyria looked nervous.

"Don't worry. We can handle it." Shay patted her reassuringly on the shoulder, rather like she did Onyx when he was a bit spooked. She knew that wasn't enough, so she was content to let Lyria prattle on about everything and nothing as they walked. It was far more conversation than she normally preferred, but it probably comforted Lyria to fill the silence with words. Shay's contribution required little more than the occasional acknowledgment that she was still paying attention.

Still, she was surprised when Lyria asked, "How did you know?"

"How did I know what?"

"About Keagan. And you. How did you know you cared about each other? Like that?"

Shay took a moment. "I didn't," she said, finally. "Not at first. I mean, I thought she was great from the beginning, which was a surprise, because I didn't really know any Elementals, and what I'd heard wasn't good. But even when I started to have feelings, I thought I shouldn't have them. I didn't think she would have them back. I was shocked when she told me how she felt." She paused. "That first night, though, we almost kissed by the fire. But we didn't, so I thought it was all in my mind." She dipped her head, hiding her smile. "Why?"

Lyria shrugged. "Just wondering." Shay was about to pursue the subject when Lyria stopped and pointed at a glow from some greater illumination. "There's the way station."

Shay nodded, drawing Vesi off to the side, where she realized she had no place to tether him. She wasn't entirely sure that dropping the reins on the ground would keep him in place as it would a Shadow mount. She sighed and hoped for the best as she drew her daggers and nodded at Lyria. "Put your lamp out. I'll leave my light here. Hopefully, he won't stray from it."

"Are we going in dark?"

"Yes. Stick close. Hand on my belt."

She was glad to see the horse remained behind as they cautiously approached the hollow. Behind her, she could hear Lyria's nervous intake of breath and knew she was frightened, yet she followed Shay implicitly, trusting her. As they drew closer to the way station, Shay saw clear evidence of occupation—supplies near the stables, fresh fodder placed near the small corral. She listened intently, detecting the movements of horses inside the smaller, one-story structure. The other structures were both two-story, and lights illuminated the windows and the doorways. Even at this distance, snatches of conversation drifted toward them. Why were there windows? It wasn't like they let light in or afforded a view. Were they simply for the sake of being?

"Shit," Shay muttered.

"There are a lot of them," Lyria said.

"Unfortunately, I think so." She turned to Lyria. "How tired are you?"

Lyria looked as if she was resisting a sigh. "You want me to fly back to the others, don't you." It wasn't a question.

"I'm sorry."

"No. We'll need everyone." Lyria looked down the passage. "Can you get us by them?"

Shay nodded. "The lights should blind them beyond the extent of the illumination. We'll cross to the other side of the passage. They won't spot us in the darkness. How long do you think you'll be?"

"Assuming Keagan and the others are already riding as fast as they can toward us, an hour or so."

"I'll go back for Vesi while you're gone. I need to make sure he's over on that side as well."

"Okay. Let's do this."

Moving quietly, they crossed the large expanse of tunnel and then crept along the far wall until they were well down the passage. Finally, Lyria was able to activate her lamp. "Stay safe."

"You, too."

She ran several paces and then dove forward, somehow caught by the air that lifted her, the illumination of her lamp disappearing quickly into the distance. Shay allowed herself that familiar, sharp pang of envy before shaking it off and making her way back to Vesi and her own lamp. She switched it off and stored it in the saddlebag. "You're going to have to trust me from here," she told him, taking hold of the bridle. "I know you can't see, but we're safer here than on a Path."

He balked at first, planting his hooves, but with a few encouraging words and slaps on his hindquarters, he hesitantly allowed her to lead him down the passage. It helped that the ground was smooth and flat, with no obstructions to speak of. She did wish she had a way to muffle his hooves but quickly discovered that if they walked close to the far wall, a deep enough layer of dust obscured the sound of their motion. They were leaving a clearly distinctive trail, of course, but hopefully there wouldn't be anyone to pick it up.

As they passed the way station, she kept a hand on his muzzle, keeping his head down so he wouldn't whinny to the horses. After they were some distance down the passage, far enough that the way station was well out of earshot, she stopped.

"Good boy." She praised him even though she still thought he was dumb as a box of rocks. Still, he had a good nature, overall, and Keagan liked him, so that should be enough for her to accept him as part of the herd. She fed him a few handfuls of grain from the bag stored in the saddlebags, then grabbed a trail bar for herself. The Lady only knew how long this would take. She had no idea what time it was, whether it was day or night, only that she had been awake for some time. She definitely wasn't getting as much sleep on this adventure as she normally did in her job as a courier.

Of course, some of that was for more pleasant reasons, and she spent some time fondly remembering those reasons as she waited for the others. It took some time, but eventually, she saw the small pinpricks of lights in the distance. As she watched their approach, she realized all the Shadow mounts had darkened their coats, as if on a Path, which was another piece of information to file away. She had no idea how it all fit together, but hopefully one day she would. She didn't speak as she moved forward to intercept them, finally dragging Keagan from Onyx's back and sweeping her up into her arms for a heartfelt hug.

"Damn it, how does she just show up out of nowhere?" Ashley said. "We were even expecting to see her this time."

After a brief second of startled resistance, Keagan returned the embrace ardently. "Are you all right?"

"Fine." Shay drew back so she could look at her, basking in the brilliant blue gaze. "The way station's up there. No indication they're aware we're here."

"Vesi?"

"Back there. He's asleep."

But he wasn't, appearing out of the darkness. Shay was pleased to realize he hadn't nickered to greet them. He was learning to move quieter, something the other mounts knew how to do instinctively. He did let out a soft snort as Keagan patted him, nuzzling her hand. Shay enjoyed her own brief reunion with Onyx before turning to the others.

"Not sure how many are there," she said, "but they have at least ten horses. Assuming those horses are pulling wagons, I can only guess their numbers. A lot more than ten, at any rate."

"Are any of them Elemental?"

"Not that I could tell."

"Awake or asleep?"

"There was quite a lot of activity," Shay told them. "What time is it, anyway?"

Torva checked her pocket watch. "Around eight. I have to admit, I've lost track. Not sure whether that's morning or night. I'm also not sure how much a passage distorts distance and time. In other passages, we're told what time it is, but I've never personally carried a timepiece to compare."

"Does it matter down here?" Ashley asked. "They seem alert, and we're operating on little sleep."

"Agreed," Keagan said, a sudden sharp bite of command to her tone. "We'll stop and rest here for a few hours. No lights. Then we go in."

XXXVI

Keagan leaned back against the wall of the tunnel, Shay curled up in her arms, fast asleep. She envied that ability—to be able to catch snatches of sleep whenever she had to, like a soldier. Keagan wished she could quiet her mind enough to do the same. Not far away, Cassius stood watch, having volunteered since she had slept a few hours at the first way station, or at least she claimed she had. Rolled up in their bedding, Ashley, Lyria, and Torva were all resting, if not peacefully, then quietly, at least. No one was tossing and turning.

Resting her cheek on the soft cushion of Shay's hair, Keagan closed her eyes, willing herself to relax. It must have worked, because the next thing she knew, Cassius was nudging her awake. Shay had slipped away at some point without Keagan noticing, because she was alone, slumped against the tunnel. Stretching out the kink in her neck, Keagan yawned and rose.

"Report."

"Nothing," Cassius said. "We're too far away to hear anything from the way station, which is good, because that means they can't hear anything from us."

"Here, eat something," Shay said, suddenly appearing with a meat wrap. "You need the energy."

It was strange, having someone looking after her needs, but Keagan was not only becoming very used to it but starting to depend on it. After eating, Keagan drew the others into a huddle.

"Okay, Torva—"

"I know, stay with the horses," she said.

"Would you rather come with us?" Ashley asked with exaggerated politeness.

"No. I'm fine," Torva shot back.

Keagan was amused but didn't show it. "Cassius and I will take point, go in, try to handle this peacefully. Ashley will stay in reserve, out of sight. Shay, slip in and take care of any problem areas. Lyria, I want you to find the highest point as quietly as you can and then keep us covered while their attention is on our approach. When I give the signal, join us."

The others went on ahead on foot, led by Shay through the darkness. Once they'd had enough time to take up position, Keagan and Cassius mounted and rode toward the way station, lights at full intensity, making no attempt to disguise their approach. They were quite close before the sentry spotted them and let out a surprised shout of alarm. Keagan wasn't impressed. They must have thought themselves truly safe in here.

Sword drawn, Keagan nudged Vesi into a gallop, and they thundered into the way station's central courtyard before pulling up dramatically. "Marshals. Elemental. Lower all weapons, show your hands, prepare for inspection," she shouted in a penetrating voice. "Any resistance will be met with lethal force."

For a few seconds, there was a sort of stunned silence, and then an arrow struck the ground, not far from Gault's front hoof. Immediately, the archer was lit up like a torch, a streak of flame that died out as he plummeted from the second-story window, consumed to ash before he ever hit the ground. The way it was done, no one could tell where the flame originated, leaving observers to assume it came from Keagan or her companion.

"Anyone else prepared to question the level of our ability?"

Another silence, this one more sullen, and then people began to appear from the buildings. Such was the influence and power of Elementals, Keagan reminded herself. They were feared for a reason. She had no doubt some individuals had remained in hiding, but they probably didn't remember a Shadow Rider was with them, undoubtedly moving about the area with deadly and silent intent. A quick glance upward took in a slight figure on the roof of the stables, a crossbow peeking over the edge.

"What's this about?" A woman stepped forward, taking command. Stout, with graying hair and a sour mouth, she was not a fighter, Keagan determined, but a leader nonetheless.

"I think you know," Keagan said calmly. "Considering where we are and how you got here."

"We're not doing anything wrong. This passage isn't claimed."

"Several murdered Elementals would disagree," Cassius said, lifting her crossbow, having forgone her usual quarterstaff in this instance.

"We haven't murdered anyone," a man in the back said.

Keagan took in the crowd that was gathering. Twenty-six people, she counted, who were slowly trying to surround them, and she lifted her hand.

"Everyone will stop moving right now," she said calmly but firmly.

"I will not tell you again to drop all weapons. You have five seconds." She began to count backward. "Five, four, three—"

Another person went up in flames, a slender man in the back who had been carrying a crossbow. He had been lifting it into a ready position and didn't have time to scream. Despite her lack of experience, Ashley didn't hesitate in combat situations, Keagan thought. She struck fast and true. But two was undoubtedly her limit in here, where little was combustible, and she had no direct sunlight to recharge her. Hopefully, no one else would test them.

"Two, one."

Weapons clattered to the ground. Keagan focused her attention on the woman. "Name."

"Patricia."

"All of it."

"Darvus."

Keagan raised her eyebrow and exchanged a brief glance with Cassius. "Relationship to Arthur?"

"He's my son."

From the entrance of the nearest building, Shay appeared, escorting three people ahead of her, daggers dripping blood. They were bound, and she herded them over to the edge of the corral, making them sit down. Then she looked over at Keagan.

"Three prisoners," she said. "Two that wouldn't surrender."

Keagan met Patricia's eyes. "We don't want to hurt anyone, but we will *not* hesitate. Is this all of you?"

Patricia was clearly shaken. "Yes. All right. We'll cooperate."

Keagan peered at her intently for a few seconds, gauging her honesty, then lifted her arm. From behind the stables, Ashley appeared like an avenging angel, stalking forward, every inch a member of a Guild family, flames wreathing her hands, eyes glowing with golden intensity, auburn hair wafting around her face, stirred by the heat radiating from her body. If they hadn't been scared of Elementals before, Keagan thought wryly, they sure as hell were now.

Lyria descended less spectacularly but impressively nonetheless, a firm set to her jaw, eyes a solid white, looking older than her years.

"What do we do with them?" Ashley asked.

"Secure them."

For the next few minutes, the others bound the prisoners with cuffs and, when they ran out of those, metal ties. Keagan remained in the saddle, making it clear who was in charge and that her abilities, not yet displayed, weren't yet needed. After everyone was secured, on the ground next to the corral, tied to the fence posts, Keagan finally dismounted and, motioning Cassius and Shay to join her, took Patricia into the building for caravan passengers, leaving Lyria and Ashley to guard the others.

Cuffing Patricia to a chair in a small office just off the large cafeteria, Keagan took a seat opposite her. "Start from the beginning. What's this all about?"

"I want a lawyer," she responded, instead, gaze steely.

Cassius looked interested. "Is there one out there?"

Patricia's mouth turned down. "No."

"Do you really think we're going to wait for you to be taken to one? Or have one brought here?" Keagan showed her badge. "This is a crown matter, involving the death of Elementals. You know what that means. Unfortunately, your rights are superseded."

"The more you cooperate, the better it will be," Cassius said gently. "Not just for you, but for your son, when we catch him. Do you really think he can stand against us? Keagan and I didn't even have to do anything out there, and we're level four. We have a five riding with us. You must realize he's sorely outmatched."

"With the stones—" Patricia said, then stopped, closing her mouth firmly.

"The stones don't affect Riders," Shay interjected suddenly, eyes shimmering with icy darkness, all sexy and dangerous. She had been standing in the corner, doing her best to look intimidating, which she managed very well indeed. "You've involved the Shadow Lands. Now you answer for it."

Patricia nervously glanced her way, and Keagan abruptly thought that while Patricia wasn't particularly impressed with the Elementals, Shay frightened her, even though she managed a sullen mutter, "Once, anyone could travel in the Shadows."

Shay's eyebrow lifted. "Indeed?"

"How was that discovered?" Keagan forced her voice to be calm.

At first, it seemed that Patricia wouldn't respond, regarding them with a stubborn cast to her jaw, but as Shay began to clean her daggers, eyeing her dispassionately, she began to talk.

"Arthur always liked to explore. He never liked farming. Even when his father was able to secure him his own land, he didn't really take to it. Not that it was good land. And he was Elemental! He deserved the best!"

Keagan detected a deep-seated bitterness there.

"Why become a farmer, then?" Cassius asked in her quiet, reassuring tone. Belatedly, Keagan realized the three of them had fallen naturally into specific interrogation roles. Good cop, bad cop, and, in Shay's case, barely-in-control, possibly-deranged cop. "He could have made a good living with a company."

Patricia let out a bitter laugh. "At the bottom rung."

"Well, he's only level one," Keagan said. Never mind that he still would have made enough gold in three months in what would take a marshal a year.

"He deserved better!"

"If only we all get what we deserve," Shay said coldly.

"How did he learn about the Shadow Realm?" Keagan tried to bring the conversation back on track.

"He began exploring the ruins near the farm," Patricia said. "Then he found the passage. Imagine, a passage that no one knew about. He tried to explore it, but creatures drove him out."

"He was lucky to survive," Shay said.

"Then he discovered the embassy not too far away."

"Embassy? What's that?" Shay straightened.

"It's when a nation establishes a diplomatic presence in another," Patricia said, her tone becoming slightly disdainful, as if Shay should know this and her ignorance was shameful. Keagan resisted the urge to slap her. "All the nations had them, back in the day. It's a building that's considered the territory of the visiting nation, I guess like the Shadow Rider stations are now."

Shay frowned. "What did he find?"

"Everything. Eyepieces that let you see in the dark, devices to drive the creatures away or call them, a key that let him enter the Shadow Realm, and a compass that guided him to wherever he wanted to go."

Keagan glanced over at Shay, whose face was dark. She couldn't be happy about what she was hearing.

"How did he figure out how they worked?" Cassius asked.

"They have symbols on them. He saw that they were like the ones around way stations and worked it out." She looked very proud. "He was always very good with things like that."

"Do you have any of these devices?" Keagan asked.

"We have one that keeps the creatures away," Patricia said. "Lets us travel between way stations without being bothered. It's in the stables with the wagons. You can't miss it."

Keagan glanced at Cassius, got a nod in return, and while she went to retrieve said device, Keagan refocused her attention on Patricia. "So help me understand this. How did it go from exploring ruins and discovering passages to kidnapping and murdering Elementals?"

"No, we didn't—" Patricia stopped, swallowing convulsively. "No one was meant to be hurt. We didn't kidnap anyone in the beginning. They all wanted to help. The stones…"

"What about the stones?"

"It's all that professor's doing. Arthur thought he could make a lot of gold from the artifacts he was finding, but he didn't know what was valuable, so he contacted his old teacher for help. He was the one who recognized the Sylph stone. Suddenly, that's all he and Arthur cared about. Finding more of them."

"Tannehill?"

"Yes. Arthur met him in that null college."

Keagan had never heard a human refer to themselves that way. "Are you Elemental?"

"No, but—"

"But what?"

Patricia just shook her head, mouth firming stubbornly.

"Where does this passage go?" Shay asked suddenly. "Where are you headed?"

"Back to the farm, eventually," Patricia told her. "We came from Amane. That's the old city on the west coast—"

"We know where it is," Shay said. "So why are you still in the passage? You should have reached the farm long before now."

"The storms."

"How do you know it's storming?"

"It's always storming," Patricia said. "I decided it was safer here as long as we had supplies. No one could find us."

"Oh, I think someone did," Shay said.

Cassius came back into the room, carrying a square box about the size of a breadbox. She carried it without effort, but somehow, it looked heavy. Cassius put it down on a nearby table, and Keagan went over to examine it.

"Why is this so large? The one your friend used in the ruins was much smaller."

"Herodotus? Where is he?"

Patricia was looking at her so anxiously that Keagan felt a pang as she shook her head. "I'm sorry. He died when the creature he called threw him aside." She hardened her heart. "Both your associates chose not to cooperate."

Patricia, obviously shaken, bent her head, tears leaking down her cheeks. "I should have sent for him, had him and Kracus join us rather than wait on the other side. He was a good man."

Keagan found that somewhat debatable, but she didn't pursue the subject. "Why was it smaller?" she asked again.

"The small ones are only good for one use," Patricia said after a moment, speaking with difficulty. "There's no way of knowing what it will call. If it's a wraith, it's cooperative. If it's not..." She left it to them to fill in the blank.

"It didn't call a wraith," Shay said. "And just how the hell are wraiths cooperative?"

"They just are," Patricia said, eyes shifting. She was becoming evasive, Keagan realized. They couldn't trust her answers at this point.

"And this thing?" Keagan gestured.

"It drives all the creatures away." She lifted her head, blinking rapidly. "The switch to activate it is on the side."

"Isn't it on?"

"We haven't needed it."

Cassius reached for it. "Just turn it on?"

"Switch it to the left," Patricia suggested helpfully.

Too helpfully. Shay's hand suddenly snaked out and seized Cassius's wrist. "No. Let me look at it."

After examining it for a few seconds, Shay cast a baleful look at Patricia. "Nice try. Seriously, you're willing to die under the claws of a Shadow creature rather than go to prison?"

Keagan was shaken. "It would have called the creatures."

"Like the one that brought out the squib," Shay said. "And if the small one lured that, I can only imagine what something this large would attract. Or how many. But the glyphs are the same as on the other device." She traced her fingertip over the markings on the box. "The glyphs on this side of the switch are like the ones on Paths. Or near way stations, I guess. They ward off the creatures." She glanced at Patricia. "Does it work using sound?"

Patricia just shook her head, not in negation of Shay's question, but in refusal to speak, her mouth twisting stubbornly, her muddy eyes suddenly glinting with anger.

"Are glyphs a language, Shay?" Cassius asked.

Shay shook her head. "I'm not sure. We just considered them symbols, but clearly, there's a lot I don't know about my people and our past."

"Tell us more about the stones," Keagan said. "What's the grand plan here? Does Darvus really think he's going to become all-powerful, gaining all four abilities at once?"

But Patricia was done speaking, and nothing they did over the next hour—cajoling, bargaining, or threatening—made a difference. Keagan drew the line at physical intimidation. They finally gave up, and, leaving her tied up inside, they gathered outside the door.

"What now?" Cassius asked.

"We figure out a way to secure the prisoners," Keagan said, rubbing the back of her neck to ease the tension there. It hadn't been a pleasant interrogation toward the end. "How secure are these buildings?"

They put Patricia and her followers in the employee building because the doors of those rooms had locks, undoubtedly to keep stray passengers from bothering the staff. They had to break them to make them inaccessible, but that was easily done by melting them with Ashley's flame. Since the rooms all had access to bathrooms, and they were given enough trail rations for a month, they'd be comfortable as far as prisons went. Still, it wasn't ideal. They'd have to batter the doors down to get them out when it was time to leave, but that was a problem for the future, though Aigua only knew what kind of mischief they'd get up to in the meantime.

Once finished, everyone gathered in the cafeteria. Keagan sat down to write her report, wondering what their next step should be. They now knew where the passage ended, and they could turn the prisoners over to the crown guards currently occupying Amane, but that didn't tell them where Darvus and Olive were. Nor would it be quick or easy to herd twenty-nine people back to Amane, even with four Elementals, a Shadow Rider, and a historian to guard them. And Keagan wasn't too sure how useful the historian would be in that capacity.

That's when she realized that, at some point since the interrogation, Shay had simply vanished.

XXXVII

Prowling around the upper rooms of the passenger building, Shay made sure she hadn't missed anyone the first time around. Her technique had been brutal and simple. Anyone she found, she came up behind them, put a knife to their throat, and told them to surrender. If they did, she tied them up, gagged them, and moved on to the next. If they didn't, if they offered any resistance, she killed them, swiftly and without mercy. She and the Elementals were outnumbered, and she knew she couldn't hesitate. It wasn't pleasant, but with the lives of her friends and of her love at stake, she did what had to be done.

She had left the two who fought back where they lay, and now she retrieved them. After carrying them one at a time down the stairs, she placed them in a pile behind the stables, where, hopefully, Ashley could deal with them later. Once the unpleasant task was complete, she cleaned up the blood, washed herself in one of the bathrooms, and began exploring. Darvus's followers had made themselves quite comfortable in the rooms, settling in for a long stay, and she rummaged through their sparse belongings, searching for more Shadow Realm devices.

To her dismay, she found a great many goggles and individual creature lures, so many she couldn't carry them all, finally appropriating a knapsack to hold them. She switched one on to repel, heard nothing, and suspected it was emitting a sound too high for her to hear. She regarded it sourly. It would have been useful to have had one during all her travels as a courier. Then it occurred to her that before she had met Keagan, she had rarely even seen a wraith, and then, only from a great distance, riding as she did on protected Paths. She could identify the larger creatures only because she had been shown what they looked like at school.

Did the scouts have similar devices as they explored? She really did need to speak to one as soon as possible. Still, the presence of so many devices implied that any of Darvus's followers could, if brave enough, travel the passage, or even a Path, on their own. She slung the bag over her shoulder and walked through the rest of the rooms, pausing in the largest one containing nicer furnishings and a king-sized bed, clearly a suite designed for wealthier patrons. She guessed there had been a class structure in ancient times, as well. As she looked around, she suspected this had to be Patricia's room, a supposition verified when she found a battered, leather-clad book on the nightstand. Flipping through it, she raised her eyebrows when she realized it was a journal and began reading it, fascinated, the time passing quickly before she realized she needed to get back to the others.

This journal could be very useful, she thought as she returned to the cafeteria, where the rest had now gathered. Dinner was just being placed at the table when she walked in. After an initial start of surprise that Shay was, sadly, becoming very used to, Keagan frowned when she saw her.

"Where have you been?"

"Exploring."

Keagan looked disconcerted at the shortness of the reply, then shrugged and continued her conversation with Ashley. Shay dumped the bag on the table and took a seat, leaning back in her chair as she put her feet up and continued to skim through the rest of the diary, flipping back and forth between the beginning and the most recent entries. She was grateful she was a quick reader. Also, Patricia was remarkably succinct in her entries, recording a lot of information with very few words, totally unlike how she'd been in the interrogation.

"What's that?" Lyria asked several minutes later, peering over at Shay as Cassius started pouring wine into glasses. This was becoming a rather formal type of dinner, Shay decided, as she took her feet off the table.

"Patricia's diary."

Everyone was suddenly staring at her. "Where did you find it?" Keagan asked.

"In the room with the biggest bed," Shay told her, giving her a smoldering look. "I was picking out where we were going to sleep tonight."

Keagan grew red as Ashley let out a snort, and Cassius smiled as she finished putting out plates and cutlery. Torva placed a large bowl of meat stew on the table with some bread rolls. "Did you find anything else?" Keagan asked with a note of forced patience. Shay resisted the urge to smile. Occasionally it was fun to tease her love. She was so serious sometimes, as marshal.

"More devices with glyphs," Shay said, nudging the knapsack. "I gathered all I could find and put them in here. I thought we could look at them later, try to figure out if they do anything other than allow people to see in the dark and deal with creatures."

"Good idea. Ashley, were you and Lyria able to find out anything about the prisoners while we were questioning Patricia?"

"Nothing much," Ashley said as she took a seat and began to fill her plate. "Other than the fact that all these people are nulls. No Elementals. What happened to them all? And why would nulls be so besotted with some low-level Chthonic who couldn't make it as a farmer?"

"To the point that they'd die for him," Lyria said. "It doesn't make sense."

"Is this man particularly charismatic?" Torva asked as she and Cassius sat down to eat.

"It's not like our dealings with him have included much conversation," Keagan said, "so I don't really know. But I don't understand it, either. Especially if he just wants to acquire all the abilities and turn himself into a tyrant."

"Oh, that's not the plan," Shay said, sopping up some stew with her bread and taking a large bite.

Everyone stopped to stare at her, and she had to finish swallowing before adding, "According to his mother's diary, in the beginning, Darvus did think he and his Elemental followers might get more varied and greater abilities from the Sylph stone, but eventually, he discovered the only effect it has on Elementals is to take abilities away. And while those abilities can be transferred to an ordinary person, the process kills any low-level Elemental, and the transferred abilities don't last very long, no more than a week. That's when they decided to go after high-level Elementals, even though they knew that would attract attention. They hoped more power meant the effect would last longer, perhaps even permanently."

"Why the hell would he want to give a null abilities?" Ashley appeared gobsmacked.

"For his mother," Shay said. "From what I read, his father is Elemental and abused both her and Arthur. When he was given the farm, his mother left his father and came to live with him. I guess he thought if Patricia acquired high-level abilities, both of them would accomplish their goals, which is basically revenge against Daddy. Not quite sure what form that revenge would take."

"Oh, no. I can't believe Professor Tannehill had anything to do with this," Torva said, obviously horrified.

Keagan also seemed horrified. "Does that mean someone has my abilities right now?"

"And ours?" Cassius and Lyria exchanged concerned looks.

"According to the diary, they concluded that they need all four to make the process work permanently, and hopefully on Elementals. I guess your abilities are still stored away in the stones for future use. After we fought him in the Badlands, Darvus made his way back to Amane, where he sent everybody home to the farm. Then he and Olive went off by themselves to retrieve the Undine stone at the Anemoi site, not knowing we'd already found it. Since now a crown presence is there, I'm not sure what happened to them. Maybe they're already in custody. Or they might even show up here next."

"One can hope," Ashley said, eyes glowing a little.

"Do they have the two stones with them?" Keagan asked.

Shay nodded.

"Does anyone think Olive's the one who really wants to acquire the abilities?" Ashley asked, sagely. "And everyone else is shit out of luck?"

"And do what? Become a new empress?" Torva asked. "Is this what Alameada actually did millennia ago? Take abilities away from enslaved Elementals for herself? Is that how she really took control? Got armies to follow her? Was she the one who actually destroyed civilization?"

"Does it really matter?" Ashley took a sip from her wineglass. "Honestly, we should just concentrate on the here and now. Anyone who suddenly gains high-level abilities without training or even the smallest understanding of how to use them will be a danger to themselves and everyone around them." She let out a snort. "I'm only glad they didn't get fire."

"Oh, they did, at least once," Shay told her. "Six of the bodies buried at the farm were the result of an ordinary human being given a level-one Salamas ability. Possibly from the man Cassius dug up. In any event, the guy who received the abilities took out himself, a barn, and four others with his flame. It was one of their many attempts to figure out how the stones worked, and according to the diary, the Elemental had volunteered to go through the process. No one thought it would kill him or that the guy who got the abilities wouldn't be able to control them, even though Arthur had apparently 'trained' him. A lot of trial and error going on, I guess."

"That's why it matters, Ashley," Torva said. "Those who don't know their history are doomed to repeat it. If we'd known about Alameada and the stones, then possibly they would have been found long before now and kept in a safe place. None of this would be happening."

"Or with everyone knowing they exist and what they can do, there would be a constant effort to steal them from any supposed safe space, which would keep happening over and over through the centuries instead of once every thousand years," Keagan stated, forestalling the argument stirring between Torva and Ashley. "Don't forget, for all our abilities, we're badly outnumbered by nulls, which adds to the resentment. Both sides want power, and some don't care what they have to do to get it."

Shay agreed with her. Only if they were in Shadow Lands would the stones possibly be safe, and honestly, at this point, who could be certain of that?

Keagan inclined her head toward Shay. "What else is in the diary? Does it mention where and when he found the first stone?"

"In Lurrera." Shay looked at Torva. "Like you thought. He used maps and the compass he discovered in the same ruins as the passage and traveled there through the Shadow Realm. He discovered an ancient Path that led directly to the palace, with a throne room containing the stone. It was blind, stupid luck."

"The palace was still standing?" Cassius sounded astonished. "How is that possible?"

"Well, that's the weird thing. Everything else was destroyed, but the palace was on this little island, untouched by the storms. He took the stone, along with several other treasures, back to his farm, but when he returned in hopes of looting more, he couldn't because, suddenly, it was all underwater. The island had sunk. Patricia wrote it was lucky he didn't drown when he opened the entry and sea water rushed through. He was barely able to shut it in time."

"Too bad. It would have saved us a bit of effort," Ashley said.

"So does that mean the stone was protecting the area, and with it gone, the hurricanes finished destroying it? The palace in Amane still stood after all this time, even after that stone was taken." Cassius frowned, clearly thinking it through. "Of course, it's not like there are ongoing firestorms in western Aquas that would have burnt it down."

"Initially, they didn't know the Salamas stone in Amane was gone," Shay said. "Darvus and Tannehill excavated for years, looking for it. In the meantime, they're experimenting with the Sylph Stone, recruiting Elementals to use as batteries, building up this following of other people who think they're going to become Elementals. It's all very secretive and sort of devout, almost like they're creating their own religion around Alameada. That's also when Olive begins to show up in the diary entries. It doesn't say how exactly she comes in, but suddenly she's selling the antiquities they find to private collectors and coming up with all sorts of gold to fund their little cult." Shay tapped the weathered, leather-covered book. "A year ago, they discovered that Heratherus, the warrior queen, retrieved the stone and took it to Naiad. They didn't know where, but now they needed access to historical records that aren't readily available. Things in the temples, and the palace, or in the Academy."

"And in private collections. The thefts I was investigating," Keagan said, eyebrows rising. "They must have grown desperate, less careful about covering their tracks." She paused, suddenly looking thoughtful. "Heratherus also must have made a huge effort to conceal the stone's existence, as well. Otherwise, why have it buried with her? Why didn't her successor take it? Did it remove her abilities at some point? Was that why she stopped being a warrior in the middle of her reign?"

"What made her a warrior in the first place?" Lyria asked. "Weren't the nations at peace?"

"Yes, but they were separate, with little interaction. And there was always some question inside each nation as to who exactly was going to rule it," Torva said, in her lecturing tone. "In Aquas at that time, several powerful Undine were making claims on the throne. There were clashes between various factions, and then, suddenly, according to our recorded histories, all the fighting stopped. Heratherus was declared the first queen of all Five Nations, and the Rite of Succession was created, setting up the system we have now." She pursed her lips. "How much did the stone impact those events? Maybe it didn't take away her abilities. Maybe it took away the abilities of her rivals and threatened those of the rulers in other nations, who had no choice but to agree to a unified government under her rule."

"The last Rite of Succession took place when I was ten and Chiesa was named successor," Cassius said. "She hasn't chosen her heir yet." She gazed at Keagan. "You know, you'd be in the running."

Shay was stunned, and from her facial expression, so was Keagan. "I'm only a level four."

"Yes, but the Rite doesn't consider only abilities and how well they're used," Cassius said. "It also takes into account the skills of leadership and diplomacy. You have both, in spades. Didn't you wonder why she knew so much about you? She's probably been watching you since you became a marshal."

"I wouldn't want the throne," Keagan said, with certainty.

"I'm not sure there's a choice," Ashley said, her expression odd, as if looking at Keagan with new eyes. "Those who are called to service know their duty." It sounded like one of their Academy platitudes. Shay swallowed hard. She knew how strongly Keagan believed in duty.

"Nonsense." Keagan managed a dismissive tone. "Of us all, Lyria is more apt to be considered than me. She's level five, after all."

Lyria was clearly taken aback as everyone suddenly looked at her. "Well, my first decree would be for the companies to work together to clean up the River Anemoi."

"And that would start the first uprising, so you wouldn't be on the throne long," Ashley said, sounding wry. "Thus ends the reign of Queen Lyria."

They laughed, but a small part of Shay wasn't so amused. The thought that Keagan could, in any way, be eligible for the throne made her stomach ache. She hoped Cassius was mistaken in her speculation.

"So what's the plan, Keagan?" Ashley asked, suddenly. "What's next?"

"We need to get out of this passage," Keagan said. "There's no point in going back to Terras, so we'll continue to Amane and meet the crown guards there. Yet do we take the prisoners with us or leave them here? It won't be easy to escort them all."

"They're set up for several weeks unless someone gets greedy," Cassius said. "Horses are a lot faster than a caravan, especially our Shadow-bred, so we can reach Amane quickly and send a squadron back long before they run out of food. Or, hopefully, figure out a way to escape."

"Normally, a small squadron wouldn't be safe in this passage," Shay said, "with the Shadow creatures roaming through here, but if we give them these devices, it might be okay. I hate for knowledge of them to get out, but needs must."

"All right, assuming that works," Keagan said, "we'll take the Path from Amane to Anemoi and see if we can pick up Darvus's trail from there. We'll leave as soon as we can."

"Does anyone else feel like we're starting to travel in circles?" Ashley asked.

XXXVIII

They were in Amane a couple of days later. The passage exited some distance from the temple, and it took another half day to make their way through the ruins, surprising the hell out of the crown contingent who had no idea it had existed. They had to subsequently arrange for the prisoners to be brought back, providing the squad with the devices and teaching them how they worked, as well as dispatching reports to Naiad. But once that was done, they were in Anemoi the following day, dashing along the ancient Path that glowed with newly restored glyphs. The time differences were hard on them, though Shay remained totally unaffected. By now, Keagan wasn't completely sure what time it was, or even what day it was. Conscious only of a deep fatigue, she felt like she hadn't rested in days, despite grabbing some sleep in Amane.

That's when things stalled. The once-small camp in the desert canyon was now a bustling community, filled with every historian that could be recruited from the Five Nations, along with two full squadrons of crown guards. Even a young Shadow Rider was assigned to courier dispatches back and forth between Anemoi and Amane, and then on to Naiad along a newly laid, crown-commissioned Path between the jungle ruins and the capital city. No one had seen any sign of Darvus or Olive, and Keagan suspected they'd been warned off by the very busy nature of the canyon long before they reached it. More people and supplies were arriving daily on boats coming up the river to a hastily constructed makeshift pier, and unsurprisingly, a few entrepreneurs were setting up temporary shops in the shadow of the nearby cliffs. Even some rough buildings were going up by the river, constructed quickly from mud brick.

Keagan did wonder how long it would be before the pool in the canyon reached the limit of sustainability and Undine started being hired to find more fresh water. Or even if they would have to start purifying what came from the river itself, which would be an unpleasant task indeed.

She'd never seen anything like it. Somehow, the crown had turned this discovery of old ruins into something new and exciting, and not at all the threat that was supposedly behind it. It was astonishing and incredibly frustrating. Since Darvus and Olive hadn't returned to the passage leading to Amane, she had no clue as to their current whereabouts, especially considering Darvus could walk the Shadows. Still, he and Olive couldn't stay in the Shadow Realm. They had to go somewhere they felt they could regroup.

Keagan gathered with the others near the pool. "Review Tannehill's and Patricia's diaries again, every detail," she told Shay and Torva. "Maybe something will give us a hint as to where they might be."

Cassius was looking around with a smile. "Honestly, how are the crown and Council keeping things under wraps? What do the people here think is going on?"

"I spoke to some of the historians," Torva said. "The Council has glossed over exactly how the temple was discovered. In the meantime, those other rooms that you told me were filled with rubble? They're uncovering a lot of valuable antiquities and gold, all of it being funneled directly into the treasury. The Arias government suddenly has a vested interest in this place. In fact, the treasure is all they're interested in." She frowned, looking very disgruntled. "Certainly not the historical value. This isn't a dig anymore. It's become sanctioned, systematic looting. And it won't be long before the other nations decide they should develop an interest in their ancient ruins, too. Everyone will be claiming historian status."

"Good thing we got the stone out of here, then," Ashley muttered.

"Terras and Urodela won't get much out of their ruins," Cassius said. "Their disaster areas are still active, even a thousand years later, but yes, I can see how Arias and Aquas might decide to reclaim as much as they can." She glanced at Lyria. "The river might get cleaned up yet, especially if some companies can make a deal to keep what they find along the riverbanks after they've reclaimed it for Arias."

Lyria suddenly looked considerably cheered. "We need to mention that to someone in charge."

"We'll talk to the Council," Cassius said. "Especially now that we have access."

"Someone in Aquas is bound to figure out they should reclaim some little ruin along the western coast," Ashley said. "Set up some piers and start competing with the eastern ports who need at least two more days to ship goods to Terras. This is going to start a sudden boom." She smiled. "It'll be very good for the economy."

"Look at you, all big picture," Cassius said. "Maybe you should be nominated for the Rite."

"Like that won't end badly," Torva said, earning a sharp look from Ashley and a smirk from Cassius.

Keagan exhaled. "Let's get to it, shall we?" she said, suddenly impatient with her companions and their banter, something she otherwise enjoyed. "While we go over the diaries, speak to the historians, again, and see if they're coming across anything that might help us regarding Alameada. If Darvus is starting a new religion, maybe someone will mention it. Ashley, find us someplace to set down for the night. We'll need to take care of the horses, as well."

Back on task, Cassius nodded. "I'll take the horses over to the corral and renew the pasture. Aside from the courier's horse, they'll have it to themselves. Then we'll start talking to people."

The others scattered, leaving Keagan to stare at the waterfall. She drew in large amounts of moisture and released it in a forceful jet back into the pool, trying to take the edge off her fatigue.

"Are you all right?"

Shay's voice made her start. Of course she hadn't seen her there. "The diary?" She didn't like the sharp note of waspishness in her tone, but she couldn't help it.

"I'll get to it," Shay told her firmly. "You're tired. You need a break."

"How can I? We have no clue where Darvus and Olive are."

"No, but they've also lost access to the third stone, their followers, his mother, the farm, both sets of ruins, and the passage," Shay reminded her. "They'll probably need a break of their own." She motioned to a nearby log that had been carved into a rough bench. "Here. Sit down before you fall down."

Keagan frowned, but she allowed Shay to lead her over, where she sank onto the rough surface, weariness dragging at her like a deadweight. Shay stood behind her, and those slender, lovely hands were suddenly massaging Keagan's neck, thumbs digging lightly into the muscles of her shoulders, soothing away the tension there.

"Oh," she said.

"Yes," Shay murmured. She removed the shield and helped Keagan out of the weapon harness, putting it aside. "We'll find them, Keagan. You can count on us. Just let it go for a few moments. Start fresh."

"Hmm, all right." Keagan surrendered to the sensation as the hands moved beneath her mail and up her back and spine. "Where did you learn this? You're very good at it."

"Stop questioning everything," Shay said. "Stop thinking. Just *be* for a little while."

Keagan tried to obey. It wasn't easy. It went against her very nature. But eventually, after a few moments, she was lost in the elegant fingers taking away her stress. Finally, Shay sat down behind her, easing her onto the ground and enfolding her in her arms. "Rest," she said. "I'll wake you when the others get back."

Keagan briefly thought about resisting, but the urge was weak, and before she knew it, she had drifted off even as it occurred to her that Shay held a certain influence over her like no one ever had before. It was both terrifying and exhilarating. As she drifted up from the dark depths some undetermined time later, she could hear the others around her, speaking in low tones.

"She asleep?" Cassius rumbled.

"Good. She was getting really cranky," Ashley said.

"Doesn't she need to know what we found out?" Lyria asked.

"Did we really find out anything?" Torva said.

"Maybe. Depends." Cassius sounded dubious.

Keagan opened her eyes. "Report."

"And she's awake," Ashley said, lips pursed.

"We may have a lead," Shay said quietly, in her ear, reminding Keagan of where she was, tucked up in her Rider's embrace, pleasant as it was.

Hastily, she rose and retrieved her weapon harness and shield, refastening them to her back. She felt tremendously better, if not completely rested, then at least filled with a renewed enthusiasm. "What have you got?"

"Amane was stripped clean, as one could expect since they'd been digging there for years," Torva said. "But this area holds a trove of information on Alameada. I checked in with several historians, who all agree that her chosen residence and favorite city was Elfenol." She glanced at Cassius. "If Darvus and his followers were beginning to worship her as a goddess, or even if they were just trying to follow in her footsteps, they might consider her home as some kind of sanctuary."

Keagan felt her eyebrows rise. "That's the best you could all come up with?"

"It's not like we have much to go on," Ashley said, which was, sadly, very true.

"All right. Where is this Elfenol?"

"It would be in the middle of the Lernaean Swamps," Torva said. "In Aquas."

"My map has it marked," Shay said. "It also marked an ancient Path that ends about ten or so leagues away from Elfenol's center, where the palace is probably located."

"But isn't that entire area a swamp now?" Keagan asked. "Didn't the whole city sink?"

Shay shook her head. "No way to know unless we go there and I open an entry."

"If we go, we'd have to leave the horses," Keagan said. "Even if the

Path does allow us to reach the swamps, we can't ride anywhere. We'd probably need some kind of boat. A canoe or flat-bottomed outrigger. How would we get that through the Shadow Realm?"

Shay shook her head. "I don't know. Carry it?"

"It would need to be pretty big, for all of us," Cassius said. "Which would be too heavy to carry. Maybe two smaller craft?"

Keagan felt a little overwhelmed by the logistics. "Where does this Path begin?"

Shay glanced at the map in her hand. "A few leagues upriver. That's why I chose it. The others that are marked don't seem accessible from their current starting points, assuming any of them still exist."

"Why wouldn't they exist?" Lyria asked.

"Well, these maps show several Paths supposedly originating from Amane and leading to various other capitals, but the only Path I found there is the one that leads here. And possibly the passage to that ruin in Terras, if it really is a dead Path. But otherwise, I didn't sense any others. Maybe they died out so long ago there's no longer any trace of them."

"I wish you wouldn't refer to them like they're alive," Ashley said. "It makes me feel like we're traveling through the intestine of a very big snake and being pooped out at the end." Lyria snorted laughter as Cassius smiled.

Keagan ignored her. "Could we get one of your scouts to lead us there?" Keagan asked Shay. "Go directly to Elfenol's center?"

"I don't think you realize how few scouts there actually are," Shay told her. "It's an extremely rare ability. Right now, only three possess it. Scout Vardis is doing most of the pathfinding for all the towns that have already paid. There's a huge backlog. The second scout is still in school since he's only thirteen, and I'd never trust an untrained child to be able to lay down a Path through leagues of swamp where no one goes. The last, Scout Atlas, should be retired, he's so old. The effort would probably kill him. I could send a request, but frankly, I was surprised when I heard the Queen managed to get Vardis to set aside her regular duties long enough to restore the glyphs on the one leading here and mark out a very short Path between Amane and Naiad. They would have needed to use obelisks to anchor the entries already prepared for another job. It must have been by a royal emergency decree, and it would have cost a ridiculous amount of gold. Plus, it takes several days to have one laid down and marked." She regarded Keagan inquiringly. "We might have the authorization, but do we have that kind of time? Or money?"

Keagan frowned, but she couldn't justify something like that.

"Where are we going to find small boats?" Ashley asked in a practical tone. "I doubt there are any around here. Where would you use them?"

"Maybe they have some smaller craft on the riverboats," Lyria suggested. "Like for emergencies or something."

"Good thought," Keagan said. "Check it out. Cassius, as quartermaster, you have the authority to commandeer anything you need."

"That will make us popular," Cassius said, but she nodded. "Lyria, come with me? It might sound better coming from a Sylph."

"Maybe," Lyria said, but she looked as if she very much doubted it. "Riverboat captains are pretty independent. Good thing we're deputized."

The two of them departed for the river, leaving Keagan to figure out what to do next. "Ashley, were you able to secure us lodgings?"

"I found a place to pitch our tents, if that's what you mean," Ashley told her. "In the corral. Means a lot of flies and the smell of manure, but I figured Shay would want to be near the horses, and honestly, it's the only place left. It's not great, but it's better than having to pitch them out there in the desert between the canyon and the river. They've set up a communal kitchen here where the fire pit and the portable cold/hot boxes used to be so we can eat there. We won't have to make our own supper."

Keagan nodded. "Good job. It'll be a lot cooler here in the canyon." She sighed, sweat trickling down the side of her face. "And it's not cool here. Let's get to it, then. We'll set up camp and get some rest."

She glanced at the huge statues of Alameada towering over them. "I'm sure we'll need it."

XXXIX

Shay really didn't like the idea of leaving Onyx and the other horses behind. Even if the Shadow Rider assigned to the canyon could periodically check on them, it was like leaving a part of herself. But she couldn't figure out any other way. If there were swamps where they were headed, it was no place for horses, and it would take far too long to follow the other Path back to the Shadow Hills and let them loose to return to the clan on their own. Plus, she didn't want any part of that hub of multiple Paths. She still got a headache whenever she thought of it.

"Hey."

Keagan came up to where Shay was leaning on the corral fence, arms crossed on the top rail. She put a comforting hand on her shoulder. "I know this isn't ideal."

"Guess I'm just not used to being without Onyx," Shay said. "I'm a Shadow Rider, after all, not a Shadow Walker. It won't be fun."

"Is any of this fun?"

Shay gazed at her. "Every bit of it," she said. "Being with you most of all."

Keagan laughed. "Okay. That's true. It has had its good points, along with the difficult times." She moved closer and leaned against her, prompting Shay to put an arm around her waist, pulling her close. They stood there for a few moments, watching the horses graze. "The crown guards are here. And Rider Amos promised to keep an eye on them."

"Yeah, but he's running messages a lot," Shay said. "We should hire someone full-time to act as groom. Can we do that?"

"Sure. There must be someone looking for work," Keagan said. "They're arriving constantly, and some of them don't even seem to know what they're coming for, other than to see what's going on. We certainly have the funds for it."

"What makes all these people suddenly pick up and come here?" Shay was amazed.

"Bored with their lives? Wanting a better one and hearing about something like this is sometimes all that's needed to make a change."

"It's almost like they've suddenly been given permission to explore."

"Well, up until now, the religions and governments have been discouraging it somewhat. It's like when Terras issued those land grants. People condemned the move as greedy, but others saw it as an opportunity, no matter how poor the farming actually was. They consider this another opportunity, even if they're not sure what exactly the opportunity consists of."

Shay shook her head, marveling at the thought, but wasn't that exactly what had happened to her? She had stumbled into something, and now, her entire life had changed as a result. She kissed the top of Keagan's head. Changed so much for the better.

It took a couple of days before Cassius and Lyria were able to secure two rowboats, having to fork over a substantial amount of gold to soothe the ruffled feathers of the riverboat captains. Presenting their badges simply hadn't been enough. Once that was done, they arranged for another riverboat to take them to where the map indicated there was a Path.

But not before they hired a tow-headed young man called Bradly who, after Shay caught him hanging around the corral and petting the horses, underwent a stringent interview. He was a farmhand out of Terras, seeking his fortune by heading west and joining a riverboat crew, but now he was missing the farm and bitterly regretting that he had ever left that life behind him. Shay decided, reluctantly, that he was probably the best they could get and agreed to let him look after their mounts for enough gold to make it back home, although Keagan assured her he was perfect and probably wouldn't try to steal them. Not that any of the Shadow-bred would put up with that sort of foolishness, of course, especially after Shay told Onyx to stay put until she returned. They'd attack anyone who tried to take them. Well, maybe not Vesi. Feed him a carrot and he'd follow anywhere, so long as it wasn't down a flight of stairs, Shay decided, sourly.

The riverboat took another two days to navigate the current upstream, possessing a large paddle wheel powered by a crystal that Keagan recharged to full as part of the deal. Shay was relieved when she sensed the Path as they approached the area marked on the map. It could easily have disappeared like the others after so long. With the riverboat moored on the bank where the captain promised to stay until their return or when a fortnight had passed, whichever came first, they unloaded the rowboats. Strapped to two small carts, they pulled them a league or so inland over the desert sand to a crumbled obelisk with markings so faded, they were illegible. Only because Cassius was so strong and could pull one all on her own did they manage it at all, and Shay learned several new curses from Ashley that she'd undoubtedly find herself using in the future.

They waited until after sunset, when it was fully dark, so it would be easier to create a large entry. Shay used copious amounts of oil to grease the wheels of the carts, making them run as quietly as possible and leaving a trail dripping behind them. It took an effort to open an entry large enough to allow Cassius to pull through one cart on her own, with Keagan and Ashley dragging the other. Once in the Shadow Realm, Shay and Lyria took point, on constant alert as they moved through the darkness. They carried some of the creature-repellent gizmos, but Shay wasn't entirely sure she trusted them. Torva walked between the carts. If not completely protected, then at least she'd have some cover if anything happened.

Shay wasn't pleased at the weakness of the glyphs bordering the Path, but they had to work with what they had. They moved as silently as possible, not speaking until Shay finally sensed the end and held up a hand. Cassius quietly set down the handles of her cart and moved to a spot beside Shay, ready to assist.

"Start at the top?" she suggested in a whisper.

Shay nodded, beginning her entry several feet above her head, making it small at first. No liquid spurted through, and encouraged, she slowly drew the opening downward until she did strike water, about a foot above the pavement. Exchanging a glance with the goggled Keagan, Shay set her jaw and wrenched the entry open as wide as she could, shuddering as she held it in place while the others wrestled the boats off the carts and out onto the surface of the swamp waiting for them on the other side. Then they piled into them, pulling off their goggles and blinking in the moonlight.

With a sigh of relief, Shay eased her grip on the entry until there was only room for her to pass through. Cassius took hold of her, helping her up into the boat as Shay allowed the entry to slide shut behind her, leaving the carts in the Shadow Realm.

"What will happen to them?" Cassius asked.

"I have no idea," Shay said. "Maybe they'll be there for the next Rider that comes through, if one ever does. Or maybe they'll just be gone. Who knows? This is all uncharted territory for me."

They looked around, checking out the area. It was calm, the water moving sluggishly around them. Moonlight glinted off the surface, while the surrounding trees and vegetation held the wind, making the air still. Not far away, the tip of a ruined obelisk jutted upward, covered with thick moss, as a cacophony of animal and insect noises filled the swamp. From a distance, they could hear things entering the water with distinctive splashes, providing disturbing evidence of substantially larger creatures.

It smelled musty, humid, and thick, a pervasive odor that made it hard to breathe. To the east, above the trees, the sky was lightening, heralding the arrival of sunrise.

"Which way?" Ashley spoke from the other boat in a very quiet tone, as if they were still in the Shadows.

Shay looked at her map. "Southeast." She pointed. "That direction." She was disappointed when she realized Keagan was in the other boat with Ashley and Lyria, leaving her with Cassius and Torva, though at least, Cassius was at the oars, clearly willing to take the first shift in propelling them through the brackish channel.

"Can you keep me on track?" Cassius asked Shay. "I'll be facing backward."

"Yes, Shay. You're in charge of navigation," Keagan said. "We'll stay on the water as much as possible. I doubt it'll be a direct route, but I really don't want to test the stability of the ground before we have to. It's a bog."

"Do you want me in the air?" Lyria made a move to stand up, then quickly sat down as the boat rocked and Ashley and Keagan yelped in protest. "Oh. I don't know how to take off without this capsizing."

"Stay put for now," Keagan told her. "Shay, lead the way."

"We're in ruins," Torva said, peering at a nearby clump of vegetation. "This city must have been huge."

Cassius started to pull on the oars, and with Shay giving directions, they began to make their way along the narrow channel of water winding through the thick vegetation, the bushes and trees around them dripping with moss and vines. As the sun rose, the heat grew steadily, tiny insects buzzing constantly around their heads, and more than once, they had to back out of one channel or another when it proved to be a dead end. It was not at all pleasant, especially when the occasional snake dropped from above into the boats. The first time it happened, into Keagan's boat, the three of them scattered as much as they could, which wasn't far. It hissed, reared back to strike, and froze solid as Lyria screamed and threw out her hand, a frosty icicle condensing in a visible trail between her and the unfortunate reptile.

Gingerly, Keagan reached over, picked up the snake, and flung it across the water until it landed with a plop, disappearing beneath the turgid surface. For several moments, they all caught their breath, hearts pounding, looking at each other, and from that point on, someone always checked above to give warning.

At one point, Shay absently let her hand trail in the water, finding it somewhat slimy. She quickly pulled it out, shaking it frantically, looking for leeches and relieved to find none. "This must be as bad as the Anemoi River," she said, looking back at the other boat.

Keagan looked back over her shoulder at her, eyes wide. "Oh, no, this is amazing water." She exhaled, shoulders rippling as she drew the oars. "I wouldn't drink it, of course." She paused. "Or swim in it, for that matter, but these wetlands are teeming with life. Vital and thriving. The river was practically dead. Very little lives in it, it's so polluted."

"Good for you, because this place is not great for my flame," Ashley said. "Even the air is wet." She motioned at Keagan. "My turn." She switched places with Keagan, both of them carefully maneuvering around each other in the small boat. The water might have been vital and alive, but neither of them wanted to fall into it. Lady only knew what lay below in the murky depths.

"Is there any sign anyone else has been here?" Ashley asked, a little breathless as she rowed. "Wouldn't they need a boat if they used the same Path?"

Shay frowned, annoyed. "That compass would give him a real advantage. He'd be like a scout, able to walk much closer to the palace before leaving the Shadows."

"Assuming it's still standing and they're even here in the first place," Torva said.

The hours passed and their initial confidence waned. It was hard to tell if they were getting any closer to the center of the city, and they couldn't see anything through the trees. Finally, Shay looked up at the sun starting to sink in the sky.

"We may have to stop for the night."

"I've been looking for someplace solid," Keagan said. "Even if it's just to stretch our legs."

"And to let me fly," Lyria added. "Are we any closer to this place?"

"Hard to say," Shay said. "We've had to backtrack so much, we may not have traveled half the distance."

"Great," Ashley muttered.

"There." Torva pointed at a hillock where the vegetation seemed less thick, as if having a harder time gaining purchase. "I think that was a bridge at one time."

As they drew closer, Shay could see that the ground was more broken concrete than mud, but it was out of the water and would provide a drier base than anything else they had found until now. They pulled the boats up onto the bank and, for a few moments, just stood there, stretching out the kinks of having sat in a cramped position for too long. Shay noticed Keagan was wincing every so often as she moved her arms, undoubtedly sore from rowing, and made a note to provide another massage before bed.

"No fire," Keagan said. "We don't want to alert anyone to our presence."

"Nothing's dry enough to burn anyway," Ashley said, though Shay knew Keagan could absorb the moisture from any wood and make it flammable enough.

Lyria looked ready to launch before Keagan stopped her. "Is there any way you can ascend slowly?" she asked. "If you lift off, you need to barely clear the tree line. I don't want to risk anyone seeing you."

A baffled expression appeared on Lyria's face. "I don't know how I would do that."

Shay remembered that normally, when Lyria ascended from a standing stop, a large blast of wind created under her shot her straight upward for several hundred feet, far higher than any tree could grow. It must have been easy in the Chimera Wastelands with the winds blowing constantly. Or even in the Anemoi Badlands, where the light desert air and blistering heat had constant rise. Here, the air was heavy and stagnant. Shay could feel the weight of it pressing down on her.

Keagan glanced around. "Suggestions?"

They all looked confused as they proceeded to make a rough camp for the night, the tents pitched in a tight radius on a small patch of ground flattened and smoothed over by Cassius. Unfortunately, any updraft that would be controlled enough to lift Lyria slowly to a low height would be too weak to get her off the ground. It also didn't help that most of them didn't really understand how a Sylph's abilities worked beyond the basics or, frankly, even how wind itself worked.

"I mean, honestly, it takes us long enough to figure out our own abilities," Ashley said as they made a supper of trail rations, dry and chewy as they were. "Now you want us to figure out a technique that no Sylph at the Academy was ever taught?"

Shay tried to imagine how the wind felt as she rode Onyx across the prairie. "How did you fly in the passage?" There would have been no natural assistance there, nor would Lyria have been able to take off straight up without hitting the ceiling. Thinking back, it seemed like Lyria had simply sprinted several steps and then was suddenly flying down the passage. Shay still remembered the blast of wind in her face, but how was it different than the other times?

"I had an endless straight line where I could take a running start horizontally and gradually lift from there," Lyria said. "That won't work here. There are too many obstacles. I don't have enough distance, and besides, the trees block any wind before it can become powerful enough to lift me." She slapped her hand on the ground. "This is firm enough to create an updraft, but it still has to be really strong and concentrated to push me off the ground."

"So it will lift you too high." Shay let out her breath, stymied. Who knew flying could be so complicated?

"A dust devil," Torva said suddenly. She had stayed out of this conversation for the most part, probably because, like Shay, she hardly felt qualified to comment on Elemental abilities.

"What?" Lyria frowned as they all stared at her.

Torva reddened. "I've seen them in Arias. How do they work? The wind going around and around in a circle, like that? It just picks things up."

Lyria's mouth fell open. "Oh, Sirocco. That's brilliant, Torva."

"Is it?" Ashley looked very skeptical.

Lyria looked at her admonishingly. "It is," she said. "I just have to figure out how to do it."

Keagan smiled. "Problem solved, then. You'll go up first thing in the morning. Try to spot any breaks in the trees where a palace could be. Or just anything that looks like it should be investigated."

She looked around. "Other than swamp."

XL

Keagan groaned as she lay facedown on her bedroll, Shay straddling her hips as she massaged her naked back, soothing out the kinks that rowing all day had caused. "Have I ever told you how much I love you?"

"Once in a while," Shay said, sounding amused.

Keagan rose a little, indicating she wanted to roll over. As she looked up at Shay, into those silver eyes, her heart sang. "Not enough, then," she told Shay, who continued to massage her shoulders, smiling as she trailed her fingers along her collarbones. "I love you so much."

Shay's smile deepened, and she leaned down and kissed Keagan, slowly, gently, with utter thoroughness. Her hands slipped down Keagan's chest, over her breasts, fingers lingering on her nipples.

Keagan groaned again. "I'm sweaty," she said as she put her arms around Shay, holding her close. "I stink."

"You smell fine," Shay said, kissing her again.

"No. You're the one that smells great," Keagan murmured. "All spice and cinnamon." She brushed her lips over her dusky cheek and down her neck. "Like rolls fresh from the oven."

"For Baast's sake, you both smell like swamp" came Ashley's voice from the tent next door, sounding thoroughly aggravated. "Would you please just shut up. Some of us are trying to sleep."

"I'm afraid I have to agree with her" came Cassius's voice from the tent on the other side, her tone far more polite. "The sleeping bit, not the how-you-smell bit." She paused. "Shay does always smell nice, though. Is that a perfume?"

Shay's body shook in silent laughter as Keagan let out her breath in exasperation. Reluctantly, she loosened her embrace and allowed Shay to settle on the bedroll beside her. No lovemaking, then. It was too bad, but just being in her arms was enough. Snuggling close, head resting on Shay's lean shoulder, Keagan shut her eyes, so grateful she was there. Slowly, she relaxed, aided greatly by the looseness of the massage, letting her mind drift.

She tried not to worry about what the next day might bring. Or what it might not. If the fugitives weren't here in the swamps, she had no idea what her next step would be. Return to Naiad? Try digging into the thefts again, search for some other target they might go after? Try to make their way to Urodela, where that ancient capital city was supposed to be buried under tons of ash and lava, on a plain surrounded by active volcanoes? Their search was beginning to feel hopeless.

Shay seemed to notice her disquiet and hugged her. "It'll be all right," she muttered sleepily.

It might not be, Keagan told herself, but Shay had a way of convincing her otherwise. With an effort, she turned off her mind and let sleep take her away.

The next morning found them sitting in the boats, some distance away from the hillock, as Lyria tried to work out how to make a twister as opposed to an updraft or a steady wind. She began by rotating her upper body back and forth, arms outstretched, apparently making the wind move in a circle around her. It looked rather silly, right up until Keagan noticed leaves and dust starting to rise around Lyria, whirling faster and faster.

"What if it throws her out?" Ashley said, clearly worried.

"Hopefully, she'll land in the water," Cassius said, calmly. She and Ashley were now in the same boat, while Shay and Torva had joined Keagan. "We'll fish her out." Cassius frowned. "She can swim, can't she? Did anyone ask?"

"Baast's tits!" Ashley swore.

Keagan readied herself, intending to manipulate a wave to catch Lyria if necessary. She felt so mighty, surrounded by all this moisture. Unlike the sea, which was almost overwhelming in its chaotic power, the wetlands were steady and strong. She felt like she could do anything she could conceive of.

On the hillock, Lyria's feet lifted from the ground, and slowly, she began to rise, a smile creasing her entire face. The joy of learning something new about her abilities, Keagan thought. There was nothing like it. For so many, such learning stopped after the Academy, restricted to the strict parameters of a company job. Only out here, while on this crazy adventure, the four of them were discovering all they could be.

She glanced at Shay, who was watching Lyria with rapt attention and perhaps even a little envy. Make that the five of them, she thought. Surely Shay was learning different things about her abilities as well.

"She's up," Torva murmured.

Keagan returned her attention to where Lyria had risen to just above the treetops, hovering in place, held up by the air twisting beneath her. It was an impressive sight, though Keagan wasn't entirely comfortable with how loud it was, a low roar, like some strange beast. Lyria remained aloft for about ten minutes, and then the whirlwind began to slow, the dust gradually decreasing as she descended. When she landed, she waved her arms, dispersing the last of her wind, and looked over at them, joy emanating from her.

Quickly, Cassius and Ashley rowed over to the hillock, brought her on board, and rowed back to where the other three were waiting. "Report," Keagan said eagerly.

"We're closer than we thought." Lyria pointed to the south. "We're a little off course, but I did see a big structure that way. There's also a large channel over there that leads to the island it's on. It's like a highway right to it, only underwater."

Keagan looked at the vegetation in that direction. "How far?"

"Not very," Lyria said. "If we can just find a break in the trees, we could be on it in no time." She turned to look at Keagan. "I saw a little trail of smoke rising from behind the structure. Like from a campfire."

A weight lifted as Keagan let out her breath in relief. That meant a human presence, and considering they were in the middle of nowhere, it had to be the fugitives. "Let's find that channel."

"Won't that allow them to see us coming?" Cassius asked as she picked up the oars and began to row south.

"One step at a time," Keagan said, setting her back to her own oars.

They reached the tree line and began to row parallel to it, looking for a break. They could see through the thick vegetation how the air was lighter beyond it, indicating an absence of foliage. Finally, they found a small, cross channel. It was shallow, their hulls scraping the bottom tangle of roots and silt, but they were just able to make it.

Lyria had not underestimated the artificial straightness of the channel, which was about thirty feet wide. They could look along its considerable length to see the island with its structure rising to the east. Remaining near the bank, hopefully they stayed hidden in the shadow of the trees as they studied it intently. Through the greenery covering it, the building seemed constructed of white marble, with pillars fronting a huge entrance. Even in its decrepitude, it was grand and lavish, clearly of some great importance.

Shay frowned. "So much for it being destroyed along with Alameada."

"As long as she's not still haunting the place," Ashley murmured.

"Does that mean the Primal Stone might still be there?" Lyria asked, seeming anxious. "The one that controlled them all? The one on her staff?"

"Aigua, let's hope not," Keagan said.

"This is not what I was expecting," Torva said, appearing awed.

"When my uncle volunteered me, I didn't want to come. He threatened to cut off my funding and have the university fire me if I didn't."

"I'm sorry." Keagan winced. "We never wanted that."

"No, don't you see? What you discovered, what you're all discovering, it's more than I would have found in a lifetime." She turned to look at Keagan. "I'm honored to be here."

Keagan nodded. "We're honored to have you," she said. "Your input has been invaluable." She looked over at Shay. "Best approach? Wait until dark?"

"That's a long time from now. Can we wait?"

"It'll be hard to get there without being spotted."

"Assuming they're in the palace and not behind it." Shay eyed the thin ribbon of smoke barely visible over the roof before dissipating. "Lyria?"

She peered at the palace, undoubtedly utilizing her telescopic vision. Now, that was something that Keagan envied, far more than the flying. In truth, a part of her didn't particularly like heights.

"I don't see any movement," Lyria said. "Not even any indication that anyone's been there. No breaks in the vines covering the front. I don't know how far back the palace goes, but that smoke is a considerable distance from the entrance."

"Let's go," Keagan said. "Stick to the side."

Rowing as quietly as possible, they approached the palace. It became grander as they neared it, statues of Alameada appearing from the water, her head and shoulders at least, and her staff. The water grew shallower, indicating the ground beginning to rise, or perhaps the remains of a staircase. Keagan reached down and created a void in the water that revealed a layer of silt that sloped upward in offset layers. Definitely a broad staircase. It must have been a sight in its heyday, she thought.

They reached the top of the staircase, where they exchanged glances and slipped out of the boats, pulling them up onto the landing.

"Torva—" Keagan said.

"No." Surprised, Keagan looked at her, and Torva held up her crossbow. "I won't stay with the boats. I have to see this through. Besides, I'm not equipped for an expedition. I'd never find my way out of these swamps on my own, so there's no point leaving me behind in supposed safety."

"Fair enough." Keagan drew her sword, and nodding at Ashley and Cassius to take flank, they walked across the ornate tile to the entryway. Keagan used her sword to hack away the vines, revealing a large, stone door.

"It has a lock," Lyria said, leaning over to examine the small panel. "The same kind as on the palace in Anemoi."

"Good thing we know how to open it," Ashley said.

After they activated the lock, the large door ground opened about halfway and refused to go any farther. Through the crack that was barely large enough to admit a body, Shay eased inside, checking it out. She sneezed as she withdrew. "The dust is inches deep on the floor. No one's been in there," she said with certainty.

"Should we leave this and search for the source of that fire?" Cassius asked. "Go around?"

"If it's near the back of the palace, then they got in another way," Keagan said. "If so, they won't be expecting anyone from this direction." She glanced at Shay. "Take point."

They entered the large foyer. It was full of destruction, the remains of shattered furniture and odd, suspicious stains here and there. The air was thick, the building clearly closed for a long time. Dank cobwebs draped from the ceiling as spiders skittered along the upper walls. Moving silently after the dark form of her Rider, Keagan did her best not to choke on the dust, pausing to pull a cloth from her tunic to cover her face. The others followed suit. It was fortunate they all carried handkerchiefs, she thought, but then, again, she didn't really know anyone who didn't. They were so useful. To filter out bad air, to tie things together, to bind wounds if necessary, to use as a small towel, to signal from a distance, to tie back hair, or even to strain liquid. Aigua. You could even blow your nose on one, if it came to that.

Shay didn't pull out a cloth. She just drew up the scarf attached to her tunic. It seemed designed for that purpose, in fact. For the Shadows? Keagan hoped she'd remember to ask about it later.

As they moved through the large room, Torva peered at the broken debris. "This isn't from time," she said. "Some kind of sustained battle took place here."

"Are you surprised?" Ashley asked. "Isn't that how the story went?"

"This isn't Elemental damage, though," Torva said. "Would they have taken on the guards without using their abilities?"

"Maybe someone else had to keep the guards distracted." Cassius nudged aside a broken sword. "It could be the rest of the rebel army, sacrificing themselves to allow the others time to get inside." Her jaw was very firm. "I guess the story's all true."

"We only know some kind of a fight took place here," Torva said, her tone gentle. "Nothing more." But her eyes were shining as she absorbed everything, almost quivering at each discovery.

"Maybe we should check out the throne room, then," Ashley suggested. "This way."

She strode off before Keagan could object, the others following, and Keagan muttered a curse. Had they forgotten why they were there?

Still, she couldn't deny a part of her was desperately curious to see that throne room.

It wasn't hard to find. The palace was designed to channel people toward it, after all. They walked through the long halls, filled with other obvious signs of struggle, broken spears, discarded swords and shields, along with armor piled in little mounds here and there, all covered with a thick layer of mold, dust, and dark stains that were probably from blood. Finally, they reached another door with a lock similar to one at the front entrance.

"Woman took her security seriously," Cassius said, her tone clipped. She was obviously not happy about all this evidence being presented to substantiate Tannehill's theory.

Without hesitation, they activated the lock. This door slid open easily, almost as if it had been waiting for someone to access it after all this time. They fell silent as they went in, astonishment and not a little awe on their faces. Keagan could barely breathe, her heart pounding so hard.

The destruction was more apparent here—artwork torn from the walls, holes in the marble, overturned furnishings, draperies ripped and destroyed, statues decapitated and toppled over. The room was three stories high, the walls broken up by balconies. Keagan wondered how they were accessed. The ceiling had some kind of mural painted on it, but it was too far away and too faded to make out what it was.

At one end of the large room stood a raised dais with a heavy throne, ornate and larger than the ones they had seen in the other palaces. In front of the dais, on the marbled floor, lay the remains of a wooden staff, along with what could only be the Primal Stone. It was shattered into several shards of dull crystal and a gray dust that sparked oddly in the light from their vapor lamps.

Then, a beam of light from Ashley's lamp fell over the throne. Something occupied the chair, a blackened, sinewy, moldering mound shaped something like...

"Aigua's balls," Keagan said. "That's a body."

XLI

"It can't be!" Torva shook her head furiously. "Anything organic should have decomposed completely long ago. It's been almost a millennium." She moved closer, shining her light on it as she examined it. "This is a mummy." She appeared flummoxed. "It's absolutely impossible."

"A 'mummy'?" Shay echoed her, frowning.

"It's an ancient burial rite practiced by an old, isolated culture in Arias," Torva said. "Organs are removed and placed in jars, and the body is packed with salt for three months before being entombed. It's not practiced anymore."

"Salt," Keagan repeated, in an odd tone. "To remove the moisture?"

"Yes, but it's not a natural occurrence," Torva said. Then she paused. "Well, it happens on occasion in deserts due to the extreme dryness of the air, but never in this kind of environment, no matter how intact this room is. It would have to be airtight, and obviously it's not. This could never happen."

"It could if all the water was sucked out of the body at the time of death," Shay said in a wry tone. "Like, say, by someone who happened to be Undine."

"Aigua," Keagan said, her expression one of complicated pride and horror. "He killed her. He absorbed all the moisture." She swallowed visibly, almost as if she had something caught in her throat. "What would that have done to him?"

"Maybe killed him, but not before he helped put her down," Ashley said, scratching at the soot on one of the chair arms. "There's scorching all over the place. That's Salamas markings. Baast took her shot. More than one. The throne's made out of steel. Little bits are actually melted along the arms. Amazing."

Behind them, Cassius was kneeling by the shattered remains of the crystal. Shay heard her breath catch and turned to look at her, concerned. "This is a Chthonic's doing," Cassius said in a weak voice as she touched the sparkling dust and broken shards. She bowed her head, tears sliding down her cheeks. "It would have taken everything Lurra had to destroy this, even if she was level five. I didn't dare try to sense the composition of the other stones, but I can tell this rock was incredibly dense. Denser even than energy crystals. I've never detected this kind of composite before."

Shay eyed a greenish, moldy stain on the marble floor not far away, with a few dirty scraps of cloth, wondering. It wasn't obvious remains of a body but perhaps indicated something organic had fallen there.

Lyria went over to Cassius and put a comforting hand on her shoulder. "This place has been turned over. There's wind damage everywhere. Sirocco kept her distracted, at least." She lifted her lamp, angling it toward a dark splotch on the marble wall, about halfway up, near one of the balconies. "Blasted him out of midair, I'd reckon. Looks like a lightning strike. Maybe when the stone was destroyed?"

Shay peered closer at the shriveled remains on the throne and then reached out, carefully extracting something from the neck area before holding it up to examine it. The blackened remains of a blade, broken at the end from where it had gone through to strike the back of the chair, still bore an insignia on the moldering hilt. She could just make out the symbol of the Shadow Lands.

"Right through the throat," she said, unsure of what she was feeling. "Stygia struck true." She looked around the blasted room. "There are no other bodies."

"They would have decomposed long before now." Torva looked up at the ceiling three stories above. "Still, the room is protected from the elements, so perhaps not everything would have been erased. No large animals could get in here. Only insect and bacterial degradation would occur." She pointed at the stain near the broken crystal that Shay had already identified. "That could be signs of decomposition. Lurra may have fallen there." She pointed to another stain not far from the throne. "And there. That's large enough for two or three bodies. Baast and Aigua. Stygia, as well, perhaps."

"Stygia walked out of here through the Shadows," Shay said. "To start rebuilding."

"It's nice to think so," Torva said in a noncommittal tone.

"Someone told the story," Shay reminded her. "Something got Tannehill started on the stones. He was the one who told Darvus about them. Darvus didn't know what he had discovered in Lurrera."

Torva held her gaze. "You're right. Something did," she said, her dark eyes lightening. "What would it take for me to be allowed to study in Aether for a while?"

"I don't know. I'll try to find out." Shay exhaled, feeling a bit overwhelmed as she tucked the broken blade into her tunic. "Assuming we get out of here. We still have the two idiots to deal with."

Keagan seemed to shake herself, as if from a dream. "Right," she said. "Let's go."

They made their way through the rest of the palace, marveling at how intact it was considering how much time had passed and that a huge battle had been fought within its walls. It had been strong. Everything around it, however, was now clearly devastated. They exited the rear of the palace onto another landing, leading to what might have been courtyards or gardens. It was hard to tell since it was all underwater. In the distance, about five hundred yards away, smoke rose from within a much smaller building, also made from white marble. Quickly, they moved out of sight, Ashley, Torva, and Cassius, crouching behind the pillars, while the others ducked behind a crumbling stone half wall.

Shay lifted her head and peered over at it, eyeing the island keenly. "Lyria?" she whispered.

"Ten people are over there," Lyria told her, voice low. "Don't know how many more might be inside."

"Damn. I thought it would only be Arthur and Olive," Keagan muttered. She glanced and then quickly ducked out of sight. "Something's in the water."

Shay looked again, saw something moving through the still surface of the pool, making tiny ripples, then noticed other little mounds that looked innocuous at first until she spotted the slit pupils in the eyes, barely raised above the surface. "Huh. They're like those reptiles in the Anemoi River."

"Gators," Keagan said. "A little different. Those were crocs. Spikes on their backs and tails. These don't have spikes, but they're still as nasty. They can be found in a few small towns on the edge of the swamps. I don't know why anyone lives there." She took another peek. "They must not have a boat."

"Negligent of them," Ashley said.

"Still, why aren't they over here? This must have been where they were headed. Why not just come the rest of the way through the Shadows?"

Shay thought about it and then snickered. "He missed."

"What do you mean?"

"He missed his entry. He came out over there," Shay said. "Now they can't get over here because they're surrounded by water and no one's about to take a swim."

Keagan frowned. "How does that work?"

"It's like what happened in the passage," Shay said. "I took three steps in the Shadow Realm, and I was leagues away in the real world. There's no way to travel such a short distance in the Realm. Maybe he picked the first standing structure his compass detected, thinking it had to be the palace." She took another quick look. "Well, that probably *is* part of the palace. It could be the servants' quarters or the stables or the kitchens. Whatever." She smiled. "He's not using a Path. There's no obelisk to draw the entry to a precise spot, which is why that's installed first. He can't make a different entry for this general vicinity. Scout Vardis couldn't, either. Hers would just layer itself over the original. It will take months for that to change. Possibly years. He made a random tear, and now he's stuck with it."

"Ha. I find a certain poetic justice in that, don't you?" Ashley asked from her pillar, a wicked smile playing about her lips.

Shay agreed.

"Oh. They're Elemental," Cassius said, softly.

They peered out to see a young man by the bank, brown-haired, throwing stones at the gators, apparently trying to chase them away. He didn't have to bend down to pick up the stones. They just appeared, flung from his hands at the mounds. Once in a while, he managed to hit one, but all that happened was a slow blink, the mound submerged, then popped up in a different place a few minutes later.

Someone else showed up, a woman who wasn't Olive, and started talking to him, gesturing forcefully. White-haired, although far too young for it. The eyes were probably a brilliant blue, Shay thought idly. The Undine was undoubtedly telling him to stop bothering the gators, lest one of them decide to make a lunch out of him. Shay wondered why they hadn't already. They must have had weapons initially, which taught the animals to keep a certain distance, but obviously not particularly powerful weapons, since they were still hanging around. Had they actually had a taste? Were they wanting more?

"Can you kill a gator with a sword?"

Keagan sucked air in through her teeth. "I wouldn't like to try," she said. "Their hides are really thick. And frankly, water doesn't bother them at all."

"I bet I could bother them a little," Ashley said. "Or my arrows could, anyway."

"Maybe," Keagan said. "They might not penetrate, but the blast might kill them or at least drive them away. Something to keep in reserve."

"If those are the missing Elementals, they don't look like prisoners, although, granted, it's not like they can go anywhere." Shay exhaled slowly. "But what if they're here willingly? Patricia's journal said some had joined Darvus voluntarily to increase their abilities. Not sure why they stuck around after they discovered the stone only takes them away. Maybe for the gold?"

Keagan looked pained. "That's…possible."

"Will they surrender?"

"Elementals, in general, have problems with authority, especially human authority like marshals. Every Elemental arrest I've ever made was a fight."

Shay met her gaze, wondering if she really had to say it out loud, but thinking she'd better. "If that's the case, and they're as fanatical as the others, some are going to die. Some by my hand. Maybe even by Torva's."

Keagan was quiet for several long seconds. "I know," she said, finally. She motioned to the others. "Back inside where we can talk freely."

As they moved back into the palace, away from the back door and deep in the shadows of the stately structure, Shay glanced over to meet Ashley's gaze. Ashley's mouth tightened, but she nodded. "Do what you have to, Rider. Baast knows the rest of us will. I'll testify to that if I have to."

"How are we going to get over there?" Cassius asked when they regrouped near the throne room "Without them attacking us in the boats or jumping into the Shadows and getting away while we're rowing toward them? I don't think announcing ourselves as marshals will work this time."

"Oh, we'll have to announce ourselves, give them a chance to surrender," Keagan said. "That's the law. But I want to already be over there, behind cover, when I do it." She exhaled, frowning as she thought over the situation. "Okay, assuming these are low-levels, they're going to try to isolate and counter us. Standard Academy tactics. Any Undines will go after Ashley, try to drown her. They'll have the home advantage here with all this moisture. If there's a Salamas, they'll focus on Lyria. The Chthonics will try to slow me down. Any Sylph will be firing projectile weapons, and those bolts and arrows will be coming a lot faster than you're used to, Cassius."

"What if they've developed different techniques?" Shay asked.

Keagan grinned at her. "That's why you and Torva are the wild cards." She sobered. "But Arthur and Olive might focus on you, and who's to say they don't have some kind of unknown ancient Aether weapon they reserved for themselves. We'll also have to be prepared in case he calls in backup from the Shadows." She looked over at Lyria. "I doubt they've got anyone who can take to the air. When the fight starts, I need you to find the highest point of cover and do what you can from above. Plus, you're crucial against any Shadow creatures that might appear. Keep an eye out for them."

Cassius stuck her hand in her tunic and pulled out a small jar. "Here's some honey," she said. "Let's keep that throat coated."

Somberly, Lyria took it while Ashley gave her an unfathomable look, her face dark. Shay watched the exchange with interest before turning back to Keagan. "Still doesn't solve the problem of closing that last little distance between us."

Keagan was quiet for a moment, mouth tight. Whatever crossed her mind, she obviously wasn't coming to it lightly. She touched Torva on the arm. "That's the bit you might not like."

Frowning, Torva looked at her, and then her eyes widened. "You want me to be the rebel army."

Shay let out her breath, feeling a stab of regret as she realized what Keagan was proposing. The rest of them, however, looked confused as Keagan and Torva stared at each other. "They don't know about you," Keagan said, her tone very rational, even if what she was suggesting wasn't.

Torva nodded, her expression tight. "You're right. They probably don't."

"Wait. What are you talking about?" Cassius was frowning, bright-green eyes darting back and forth between them. It was always disturbing when she started looking like that, dark brows lowered, square jaw set and tight. Like an avalanche of boulders about to slam through a town.

"Can you do this?" Keagan asked, ignoring the outburst. "Because you don't have to. It's just the best idea I can come up with."

Ashley scowled mightily. "You'd better not be thinking what I think you're thinking." A little surprising, coming from her, Shay thought, but perhaps even she had embraced Torva more than she wanted to admit.

Lyria glanced around. "I don't know what's going on."

"I'm going to cause a distraction," Torva said, still holding Keagan's gaze. "Row over there, talk a big game, get them all confused while you sneak in behind enemy lines." She paused. "How? Swim?"

Ashley was appalled. "In that water? With those reptiles?"

"Lyria can cool the water around us, set up a buffer. Reptiles hate the cold. They'll avoid us."

"This is insane," Cassius hissed. "They'll kill her."

"Why?" Keagan asked, finally breaking eye contact with Torva to regard Cassius with that cool, impassive, marshal expression. "She's a human historian who's come out to explore the ruins. In a boat they'll be overjoyed to have. She'll tell them all about what she's found in the palace, rave on about a theory turned fact, show them the broken remains of the Primal Stone. They'll think they have a true believer on their hands. Even better if they recognize her name as belonging to a relative of a Council member. They'll want to replace Tannehill somehow. Darvus will be able to start rebuilding."

"And when the fighting starts?" Shay asked quietly.

Keagan looked at her, eyes soft and sad. "You get her to cover. They won't see you coming."

"Well, as plans go, this is absolute horseshit," Cassius said, clearly furious.

Shay blinked. That was a little more vulgar than she was used to from the woman.

Keagan spread out her hands. "What's your plan, then? I'm certainly open to suggestions."

Torva put her hand on Cassius's arm, calming her. "It's all right," she said, her tone unexpectedly gentle as she looked up at her. "I can go on for hours about history. You know that better than anyone."

Shay felt her eyebrows rise. She did? That was unexpected.

"It'll be dangerous," Cassius said.

"Like this whole trip here has been?" Torva smiled wryly. "You've all gone out of your way to protect me, so far." She managed a small smile and looked at all of them.

"Time for me to take point."

XLII

They didn't so much swim as they simply floated over on tabletops they scavenged from the palace, their upper bodies resting on the wooden surfaces as Keagan used her abilities to move them through the cool water. Well, it was more than cool. It was cold, with Lyria taking no chances. No ice was forming, but Keagan thought it was barely short of that. Keagan frowned at her, and, chastened, Lyria lightened her touch and allowed the water to warm a little.

Torva had arrived at the island a few hours earlier. They had watched covertly from the palace, ready to move immediately if it seemed like things were going wrong, but Darvus and his followers had seemed delighted to see her. Now they were all gathered next to a fire pit set up in a small courtyard to listen to her story, giving Keagan a firm count. There were sixteen of them: Arthur and Olive, and fourteen others. Eight were Elemental, easily identifiable: two Undine, four Chthonic, a Sylph, and a Salamas. The rest were obviously fighters, presumably mercenaries. This was clearly what Arthur considered his army, brought to Elfenol to plan their next move, having sent his mother and the rest of the noncombatants home to the farm.

At least that's how Keagan interpreted what she was seeing, and was now hearing, as they drew closer to the island. The gators had moved to the far side of the lagoon, well clear of the frigid current suddenly flowing here in the shade of the thick mango trees. Keagan hoped the cold would also keep any other pests away, including any bloodsuckers.

Torva was in full lecturing mode, explaining all she had found in the temple, gesturing with the remains of the Primal Stone, keeping her audience enthralled. She had truly embraced her role, which, frankly, was what she had to do in her position as undercover agent. Easing to a stop against the bank, Keagan and the others quietly stepped out of the water and across the fern-covered bank, moving in behind the building, where they pressed themselves against the wall.

"They don't have anyone keeping watch," Cassius said, her voice so low it was barely audible.

"They think they're safe here," Keagan said. In fact, that had been a constant weakness, she thought. Possibly they had spent so many years operating without any authorities noticing, moving among old ruins just like this, that even now they didn't seem to completely grasp the fact that they were exposed.

"Why didn't you move the rowboats through the swamp the way you did us, just now," Ashley muttered. "It would have been a lot faster." She wrung out her hair, her boots squelching.

"The boats are heavy, especially with all of us and our supplies in them," Keagan said. "It would have been exhausting to move them any distance. A waste of resources."

"I hate fighting wet. It's inhibiting."

"You'll get over it." Keagan touched Shay's arm. "Get into position," she told her. They shared a look, a multitude of unspoken thoughts and promises passing between them, and then Shay nodded sharply and melted into the dusk.

"Lyria?"

"Ready," Lyria murmured and nodded at Cassius, who stretched out her arms, hands linked together. Lyria stepped into them, and, with a soft grunt, Cassius flung her up the side of the building, Lyria adding just a little touch of updraft to carry her the rest of the way to the roof. She vaulted over the edge and disappeared, taking position overlooking the courtyard.

"You two, with me," Keagan said. They moved to the corner of the structure, where Keagan peered around the corner. "Damn it."

Olive was just coming out of the building, walking toward the courtyard. In each hand, she carried the Salamas and Sylph stones, cradling them in her palms like they were eggs, fragile and precious. The Elementals around the fire shifted uneasily, moving away a little, but in an almost instinctual way rather than with conscious apathy. Keagan still wasn't sure what they thought they would gain from all this.

Keagan had also been hoping the stones would be kept in a protected area, not easily accessible when the fight started, rather than right there, ready to go. She heard Torva exclaim excitedly when she saw them. She took one from Olive, studying it avidly. Then she said something else, reaching for the second one. Olive seemed to hesitate, and then at Arthur's nod, she reluctantly handed it over. Torva looked as if she was comparing them, mouth moving a league a minute. She was doing everything she could to keep their full attention. Keagan couldn't wait any longer.

She drew her sword, held up her badge, and stepped around the building. "Elemental Marshal! Everyone, drop your weapons, facedown on the ground!" She saw Shay emerge from the shadows behind Torva, dragging her and the stones back toward the shelter of some trees. "Any resistance will be met by lethal for—"

Keagan didn't have the chance to get it all out before two mercs sprang toward her, drawing their swords. Relieved to have the stones out of play for the moment, she met their attack head-on. At the same time, she sensed a gout of flame shoot toward her from the side, which she easily doused with a stream of water that flew on to knock a young Salamas teenager off his feet.

Flames suddenly lit up the darkness as, not far away, Ashley tussled with the two Undines and a male mercenary. Beyond her, Cassius was swinging her stick and knocking people aside, left and right, including the Sylph, who had been trying to shoot her with a crossbow.

Keagan turned aside one blow with her shield as she parried the other's sword away. The first one, a rugged man who clearly had some skill, suddenly grunted as a bolt struck his chest, blunted by his armor. From Torva or Lyria, Keagan thought, though the angle implied it had come from some height. Lyria must have been aiming somewhere else. He staggered and went down, leaving her to drive her sword through his gut, blood spilling hot over her hand.

She swiftly pulled it out and turned to meet the next attack from a Chthonic with her shield, though the force of his bull rush knocked them both down. She grunted as she hit the ground, his much greater weight bearing down on her.

"Off me," she snarled, slamming the hilt of her sword into his temple, dazing him. Quickly, she pushed him off and rolled away, leaping to her feet. She kicked him soundly in the ribs and then stomped him in the groin. "Stay down."

The air around her was filled with shouts and curses. She couldn't keep track of everything that was happening in the flickering distortion of firelight, both from the pit and from random Salamas blasts that had found flammable material. She couldn't see where Arthur and Olive were, and then, from the corner of her eye, she saw Olive wrestling with Torva. She took two steps in that direction before another Chthonic suddenly engaged her, this one a woman, though not nearly as large or powerful as Cassius. She wasn't bothering with weapons, using her abilities to fling dirt at Keagan as fast as she could.

Keagan intercepted the stream of gravel on her shield, bringing her sword around in a full swing to slice down her attacker's chest. After a second of shock, the woman looked down at her wound in complete befuddlement, then screamed as she fell, clutching her torso. Keagan darted around her and headed to where she had seen Torva. She was horrified to see her historian crumpled on the ground, Olive just turning to face her with a maniacal expression as she lifted the stones like she was offering them to the gods.

Keagan skidded to a stop, frantically trying to backpedal as a light pierced the night, gold and red, swirling around Olive in a burst of color that nearly blinded Keagan. From farther away, she heard an unnatural screech and was dismayed to see the familiar streak of darkness open and dark creatures begin to spill out. Things were becoming very complicated yet very slow, at the same time, as battles were wont to do.

It belatedly occurred to her that she was not unconscious, nor had her abilities been taken. She wrenched her attention back to Olive, astounded to see her standing there, water and earth flowing around her in some weird dance, wind lifting her hair.

"Bow to me, bitch," she told Keagan. "I am your Empress."

Okay. Apparently Olive hadn't used the stones to try to take away Keagan's abilities. Instead, she had taken what had been stored into herself. Not great, but better than the alternative, Keagan decided. So she was facing a combined level four and five from three different specialties, all wrapped up in one person. It was highly unlikely Olive knew how to use the abilities in their best incarnations. At least no fire was mixed in there, too. Keagan could handle this.

That was all she had time to think before a gigantic wave of water washed over her, knocking her down and sending her skidding along the ground. It was both painful and profoundly humiliating. She made a move to get up, snorting out the water that had gone up her nose, stinging sharply, when a sudden scream left her curled up in a ball, hands over her ears. Lyria was taking care of the Shadow creatures, she hoped, but in the moment, the sound was thoroughly incapacitating.

It took another minute for her to stumble to her feet and retrieve her sword. A glance revealed the scream had knocked back everyone else a little, including Olive. She was just rising to her feet, face twisted with fury. She combined water and mud into the shape of a large arrowhead and shot it toward the roof of the building with incredible velocity.

"No!" Keagan sprinted toward her, anger blasting hot and red through her chest. "You leave her alone." She heard the mud slam into the building and onto the roof, praying that Lyria had avoided it.

From the side, she saw Cassius running toward them, and a pit suddenly opened up beneath Olive's feet, as large as any Keagan had ever seen Cassius manage. It had to be fifteen feet deep and that wide across. Clearly startled, Olive looked down and fell several feet before catching herself on a fierce updraft of air. Ashley, coming from the other side, did her best to take advantage of that updraft, shooting flames at the base so that they blasted up to engulf Olive.

She screamed and surrounded herself with water, dousing the flame, but was clearly hurt, skin blistering visibly. Ashley would be the key, Keagan realized. That was the element Olive didn't have, though the power of her water enabled her to knock Ashley off her feet, keeping her down with a steady stream.

"Cassius, we'll keep her attention," Keagan shouted on the run as she leaped off the edge of the pit and grabbed Olive around the waist briefly before being knocked back by a huge gust of wind.

But the move had diverted the water pummeling Ashley, and she staggered to her feet, completely soaked, coughing and spitting. She used her hands to wipe her face and, with clear effort, tried to generate flame, though at this point, it was sparking weakly, more smoke than anything truly combustible. As Cassius flung rock after rock at Olive, Keagan forced herself up once more, glancing around to check for additional threats. No more Shadow creatures seemed to be nearby, and everyone else was apparently out of action. Near the entry, Arthur was standing in place, watching Olive. Keagan was too far away to see his expression, but she did detect a flicker, a dark shape rushing toward him, and knew Shay would engage him. She was relieved beyond measure to spot a slender form swooping around the sky in the distance, meaning Lyria was unharmed.

Taking all this in required seconds, and then she was rushing toward Olive again, intending to engage her long enough for Ashley to dry herself and try again. She didn't know how long that would require, so she swung her sword at Olive, gleeful when she managed a shallow slice across her leg. She didn't have time to enjoy it, though, blasted away once more, this time with a combination of water and wind, like being struck by an out-of-control cart. Then lightning started to flash, striking the ground around her.

Aigua's balls. That wasn't something even Lyria could do. Keagan flinched away, the smell of ozone sharp in her nostrils, terrified that one of her companions would be struck. It occurred to her in a distant way that she could also be hit, which would probably kill her instantly, but she couldn't worry about that. She didn't pick up her sword this time, aware that she didn't want to be carrying anything long and metal, though she *was* wearing mail.

Exhaustion threatened to overwhelm her, and she didn't so much run toward Olive again as she skittered sideways in a crablike motion, legs about to give out. Frantically, she considered plan after plan of attack. She could see Cassius crumpled in a heap at the bottom of the pit. Only unconscious, Keagan hoped with every fiber of her being, but maybe worse.

Fire. They needed fire. A glance at Ashley noted that she was still trying to generate some as she took cover from the lightning in the trees, though that wasn't exactly a better spot. They needed the fire to work. How did fire work? What would make it work better?

"Lyria," she shouted as she staggered the last few feet toward Olive. "Help Ash!"

She could scarcely believe what she saw as she looked at Olive. The woman was surrounded by her elements, wind and rain and rocks continuing to swirl around her. A cruel smile edged her lips as she watched Keagan approach, clearly starting to enjoy herself. Her hair had altered color, becoming white with streaks of gold and brown, her eyes a solid white but sparking with flecks of blue and green. The sight was terrifying.

"I'm going to bury you, Marshal," Olive told her in a voice that echoed oddly. "Then I'm going to dig you up and rip you apart."

"Well, that's not nice," Keagan said, drawing as much moisture as she could from the vast swamps around them. "Let's do this, then."

She channeled everything she could through her hands, blast after blast of water rushing through her. Water conquered everything, she told herself. Eventually. Doused the hottest flame. Used the strongest wind to make it surge. Cut its own path through earth, eroding rock, changing the very face of the land itself. Except it wasn't even affecting Olive, she realized helplessly. At most, it was keeping her attention as Olive took all that water, gathering it to herself. It was going to come back at her, Keagan realized in a moment of despair. Only combined with lethally sharp-edged rocks and powered by a hurricane-force wind, a storm-surged lahar of epic proportion. She wouldn't be able to stop it.

"Hey, Empress Null." Startled, Keagan faltered in her attack as she looked to her left.

Ashley stood proud, completely dry, reddish hair wafting in the wind, eyes glowing gold. Beside her, hand on her shoulder, Lyria's eyes were white and focused as she fed something, some sort of gas, to Ashley, something invisible rippling in the air between them.

"Let's go to work!"

Desperately, Keagan stopped her attack and dived for cover into the pit next to Cassius, shielding her head as a blast of heat scorched around her. She drew in every drop of water she could, from the ground, from the vegetation, even what she could from above, from Olive's heavy reserve. Olive was suddenly screaming, not noticing that Keagan was stealing her excess moisture. Covering herself and Cassius in a protective layer of water that threatened to boil off at any second, Keagan held her breath, curled up in a fetal position. Only the fact they were out of the direct path of the blast kept them alive, but it was brutally hot.

Then it was over. Something fell down beside them, and she lifted her head to see the smoking, shriveled, blackened form of something that didn't quite look like a woman anymore. The sudden resemblance between the two would-be empresses was truly remarkable, Keagan thought in a daze as Lyria slid down the slope of the pit, scrambling to Cassius's side.

"Cass, are you all right?"

Cassius groaned and stirred. "Lurra's tits." She slurred her words. "That hurt."

Ashley looked down from where she stood over Keagan, holding out her hand. "Sorry. I didn't think I should hold back."

"I'm glad you didn't," Keagan said, as she was hauled to her feet. "Good job, deputy."

Ashley's smile was wide and unabashed as she helped Keagan crawl out of the pit. At the top, Keagan looked around at the devastation. It didn't take her long to see what was missing.

"Where the hell is Darvus?"

Torva staggered out of the darkness, holding her side where crimson spilled. She pointed at the entry. "In there," she said shakily. "Shay went after him."

To Keagan's horror, the entry abruptly closed and faded away before her eyes.

XLIII

Shay landed in a crouch, one hand clutching a dagger, the other on the ground as she looked up. "Hey, you little prick," she screamed, not caring how loud she was. "You're not getting away this time."

Darvus whirled, the goggles he wore making him look ridiculous, the sword in his hand quivering. "No." Shay wasn't sure if he was protesting her presence or just the general state of affairs.

"Running away? That's hardly the act of a gentleman," Shay said, rising to her feet as she stalked toward him. "What about Olive?"

When he had first torn open the entry, she had been staggered, though the pain wasn't nearly as bad as the other times, perhaps because she had adjusted to it a little. Or perhaps because she had been ready for it when she saw him pull out his device. She had been on the other side of the courtyard and had sprinted toward him, not surprised by the creatures suddenly appearing. She ignored the rest of the battles going on around her, even what was happening with Keagan. She had to stay focused, though she was peripherally aware of some odd light coming from that direction.

A blast of flame hit the first wraith emerging from the Shadows, making it wither and die. The second creature made it farther away from the entry and, subsequently, took longer to die beneath the fire. She realized that, for a few seconds after entering the world, the Shadow creatures retained their solidity and, thus, could be killed with physical means. But several were spilling from the opening, drifting across the courtyard, not seeming to care who they attacked. One eviscerated the young Chthonic who'd been throwing rocks at the gators. Regardless of how he had gotten there, choosing to be or not, no one deserved that.

Scattered bolts from behind her came from where she had left Torva, and she ducked, not wanting to be struck by a stray missile. She focused completely on Darvus, even when Lyria's scream shattered the battlefield and forced her temporarily to her knees, along with all the others. The scream didn't just dissolve the wraiths. It did something to the entry, making it ripple and waver, as if it were being forced shut.

Darvus seemed oddly unaffected, somehow remaining upright, but stiff and still, almost as if he'd been shocked senseless. He appeared to be looking at something over Shay's head, his facial expression twisted, as if he was seeing something terrible. Then he fumbled for his goggles hanging about his neck, wrenching them up to his face, covering his eyes.

"Oh no, you don't," Shay shouted, sprinting the rest of the way. He ran for the entry, and she was right behind him, diving through before he had a chance to close it, tucking and rolling as she hit the ground. The strength of her lunge had taken her some distance inside, and now she couldn't feel the entry behind her.

Something to worry about later, she thought as she approached him. He waved the sword at her, threatening her. "Stay away."

"Why not call for help?" She was taunting him. "Let's try for something bigger than wraiths this time."

A part of her wondered what the hell she was doing, letting her mouth get ahead of her brain, but she was filled with a strange sort of elation. Perhaps because she knew it was time to end this once and for all and get on with her life with Keagan?

He lunged at her, and she grabbed his wrist, twisting hard to make him drop the weapon. It fell to the ground with a clatter. With the other, she grabbed at the device on his belt, the whole reason he had access to the Shadows in the first place, wrenching it away. Dropping it, she stomped on it as hard as she could, smashing it into pieces. He swung his other fist at her awkwardly, connecting with the side of her head, making her wince, though the blow probably hurt his hand more, she told herself. She ducked smoothly beneath the next swing, and then she blocked the third with her left forearm. With her right, in a blur of motion, she stabbed him twice with her dagger, once in the gut, above his navel, and another just below his rib cage.

Shocked, he staggered back, clutching his torso. "Wonder what that's going to attract?" she asked idly as blood spilled down his leg and onto the ground, rough and rocky, unlike the smooth pavement of a Path.

"You can't do this." He grunted.

"Oh, I think I just did."

In the distance, she heard a shriek. She couldn't detect the Path that had brought her and her friends to Elfenol. They must have entered the Realm just beyond the extent of her senses. She'd have to wander around and hoped she could pick up its trace, undoubtedly chased the entire time by whatever was heading her way. Something to look forward to.

She shook her head. "Why'd you do all this? Was it just to get back at Daddy?"

He sat down abruptly, a twisted smile on his face. "He was a monster," he said, his breath suddenly coming hard. "A real one. Not like the things in here. They can't help what they are. He could have been different but chose not to be."

"That's too bad." Shay watched with narrow eyes as life drained from him.

"They're Riders, you know."

"What are?"

"The wraiths. They're Riders who've lost their way over the centuries. You should talk to one sometime instead of just trying to kill it."

Shay opened her mouth to retort, stunned, but it was too late. He was gone, toppling over with the boneless, liquid release of death.

"They are not!" she muttered, anyway, both frustrated and horrified. Could that possibly be true?

Another shriek sounded, this one closer. Shit. She needed an entry. She dashed over and began to search his body for the compass. Where was it? She'd need it to get back to the palace. Wouldn't she? She closed her eyes as it suddenly struck her that it didn't matter where she was. She was probably still in the general vicinity of Elfenol. All she had to do was open an entry, and it would layer over the one Darvus had made. She also realized she'd need to take him along. She couldn't just leave him here. What if he turned into a wraith, for Lady's sake. She reached down and grabbed Arthur's collar, dragging him behind her as she prepared to make an entry.

A flicker in the corner of her eye made her turn, and she drew her dagger again, ready to fight. But it wasn't a wraith. It was more solid. A female form, slender and dark, long, straight, black hair falling down around her narrow, dusky face, framing the silver eyes. She walked easily, her leathers black and worn, boots pulled high to mid-thigh, several small daggers stuck through hoops on her belt. They had an insignia on the hilts, the same one that was on the broken dagger tucked inside Shay's tunic. Beside her strode the bulk of a huge horse, with bloodred eyes and foamy nostrils. They stopped a few feet away, regarding Shay for a long moment as she looked back, struck dumb, completely flummoxed.

"Yes, Rider," the woman said finally, smiling ever so slightly. "I think you'll do."

Shay finally found her voice, forcing it past numb lips. "Stygia? Our Lady of the Shadows?"

Then Shay was falling backward through an entry that had suddenly generated from nowhere, still clutching Darvus's collar, dragging the corpse with her into the real world. A glance revealed she was exactly where she had started out. Before her eyes, the entry shimmered closed and disappeared in an instant, without any input from her.

"What the fuck was that about?" she muttered, lying flat on her back in the flickering light of several small fires. She sat up gingerly, immediately engulfed in an embrace. "I'm all right, Keagan," she said, hugging her in return, arms circling that solid form that made her feel so many things it was hard to decipher them all. "I'm fine."

Nearby, Ashley prodded Darvus's corpse gingerly with the toe of her boot. "Well, that's done and dusted."

"He wouldn't surrender," Shay said in a mild tone. "What about the others?"

"Everyone's fine," Keagan said, drawing back to peer into her face, studying her intently. Almost as intently as Stygia had. Shay's mind shied away from that thought like a foal from a snake. It was too weird to contemplate. "Torva was stabbed, but it's just a flesh wound. She'll recover. Cassius is with her."

"Oh," Shay said, trying to absorb that situation. It was hard to think. "That's good. What about the bad guys?"

"Oh, you should have seen it, Shay," Lyria said. "Ashley was awesome."

And with Lyria helpfully describing everything that had happened on their end while Shay had been otherwise occupied, Keagan pulled Shay to her feet. As the enormity of what Lyria was describing began to sink in, Shay stared at Keagan, eyes wide. Keagan managed to shrug.

"It all happened really fast," she said.

The modest tone and the demure expression made Shay laugh out loud, and wrapping her arm around Keagan's shoulder, they walked over to the fire pit where Cassius was tending to Torva. They sat down and, for long moments, gazed at each other and the flames.

"Anyone else alive?" Shay asked, finally, feeling the exhaustion tug at her.

"Not sure," Ashley said. "If they are, they're having the good sense to keep their heads down and let us catch our breath."

"Good of them."

"I thought so."

They spent several more minutes gathering themselves, and then, without having to say anything else, Shay, Keagan, and Ashley forced themselves up and went to check on the fallen. They discovered four survivors: the teenage Salamas boy; the Undine woman; the older, male Chthonic; and one mercenary, none of whom wanted any more to do with this fight. They immediately surrendered, sitting in stunned heaps on the ground, weapons left far away so there would be no question as to their willingness to cooperate. Keagan cuffed the Elementals, neutralizing their abilities, and bound the merc with metal ties.

A search of the building revealed it to be a combination of stables below and servants' quarters above.

"Cheap bitch, this Alameada," Ashley muttered. "Could have been two separate buildings. Who wants to sleep above that smell?"

"Well, they were probably slaves," Shay said. "Considered to be little better than animals."

They found a relatively secure room, undoubtedly used for storage, and put the four prisoners in there, leaving them with a bucket and some bedrolls.

"You saw what I did to your boss," Ashley told them before shutting the door. "Don't make me have to come back here before I need to."

Then, they gathered the bodies and stripped them of identification and belongings before laying them out in neat rows. Shay finally found the compass in Darvus's trouser pocket and tucked it away in her tunic. She couldn't wait to figure out how it worked.

With an impassive expression, Ashley cremated the remains.

"What a waste," Keagan said, while she and Shay watched, because that was the proper thing to do. "It's too bad we can't take them back to their families."

"Assuming they had any," Shay said.

She understood why it was impossible, though. In this swampy environment, decomposition would be swift. Besides, they had no way to transport them. Shay would be damned if she would carry rotting corpses through the Shadow Realm, especially now that she knew it was occupied with more than just creatures.

That would be rude.

They did place a little bit of ash in small containers, marking who each one was, placing it with their personal effects in individual evidence bags. At the very least, they could carry that much back to Naiad. Keagan looked down at the bag holding Arthur's belongings. "I'll inform Patricia myself," she said. "She deserves that much."

The next day, they left the little rowboats tied to the obelisk, while Shay opened an entry. To her great surprise, the carts remained just inside, and they put the prisoners in them, warning them to be silent while they walked the Path back to Arias. Fortunately, the riverboat had waited as requested, the promise of gold too much to give up, even after a few days, and the trip downstream was a lot faster than the trip up, carried by the powerful current. The canyon community seemed even louder and busier as Shay ducked beneath the corral railing and wrapped her arms around Onyx's neck.

"You won't believe who I met," she told him in a whisper. "In fact, I don't think anyone will."

They left the prisoners with the crown guards before making their way along the river to the Path leading to Amane. They didn't stop long in the ruin before taking the brand-new Path to Naiad, exiting not far from the city gates. Shay eyed the freshly carved obelisk, set in the shade of some large trees, and wondered if she'd be riding back to Amane any time soon.

She dearly hoped not.

They waited at the main marshal station in downtown Naiad while Keagan handed her reports over to the desk clerk, instructing him to make sure they reached Abraham directly. He seemed unimpressed but promised to put them on the chief's desk personally. Then they wearily rode through the streets leading to the Rider station by the harbor where Shay normally stabled Onyx. They dismounted and had their Shadow-bred mounts led away by the grooms, who were very familiar with the spirited animals. Shay slung her saddlebags over her shoulder, the two stones tucked inside them. She and Torva were the only ones willing to handle them, and they had all decided that they might be safer with Shay until they could turn them over to the authorities.

"What now?" Ashley asked.

"The Queen and Council will want to see us in the morning," Keagan said. Shay could see how weary she was. "We'll give a full report. For tonight, you're booked in the Lion's Head Inn."

"Oooh, fancy," Lyria said with a tired grin.

"Not me. I'm headed home," Shay said. "My apartment's just down the street." She lifted a brow at Keagan. "You're welcome to join me, of course."

Keagan managed a smile. "Actually, as good as that sounds, I need to check in with my own place. I don't even know if I left the lights on. I'm sure I left my supper dishes in the sink. I can only imagine what they look like, now."

Shay was disappointed, but she understood. Or thought she did, anyway, though she still had an acid pang in the pit of her stomach. She worried that killing Darvus had changed her in Keagan's eyes. Was she starting to distance herself?

"The rest of us can catch a cab to the inn," Cassius said. "We'll see you in the morning."

While they flagged down their respective horse-drawn carriages at the street corner, Shay wandered down the sidewalk to her building, feeling somewhat bereft. A part of her couldn't quite believe it was over, even as another part of her wondered what would happen next. Upstairs, above the bookstore that had closed for the evening, she opened the door of her apartment and sneezed at the light layer of dust.

Dropping her saddlebags over the stand designed for them, she moved through the small kitchenette, the cold box humming in the corner. It felt oddly normal, so very familiar, as if she'd just returned from a long courier run. The small living area held a battered couch that beckoned invitingly, but she wouldn't get up again if she sat down. Why sleep there, when she had a perfectly good bed in the next room, as empty and lonely as it suddenly seemed.

She did force herself to take a quick shower. Even if she had gotten used to how she smelled, that didn't mean the neighbors had to. Drawing back the covers, she finally lay down in the bed, looking up at the familiar ceiling as the sounds of the city wafted through the window.

It was finished. So why did this little voice in the back of her mind insist that, perhaps, something had just begun?

XLIV

"I am solely responsible for the actions of my team," Keagan said, forcing herself not to direct a dirty look at anyone. She stood in the large conference room, in front of the Queen and Council, decidedly weary of explaining herself. "They acted under my authorization."

"We can't have nulls killing Elementals." Leanna Dewitt was apoplectic, her face reddened and blotchy. The Terras head of state couldn't seem to wrap her mind around everything that Keagan had told them, fixated instead on the death of Darvus to the exclusion of all other details. "It sets a dangerous precedent."

"Then he shouldn't have been trying to turn nulls into Elementals." Nigel Dunbar leaned back in his chair, hands linked across his expansive belly. The fringe of red hair bordering his balding scalp stuck out in all directions, and his golden eyes were narrowed as he regarded his fellow Council member. The Urodela representative seemed to be the only one on the Council sympathetic to Keagan and her team. Perhaps because of his friendship with Ashley's father. "If you ask me, this Shadow Rider did us a favor. Or would you prefer the public spectacle of a trial? Let everyone know what happened?"

Beside him, Damian Lynch prudently kept his mouth shut as everyone debated what they clearly saw as an Elemental issue. As a null, he was probably wise to do so. That schism always simmered just below the surface, even on the Council. Keagan noticed that he hadn't asked about his niece, Torva. Perhaps the rest hadn't realized they were related, and he wanted to keep it that way.

"A trial would be completely unacceptable," Fiona Ralston declared in her harsh voice. As the leader of Arias, she was clearly thrilled with the gold suddenly pouring into her nation's coffers from the site at Anemoi, but that didn't prevent her from finding fault with everything else Keagan and the others had accomplished. As if she could have come up with better plans on the fly. "We can't ever let it be known such a thing is even possible. We'll have riots." She turned her sharp features toward Queen Chiesa. "What will happen to the stones?"

"They'll be transported to Aether," Chiesa said, inclining her head regally. "The clans will know how to keep them safe."

That remark provoked another outbreak of raucous discussion, where everyone kept trying to talk above the next person, and Keagan wondered if she should leave. This meeting had been underway for hours, and it didn't seem like it was going anywhere. Inadvertently, she caught Chiesa's eye, struck by the weariness she saw there. Nope, she thought. No way would she agree to go through any Rite of Succession. What was the appeal?

Now the discussion had turned to the missing prisoners and what should be done about them. They couldn't leave Darvus's mother out there, possibly recruiting others to follow some crazy new religion. Keagan was still fuming over that. What was the point of doing all the work to catch Patricia and the others in the Marl passage if the crown was promptly going to misplace them? It wasn't even like they were being transported from another nation. They should have paid Aether to use Riders to transport the prisoners along the new Path between Amane and Naiad, rather than taking them by ship around the northern point. It would have been so much faster and wouldn't have afforded any opportunity for the guards to lose them to pirates. Assuming it had been pirates and not some kind of inside job, Keagan speculated darkly. The whole situation felt wrong to her and warranted further investigation.

"Enough," Chiesa said, finally, her patience clearly exhausted. "It's decided. There will be no further action taken against Rider Kendrith. She performed her duties as outlined by My will. It is so." The Queen rose from her seat, and hastily, the others followed suit. Keagan was impressed, despite herself. Maybe being the ultimate authority provided an occasional perk.

Outside, in the large foyer, Keagan found the others waiting for her. She exchanged a smile with Shay, dearly wishing she had taken her up on her offer the night before instead of going home to moldy dishes and food gone bad in the cold box. After cleaning that up, and enjoying a long bath, she had fallen into the bed and promptly did *not* fall asleep, tossing and turning all night, wishing Shay had been there. She even considered going to find her but then realized that while she knew Shay lived near the Rider stables, she didn't know exactly where her apartment was.

"What did they say?" Ashley asked.

"No further action to be taken," Keagan said.

"Well, of course not," Cassius said, as if that logical outcome could have been predicted. Keagan had been much less confident that the Council and Queen would do the right thing. She still wasn't sure they did it because it was right or because it was simply politically expedient.

"What will happen to the stones?" Torva eyed her curiously.

"Escorted to Aether." Keagan looked at Shay inquiringly.

"I've already been tasked with that job," Shay said. "I have no idea what the Clan will do with them. I have a lot to talk about with my parents when I get home."

"And the last stone? The Terras Stone?" Lyria was looking a bit down, less like her bubbly self.

"Assuming it's in Urodela," Torva said, "then it's buried under so much lava flow and ash, there's no recovering it."

"Except," Shay pointed out, dryly, "every other stone had somehow been protected from the mass destruction around it. Amane, Anemoi, Lurra, and Elfenol were all leveled, but not the palaces."

Torva stared at her. "I don't think that would be the case with volcanic debris," she said, but she spoke tentatively, and her face was clearing, as if she was becoming excited at the thought of it still being in reach.

"And if we've thought of that," Cassius said, "someone else might."

"Who, Patricia?" Keagan shook her head. "Without her son, she can't do anything on her own. We'll find her."

"But she might not be on her own," Ashley said. "Don't forget her followers. They started their own religion, for Baast's sake. Plus, I don't believe they could have funded all this, not even by selling antiquities, so someone must have been bankrolling all this through Olive. They weren't getting their hands dirty, but they weren't supporting this endeavor without believing in a payoff of some kind. And you know that's not ordinary money, Keagan. Not even Guild money. Pockets that deep have to be Elemental."

Keagan wanted to argue the point but couldn't. It was too accurate an assessment.

"But whoever it was, they no longer have access to the stones," Shay said. "It would be impossible to find the fourth without attracting some kind of attention. They may just decide to cut their losses."

"Can we really hope for that?" Ashley raised her thin eyebrows in perfect arches.

Keagan shook her head. She couldn't bring herself to offer any consoling words, especially when she didn't believe in them.

"So, what now?" Lyria looked back and forth between them, eyes starting to glisten. "Is this it? We just...what? Go home? Back to our lives? Our jobs? Like nothing happened?"

They exchanged glances. "I'm not sure what else there is," Torva said quietly. "For my part, I'll write all this up, and assuming I'm allowed to publish, our history will have a new slant. Everything we've learned about Alameada and the empire will become public knowledge, and Tannehill will finally have his theories established as historical fact.

"But as Ashley has pointed out so many times, the average person simply won't care. After that, I plan to return to Elfenol to conduct a proper dig and see what else I can discover, assuming I get there first. Aigua knows, plenty of treasure hunters will be rooting around the Wilderness now."

"Well, I'm not getting any younger, but I might look into the marshal service," Cassius said. "I'll probably find it more interesting than what I've been doing."

"Chances are, it won't be nearly this exciting or complicated," Keagan said, thumping Cassius's shoulder lightly. "But you have good instincts, and we can certainly use you. I'll put in a word with Abraham."

"Thanks."

"Maybe I'll do that, too," Lyria said. As they all looked at her, she frowned. "What?"

"You're level five, sweetie," Ashley told her gently. "There's no way the companies are going to give you up to public service."

"What say would they have?" Lyria sounded belligerent.

"The same say they've always had." Ashley patted her shoulder. "Gold. Didn't you tell me you send most of your salary back home to your family in Arias? That you're the one who's actually supporting them? Marshals pay next to nothing. Can you afford to become one? At your age?"

Lyria's expression crumpled. "No," she said in a small voice. "I can't."

"But now you know what you're capable of, what you're worth," Ashley said, her tone softer. "You can write your own ticket, Lyr. Seriously, let me put the word out. You can go where you want, choose a job that interests you, and demand the highest salary. I'll make sure of it. And in a few years, once you're really established, then you can decide how you're going to change the world."

"And by that time, you might not settle for the marshals," Keagan said, smiling. "You'll be in a position to change things on a much higher level."

"What's our travel situation?" Ashley asked.

"You've been given transport however you want to go, whenever you want to go, free of charge," Keagan told them.

"Including being escorted by a guide along the Paths," Shay said. "If you want the fastest way."

"I can find my own way back to Urodela." Ashley looked over at Lyria, smiling. "Care to join me? A ship to Terras and then a few passage caravans? It'll take longer, but I'm not really in a hurry. Are you?"

Lyria hesitated, her expression odd. "No. I mean, yes, I'd like to travel with you." Then she looked at Shay. "Oh, does that mean I have to give back Vindur?"

Shay tilted her head slightly, seeming to assess Lyria. "How often will you be able to ride?" she asked. "Where will you keep her while you're working? A Shadow-bred can't be stabled for long periods, not even at a Rider station. It's simply not acceptable."

"They'll be happier back in the Shadow Lands, you mean." Ashley sighed, clearly no more pleased about the situation than Lyria, but she also seemed to know she didn't have much choice. "I'll miss Fuoco, but I won't be able to give her the attention she deserves."

"Being a marshal puts you out on the road a lot, doesn't it?" Cassius asked, sounding hopeful.

Keagan eyed her. "Usually," she said. "Especially if you're assigned to a country district. The little villages are a good distance apart, and it takes time to ride a circuit patrol."

"You want to keep Gault?" Shay looked at her briefly. "I suppose you could, assuming you're riding every day. If that changes, you'll let me know."

Cassius beamed. "Absolutely," she said. "Thank you."

They turned to Torva, who blinked. "Um, I don't really ride a lot." Clearly, she wouldn't miss the old gray mare at all.

Keagan looked around, seeing the sadness starting to descend. This couldn't be how they left it, she decided. "Hey, let's have one final dinner tonight. My treat."

"On your salary?" Ashley said, grinning crookedly. "I'd like a better class of restaurant. Let's make it my treat, at the Lion's Head."

There, at Naiad's most expensive restaurant, they ate and talked, reminiscing about all that had occurred, laughing about incidents that had been terrifying at the time. They promised to stay in touch, even though a part of Keagan wondered if that were truly possible, separated as they were, spread out through the nations. Ashley and Lyria might, she thought, since they were both in Urodela, but were they even in the same city? She glanced at Shay, relieved that, at least, they both lived in Naiad. But what would Shay choose to do now? How long before her next courier run?

She refused to cry. Marshals didn't do that. Her eyes were stinging, though, throughout the evening. More than once.

And then, finally, they couldn't linger any longer. The restaurant was closing for the night, and it was time to pay the bill. Everyone planned to leave first thing in the morning, prepared to return to their lives, even if they weren't especially excited about it. As Ashley settled her account, Keagan went with her, leaning against the counter. "Hey, so about you and Lyria."

Ashley glanced at her sideways. "What about her and me?" Her tone was a touch icy.

"Just don't get her into any trouble," Keagan said. "I don't want to see any arrest reports show up on my desk."

Ashley exhaled loudly, clearly exasperated. "We'll be fine."

"Yeah." Keagan leaned closer and lowered her voice. "Don't hurt her, Ash."

An expression very much like pain ghosted across Ashley's face. "Never." After a pause, Ashley seemed to recover, narrowing her eyes. "I was going to have the same conversation with Shay, but maybe I should have it with you. I've come to like her better, anyway. Don't fuck this up, Keagan."

Keagan caught her breath. "I won't."

"You better not, because while she doesn't have to worry so much on her end if things go tits up," Ashley said, "you'll have two Shadow Lands Clans after you."

"I know."

Then it was farewells, and hugs, final promises to write and stop by the next time they were in town, until finally, just Shay and she stood on the sidewalk outside the inn. Shay glanced at her, head tilted slightly.

"So if I were to invite you home this time?"

Keagan smiled. "I'm definitely accepting that invitation."

The cab ride home was excruciating, sitting so close to each other in the coach, legs pressed against each other's, hands clasped, Keagan's head resting on Shay's shoulder. They got out in front of a little shop that sold books, one, Keagan realized with surprise, that she'd been in countless times before. Was it possible that Shay had been so close all that time and they'd never crossed paths before that terrible moment in the Shadow Realm?

It was truly astonishing how life worked sometimes.

Upstairs, in Shay's apartment, Keagan assessed it without conscious thought. Sparse and uniformly tidy. Devoid of knickknacks and excess furniture, with only a few photos of Shay's family on the mantle. Lots of books, tucked neatly on shelves, and a single painting hanging on the wall above the sofa, of the plains set against a backdrop of mountains. Keagan wondered who had painted it, since it was clearly of the Shadow Lands.

"Something to drink?" Shay suddenly seemed a bit reserved, and Keagan moved over to take her hands, holding them tight as she looked into those shimmering eyes.

"I just want you, and only you," she said quietly. "Now, and forever."

Shay smiled, pulled her close, and kissed her deeply. Before long, the kiss grew passionate, and now, it was all hands and lips, urgency tugging at them as they divested each other of their clothes. In the bedroom, Shay paused, looking down at her, hands cupping Keagan's face.

"I love you," she said, and just like that, the urgency was gone. Then it was soft and gentle, lovemaking as slow and lingering as it could be, and twice as delightful. In Shay's bed, they explored and caressed, having the time and freedom that they hadn't enjoyed until now.

Afterward, Keagan lay snuggled against Shay's side, head on her shoulder. "I could get very used to this," she said, quietly.

"Me, too." Shay paused. "I suppose it's too soon to ask about living arrangements."

"Maybe," Keagan said. "For most people. But I want to be with you, Shay, every day."

"Mine or yours," Shay asked, that practical note in her voice. "Is your place bigger?"

"Not by much," Keagan said. "It's near the marshal office." She paused. "What about if we find one together?"

"An apartment?" Shay hugged her. "Or a house?"

"Oh." Keagan exhaled slowly. "I've never lived in a house."

Shay chuckled. "To be fair, neither have I. It's been winter quarters or a migration wagon, or the Rider School dorm."

Keagan nodded. "Yeah, so maybe we look for a house. With a garden in the back."

And as she dozed off, her dreams were filled with a future that she had never before imagined.

EPILOGUE

The wind blew swift and clear over the long grasses as Shay and Keagan rode toward the camps where the Clan had settled for the night. Spread out as far as the travelers could see, herds of grazing horses ignored them as they rode past, far more interested in greeting the Shadow mounts they had brought back from Aquas and turned loose as soon as they could. The old gray mare cantered across the plain like she was a yearling again.

To the west, long streaks of red painted the mountains a final time for the day as they entered the camp, passing by the big wagons that were the lodgings during migration. The dusk was lit by the various fire pits for the evening meal as the smell of roasting meat filled the air.

They drew up at the largest wagon, in the center of the camp, and Shay smiled when she saw her mother in the doorway. Her father, near the fire, waved and started toward her. As she dismounted, she felt a sense of belonging and home that enveloped her like a warm cloak. Or maybe that was from the woman walking beside her.

"Be welcome at our hearth, Keagan Riley," Calvin said, taking both of Keagan's hands in his.

"Thank you, Sie Rylak," Keagan said warmly. "And thank you both for granting me special dispensation to visit the Shadow Lands."

"Well, if things continue as they are, you'll be of the Clan, with all the freedoms and responsibilities that entails," Diana said with a smile as she joined them. She looked at Shay. "Right?"

Shay's face heated as her parents chuckled. Inside the large wagon, they took a seat at the table that folded out from the wall, and she passed over the stones, handing them to her mother. Beside her, she could feel Keagan shifted uneasily on the bench, suspecting she wasn't even aware that she was leaning away.

Diana looked at the stones, her lips tight, turned down at the corners. "Such small things to cause such large problems."

"What will you do with them?"

"Put them someplace safe," Diana said, somewhat less than helpfully, as she tucked them into a small box that she pushed over to the side of the table. It was a plain wooden chest that didn't even have a lock. Her gesture seemed very nonchalant.

Shay wanted to sigh. "Why would the Queen think they'd be safe here?"

"She knows the Shadow Lands. Chiesa rode two years with the Kendrith Clan, you know."

Shay stared at her. She knew her jaw had loosened, and she shut it with a snap. "No. I didn't know that. Why didn't you tell me?"

"It was before you were born," Calvin said, somewhat carelessly. "When she was chosen as a possible successor. It's part of the Rite, of course. How else could the throne govern our nation, along with the other four, unless it knows how we do things." He looked directly at Keagan, who seemed to pale.

"So will you continue to ride courier for the crown, dear?" Diana asked, regarding Shay evenly.

Shay was perplexed. "I'm not sure yet. I'm still exploring my options." She exhaled. "I didn't really understand I had options before now."

"You're a Rider," Diana said, with complete certainty. "The Shadow Realm calls, regardless of why you ride its Paths. Or in what capacity."

"Did you know about Alameada?" Keagan asked suddenly. "And the real story of what happened all those centuries ago?"

Diana and Calvin exchanged a glance. "We're aware there were other versions of history offered up outside of the Shadow Lands," Calvin said. "But we have no control over how the other Nations interpret the past, or even how they want to present it to those who attend the schools there."

"But why?" Keagan frowned.

"Does it make you feel better to know how Elementals were treated then, in that empire, as opposed to how they're treated now in our current civilization?"

Keagan frowned. "Unpleasant truths shouldn't be altered just because they make a few people uncomfortable."

Diana lifted her brows, but Shay could tell that Keagan's response pleased her.

Keagan persisted. "The Shadow Lands had a hand in how the world recovered from Alameada's mistake. Why do it the way you did?"

"It was the will of Stygia. I think, at the time, it was the most expedient way. The abilities of the Elementals allowed society to recover that much faster, especially if they were willing participants, rather than enslaved." She smiled gently at Keagan. "There are not so many of you, after all, that our world can afford to waste you, especially at the higher levels."

Shay almost told them about who she had seen in the Shadows, but somehow, she didn't, and the urge passed, almost as quickly as it had occurred. She still hadn't told Keagan. She wasn't sure what she would say, anyway, or how she would say it. Instead, she reached over and tapped the chest.

"Torva Lynch would like permission to study our chronicles."

"Yes. She said as much at our dinner," Calvin said. "We're considering it. I don't think it will do any harm, but there are as many closed minds here on the plains as there are in the rest of the nations. The conversation continues. We'll let you know when we reach a consensus."

"Now, about the Solstice," Diana said, clearly ending the conversation about the larger world and getting down to what was truly important to her. "You'll both be there, of course." Shay opened her mouth, and Diana held up a finger, shutting her down. "No. You've missed both Winterfest and the New Year's celebration. You will *not* miss Summer Solstice."

Shay exchanged a glance with Keagan and then did what countless daughters had done before her and would do long after her. She obeyed.

"Yes, Mother," she said. "We'll be there."

Together.

Sky Rider

(Book II in the Elemental Riders Trilogy)

Lyria Hawke is a fifth-level Sylph, one of the most precious and valuable resources her nation has to offer. So why did someone just try to kill her? Meanwhile, her closest friend, Ashley Van Vuur, a member of a prominent Salamas Guild Family, is attacked as well. Is it because of what happened with the Element Stones? With a little help from their friends, they're on a quest to find out what's behind it all. Before it's too late.

About the Author

Living in Nova Scotia, her physical travel has been limited to Canada and the US, but thanks to the creation of others in countless books, TV shows, movies, and video games, Gina's mind has been able to travel light years, from one end of the galaxy to the other. Previously a writer of science fiction and mysteries, this is her first foray into fantasy and she hopes others will have as much fun reading this trilogy as she did writing it.

Books Available From Bold Strokes Books

Back to Belfast by Emma L. McGeown. Two colleagues are asked to trade jobs. Claire moves to Vancouver and Stacie moves to Belfast, and though they've never met in person, they can't seem to escape a growing attraction from afar. (978-1-63679-731-1)

The Breakdown by Ronica Black. Vaughn and Natalie have chemistry, but the outside world keeps knocking at the door, threatening more trouble, making the love and the life they want together impossible. (978-1-63679-675-8)

The Curse by Alexandra Riley. Can Diana Dillon and her daughter, Ryder, survive the cursed farm with the help of Deputy Mel Defoe? Or will the land choose them to be to the next victims? (978-1-63679-611-6)

Exposure by Nicole Disney & Kimberly Cooper Griffin. For photographer Jax Bailey and delivery driver Trace Logan, keeping it casual is a matter of perspective. (978-1-63679-697-0)

Hunt of Her Own by Elena Abbott. Finding forever won't be easy, but together Danaan's and Ashly's paths lead back to the supernatural sanctuary of Terabend. (978-1-63679-685-7)

Perfect by Kris Bryant. They say opposites attract, but Alix and Marianna have totally different dreams. No Hollywood love story is perfect, right? (978-1-63679-601-7)

Royal Expectations by Jenny Frame. When childhood sweethearts Princess Teddy Buckingham and Summer Fisher reunite, their feelings resurface and so does the public scrutiny that tore them apart. (978-1-63679-591-1)

Shadow Rider by Gina L. Dartt. In the Shadows, one can easily find death, but can Shay and Keagan find love as they fight to save the Five Nations? (978-1-63679-691-8)

Tribute by L.M. Rose. To save her people, Fiona will be the tribute in a treaty marriage to the Tipruii princess, Simaala, and spend the rest of her days on the other side of the wall between their races. (978-1-63679-693-2)

Wild Wales by Patricia Evans. When Finn and Aisling fall in love, they must decide whether to return to the safety of the lives they had, or take a chance on wild love in windswept Wales. (978-1-63679-771-7)

Can't Buy Me Love by Georgia Beers. London and Kayla are perfect for one another, but if London reveals she's in a fake relationship with Kayla's ex, she risks not only the opportunity of her career, but Kayla's trust as well. (978-1-63679-665-9)

Chance Encounter by Renee Roman. Little did Sky Roberts know when she bought the raffle ticket for charity that she would also be taking a chance on love with the egotistical Drew Mitchell. (978-1-63679-619-2)

Comes in Waves by Ana Hartnett. For Tanya Brees, love in small-town Coral Bay comes in waves, but can she make it stay for good this time? (978-1-63679-597-3)

Dancing With Dahlia by Julia Underwood. How is Piper Fernley supposed to survive six weeks with the most controlling, uptight boss on earth? Because sometimes when you stop looking, your heart finds exactly what it needs. (978-1-63679-663-5)

The Heart Wants by Krystina Rivers. Fifteen years after they first meet, Army Major Reagan Jennings realizes she has one last chance to win the heart of the woman she's always loved. If only she can make Sydney see she's worth risking everything for. (978-1-63679-595-9)

Skyscraper by Gun Brooke. Attempting to save the life of an injured boy brings Rayne and Kaelyn together. As they strive for justice against corrupt Celestial authorities, they're unable to foresee how intertwined their fates will become. (978-1-63679-657-4)

Untethered by Shelley Thrasher. Helen Rogers, in her eighties, meets much younger Grace on a lengthy cruise to Bali, and their intense relationship yields surprising insights and unexpected growth. (978-1-63679-636-9)

You Can't Go Home Again by Jeanette Bears. After their military career ends abruptly, Raegan Holcolm is forced back to their hometown to confront their past and discover where the road to recovery will lead them, or if it already led them home. (978-1-636790644-4)